C70321773%

THE GARDEN OF ANGELS

Also by David Hewson

The Nic Costa series

A SEASON FOR THE DEAD *
THE VILLA OF MYSTERIES *
THE SACRED CUT *
THE LIZARD'S BITE
THE SEVENTH SACRAMENT
THE GARDEN OF EVIL
DANTE'S NUMBERS
THE BLUE DEMON
THE FALLEN ANGEL
THE SAVAGE SHORE *

Other novels

CARNIVAL FOR THE DEAD
THE FLOOD *
JULIET AND ROMEO
DEVIL'S FJORD *
SHOOTER IN THE SHADOWS

* *available from Severn House*

THE GARDEN OF ANGELS

David Hewson

SEVERN
HOUSE

First world edition published in Great Britain and the USA in 2021
by Severn House, an imprint of Canongate Books Ltd,
14 High Street, Edinburgh EH1 1TE.

Trade paperback edition first published in Great Britain and the USA in 2021
by Severn House, an imprint of Canongate Books Ltd.

severnhouse.com

British Library Cataloguing-in-Publication Data
A CIP catalogue record for this title is available from the British Library.

ISBN-13: 978-0-7278-5011-9 (cased)
ISBN-13: 978-1-78029-756-9 (trade paper)
ISBN-13: 978-1-4483-0473-8 (e-book)

This is a work of fiction. Names, characters, places and incidents are either the product of the author's imagination or are used fictitiously. Except where actual historical events and characters are being described for the storyline of this novel, all situations in this publication are fictitious and any resemblance to actual persons, living or dead, business establishments, events or locales is purely coincidental.

All Severn House titles are printed on acid-free paper.

Typeset by Palimpsest Book Production Ltd.,
Falkirk, Stirlingshire, Scotland.
Printed and bound in Great Britain by
TJ Books Limited, Padstow, Cornwall.

Wenn die Generation die den Krieg überlebt hat nicht mehr da ist, wird sich zeigen ob wir aus der Geschichte gelernt haben.

When the generation that survived the war is no longer with us, then we'll find out whether we've learned from history.

Angela Merkel, July 20, 2018

PART ONE

I must have been four or five. Nonno Paolo was reading a night-time story, the two of us alone in my little room on the third floor at the front. It was a history book. Something real, true, in which a man, an ancient king or an emperor, was at the end of his reign, assessing his achievements and his failures too, wondering what came next as he lay on his death bed.

Was that a special kind of bed? the child me asked. One they kept for the occasion? Could you avoid dying altogether if you never slipped beneath its sheets?

He used to read to me out of guilt I think. Usually Dad was on the road, in America or Japan, Russia, France, there to sell the famous velvet of the House of Uccello. That was what we, among the last of the traditional weavers of Venice, did. Mum had packed her bags and gone back to live with her parents in England. Venice, it seemed, was not to her taste. Any more than us. Before long she had a new husband and a new family too.

No, Grandpa said. A death bed wasn't something special. Just the place you found yourself when the time came. Any bed would do.

Even now, so much later, I can summon up the brief world of childhood. The sounds beyond the windows of my neat little bedroom in the Palazzo Colombina. Vaporetti and motorboats, the gentle lapping of idle waves against crumbling brick and the rotting woodwork of our private jetty. Gulls squawked, pigeons swooped and flapped their airy wings. Sometimes I'd hear a gondolier sing a snatch of opera for the tourists. There was the familiar smell of the canal: diesel and chemical, the faintest whiff of decay behind. That last was always there.

'Did someone die in my bed?'

'It's brand new, Nico!'

'Will I die in it?'

He laughed, reached out and stroked my hair. Nonno Paolo's face was narrow and grey, marked by angular cheekbones that made me think he looked like a genial statue come to life. He had a kindly smile, though he often seemed exhausted from working seven days a week, tending to the affairs of our company and busy weaving outlets.

'Of course not. This is a child's bed. Soon you'll grow and we'll buy you another. There are lots of beds ahead of you in this life. Lots of excitement. Growing up in this busy world of ours will be such an adventure. You want an adventure don't you?'

'I suppose.'

'All boys want adventures.'

'But I will die? One day?'

He waved his hands in exasperation.

'That moment's so far off you needn't worry about it. Just think of . . . now. This week. Saturday when Chiara will take you to the Lido. You can play on the sand. Go paddle. There'll be ice cream. Other kids to play with.'

Chiara Vecchi was a large and bustling woman who'd once worked for us as a weaver, then later, after my mother left, became an essential helpmate, fetching, cooking, ferrying me to school when no one else was around.

'I don't want you to die. Ever.'

Grandpa closed the book.

'You're too tired for this.'

'No . . . I want a story. Another one.'

He bent down, kissed my forehead and ran his fingers through my hair.

'All in good time, little boy.' His genial face clouded over with an expression even a child like me could read. Doubt and perhaps regret. 'Though whether you'll thank me for the one I have in mind . . .'

Before I could say another word he bent down and kissed me again. Then he went to the end of the bed, turned on the TV and flicked through the channels until he found a cartoon.

June 1999. I was now a nervous, gangly fifteen-year-old, walking into a private room in the hospital of Giovanni e Paolo. It was my turn to sit by the bed. I so wanted to be elsewhere. On the beach at the Lido, listening to music, trying to keep up with my peers. Chasing girls if I could only work out how. My father was so good at that. He didn't seem to have passed on the talent.

More likely I'd be out with my cameras somewhere, taking

pictures of the wild marshes by Torcello or the dunes of San Nicolò. Photography was my one hobby, an obsession almost. Grandpa had set me up with an account at the camera shop near San Giacomo dell'Orio. They loved me since I spent a fortune there on SLR bodies, lenses, film and developing. Not a cent of it down to me of course.

All the walls were white. The corridors rang to echoing footsteps and quiet voices. The place reeked of an antiseptic medical smell that caught the back of my throat. Or perhaps that was just fear. On one side of the room two long windows looked out over Fondamente Nove and the lagoon. The placid water shone, swimming in the kind of heat you never normally got till late July. Heavy, humid, tiring, filled with buzzing, biting insects.

The moment I entered, head down, visibly unenthusiastic I imagine, Nonno Paolo gestured at the chair beside the bed. I'd never seen him so frail. That alone – I was a child still even if I didn't know it – made me want to run from this brightly lit cell with its chemical stink and the insistent, rhythmic whirr of the fan in the ceiling.

It was hard to imagine a world without him and, being the child I was, anything hard was to be avoided. To tell the truth I couldn't begin to understand how the Uccello could possibly live without him overseeing the daily running of our palazzo and the small, male household it contained. He was our rock, a fixture I assumed would always be there. Except soon, they all said, my father, the nurses, the doctors and Paolo Uccello, the patriarch of one of Venice's most famous fabric houses, would be gone.

'I gather,' he said, his voice frail but not without authority, 'there's been trouble at school.'

The truth was I'd barely been a part of it. My sin was one of omission. I'd been suspended for a week, along with Maurizio Scamozzi, the ringleader, and two other boys. It wasn't the first time Scamozzi had got us in trouble and frankly it was mostly a mix of curiosity and fear that made me go along with some of his stunts. Getting kicked out of school, even temporarily, was new though.

'Sorry,' was all I could manage.

'What happened?'

A boy had been bullied. I'd been there, watching. Not taking part. Not intervening either.

'I know I should be punished,' I said. 'One week's suspension—'

'No matter.' He swept the air with his right hand. It was such a feeble gesture for a man I'd always regarded as strong and healthy. 'I wanted you to come and see me anyway. There's something you need to read.'

Nonno Paolo seemed the tallest man in the world when I was tiny. Age and illness had bent and greyed him. Now he lay beneath a single white sheet on the hospital bed, propped up by a couple of pillows, a book and a jug of water on the chest of drawers between him and the open window. Outside was the quiet stretch of Fondamente Nove that led eventually to the gigantic, mostly closed and abandoned boatyard of the Arsenale. Since it was Sunday the stretch of lagoon that ran over towards Murano was busy, rowers sculling across the mirrored surface, vaporetti working their way to and fro, back to the city, across to the Lido.

'See that?' he asked pointing at the window.

The small cemetery island of San Michele sat between us and Murano, its walls decorated with castellated gothic ornaments. There was a church by the jetty to receive visitors, the living and the dead. The place looked like a cross between a castle and a giant's tomb.

'You've been ill before,' I told him. 'You'll get better. We'll have you home in a week or so. Dad told me. He—'

'Your father told you no such thing. Soon they'll be ferrying me in a casket across that water.'

I didn't know what to say.

'This boy you were picking on. Who was he?'

'I wasn't picking on him. I was just there.'

'And did nothing?'

A vaporetto for the Lido cruised past the window. If it was summer and school was over I might be on it, all my beach things in a bag, joining some of the crowd from school headed for the sea. Enough money in my pocket to buy ice cream and drinks. We'd swim in the flat grey water of the Adriatic, play football, lie on a sunbed, maybe talk to one of the foreign girls staying at the hotels. I could close my eyes, let the sun beat down on my face, listen to the Walkman I got for Christmas. In the evening there were discos and I could usually persuade someone to buy me a beer. The music was so loud everything else went out of your head and I liked that. It seemed a part of being young.

Or else I'd just stuff a few Nikon bodies and lenses in my camera bag and head off on my own into the wilder parts of the lagoon. Maybe the southern littoral strip this time of year. The wild beach of Ca' Roman on Pellestrina. Or take the seasonal boat from Zattere, past the Cipriani Hotel across the lagoon to the beach resort at Alberoni.

I liked being with the other boys. I enjoyed time on my own too. Perhaps that was the way I was brought up. Sometimes I'd wonder what it was like to have a brother or sister, a family around you, women, girls, noise, argument, life. Not just me, Dad and Nonno Paolo who always seemed to be engrossed in business. Our footsteps echoed round the stone floors and staircases of the Palazzo Colombina like the pitter patter of lonely ghosts. It might have been different if Mum had stayed and I'd had a younger brother or sister. I don't know and Nonno Paolo always told me that it was pointless speculating about anything you couldn't change. We were the Uccello, three generations of men, trapped together in that dusty palace on the Grand Canal. There was no escape, only the long wait to find out what came next.

'I said I'm sorry. I know I should have stepped in.'

'Who was he? The victim?'

It was some teasing that got out of hand. Maurizio had started it, then his thuggish mate Scacchi had joined in. All I did was step back. I never expected it was going to get physical.

'I've apologized.'

'Who . . . was . . . he?'

'An annoying little kid. American. Maurizio told him he didn't belong here. He got mad at that. If he'd just walked away . . .'

'People do get mad when you tell them they don't belong.'

'I didn't touch him. I just watched.'

'You think that absolves you, Nico? Just watching. Not . . . punching.'

'I'm sorry. I won't do it again.'

'What was he called? This American?'

'Carmine. Maurizio says he's one of the new Jews. The foreigners. They're taking over the ghetto like it's theirs.'

He shuddered.

'A Scamozzi cares about the ghetto?'

'Maurizio says it's for us. Italians. Not them.'

'The Scamozzi have been here for centuries, Nico. They think they own everyone. Everything. The ghetto belongs to the Jews, doesn't it? We made them live there, behind its walls. The first ghetto there ever was. A prison. Somewhere we could keep them, watch them, have them do our bidding, then send them back behind those walls. A yellow star or something on their chests.'

I mumbled, 'It's not like that now.'

The look I got then was one I don't believe I'd ever seen before. It was almost as if there was a trace of hatred in it.

'Your punishment—'

'A week's suspension.'

'Which will include a history lesson.' He reached over to the bedside cabinet and dragged open the drawer. 'Look inside, boy. Here's your homework.'

There were five envelopes in there, fat, manila ones. Each numbered.

He took out the first and passed it to me.

'This was finished not long after your grandmother died. I'd written the first part in secret, you see. I never wanted her to know. Oh, and before you blame your Jewish schoolmate for landing you with this burden, best I say. It was coming your way in any case. This is a story I've been saving for you ever since you were little.'

'What?'

'I wrote this for you. Only you.'

'Why not Dad?'

He seemed, for a second, bothered by that question. Almost guilty.

'Because that's the way it is. One day you'll understand. Or so I hope. Though how long . . .' He stopped and thought for a moment. 'I can't know everything. There are five parts to this tale. You'll take this first one away, read it, then come back and we'll talk about it tomorrow morning. After that you depart with the next. We do the same until the week is over. Don't worry. We'll be done with it all by Saturday. You can spend the weekend with your friends, on the beach, swimming, chasing skirt on the Lido, the way you should. I apologize for the interruption.' Again that awkward look crossed his face. 'It's either now or never.'

When I started to open the envelope, his shaky fingers, skin tight on sinew and bone, closed on mine.

'Not here. Alone in your room back in the Colombina. Your father knows nothing of this. Promise me it stays that way until you've heard the whole story and I am gone from this world. Then the tale is yours to do with as you wish.'

Of course I promised.

'This is the untold story of your family. Our recent history. Mine mostly. No dark secret left unrevealed. No cruel deed. No betrayal. No . . .' He coughed again and this time it went on and on. 'No blood spilt without it leaves a stain.'

History. Of all the subjects they threw at us in school I hated that the most. So dry, so boring, so distant.

'You don't want to hear it, do you?'

'I think it might be best if Dad . . .'

'It's not for him! I said! It's for you. No one else. I was born to tell this story. And you were born to hear it. Don't worry. It's quite an escapade. We start during the last war, which ended just fifty-four years ago. *Fifty-four years*. The blink of an eye for an old man like me. I can see it like it was yesterday. The people . . .' His voice was breaking. 'Those who won. Those who lost. Those who were trapped in the middle not quite knowing where they belonged.' He tapped my shoulder. 'Those who simply waited, watching, thinking the darkness and the pain and the sacrifice would never touch them if only they could stay in the shadows.'

He was Nonno Paolo. Someone I loved as much as any on this earth. Of course I'd read it if he wanted. I'd do anything he asked.

'If that's what you want, Grandpa. I'm . . . flattered.'

A chuckle again, grim this time.

'You haven't read it yet. You'll soon know things that your own father could never guess at.' He tapped his nose, smiled and I saw again the kindly figure who once sat over me in bed reading fairy tales about Pinocchio and the Befana. 'Then you'll have to decide what to do with them. Secrets between us, see. Dark ones, deep ones. Time is short, now, Nico. On your way.'

As usual the Colombina was empty. Father was away on business again.

I could have phoned up some school friend and asked them round to play table tennis in the games room. Or wandered round to the Rialto where they'd probably be setting up some music, a

DJ, a band even, in the markets for the evening. Or take my camera down to Salute and photograph another sunset, a glorious ball of orange fire falling across the city rooftops.

But Nonno Paolo, the grandfather I adored, had set me a task. So instead I got myself a can of chinotto, walked up the long stone stairs to my shuttered room, settled on my single bed and turned on the lamp.

THE WOMAN IN THE LAGOON

Tuesday, November the thirtieth, 1943.

She came out of the leaden winter water just after eight in the morning, bare, bruised arms, battered face white and waxy, stocky frame wreathed in seaweed, twisted like a dying saint in one of the many martyrdoms that adorned the church walls.

Above the fading morning mist gulls squawked hungrily, sensing food. Paolo Uccello didn't look too closely but it appeared the fish had been there already. A hard winter sun was struggling to burn through the fog. Its efforts set the faintest shadow of the campanile tower of San Pietro across the scene on the mud and pebbles. He was coming to hate the cries of the seabirds. They followed him everywhere.

The war seemed endless and worse now since the Germans had come to occupy the city the previous September, the same day the king, Victor Emmanuel, had announced an armistice with the invading Allies and fled Rome for Brindisi with his provisional government. Italy was in agony, cut in two, the bloody dividing line contested all the way across the middle, slowly moving north. The invaders had dug in along the German defensive lines that straddled the country from Campania to Abruzzo. A new 'republic' had been born, nominally under the control of Mussolini, though everyone understood it was Berlin that called the tune. Il Duce, hidden away in Salò across the country in Lombardy, was little more than Hitler's puppet, not that any dared say it. Italian soldiers, confused as any about who to follow, had either fallen in with whichever side was nearest, or been rounded up by the Germans and, in some cases, slaughtered. More and more were simply laying down their weapons, slinking off into the countryside to try to find a way home, risking immediate execution if they were caught.

Most of this Paolo Uccello tried to ignore. Politics were like the world at large, best avoided. Just turned eighteen, shy and skinny, he was alone now his parents were dead, a teenage hermit spending his days and nights in the old family weaving workshop hidden away at the very edge of Castello close to the Arsenale. Still, he had to venture out for food, on this occasion to join the queue for a dry, flavourless loaf from the bakers in via Garibaldi. It was on the way home that he encountered the commotion by the waterside on the church green. Men he recognized from the boatyard round the corner, cursing and weeping as they waded into the pebble shallows where a corpse floated, pecked at by the occasional gull until they shooed them off.

It was impossible not to stare. The miserable, drenched creature emerging from the filthy waters of the tiny harbour wore a tattered red dress, sleeveless, ripped at the front and the hem, which clung to her hefty, short body like a gaudy shroud. He didn't want to look too much at her face, not when he realized he recognized her of old.

Father Filippo Garzone stood on the bank, his face the picture of misery. Next to him was Chiara Vecchi, the woman who'd worked the Uccello family looms for as long as Paolo could remember. A widow though not yet thirty, her husband had died somewhere in the fighting. Perhaps for the partisans or as a deserter from his unit. Paolo wasn't sure and didn't dare ask.

The priest and Chiara watched in silence, which was for the best since, next to them, three German soldiers and a stern-faced man in a dark overcoat were seated on the benches by the path, the troops cradling their rifles, the civilian smoking a cigarette. Their interest in the corpse seemed minimal.

'I told you . . . I said . . . It's Isabella!' cried one of the boat builders dragging the sorry, sodden shape on to the mud. 'Oh, for the love of God . . .'

The rescuers were clucking over the corpse, one of them trying to cover her bare limbs between making the sign of the cross over his fisherman's sweater.

Isabella Finzi. A fierce and argumentative spinster who'd run a vegetable stall in the Salizada Santa Giustina until the police closed her down. A Jew. They could only sell to their own kind these days and Isabella Finzi would have no truck with that, even if she could afford it. As Paolo watched, the civilian got up from the seat, showed an ID to the men and spoke to them in rapid Venetian. A local, a cop he guessed, or what passed for one these days, judging by the chilly reception he received. The man had an easy, confident air about him and a hard and vulpine face that ran from smile to scowl and back again in seconds. He said something, then went back to his seat.

The Finzi woman had been a presence in Castello for as long as Paolo could remember, one his parents tried to avoid as much as was possible. It was unwise to fraternize with Jews, especially one with a temper. He could recall her yelling at him when he had the temerity to squeeze an orange once. Perhaps he was seven or eight, and in any case his mother bought the fruit immediately. Money always quelled arguments with that kind, she said.

The time before the war seemed so distant, as was the memory he had of the Uccello family then, back when they were halfway affluent. Mother, father, son, working away at the small business of hand weaving in their little workshop in the Giardino degli Angeli, just across the bridge from San Pietro on the way to the Arsenale. A private haven, itself only accessible by a tiny wooden bridge across the *rio* that led to a door in a high, red-brick wall. Thinking back, it was as if they were different people living in a very different world. Now, barely old enough to sign legal papers, he found himself the owner of the company and its little home, an outbuilding in the ruins of what was once the palace of a fine Venetian family. Little more than a child, certainly in the eyes of the locals who'd shunned the Uccello mostly over the years. Except for Chiara Vecchi, a kindly woman who was doing her best to take the place of Paolo's dead mother. Treating him like a child. Which he wasn't, not that she seemed to notice.

Since they shut down Isabella Finzi's market stall after the Nazis arrived, the woman had taken to buying cheap wine, wandering the streets, bottle in hand, yelling abuse at Germans and any Italian Fascists she came across. On occasion he thought he'd heard her bellowing in the alley across from the bridge. A dangerous habit in these perilous times. Surely someone – Father Filippo, perhaps, always keen to guard his parishioners, even the Jews – must have warned her. Not that she was the kind of woman to heed advice, however earnestly it was offered.

Chiara Vecchi stood on the bank, arms folded, rocking to and fro on her heels, her broad face stern and angry, looking as she always did to Paolo, older than her years. Next to her the priest in all his dark robes was shaking his head as he crossed himself and mumbled a prayer. The men heaved the body up from the shore on to the grassy bank, as tearful as they appeared furious. On the bench one of the soldiers yawned and stared at his watch.

A tall, elderly man, stiff-backed and serious, strode up to join the mournful group around the body. Paolo's mother adored old paintings and had passed that love on to her son. At weekends she'd taken him round the city to the galleries and the churches, showing him all the many canvases, some famous, some barely known. Now he could only wonder which artist might have best captured the scene in front of him. Bellini, perhaps, or the living and the dead before him could all be players in one of those striking, realistic depictions of grief-stricken locals that Tintoretto produced for altars everywhere.

The newcomer took the priest's arm, squeezed it and said, in a loud voice that all could hear, 'I'm so sorry, my friend.'

'Aldo,' Garzone murmured, wiping at his face, then shook the fellow's hand, which brought a caustic, obscene curse from the police officer.

Paolo knew who Aldo Diamante was and understood why the cop would disapprove of any Venetian who gave him the time of day. When he was small and quiet and seemingly sickly his mother had taken him to the hospital of Giovanni e Paolo. There Diamante, wearing a white physician's coat, a stethoscope round his neck, had given him a piece of candy, sat him on a bench, removed his shirt and run the cold metal disc over his chest. It was a long examination, and the doctor had apologized for the pain Paolo had felt when he'd taken some blood. But a few days later they were called back to his office where Paolo was placed firmly on a seat and told to eat his greens and take more exercise. He was, Diamante had declared, a sensitive child, not sick, merely tall for his age which had expended some of his natural strength and left him a touch fragile. This was a rare and perhaps unwanted condition in Castello, a place for physical labour, not the lazy pastimes of the fey aristocrats of San Marco and Dorsoduro. But it was nothing that time, physical activity and a good diet could not cure.

The old doctor's days in Giovanni e Paolo were over. Mussolini's Racial Laws dictated that a Jewish physician could treat only Jews, just as a Jewish stallholder like Isabella Finzi must serve none but their own. Paolo had heard that Hebrews were even barred from having their names in the phone book, which must have made the work of a man known for answering emergencies at any time of the night or day quite impossible. In place of a doctor's coat the Fascist authorities called the Black Brigades – or more likely the Germans behind them – had intervened and forced Diamante to become president of the city's Jewish community, a role that was vacant since they'd placed the incumbent rabbi in custody on the Lido ahead of his deportation to a fate none could guess.

All of this came from Chiara, naturally, in whispers between sessions at their two working looms. They were not, she said, matters to talk about beyond the walls of the workshop. Gossip was dangerous; there was always someone ready to pass on idle criticism of the Fascists or the Nazis to the authorities in return for money, preferment, or simply the closure of an old grudge. Though quite why she gave Paolo this warning he didn't know; he didn't mix with anyone if he could help it. Nor had his parents. Most of the locals seem to ignore the Uccello. They were outsiders, once well-off, to them anyway, now on hard times and no use to a soul. If he tried very hard, closeted inside the Giardino degli Angeli, he could almost fool himself the war barely existed.

But not now.

Chiara marched over and took Paolo's arm.

'You don't need to see this,' she said in a voice so low the Germans wouldn't hear. 'It's not a sight to remember. We have that job to finish, don't we?'

'Three banners. We can do it.'

'It's work, Paolo. I know you've been grieving but you should have told me earlier. We're short of time.'

He didn't want this discussion.

'I recognize her. The dead woman.'

'We all do.' She scowled at the uniformed figures on the bench. 'Please. Let me take you out of here.'

'I'm eighteen, not a child,' he said and didn't move.

Diamante had crouched down over the sad corpse on the grass. Isabella Finzi's arms were wrapped around her chest. There were bruises, purple and red, livid, everywhere on her bare skin. As if she'd been beaten. Tortured even, a thought that made Paolo want to look even less. He'd heard that went on when the Black Brigades or the SS thought they had hold of someone who possessed some secrets. Though it was hard to believe a deranged woman fell into that category. It would be sensible to do Chiara's bidding and return to the workshop and his little house, a quiet, safe place away from the city and an anxious, strife-torn world he couldn't begin to comprehend.

He didn't like to be close to the dead either. A month earlier, when they brought his parents back in coffins after the Allied air raid that caught them in Verona, he'd been forced to identify their mangled corpses. Paolo wept all night afterwards, alone in his room at the water's edge, behind the conservatory workshop where the three of them had lived and worked. Sometimes, in dreams, his mother's dead and damaged face still came back to haunt him. He'd begged them not to go to Verona. Travel was always perilous and their home, hidden away at the edge of San Pietro, as safe a place as any in Venice. But they had to leave, his father insisted, as a pair, the way they always worked. The customer was from Turin, visiting Verona only briefly and demanded a personal meeting. It was an important and valuable commission, one they needed since work and money were so short.

Chiara tugged at his arm.

'In a minute,' he snapped.

They were buried in the public cemetery in Mestre the day a letter turned up confirming the commission they'd been seeking: three small banners of handwoven fabric to a specific design, with a deposit paid through a bank in Turin. His father had been right; they were short of commissions. Still, it wasn't worth dying for in smoke and rubble and fire the night American bombers rained their deadly cargo on the Veneto, mistaking a civilian street for a military encampment.

Just a moment or two. This he had to see, not that he quite knew why.

'Alberti.' Diamante spoke in a firm, loud voice, the same he'd used in the hospital talking to a skinny young weakling called Paolo Uccello. The man he was addressing was a sour-faced fellow in the kind of dark and heavy overcoat locals preferred in midwinter. 'Come here, please.'

The chap grunted something foul in rough Venetian, stamped out his cigarette beneath his boot, then wandered over to the group arranged around the broken shape on San Pietro's thin winter grass.

Isabella Finzi must have been forty or so, a strong woman with fierce eyes and a hawk nose. Some of the men used to chase her, his mother said, but not for long. Her fury and her madness soon saw them off.

'What do you want?' Alberti demanded.

Paolo recognized the name. Chiara had warned him to steer clear if ever he should hear he was in the vicinity. A former local Carabinieri officer who'd been moved to the new National Guard Mussolini had invented to replace the military police force of old. The man had a reputation even when he wore the dark blue uniform of the Carabinieri. Always happy to gossip while they worked, she reckoned he was as crooked as those he sought to catch, well-known for demanding bribes from storekeepers, money, fish, meat, cheese, anything he fancied. Favours from the ladies he wanted too.

'This woman has been beaten. There are abrasions on her arm. A contusion on her forehead. My opinion is she was attacked and thrown into the water to die. Raped possibly. If you take her in for examination . . .'

The man barely glanced at the wounds, the bruises, the cuts, the injuries the physician was indicating.

'Who are you to say?' the fellow replied. 'You're no doctor any more. This crazy bitch . . . we all knew her. Yelling at people in the street. Drunk as a whore. Wandering round at night.'

He walked forward, stared at the corpse, then spat at the muddy beach.

'My finding is she was out here full of wine, fell in and drowned. That will go down on my report. An accident. Jews rarely kill themselves.'

'Balls!' Diamante yelled.

The priest took his arm and tried to shush him.

'Balls! Look at her, man. You're a Venetian. One of us. You grew up here, Alberti. I treated your sister—'

'Not any more. Those are the rules. We don't let Jews get their sweaty fingers on our folk now.'

'Rules. Rules.' Father Filippo was trying to push the old doctor back. 'What rules say you ignore a woman violated in the night? Her life snuffed out like it didn't matter? Do you not know your duty?'

The cop simply laughed.

'My duty?'

'Please, Aldo.' The priest begged as he stood between them. 'This serves no purpose. We must deal with poor Isabella.'

'My duty?' Alberti repeated, pushing Garzone out of the way. He was a good head shorter than Diamante, with the build and the attitude of a street bully. 'My duty is to keep Mussolini's law. Which says . . .' He turned and grinned at the Germans. 'You don't count. Not now. So shut your Jew mouth and go home.' He nodded at the body on the shingle. 'And take this piece of shit with you.'

'Luca!' the priest cried. 'Think of what you say.'

'Oh, I think of it, Father. We've been told. All of us. This country's going to be cleansed. You mark my words. Once we have public order under control. And the terrorists up against a wall. Now, Diamante. Remove this Jewish whore of yours. I don't care what you do with her.' He turned again and winked at the Germans who were already getting ready to leave. 'We've better things to do.'

With that the four of them marched off. When they were almost out of sight one of the men who'd dragged Isabella Finzi from the earth aimed an imaginary pistol at their backs and fired three imaginary shots.

'*Bang*,' he murmured.

Bang.

Bang.

'Stinking *Crucchi.*'

Crucchi. It was an insult for the Germans that was never said within earshot. 'That treacherous bastard Alberti . . . he'll get it one day too.'

Paolo recognized the man: Rocco Trevisan, owner of a small boat he used to fetch and carry cargo around the city, on occasion goods for the looms when they were busy. A quick-tempered individual from the tenements close to the shuttered pavilions of the Biennale, strong-willed, bossy. A communist, Chiara said, not that he understood what that really meant. There were little bars around via Garibaldi where men like him drank and argued and occasionally fought of an evening. Places those seeking a safer life always avoided.

'You got an undertaker who can deal with her?' the fellow next to Trevisan asked.

'Of course,' Diamante replied.

The chap frowned.

'Crazy old Jew but what the hell?'

'She was a Venetian,' Paolo cried. He couldn't help himself. 'They shouldn't treat us like . . . like we don't matter.'

Trevisan glared at him and called for a boat.

'Paolo.' Chiara Vecchi's stern gaze was on him. 'I asked you not to witness this. Now you make these outbursts. It's not wise.'

There was a heat in him he barely recognized.

'I know what's right and what's wrong.'

For some reason both Father Filippo and Diamante were gazing at him then, and the old doctor cast a glance in Chiara's direction too.

'You're leaving here if I have to drag you,' she declared, pushing him quite forcefully towards the wooden bridge that led towards home.

'I told you. I'm not a child.'

'Nevertheless, I promised your mother . . .'

The priest rushed to join them and there was a firmness in his voice even she couldn't miss.

'Leave this to me, please. I can take the young man back home . . .'

Chiara cast the man in black a glance that was almost hostile.

'No need, Father—'

'I insist,' he said and seized Paolo Uccello by the arm.

The workshop of the Uccello began life as an elegant pavilion in the garden of a palazzo belonging to an aristocratic clan from Vicenza. Made rich by trade, they'd built themselves a mock-Palladian mansion in the shadow of the Arsenale boatyards, complete with arbours, bowers, rose beds and fruit trees, a shady retreat from the searing heat of summer.

During the turmoil of unification the family backed the wrong side and found themselves ruined, washed away on a tide of political *acqua alta* that sent them scuttling from the city. As arguments built over debts and titles and ownership, the palazzo was abandoned, looted eventually by locals seeking stone for their own homes and to shore up the banks of San Pietro across the canal. Behind the remaining high wall and narrow channel of water crossed by its private wooden bridge, only the pavilion, its conservatory and the gardens survived, out of sight in a solitary quarter of the city few visited any more. There was no reason. The Arsenale to the west was a forbidden military area while San Pietro and Castello to the east and south were poor, working-class districts where many struggled to pay the rent. To the north, past an old, ruined, hexagonal watchtower, lay the sluggish lagoon stretching out towards the little-used islands of Certosa and Le Vignole.

It was a secluded, private hermitage in a city where, the wealthy apart, most people lived on top of one another, crammed into terraced tenements, family upon family. The ruins had remained empty until Paolo's grandfather, an enterprising fabric merchant with ambition, hit upon an opportunity and picked up the deeds for a pittance. Silk weaving had virtually vanished from Venice in the early nineteenth century after Napoleon closed the republic's fabric school on Fondamenta San Lazzaro. But Simone Uccello, who Paolo remembered only dimly since his grandfather had died when the boy was four, had discovered the equipment for the old school remained in the shuttered building. He was canny enough to pay the city chickenfeed to clear the place, rescuing sixteen wooden looms and sufficient equipment to restart a weaving business from scratch.

This was the 1880s. No one had used a Jacquard loom in decades, though a few old hands remembered how. With their help and some reference books, Simone created a small, highly skilled weaving shop which, after a few years, was able to replicate the finest velvet of the Venetian Republic at its peak, directly from the patterns they'd used.

Europe was entranced by these sumptuous fabrics from another age. Prosperous decades followed. By the early twentieth century the House of Uccello was a small but established business producing a range of fabrics to traditional patterns, for wealthy locals, for those elsewhere in Italy who could pay the price. At its height in 1928 the company employed sixteen weavers full time, one for each of the Jacquard looms. Their work won medals in Turin and Paris, New York and Barcelona. Uccello velvet could be found in grand houses in England, city halls in Copenhagen and Reykjavik, opera houses and the ballrooms of grand ocean liners.

The prosperity was already starting to fade when Paolo came into the world. The economic woes of the 1930s made handmade velvet a luxury few could afford. At the age of twelve he was removed from school, a place he hated, and joined the family business, learning the way of the loom as an apprentice with the idea that one day he would take over from his father as company director.

Even so money, something the family had once taken for granted, was short. Paolo soon realized the early curtailment of his education was as much to do with cash as anything else. They needed cheap labour. They needed commissions. When he turned thirteen the family was forced to abandon their beloved apartment on the Zattere in Dorsoduro with its splendid view of Palladio's Redentore across the Giudecca Canal. Father had converted some spare warehouse space at the back of the workshop into two-bedroom accommodation and they would now live there.

Still the work dwindled. When the looms broke down they became uneconomic to repair and were sold for scrap and firewood. By the time his parents left for Verona on that last, ill-fated trip in July, there were just three left. The family had been reduced to eating cheap pasta and vegetables most days, avoiding creditors whenever possible. Chiara Vecchi had first worked for his father when she was thirteen. Now, yet to turn thirty and widowed, she was the last worker left as they struggled to get by in the strange, artificial world that war had imposed upon Venice.

It seemed the cruellest irony that Verona gave the drowning company a lifeline and sent back Paolo's parents in their coffins. A few days after the funeral in Mestre the order arrived, with a down payment of ten thousand lire – the equivalent of almost five hundred American dollars – and the promise of a further twenty thousand upon production of the final item, three small identical banners to a specific pattern. The bank had looked at him sideways when he came to deposit the cheque, inquiring if he was old enough to handle the company accounts. Legally he was, just, even if he relied on Chiara to tell him how they worked.

The detail of the commission was easier. His parents had produced a detailed template already and the punch cards for the loom to make the pattern, so desperate were they for the contract. Sitting in the garden, on the old wooden bench beneath the orange trees, weeping at the memory of his lost parents, the letter in his hand, Paolo had known he had no choice but to accept. Who the customer was scarcely mattered. Work was what he needed, to occupy his mind, to give the ever-loyal Chiara some money too. To blot out the fractured world beyond the red-brick wall of the sanctuary the Giardino degli Angeli offered him.

The birds were singing as he went over the letter from Turin. The last of the goldcrests, a flock of them, tiny, bright shapes scattered through the orange and yellow fruit on the branches. Their melody – two notes, high-pitched, repeating seven or eight times – was the rhythm his father had told him to think of when working the loom, pushing the weft yarn with a beater to make the pattern the punch card demanded.

Si-dah-si-dah-si-dah-sichi-si-piu.

Uccello. Their name meant 'bird' so perhaps it was simply a joke. Soon the goldcrests vanished, headed south to escape the freezing Venetian winter. They, at least, could fly the beleaguered city whenever they wished. No birds sang at all as he walked back from San Pietro, Father Filippo Garzone by his side.

They stopped in the garden, next to the fallen head of a weather-beaten angel. Shattered sculptures from the old, ravaged palazzo ranged across the lawn, heads and torso and arms. His father had tried to sell some when they were struggling, but there were no rich foreign tourists around in wartime. So they stayed where they were, like fallen victims of a long-forgotten battle.

'You have a lovely home, Paolo. Many would envy you.'

Father Filippo was a familiar figure, a man who pottered around the northern quarters of Castello in his dark priest's robes, stopping to talk to everyone. He was fifty or so, not stout like some of the priests who were forever cadging food and favours from their parishioners, but almost skeletal, as if he was sick or starving himself in sympathy with the privations of his flock. His hair was long, chestnut shot through with grey, his voice had the accent of his native Vicenza. Had he not joined the church he would have made a good hotelier or restaurateur in Paolo's opinion. There was always something charming about him, a steady, patient temperament that sought calm amid strife.

Technically the Uccello were of his parish since it extended across from the island of San Pietro to take in the terraces running to the Arsenale. But they had never been frequent visitors to his services, or inclined to confession. Work got in the way, even on Sundays, father said. There was more to it than that. His parents were business people first and Catholics second. Enthusiastic believers busily crossing themselves if there was a clerical commission to be won. When they'd dried up years ago, so it seemed had their faith.

'What would they envy, Father? My parents are dead. I've no idea how we can keep the looms working. Even if I want to.'

Garzone briefly closed his eyes as if in pain.

'I apologize. A priest says stupid things as easily as anyone else. I meant . . .' He gestured at the garden. 'This. Seclusion. Solitude. Peace.' He smiled. 'Well, as much as one can call it peace in times like these. A private peace. Which is a start. How are you coping? Is there anything I can do to help?'

He didn't know how to answer those questions. The memory of the dead Isabella Finzi, drenched, stiff from the cold lagoon, wouldn't leave his head.

'I'm trying my best.'

'And Chiara . . .?'

'She helps.'

'We need friends in times like this. I'm sorry you witnessed all that, Paolo.' The priest was always good at reading someone's thoughts. 'I wish you hadn't. Sometimes one should try to walk on.'

There was a curious note in the man's voice. Almost as if he was fishing.

'I was passing. I saw something happening. I couldn't . . . not watch.'

Garzone nodded.

'Does Chiara bring you news?'

'Sometimes. And I listen to the radio.'

'It's easiest to stay behind these walls. Keep your head down. I know we don't get real news here. Not *true* news. But word gets out. The Americans and the British are coming up from the south. Now they have Rome firmly in their sights, this can only go one way. The Germans are losing and they know it.'

'The ones you see here don't seem to. They look like victors. More so than ever.'

Which was true. But Venice, everyone said, was unique, an island attached to the mainland by a single slender bridge. It had little in the way of military importance, being at the edge of the Adriatic in the north east. The Americans and the British wouldn't bomb the city because of that and its heritage, or so it was rumoured. The Germans and the Fascists used the place principally almost as a leisure destination, somewhere they could go for a few days to escape the shock of conflict. One night, after some wine, his mother had grumbled that there were more brothels in Cannaregio now than had ever existed before the war. Ribald theatres and nightclubs had set up too. The bars in San Marco and the fancy hotels on the Grand Canal and Riva degli Schiavoni were as busy as ever, though with visiting Germans and Italian Fascists, not the international set of old. Even La Fenice kept up its opera programme, with well-known names.

'The Crucchi we see here in Venice are mostly inadequate fools, Paolo. That's why they're here. Not out terrorizing ordinary people in the countryside. Murdering partisans or anyone whose face offends them. We must be patient. We must wait.'

Again it seemed as if the man was looking for something.

'How long? How long must we wait?'

'I don't know.'

Paolo didn't believe that.

'My father told us the Americans and the British would invade France soon. When they do, that's where they'll try to win this war.' History. He still remembered some of that from school. 'If they came through Italy they'd have to make their way across the mountains, like Hannibal in reverse. Why take the trouble when they can go straight to Berlin the easy way?'

There was that friendly nod again.

'You're rather more in tune with affairs than I realized.'

'I'm not a child!'

'How could you be?' Garzone said in a quiet, considerate tone. 'After what you've been through.'

'So even if Italy is liberated we may be the last. They could be here years.'

'Possibly. But we will be free one day. This war will end. Your world will turn to good. It always does. God demands it. So do men eventually. Mussolini and the Germans will be defeated. Of that I have no doubt. Nor do many of us in Venice, not that we say it out loud in public. That would be unwise.' A quick and inquisitive look then. 'This radio of yours . . .'

'It's not against the law.'

'That depends what you listen to.' He took a deep breath. 'May I see?'

'Why?'

The priest drew his cloak around himself.

'If it's a problem . . .'

'Shouldn't you be taking care of Isabella Finzi?' Paolo asked.

'She's a Jew. Diamante will find one of their undertakers.' He took Paolo's arm for a second and leaned down, then said, almost in a whisper, 'How do you feel about the Americans and the British? Do you blame them for your parents' deaths?'

It seemed a strange question.

'They dropped the bombs.'

'Yes. They did. Bombs kill and maim. Anonymously, those who dispatch them believe. The newspaper said the aircraft were aiming at civilians deliberately. But they're run by the Nazis. You can't believe a word they print. A friend from Verona told me the target was an army barracks. They mistook the railway for something else.'

Paolo wasn't minded to answer that question. Still the priest persisted.

'And what of the partisans . . . the Italians fighting the Black Brigades *and* the Germans?'

'What of them?'

'Are they brave? Are they foolish? Are they your enemy too?' Garzone hesitated, as if unsure of the answer himself. 'Or should they behave like the rest of us? Stay quiet, obedient. Tame. Hope to get through the day until finally we are free.'

'What do you think?'

'I think I don't know.' The priest smiled and looked around the garden. 'If I lived in this place I believe I'd want to stay behind these walls until the sun broke through those clouds and the war was over. My work, my duty . . . they make that impossible.'

Chiara hadn't wanted Garzone to accompany him home. She must have had a reason.

'I was simply seeking your opinion, Paolo. Whoever it was murdered Isabella, because murdered she surely was, the police and the Germans will do nothing to bring the fellow to justice. Even if that policeman Alberti wished it, the Nazis would stop him. They think we belong to them now. Theirs to do with as they wish.' The man in black put an arm around his shoulders. He had a firmer grip than Paolo expected. 'Bombs are indiscriminate, though I know they've caused you pain. The Black Brigades, the SS . . . they inflict agony deliberately and choose the ones they slaughter. An accidental death is a tragedy. A deliberate one cold-hearted murder. These people are beyond the Lord. They grin in their victims' faces as they wield their blades and prepare the rope. I know you're happy in your little hermitage. But the world outside blows in on the wind and rain. Can you remain content here forever, Paolo? If there was the smallest, safest opportunity to offer a spark of hope against the darkness . . . would you reach for it?'

If only it was summer and he could hear the birds singing again. Though, he wondered, too, how many times he could sit in this garden crying over his mother and father. What they would say? Politics never interested either of them. Right and wrong, though. They mattered. That, he now realized, was the cause of his outburst in the thin grey fog of San Pietro. It was their dead voices in his head, protesting at another innocent lost to the cruelty of war.

'I'd very much like to see that radio of yours,' the priest added. 'Mine is old and will need replacing soon, I fear, since the chances of repairing it these days . . . Well . . .' He lumbered towards the dusty glass of the conservatory. 'This is a conversation we should continue inside.'

Luca Alberti was thirty-nine. Police work was the only job he'd known. First in the Carabinieri building near the Greek church in Castello where he'd soon risen through the ranks. Then, after the creation of Mussolini's new puppet state, as a captain in its replacement, the National Republican Guard.

The landings of the Allied forces in the south had divided Italy in more ways than one. Il Duce was first under arrest after the coup in Rome, then freed by a daring German raid and taken north to start his phoney republic under Hitler's fist in Salò. The Italian military caught on the wrong side of the line as the Nazis took control faced a grim choice: side with the old guard or risk being shot if the Germans feared they might defect to the new. Nor had the battlefront changed much in months. The British and Americans had made slow progress north as the wettest and vilest winter in years came to greet them. For the Nazis in the Veneto, the Black Brigades and the rest of the Fascists left working for Mussolini, the greatest local threat came from the disparate forces of the partisans fighting a guerrilla campaign of assassinations and strategic bombings of railway lines and military installations.

In Venice, Mussolini's artificial state now found itself in a strange, almost idle lull. There were still a few who believed that the Germans would prevail, or perhaps even that there would be an armistice allowing two rival Italian nations to exist, north and south. In his gut Alberti understood there could be no such solution. The king and his government had sided with the invaders and knew which way the war was headed. One day they would come, perhaps not soon, but the end was inevitable and when it arrived it would be bloody.

By that time he'd be gone, out of Italy altogether. He had money. He had contacts too, and nothing to keep him in Venice. The year before his wife had left him and taken their son to live with her parents in Chioggia. She'd become sickened by the fact that, more and more, he was working alongside the Fascists, tracking down partisans or those who were intellectually hostile to the regime, men and women who might be executed in public or simply disappear. What really got to her was when he began paying a madame of one of the brothels for German lessons and a few tricks on the side.

His original job was a perilous occupation, one that offered little opportunity for reward and much for retaliation by a public who hated collaborators. Then came September and the German occupation. With it he was offered the opportunity to move entirely into the Nazi's camp as a liaison officer between occupier and occupied. His new office was in Ca' Loretti, a palazzo on the Grand Canal at the Rio de San Moisè, a little way along from the shuttered Harry's Bar. Once an aristocratic home, the four-storey building was a minor sight among the grander palaces of the area, middling Venetian Gothic, a crumbling pile dating from the late sixteenth century. For the previous fifty years it had been used as council offices and was as cold and spare within as any other public building in the city. Now it was nominally under the control of Mussolini's Italian National Guard. In truth, as everyone in Venice knew, it was home to the SS, a place to be avoided at all costs by guilty and innocent alike.

Anyone brave enough to walk the narrow alley by the side to the Grand Canal might on occasion hear screams from the cells at the back where torturers, local and German, went about their work. It was common knowledge that the garden courtyard where council workers once took their lunch breaks was now used for summary executions, the victims, taken out in rubber sheets to waiting boats by the building's private jetty.

Alberti, a local who knew the lie of the land, the people, the language, Italian and Veneto, the way the unique city worked, had proved a natural for the tasks the Germans sent his way. The financial rewards were reasonable and came with plenty of opportunities for bribery and extortion among those he caught working the black markets, running brothels, smuggling tobacco and illicit booze across the Adriatic.

As icing on the cake he'd been allotted a place in the Hotel Gioconda around the corner. This was an establishment entirely in the hands of the Germans who required secure accommodation for those working in Ca' Loretti. Its sixty rooms were luxurious by Venetian standards, once occupied by wealthy Europeans enjoying the Grand Tour. Of an evening the bars and restaurants served as salons where military men on brief breaks from the war paraded their mistresses and the occasional spy went about his or her business. The upstairs ballroom at the canal front was used for military banquets and doubled as a casino at times. On the floors above some of the suites were home to a few of the most beautiful and expensive whores in the city.

For the visiting Nazis, Venice was a welcome break from the muddy, violent, bloody business of warfare. But never one to be taken lightly. There were always partisans to be considered. Two months before, a drunken Austrian officer had been caught lurking in the Strada Nuova and shot dead on the spot.

Alberti had immediately raided the homes of the partisan sympathizers he deemed most weak when it came to pressure. Under the lightest torture names were swiftly revealed, the culprits apprehended and immediately executed in the street. Then, to his dismay, the Germans satisfied their continuing lust for blood with reprisals. A dozen known anti-Fascists came under suspicion, a teacher, a gondolier and a baker among them. They were dragged from their homes, made to kneel on the old cobbles and dispatched with a single bullet to the neck, their bodies left to rot out in the open for three days with the locals under pain of death not to touch them.

He'd hated all this. Their executions seemed unnecessary. Had the Nazis understood the Venetians as well as he did, they might have appreciated they had only increased the dangers they faced, not diminished them. A man could only kick a dog so much until it gave into its own nature and kicked back.

The single page report on the Finzi case was on his desk. That morning they'd picked up the soldier responsible, the lowest form of Nazi grunt, drunk in a bar near the Piazza San Marco, boasting to all and sundry of how he'd raped a Jew the night before and thrown her in the canal. He was now confined to barracks on Giudecca. The man's fate was in the hands of Ernst Oberg, the SS officer in charge of Alberti's department, running security operations from an office overlooking the courtyard at the back.

Oberg held the rank of Hauptscharführer, squad leader, a position Alberti understood to be unique to the SS, the highest an enlisted man might gain. Being the boss he'd claimed the place by the window. Midway down the room, to left and right, sat his German underlings: Gustav Sachs and Rudolf Sander, two low grade SS men who relished being away from real fighting, all the more so in a city that allowed them to indulge whatever vices took their fancy. Alberti was given the shadiest, most cramped space of all, near the rear wall. There was a hierarchy in all this, naturally, and as a Venetian, he was at the bottom.

There were Crucchi Alberti could deal with and Oberg was one of them. He almost admired the chap in a way: intelligent, thoughtful, always willing to talk an action through before embarking upon it. A slight man in his early forties, a teacher before the war, in recent weeks he'd begun to look drawn, ill perhaps. He avoided the bars, the casino and the brothels and mostly read in his suite at night, alone as far as Alberti understood.

In the months since the Germans seized control of Venice, Sachs and Sander had quickly established they couldn't be more different. The two of them lived on booze and women and relished the job of harassing Venetians, innocent or not, whenever they had the chance. Alberti knew he had to watch his tongue around them. The SS was as riddled with gossip as the city itself. If Oberg displayed any reluctance to carry out the orders he received from command, then his underlings would surely be keen to pass that on to those who might do the man damage.

'This soldier who murdered the woman last night.' Alberti tapped his finger on the single-page report in front of him. 'He's confessed. What happens now?'

'She was a Jew,' Sachs butted in. 'Give him a medal and a promotion.'

'No.' Sander wagged an admonitory finger at him. 'He must be punished. Tattoo the Iron Cross on his dick. That way he gets a penalty and a reward at the same time.'

The two of them guffawed at that, their belly laughs echoing round the room. Oberg sighed and stared out of the window. The few trees in the courtyard were losing their leaves. Somewhere distant there were shouts and screams. A woman perhaps. When they were being tortured it was always hard to tell from the sounds alone.

Then came a crack, a shot and silence.

'I just thought—'

'None of your business,' Sachs cut in. 'The fellow's one of ours.'

Alberti shoved the report to one side.

'Perhaps I got a copy of the paperwork by accident then.'

Oberg lit a cigarette and he thought, *You shouldn't be smoking, chum. You don't look up to it.*

'He'll go back to active service. In the field,' Oberg said. 'In Germany. That will be punishment enough. Perhaps as good as a death sentence. Who knows?' He stared at Sander then Sachs. 'If you'd like to volunteer to join him I could always ask.'

They glanced at one another.

'Work to do here, boss,' Sander said. 'Lots of it.'

Oberg retrieved a report from the pile on his desk, walked over and placed it on Alberti's desk.

'Indeed. Look at that will you?'

He made out he was reading the thing, but he kept listening too. And anyway it was a file he'd got sight of the day before. An interesting one.

Sachs plucked up the courage to speak.

'Picking out Jews one by one's a lot of effort for little reward, it seems to me. Why can't we just grab them all out of the ghetto in one go?'

'This is Venice, not Warsaw. Tell them again,' Oberg ordered. 'Perhaps one day it'll stick.'

That, Alberti doubted. But he did repeat what he'd said to most of the Germans a million times. Hunting Jews in a city like Venice wasn't simple. A few lived in the ghetto, for sure. But mostly they were ordinary citizens, ordinary-looking too, indistinguishable from their neighbours. Many ran small businesses and a good number were secular, rarely visiting the ghetto, the synagogue or a rabbi except when some ceremony called for it. A good few had supported Mussolini in the beginning, being families with commercial interests who saw him as a buffer against the threat of communism. It wasn't simple to identify people who didn't wear badges, yellow stars, strange hair styles. The average local Jew saw himself as an Italian first and Hebrew second, and had done ever since Napoleon brought discrimination to an end, only for Mussolini to reintroduce it just before the start of the war with his Racial Laws. There was also the plain fact that they had no legal power to round them up. Not yet. The Germans didn't feel bound by any laws but Mussolini usually did for some reason. If the seizure of the Jews was to happen in any organized way it would surely be heralded by some announcement of how they were a stain upon the nation, one that needed to be removed, along with legislation to make their detention possible.

The two underlings listened, then Sander said, 'So how do we find them?'

'Is it a priority?' Alberti asked. He'd made those threats that morning when they fished out the Finzi woman to make sure Aldo Diamante knew his place. But they were empty and the old man probably knew it. There were much bigger fish to fry than the timid community of Jews spread across Venice, Murano and the Lido.

'I've asked their president to compile a list,' Oberg said. 'He's working on it. Slowly, I imagine, though to be fair I doubt it's a simple task. Venice, not Warsaw. How many times do I have to repeat this?'

'Well.' Sachs banged his fist on the desk. 'When we've got it we'll round the buggers up.'

'Then what?' Alberti asked.

Sachs grinned, pulled out his lighter, sparked a flame, grinned even wider while Sander opposite laughed.

'That's what I hear anyways.'

'And how do you propose we get them out of here?' Oberg asked.

'On the railroad,' Sander said, and sounded a little puzzled.

'They're principally occupied with military traffic.' Oberg stood up and went to a map of the north of Italy, stretching from Genoa to Venice and into Austria. He ran his finger along the train line running across the country to Milan and the alternative north to Munich through Verona and Bolzano. 'There's no capacity east to west. The mountain route keeps getting shut by damned partisans and their bombs. Only last week . . .' He glared at the men. 'You don't even know what I'm talking about, do you? You don't even read the daily reports?'

Sachs and Sander shuffled awkwardly in their seats.

'There was an attack in the Vallagarina valley near Rovereto,' Alberti said, tapping a finger on the papers on his desk. 'They blew up the track.'

'They did.' Oberg got up and deposited another report directly to Alberti, quite deliberately. 'It's going to take us a week or more to clear. God knows they were prepared.'

When he looked at the new report, Alberti realized the intelligence had been updated. At first it was claimed the entire partisan team, six men and two women, had been cornered, five of them killed during the shootout, two committing suicide, one taken into custody though seriously wounded. The latest news came from interrogation of the survivor. It seemed two of the gang had evaded capture, one, a woman, the leader. Regional headquarters wanted their heads, an order Oberg could not ignore.

There were two photographs with the report, a man and a woman. A name for each written at the foot along with a one-page report. Giovanni and Micaela Artom, aged twenty-one and twenty-three respectively. Brother and sister from a middle-class, Jewish family in Turin. They looked too young to be trouble and scarcely Hebrew at all. Just everyday, dark-haired Italians staring at a police camera with the belligerent hatred most people wore, guilty or not.

They were both at university in Padua, the brother studying literature, the sister medicine. Earlier in the year they'd been picked up as suspected partisans, then released for some reason. Only later was it discovered they were part of the local cell, a unit they'd formed after the capture and execution of their parents. Micaela Artom, Mika to her comrades, was the ringleader.

'Diamante's list will go to a Jew hunter Milan is sending us,'

Oberg said. 'One of their own who's decided to help us. He can work out what's true, what's bogus, who the old man's trying to hide from us.'

Sachs chuckled.

'Why the hell would a Jew want to do that?'

'He probably thinks he'll live,' Alberti said.

Oberg carried on.

'Till we have specific orders I have no interest in Jews. Except for this pair. They were behind that attack. Their fellow terrorist began to talk before we shot him. He said the woman was as ruthless as anyone he'd ever met and familiar with explosives and weaponry. The brother was the propagandist. He was wounded escaping. It seems they're on their way here.'

Alberti found it hard to suppress a groan. Hunting anyone on the run was never easy. In normal cities there was a network of informers to work with. Streets and squares and communities that could be mined for information. Nothing was so simple in Venice. The locals regarded themselves as a race apart. They had long memories of occupation, by the Austrians and, earlier, the French who had brought to an end an independent republic that had lasted a millennium. People rarely talked easily and never to strangers. Which was why the Germans tolerated him.

Then there was the geography. The place was mostly a spider's web of alleys, dead-ends, waterways, abandoned warehouses and teeming tenements. It was a simple task for a fugitive to avoid the handful of large public squares, impossible to police the streets with any great success. If a fugitive was concerned they were closing in, all the rogue had to do was steal a boat at night and sail out to one of the islands, Burano, Torcello, Sant'Erasmo, and vanish into the remote marshes.

If he'd been a Jewish partisan on the run Venice was exactly the place he'd head for. With one proviso. You had to know someone. At a time like this no local would tolerate two dangerous strangers without an introduction.

Castello. Via Garibaldi. The drinkers, the troublemakers, the communists in the warren of terraced streets there. Not far from where he'd been that morning watching a handful of surly men drag the corpse of Isabella Finzi from the water. That was the place to start even if it was a perilous district for him to wander alone.

'Alberti,' said Oberg, staring at him.

'Sir?'

'These are your people, not ours. If anyone's going to find them it's you. Where do we start?'

After a moment he said what was in his head anyway.

'You take that idiot soldier from his barracks and hang him out in public for all to see. Then invite a response. People here aren't ungrateful. The Finzi woman was one of theirs. They understand an eye for eye. It might loosen a tongue for me. That's all I need. One tongue.'

Sachs and Sander banged their desks and swore, a stream of vile epithets about Jews and traitors and enemies.

Oberg waited for them to calm down, then said, 'You know I won't do that. I can't hang one of ours for killing a Jew.' He laughed, without any humour and lit another cigarette. 'Imagine the precedent it would set.'

It was the answer he'd expected.

'Do we believe they're here already?'

The German exhaled a grey cloud of smoke.

'We only have the word of a dead terrorist who thought they'd be headed this way. You tell me.'

'Then,' the Venetian said, scooping the photos and the reports from the table, 'I will ask around.'

Outside he bought himself a caffè corretto in the Marino, a safe bar opposite the palazzo entrance, somewhere all the Germans used, watched over by the building guards at the entrance. Double the grappa for free as usual.

Alberti flipped a few lire on the counter.

'How's things?' wondered the young lad behind the counter. 'Busy?'

Beppe was his name. He'd washed dishes in Harry's Bar down the way before it got closed. A simpleton.

'You know better than to ask questions like that.'

The kid blushed, the blood suffusing his pale cheeks. He looked terrified in an instant.

'Don't say that to anyone, sonny,' Alberti told him. 'They might not be as forgiving as me.' He picked the coins off the counter. 'There. You can pay for this one. Be grateful you got off lightly.'

* * *

The morning mist was persistent but there was a little more light coming through the haze. Falling through the long conservatory windows, which still had the style of the original garden pavilion, the day cast the workshop in a soft, cold light. The priest smiled at the sight that greeted him. Three looms set for weaving, a small banner partly completed on each one. Paolo and Chiara had taken turns in moving to the spare loom from time to time to keep each piece of fabric roughly at the same stage of production.

'This is like your own secret Aladdin's Cave,' Garzone declared.

Paolo said nothing. They walked past the machines and creels and storage cabinets and reached the door to the living quarters his father had created when money began to run short. A main room which served as both dining room and kitchen. One large bedroom for his parents on the left, now unoccupied since he preferred to stay in his own on the other side. A bathroom took up the space on the right to the rear, feeding waste directly through a drain into the lagoon, which was probably illegal, his father said; they were supposed to put in a *pozzo nero*, a cesspit to be drained by one of the boats that carried out that foul-smelling task around the city. But hidden away at the very edge of the city, they could probably escape that expense. If the council did find out it might take them years.

A pair of small windows looked out of the back towards the lagoon. In the grey fog the far wall of the Arsenale was just visible with its own hexagonal watchtower, a larger version of the Uccello's ruined equivalent ten metres beyond the window.

Garzone sat at the table and unbuttoned his cloak. Paolo unplugged the radio and placed it in front of him.

'Very nice. I will remember the make. This is a large place for one young man.'

'It's where I live. It's where Chiara and I try to earn a living.'

'Ah.' He gestured back at the workshop. 'The weaving.'

'The weaving, Father. What do you want?'

The priest smiled. He had grey and very bushy eyebrows which, when Paolo was younger, reminded him of the caterpillars his father used to pick off the fruit trees, cursing every one.

'A very direct question, Paolo. People out there, if they think of you at all, doubtless believe you're still a child. A frightened little boy. Hiding away here now your parents are dead. Too scared to emerge in the light.'

'Am I supposed to care?'

'One should always take note of what others think. But it's not quite as simple as that, is it? Would you have some tea?'

Paolo poured him a glass of table water from the bottle he kept by the sink.

'Thank you,' Garzone said and didn't touch the glass.

'They'll do nothing about Isabella Finzi?'

He frowned and the grey eyebrows furled more than usual.

'The Crucchi? Of course not. One dead Jew? They've bigger things on their mind. They're the new masters of Italy. At least the part they control. Takes a little while to understand you've got your fists round something so precious. Especially when they're so full of hate.'

'What about our own people? The police?'

The wry, hurt smile again.

'Our own people? What does that mean anymore? There are all kinds of Venetians, all kinds of Italians now. Fascists who wish to do others harm. Fascists who don't and regret they signed up to Mussolini's accursed ideas in the first place, and now have no idea how to retreat from them.'

Paolo understood that last. His parents had thought Il Duce a decent man, perhaps a necessary one, for a while, someone who put Italy's interests before those of other nations. Even towards the end they were never openly hostile, though perhaps that was because it would be bad for what little business they had and expose them to accusations of disloyalty, or even treason.

'Then,' the priest continued, 'you have those who wish to fight his failing regime. The partisans. Who aren't a single group by any means. Some are the people who openly opposed him through the ballot box before. Centrists, democrats, Christians. And others . . .' He stopped and scratched his cheek as if trying to decide his own position here. 'They have a lower opinion of what we used to call democracy, perhaps because it gave us Mussolini and Hitler in the first place. Communists. Marxists. Who again tend to divide into different groups at times in ways I fail to understand.'

'You seem to know a lot.'

'Unlike you I talk to many people. All kinds. Ones who approve of me. Ones who are wary. Like you.'

'My parents weren't really believers. Not unless there was money on the table. They liked a quiet, private life.'

'They barely knew anyone here, Paolo. You came from Dorsoduro. You had money. You're not like the people here, are you?'

It was true. They didn't mix. Didn't make friends. He doubted most of the locals even realized they were there most of the time.

'It wasn't my choice. Or doing. We weren't aloof.'

Garzone shook his head and continued, 'Of course not. These streets . . . the people here have grown up living on top of one another. It took years before they regarded me as one of their own. And I'm their priest. They're ordinary folk, dissatisfied with the present situation, desperate for the war to come to an end. Determined that when it does their friends and families will survive if possible.' He leaned forward and rapped his fingers on the table. 'You see the dilemma? When the world turns dark do you stay hidden and wait for the light to return? Or do you try to strike a small flame oneself? And know it may snuff out your own life along the way?'

Paolo returned to the kitchen range and retrieved a bottle of his father's grappa from the cupboard. Two glasses. He poured a large one for the priest, something smaller for himself.

'There are those out there who doubtless think you too young to be drinking this stuff,' Garzone said, raising his glass. 'You're a stranger to everyone here.'

He wasn't going to say it but he hated the strong taste of his father's grappa. There was a point to be made here. That was all.

'Let them think that. I'm eighteen. Of legal age. We came here from Dorsoduro because the money was running out. If they hate us for once having it tell them to be happy. It's gone now.'

The rough and fiery taste of the spirit made him cough.

The priest got up and walked to the window. At the back of the building a brick patio extended out to the lagoon and the ruined tower. A rough-hewn staircase led down to a small jetty where the grey water lapped against steps covered in hanks of green seaweed at the foot. Occasionally during the summer they'd sit out on the patio with chairs and enjoy the sun. Sometimes a boat would turn up, a fisherman offering his catch. That would never happen again.

'I remember your father saying you had a cellar. Imagine that. Not many of those about.'

Paolo kicked the kitchen carpet to one side to reveal the trap door. Once, when the place had been an aristocratic mansion, there'd been a lower level water gate for deliveries, opening straight out on to the lagoon. The exit had long been blocked off but the storage space remained, unused for years.

'What is it you want me to hide? Guns? Explosives? What . . .?'

'No. Something perhaps more perilous. Two people not far off your own age. Brother and sister from Turin. He's been wounded. She is . . . dangerous, I gather. A hardened fighter.'

'Terrorists?'

'Partisans. They're on the run. If we don't find them somewhere safe I fear the Germans will seize them. Which could lead to many more deaths than their own. We . . .' He rapped on the window. 'If you're agreeable we could arrange for them to come this way tonight. No one will see. The boat will have no lights.' He laughed. 'You're in the shadow of the Arsenale after all. A place full of the military. What better place to hide than under their noses? The last place of sanctuary they'll ever look.'

Paolo said nothing.

'They can stay in the cellar for a few days until we find a way out. They'll do no harm. The two of them will never set foot outside this place all the time they're here. As I said the brother's wounded. The sister has some medical knowledge. She can look after him until we find the means to smuggle them somewhere else.'

Still he kept quiet.

'That will be as soon as we are able.' The priest was sounding desperate. 'I can't promise how long but it will be a matter of priority to get them out of here. By way of reward you must buy food at one place only. Gallo's in via Garibaldi. Do you know it?'

'No. We always shop at the store by the bridge.'

'Good. Then he won't know you either. Which is for the best. Tell him you've friends visiting from the mainland and would like something special for them. Gabriele will be ready and make sure you get enough for three in return. As well as a fee to compensate you for your trouble.'

'I don't want your money!'

'Everyone wants money, son.' The humour in his voice had gone. 'If it's more you're after go to Ca' Loretti and tell the Crucchi what I've said. Or slip the word to a waiter at one of their brothels. They'll surely pay you well.'

Paolo sipped at the grappa and thought he might carry on until he liked it.

'Does Chiara know about this?'

The man in black shook his head.

'I suspect she can read my mind. Couldn't you see that in her eyes? She wants to be safe. She wants the same for you. Why not? The poor woman's already lost a husband and now you, orphaned . . . I think she feels you're as much her charge as her employer. All of which I appreciate. But . . .' He finished the glass and pulled his coat around him. 'I'm a man of God. A man of peace. I live on the horns of a dilemma, with secrets I fear to share, even in confession. Except a few with you. Well . . .'

Garzone got to his feet.

'If you feel disinclined to help I won't hold it against you. No one will. Just don't mention Gallo to anyone. Gabriele is a kindly, brave man, but terrified, as he deserves to be. I shouldn't have spoken of him. You don't have to give me an answer now.'

'Good. I won't.'

That disappointed him.

'If . . . if you're willing to allow them in, then leave a light on in the window tonight. A boat may pass. If the place is dark they'll know.'

Paolo walked to the door to the workshop and held it open. The priest took the hint.

'If you should decide to take this path, know it's not easy,' he said as they went past the idle machines. 'No one will come to visit you. I would advise you live as you do now, staying out of sight as much as possible. Do nothing to indicate there's anything here that's changed. Go out at the same time. Come back at the same time. Your daily routine must not alter. Chiara Vecchi I would trust with my life. The same cannot be said of others. There are men and women here who would betray their neighbours over the bark of a dog or a cold glance in the street. That is how we are. And as you say . . . to many of them you're a stranger. An alien Nicolotto in the territory of the Castellani. It's curious how old enmities still live on in this place. Even in wartime. At least you're not fighting one another on bridges anymore. Though . . .' He put a wrinkled finger to his chin. 'I must admit you seem a stranger to me mostly. Not just because I never see you in the congregation. Still, we all have our secrets, I imagine. Even priests.'

* * *

Garzone marched up to one of the orange trees, pulled off a fruit and only afterwards asked if Paolo minded. No, he said. He could help himself to as much as he wanted. So the priest tore three more off the tree and stuffed them into the pockets of his cape.

'This weather,' he said, waving his hand through the mist, 'it will lift. It always does. We expect life will be the same afterwards. Which is impossible, of course. Venetians like to think they live outside of time, on this little island of theirs, protected by the lagoon from the horrors of terraferma across the way.'

He retrieved an orange from his pocket and ran his nail through the pithy skin, prising out a segment.

'If only that were true.' He took a bite and the juice ran down his chin. 'Good day, young man. I apologize for attempting to embroil you in our troubles. I apologize, too, if it felt as if I were talking down to you. I realize now you're not the adolescent I assumed. Which is understandable. These are not times for the naïve. Were I not desperate I can guarantee I would leave you here alone, with your looms, your weaving, with Chiara Vecchi and the peace you seek.'

Paolo Uccello watched him go, a dark, slightly hunched figure wandering down the zigzag path to the wooden bridge across the narrow water. Then he went to the garden door and locked it. Chiara wouldn't be back until the morning and she was the only other person who now possessed a key.

Back in the kitchen he tucked away the grappa bottle, opened the trap door to the basement cellar, walked down the slippery steps. It was cold and the air was poor and foetid. His father had stored so much here over the years: design cards, drawings, patterns, all wrapped up in oilskin packets to keep out the persistent damp. The lapping of the lagoon whispered through the bricked-up water door where gondolas had once arrived to take the aristocrats of the old palazzo to salons, casinos, theatres and *ridotti*. Beyond the stained and dirty glass of the window, a metre high, with a tiny tracery design copied from the Doge's Palace, the murk was setting in again.

There was an ancient table with a candle set in the centre, a single rickety chair on the side facing the outer wall where all the oilskin wallets and chests were stored. He sat down in the dark, listening to the waves, wondering where the corpse of Isabella Finzi was. How soon she'd be laid in the ground and where.

* * *

Alberti was a Cannaregio man by birth but from his Carabinieri days he knew where the Castello misfits hung out. A bar run by a deaf, ill-tempered, old woman called Greta who, rumour had it, was once madame of a long-vanished brothel beloved of fishermen. It was a low-ceilinged dive close to the point at which via Garibaldi gave way to the canal it used to be before Napoleon came along with his ideas of reshaping the city. The Frenchman wasn't alone in that. During the 1930s Mussolini's builders had created a new waterfront at the foot of the street, extending it towards the tip of the city proper with the name Riva dell'Impero. This addition was almost elegant which was more than could be said for the warren of terraced slums that ran back into Castello behind, ancient cheap housing for manual labourers from the Arsenale shipyard.

The place was essentially Greta Morino's front room turned into a public bar with a few tables made out of painted barrels. There, each night until the last customer staggered home, she sold beer, wine, spritz, coffee and cigarettes, much of it smuggled he had no doubt. When she felt like it, the old bird cooked steaming pots of cheap soup, cans of tomatoes spun out with what vegetables she could find or the old pauper's standby of *pasta e fagioli*. These she sold for a few lire but only to the local men and a few women she knew. A worker's lunch, said the sign on the door, for no one else.

She was probably part of the communist cell which he knew was active around via Garibaldi. In her case that was, he felt, more because it offered an opportunity to whine than anything to do with politics. Had the communists been in charge she'd probably be a secret Fascist.

The place was almost full when he marched in that afternoon and, as he searched for small change in his pocket, took out his Walther P38 and placed it on the shiny, scratched, wooden surface of the bar.

'A fellow's in need of a *caffè corretto*, Greta. A double shot.' He grinned at the unsmiling faces staring back at him. Rocco Trevisan, the ringleader of the men who'd dragged Isabella Finzi out of the drink that morning, was among them. 'Chilly work out there in this weather. You guys did well. I'm grateful. We all are. I imagine the poor old bat's in the ground now. The Jews like to get rid of them quick.'

The old woman didn't move and he could see why. She was

waiting for the nod from Trevisan. When it came – and only then – she moved and made the drink.

It wasn't good grappa. There was so much fake and counterfeit junk around. At least in the Marino opposite Ca' Loretti they didn't dare serve anything but the real thing. If she could have spat in the cup without him seeing, she'd have done it for sure.

'Luca,' Trevisan said and raised his glass.

Alberti put the Walther back in the leather holster he wore around his chest. He'd arrested this man once when he was in the Carabinieri. A fight in a bar near the Arsenale. Trevisan had taken a knife and cut some drunken idiot from the ear almost to his mouth. Six months in jail for that and when he came out he seemed more popular than ever.

'Such a shame I have to carry a weapon around here.' Alberti frowned. 'In my home town. Such a shame.'

'We all make choices, mister.'

That came from a redhead in her thirties, someone he didn't know, good-looking in a hard-faced kind of way. Maybe, he thought, she was warming Trevisan's bed given the way the two stood together like a team.

He pushed the vile coffee to one side and halved the coins on the counter. There were limits to what he'd take.

'Someone has to, lady. In case you hadn't noticed the Germans are here and they're not leaving soon. The Black Brigades come and go as they please. Would you rather they ran free as birds across this place? Or that one of your own stood in the way at times.'

She laughed and said, 'Oh, so you're a hero?'

'No. I'm doing a job someone's got to. There are people hereabouts who owe the fact they're still breathing to me. Maybe they don't know it. Maybe they never will. I don't ask for thanks. I don't even ask for understanding. But that is how it stands—'

'Be quiet, man!' It was a tall, bearded stranger at the back who bellowed at him. One of the bunch down by the water in the mist that morning. 'We all heard you today. Sucking up to the Crucchi. Telling a decent fellow like Diamante to shut his Jew mouth. You should be ashamed of yourself.'

Alberti nodded.

'Maybe I am. But I've got a job to do and part of that is telling people what they want to hear. You think I should argue with the Germans? You think I should march into the office of some SS boss and tell him he's being a fool? What benefit would there be for any of you there?'

'That poor woman . . .' He wondered if perhaps the fellow was a relative. 'She was abused. Murdered—'

'By a drunken German soldier. An infantryman from Munich. They're going to put the moron up against a wall in the Arsenale tomorrow and use him as shooting practice.'

Silence then.

'You don't believe me?'

'Why should we?' the redhead asked.

'Why would I lie? I'm risking my neck telling you this. You don't think it'll be in the paper, do you? Hermann Schulz. Foot soldier with the Seventy-First Division Kleeblatt. Gets shot by his squad mates. There. Satisfied?'

The old woman behind the counter muttered something that sounded halfway approving.

'If you like,' Alberti went on, 'you can pass on what I just told you to one of their grubby little informers. They could put me up against the same wall. If it makes you happy . . . Greta, gimme a good grappa this time. I'd like to leave here without the taste of someone's piss in my mouth.'

She poured a small glass and put it on the counter. He downed it in one.

'What you have to understand, all of you, is that life's complicated right now. The Crucchi are here, like it or not. They rule, like it or not. They will take any of us – you, me, old Greta here – right out into the street at any moment and cut your throat. Not a second's hesitation.'

'Tell us something we don't know,' Trevisan demanded.

He pushed the glass away. It was half-decent so he'd won a small victory there. Then he barged his way through the bunch at the counter and got right up to Trevisan.

'I'm not asking you to like me, Rocco. Just understand this. If I don't do this job someone else will. And it'd probably be some vicious Black Brigades hoodlum from Milan who'd be ten times worse. I'm here to stand between you and them. To try and keep the peace until times get better. If you don't like that, then follow me home one night and we'll argue this out in a dark alley between us. When you want to rise up and take these bastards on yourself' – he punched Trevisan in the shoulder – 'you let me know. Maybe we can talk about it. But we will lose. We will all die. And when we're dead they'll rape your wives and kids and kill them too. Every German that goes down they want a dozen Venetians in their place and they don't give a shit who that might be. Understood?'

'You said your piece,' Trevisan replied.

'Not quite finished. There are two partisans on their way here. Jews from Turin. They screwed up trying to place a bomb in the mountains. The rest of their team's dead. Bunch of Germans with them too. The SS have got a bead on the pair. Won't be good when they're caught. Won't be good for anyone who hides them either. Or knows where they're hiding and doesn't say a word.'

He opened his jacket so they could see the pistol in the shiny leather holster.

'I came here because I wanted you all to know this. I want you to understand the risks. These are not our people. They're terrorists. Communists or worse. They will bring down anyone who falls for their lies. Not just you. Your families too. If—'

'We're not informers,' the woman butted in. 'You've a nerve.'

'I'm not asking for that. If they turn up here just send them on their way. Don't hide them. Don't listen to their lies.' He turned to each of them in the bar. 'I'm trying to make sure as many of you live through this. You and your families. I want this city back the way it was before the war. That's all. Now . . .' He pushed out his chest and waved a finger at the gun. 'If you think that's all bullshit and I'm just one more piece of Nazi slime feel free to use it. Huh?'

The redhead was on the weapon in a flash, seizing it from the holster, pointing the barrel in his face.

'You two-faced shit . . .'

'Do what you like, lady. I'm just a product of the time.' He shrugged. 'I doubt they'd want as many dead for me as one of their own. But to be honest with you, I really don't know.'

'Give him back the gun,' Trevisan ordered.

'No . . .'

'Dammit.' He took the Walther off her. 'Here.'

Alberti shrugged, smiled at the woman first, then Trevisan, and placed the gun back in his holster. They weren't to know it wasn't loaded and he had another weapon, a smaller pistol, tucked in his waistband.

'Thanks, Rocco. I was breaking into a sweat there.'

'We heard what you got to say.' Trevisan nodded at the door. 'Leave it there. Stay away from here. I might not be around next time.'

He went out into the street, watched every step of the way.

Maybe, he thought, he ought to wander round to Giardini. He'd heard film crews had decamped there from Rome and were aiming to make the kind of gung-ho movies Il Duce loved. He could cut it as an actor. He already had.

Paolo Uccello sat at the kitchen table, reading up on the commission placed by a man called Ugo Leone. The windows were all shuttered. Nothing could be seen from the outside at all. The simple box file his father used for orders sat in front of him. The order was the most recent so naturally it sat at the top. Chiara's worries about getting the job done on time had rattled him. She knew weaving so much better. He'd been a fool to treat the job, so closely associated with his parents' deaths, as nothing important.

The letter was typed as if from an office and demanded three identical small banners, all to be delivered to the Gioconda by Tuesday December the seventh, a week away. The velvet was to be made up of two patterns, rampant lions with a pile of scarlet silk along with leaves and decorative emblems in dark blue with a fawn silk background. The pattern would repeat every fifty centimetres and the fabric was to be finished in *soprarizzo*, an ancient technique used only for the most expensive commissions such as those for the Doge or highest ranks in the Church. This gave the final fabric an extraordinary texture, the base soft and curly for the borders, the top hand cut to emphasize the pattern, here, the lions. The results were beautiful. It bestowed a kind of life to the fabric, an extra dimension, delightful to touch. No customer could resist running their fingers over the brush-like master and the soft, subtle background. They usually stopped when they heard the price.

He'd initially believed the payment was generous but now he was thinking more clearly it was obvious how desperate his father had been for the work, any work. Such an order in soprarizzo should have cost far more, perhaps double. The technique was time-consuming and demanded careful labour with a blade and a variety of needles alongside all the usual, tedious weaving. He was glad they'd started when they did.

'We can do this, Chiara,' he muttered to himself.

He hadn't looked in the file for weeks. There seemed no need. Now he saw there was an unopened envelope among the correspondence. A scribbled message from Chiara on the front said the postman had handed it over while Paolo was out shopping. She must have forgotten to mention it, as he had forgotten to look. It bore a Turin postmark from ten days before.

Heart in mouth, he ripped open the envelope. Maybe they'd cancelled the whole thing and they'd be asking for their money back. Almost all of it spent.

But no, it was worse. A brief note from Leone, handwritten.

> My travel arrangements have altered. I now wish to pick up the banners on Saturday, the fourth of December. Since this is only a few days earlier than previously agreed I assume, Uccello, this will be met. There will be great and important men in attendance. I must advise you it would be perilous to your reputation if not your person if you were to disappoint them and me.

He stared at the letter, wondering what he could do. Tuesday would be tight. Saturday impossible. Even if he and Chiara tried to work night and day they'd never meet such a deadline. Weaving was hard, tiring work and the soprarizzo something only she knew. He couldn't possibly give this man from Turin what he wanted when he demanded it. Nor could he return the deposit.

Or run. Where? How?

Paolo Uccello tucked the letter in the folder with the pattern and placed it in the office desk next to the looms. Then he went back into the kitchen.

The priest's business was his alone. True, Paolo had been outraged by the way the Finzi woman had been treated. But cruelty seemed to be a part of this world and nothing he could do would change that. He was an orphan, eighteen, timid and happy to be that way. The American bombers had killed his parents. Accidentally or not they were still dead.

A couple of rebellious Jews on the run after fighting a reckless guerrilla war against the Crucchi were none of his business. A commission for a piece of soprarizzo velvet, perhaps from a Fascist who might do him and Chiara harm . . . that most certainly was. There was only one solution. They needed another pair of hands to work the third Jacquard loom.

He got two candles from the cupboard and lit them, then threw aside the carpet, lifted the trap door and walked downstairs into the cellar. There was a small table in the centre of the damp, dark place.

Those flickering lights by a tracery window stood between him and whatever happened next. Let fate decide. There was nothing else he could think of.

Paolo made himself some food. Drank a little more of the grappa his father had left and decided he didn't like it. He was about to go to bed when he heard the waves beyond the window shift their rhythm, as if there was a boat out there, disturbing the gentle beat of waves against the steps down from the patio.

Footsteps shuffled up the stairs and there were voices, a woman first, then a man, low.

Their rapping on the wood was so loud and insistent it made him jump.

Paolo's heart was in his mouth as he got up. The door was little more than ajar when it slammed back into his face, someone swore on the other side, a woman's voice, and he found himself flying to the floor.

Two people, the rain, the cold wind all around.

The door slammed shut but not before he could see something outside. A spotlight sweeping through the stormy night, left and right, hunting.

Something sharp and cold pressed against his neck. The point of a knife. It had to be, even though he couldn't see it.

'Keep quiet and I won't cut you,' the woman said, stamping her knee hard on his chest.

They stayed like that for a minute or more as the sound of a motor launch grew nearer outside. The spotlight was so bright it cast little motes of white through the slats in the shuttered windows.

Over the rattle of the engine there were distant voices, low, hard, male. Foreign. It took him a moment to realize they were speaking German.

The knife point pricked his skin and he couldn't help but squeal.

'I said keep quiet,' the woman whispered so close he could feel her breath warm against his face.

PART TWO

The pages Nonno Paolo gave me were old but they had the letterhead of the House of Uccello on them. A design from years back, paper he used up for everyday notes since he always hated waste. I knew the Palazzo Colombina inside out, every room, every last dusty corner. On the top floor, the mansard overlooking the canal, he kept a private study, a place he retired to from time to time, to read he always said. It was always locked but I knew where he hid the keys. In a cabinet by his bed. A place I'd seen him put them back when I was little.

I went into his room, trying to dismiss the thought he'd never see this again. The keys were where I expected. Feeling like an intruder in my own home, I took them and went upstairs. The place was small with a roof so steeply pitched I had to bend down as it narrowed towards the far wall. More like a cell than a spare bedroom for visitors. Or perhaps, in the old days, somewhere a servant lived.

There was a single window looking down to the Grand Canal. A desk was pushed up against the sill, a portable typewriter on it, a single office chair in front. A blank sheet of paper was in the machine. I'd never used a typewriter. We were all about computers. The pages Grandfather had given me had corrections and scribbles in pencil the kind of which I'd never seen before. I sat down, tapped out a few words on the funny physical keyboard, my fingers quickly falling between the letters. Then I worked out how to turn the page out of the back and looked at the results.

This was where he'd written his story. I could see it from the letters on the page and the fact it was clearly the same old and yellowing paper, a little damp from age. Day after day, week after week, he must have come in here at night. For years. I'd heard him padding round the floors sometimes and thought it was just insomnia. But no. He was writing something. A story about a part of his life, though he set it down as if he was an observer, someone watching all this from afar.

I shouldn't have been there. But since I was – and I understood in my heart he wasn't coming back – I thought I'd make the most of the opportunity and went through the drawers. There were three of them but the bottom one was firmly locked and none of the keys I had worked.

In the first were piles of old letters bound together with elastic bands, personal, from people I didn't know. Some nearly forty years old, to do with the business.

The middle contained nothing but a photograph. It was dated 23rd June 1937. A man and a woman, my dead great-grandparents I assumed, standing stiffly, proudly, next to a loom in an airy glass building much like a large garden conservatory. The Giardino degli Angeli in San Pietro was sold before I was born. It was a piece of our past that didn't concern me. But this was their workshop before the war when the Uccello were starting to struggle and had moved there from their apartment in Dorsoduro. I shivered as I gazed at it. Those dead faces seemed to be looking right at me. Grandfather, it must have been, stood between his parents, unsmiling, twelve years old, not far off my own age. I thought we had no photographs going back before the war. Nonno Paolo always said they were lost in the chaos. His own parents had died in a bomb raid somewhere. This was the first time I'd laid eyes on them and I wondered: why would he keep this one photograph hidden? Not that I recognized anyone in it, even him.

For the first time ever in the warm, familiar surroundings of the Palazzo Colombina, I felt scared. Shivering, even on that sticky summer night, I put the picture back, carefully, the way I found it, as if he might know. Then I rattled the bottom drawer, the locked one, hard. It still wouldn't budge and for that I felt quite grateful.

The following morning, before I set off for Zanipolo and the hospital, Chiara turned up, ostensibly to do a little cleaning though I felt sure her principal purpose was to see I hadn't burned the place down. A maid came to do the real work five times a week.

I'd finished breakfast: coffee and a cornetto from the bakers round the corner. She asked after my grandfather and shook her head when I said he seemed no better.

'Paolo's so young. Cancer's a terrible thing.'

He was seventy-four or so which didn't seem young at all to me.

I toyed with the cornetto and said, 'I have to do a project for school. I was thinking of writing something about the war.'

She was looking at me as if I were mad.

'You've been kicked out of school for a week, Nico. Your father told me. You . . . of all people, getting mixed up with that Scamozzi crowd.'

'I said I'm sorry. It doesn't mean I can't do school work. The war—'

'Why on earth would you want to write about that?'

'Because I don't think anyone else will. No one ever talks about what happened. Not much.'

She picked up the plates and the cups from the table and placed them in the dishwasher. Which was unnecessary. I normally looked after that myself.

'Some things are best that way.'

'If we sat down together and you talked to me . . . I could record it. Just your memories . . .'

'Memories?' Her voice had become hard, her face flushed. 'In June 1940 that idiot Il Duce made us sign up for Hitler's madness. It was five years before Venice was free of those monsters. I lost a husband I never could replace even if I wanted to. You want me to sit down and talk to you about it over a coffee and a biscuit like it was a little holiday one summer?'

I'd never seen her angry before. It seemed wrong, and I felt bad for making it happen.

'Sorry. I didn't mean to upset you. I mean . . . I could always ask my grandfather—'

'The poor man's dying, Nico. Let him leave this world in peace. That time's gone and God willing it's never coming back. Now is there anything you want me to ask the maid to do when she turns up?'

'No. Not really—'

'So let's not talk of this again.' She went for her bag of shopping. It was to be a short visit for once. 'Think of something else. Someone of your age should be looking to the future not the past. Leave that to us. There are things that should be remembered. There are others that should be left to die with the old.'

An hour later I was back at the hospital, watching San Michele, the cemetery island, shift like a mirage in the summer heat across the water.

'Well?' He didn't look any different. The doctors seemed to

have no idea how long he might live. Not that they foresaw him leaving the hospital, or that he showed any sign of expecting to return home. 'Did you read it?'

'Of course I did.'

'Did it bore you? Be honest, Nico. If you want to go and mess around with your pals. Chase girls. Take your camera out somewhere. I know how much you love that. I won't be offended if you've no interest in an old man's memories—'

'I read it and I want to read the rest.'

I couldn't work out whether that pleased him or not. So I added that I found it strange he should write about himself as if he was another person.

'A stylistic objection? Are you my editor now?'

'No. It sounds odd. That's all.'

'Think about it. I'm telling the story of several different people. I'm imagining the conversations they had when they weren't there.'

'You mean making it up?'

'That's what storytelling entails in case you hadn't noticed.'

He started coughing and it went on so long I walked out into the corridor and tried to find a nurse. By the time I got back with her he seemed fine again and politely but firmly said she'd be better off serving patients elsewhere.

'That's the way I felt I had to tell it, Nico. I'm sorry if it confuses you. What do you know of the war?'

'Not much.'

'Don't they teach these things in school?'

They did, I told him, up to a point. No one said you had to listen. And, as Chiara had shown that morning, there was always a sense of embarrassment when conversations turned to that time, especially among the old. Italy had backed the wrong side. As Mussolini lost the war, the country came to be divided for a while, north and south. Peace only seemed to bring with it more arguments and divisions. Italian politics seemed so endlessly complex no one of my age took the slightest notice. We were too young to waste our time on that.

'I still think maybe you could show it to Dad. It's more his—'

'I said already. It's for you, not him.'

'Why?'

He blinked, gasped for air for a moment. I thought, *He really is dying here, minute by minute. I can see it now.*

‘That,’ he murmured, ‘I can’t tell you. It’s something you need to find yourself.’

‘I don’t understand.’

‘Perhaps you never will. And that’ll be for the best. Sometimes you hand someone a gift and you never know if it’s right or not. Just that you want them to have it.’

He looked exhausted, terrible.

‘It’s OK, Grandpa. You’re tired. Have a sleep.’

‘Sometimes it takes a while. For someone to appreciate that gift. Sometimes it never happens at all. Maybe you’d be better off going to the beach, Nico. I mean that.’

‘I’m going to read your story. I’ll come here every day until it’s finished.’

He closed his eyes and made a snuffling noise that sounded like a snore. I got to my feet and took one step towards the window and the bedside cabinet.

‘The second envelope marked “The Visitors”,’ he said, making me jump. He hadn’t moved a muscle. ‘Nothing else. Or I’ll know.’

THE VISITORS

'God I need a drink,' the woman said when the sound of the German boat vanished and all they could hear was the rhythmic lapping of the waves beyond the window.

She took her knee off Paolo Uccello, stuffed the knife into her jacket pocket and went straight for the grappa that was still by the sink.

As Paolo clambered to his feet the man limped to the table, sat down and let his head fall into his hands. There was what might have been a tourniquet on his right leg, blood seeping through his muddy khaki trousers.

'We need food,' she said, no please or thank you.

Paolo got the last of his *bigoli* out of the cupboard, a can of anchovies and an onion and started to put a meal together.

When he told them his name she said nothing, just poured another grappa. Looking at them now he realized she was the older by a couple of years and probably the boss too. A sharp-eyed young woman with dark hair, short, roughly cut, swept back from a face that was olive and perhaps more than a little grubby. The brother shared much the same looks. He guessed they seemed Jewish, not that he was very good at labelling people unless he was told. If he didn't know he might have thought they were from the south, Calabria or Sicily. They had plenty of people like that, his father used to say. Arab blood. Which was the same as Jewish anyway.

They sat at the table waiting for the food. She took out a pack of cigarettes and said, 'Do you smoke, Paolo?'

'No. My father hated it.'

'But he's gone, isn't he? Just you here now. Take one.' She insisted. 'You're going to need a cigarette from time to time. People round us usually do.'

'That's true,' her brother said and grabbed one.

Paolo followed his lead and coughed as the brother lit it for him. But he kept smoking as he cooked, which felt grown up in a childish sort of way.

When he came back with three plates of food he said, 'They told me to put you in the cellar. I don't think that's a good idea. It's too cold and damp. Take my parents' room. There's a double bed. Space. Some clothes in the cupboards too. I didn't . . .' He realized he'd done so little since they died. 'I didn't bother to take anything out. Have whatever you like.'

'My name is Vanni Artom,' the man said, holding out one hand across the table while he scooped at the pasta with his left. 'This is my sister Mika. She doesn't do small talk.'

'Sorry, brother,' she said with a wry smile. 'Not much chance of late.' She put her elbows on the table, cradled her head in her hands and smiled at Paolo. 'I'm sorry I stuck a knife in your neck. The Crucchi weren't far behind. You heard. I thought it . . . wise.'

Paolo said he was sure it was, then pointed at Vanni's leg.

'You're hurt.'

'True. A German mosquito bit me.' He smiled at his sister. 'I'm on the mend. She's a doctor. At least she would have been if they hadn't kicked us out of university.'

'And you?'

'I would have been a . . .' He thought about this. 'A poet, I think.'

'No money in poetry,' his sister pointed out.

'A journalist then. It's all rather academic now, isn't it?'

She'd nearly finished the food and was lighting another cigarette.

'This is good. What do you call it?'

'Bigoli in salsa. My mother used to make it. She said the anchovies should come from a jar not a tin. But it's not easy getting jars at the moment.'

The woman laughed.

'We heard you were all having a tough time of it in Venice.'

'The Americans killed my parents,' he said and wanted her to know there were limits. 'That was tough enough.'

'The Germans murdered our entire family,' she shot back. 'Lined them up against a wall. Made them kneel and put a bullet through their heads. Mum. Dad. Aunt and uncle. Our little sister too. She was seven.'

'This isn't a contest in misery, Mika,' Vanni told her.

'No. I'm sorry. I'm sorry for everything. Sorry we're here.' She held out her hand. Paolo shook it. 'Apology accepted?'

'It is.'

'Thanks. We've been running from them for a week. Barely eaten. Barely stayed alive. Forgive our rudeness.'

Vanni looked ready to point out it was on her part alone. But then he seemed to think twice of it and kept quiet.

She got up from the table and looked round the kitchen.

'I need to change the dressing on his wound. Do you have an old sheet or something I can use?'

'I told you. Take whatever you want in my parents' room.'

'Come, brother. After that I need a shower. I'm filthy.'

'Wait.'

There were things Paolo had to say. They had to stay away from the windows. The German patrol boats ran in and out of the Arsenale docks all the time. Anyone on board could see things from the lagoon side of the house. The rest, the workshop, was protected by the wall around the Giardino degli Angeli. If they stayed inside until someone came for them they'd all be safe. He could fetch everything they needed.

'*Grazie*,' she said with a sigh. 'Though I believe we can teach you more about hiding than you can teach us.' She squinted at him and asked, 'Are you still at school? They said you lived here alone.'

'I do. I'm eighteen. I left school years ago. This is what I require if you're going to stay here. If you can't abide by my rules I'll be forced to ask the priest to find you somewhere else.'

'You seem quite grown up for eighteen,' Vanni said.

'I'm on my own. This is my home. This is my little company to run. I have no choice. If you can't abide by what I say I will ask Garzone—'

'There.' She pointed a dirty finger at him. 'First mistake. You never say a name. Not around strangers.'

'We're not strangers,' he replied. 'We're people in a hole who don't know one another. I hadn't finished.'

'Oh?' She put her hand on her hips. 'What else?'

'In return I want your help.'

Vanni and Mika took themselves off into his parents' old room. They didn't emerge until midday on Wednesday, woken perhaps by the constant rattle and banging of the Jacquard looms at work.

Paolo and Chiara Vecchi had started them up at just after eight that morning, weaving the ornate velvet millimetre by millimetre. He hadn't dared tell her he'd got the delivery date wrong.

Si-dah-si-dah-si-dah-sichi-si-piu.

Sometimes, when he'd spent hours at the Jacquard, he heard that short, fast refrain in his sleep, found himself waking to the sound of the beat being drummed by his fingers on the bed.

They broke off for a brief break around one, Chiara to eat a *panino* at the sewing table by the long window by the side while he went inside for a while. The Artoms were back in the bedroom. They didn't appear and he wasn't sorry. He never mentioned them to Chiara, naturally, and had no idea if she'd guessed there were others in the house. When he returned she said barely a word.

The looms were hard, physical work. She was a strong woman, more robust than him since his arms remained spindly in spite of the exercise. Thick-set, rosy-faced, always healthy, she'd learned lace-making on Burano as a child, then moved to the city when she married to join her husband, a carpenter in the Arsenale. He had a small apartment near the church of San Francesco della Vigna, a grand Palladian building which Chiara boasted marked the spot where Saint Mark was shipwrecked during a storm, to be greeted by an angel who told him his coffin would one day rest in the lagoon. She was a religious woman, to the point of superstition at times, and seemed to regard Filippo Garzone with some suspicion since he came from another parish, the isolated island world of San Pietro.

Chiara had an anxious bustle about her. There were never idle moments. She was always active whether it was at the Jacquard, knitting a shawl or in her kitchen, making meals for the elderly she helped care for with some nuns from a nearby convent. Idle fingers, she said, were an insult to the Lord.

At the door she looked back at the looms, the few centimetres of fabric they'd produced that day, still on the frame, and offered to work another hour or two. He'd have none of it. They were both exhausted and tiredness only led to mistakes that would take longer to remedy than they did to commit.

'You're a godsend, Chiara. Go home and rest.'

'Soprarizzo,' she muttered putting on her coat. 'I need to teach you, Paolo.'

'You do. But not now.'

'Thank goodness we've got a little time.'

His heart sank. He had to tell her.

'I got the date wrong. They expect it by Saturday afternoon.'

She shrieked and uttered a rare curse.

'Don't be ridiculous. Look at how far we are now. Three looms to work and just the pair of us to manage them? And you not so sure with the scissors? Tell your customer. If they want quality we can't be rushed.'

'We can make up some time.'

'How?' She pointed to the garden, the trees, the stumps of masonry lying around on the thinning winter grass. Once the bowers must have been full of statues, graces, angels, saints. Now all that was recognizable was a fragment of face, of arm, of stony, shattered feathers. 'Will this be magic time, Paolo? Will your fractured cherubs come and help us weave this work?'

He had no answer. Chiara looked angry, lost, not the usual confident woman he'd grown up with, more than an employee, a close and valued friend of the family.

She came close, took his arms, whispered in his ear.

'There are no angels left in Venice. Only devils and those who've lost their wings. Don't be so naïve. You're not a child anymore.'

'I'm aware of that,' he said rather testily and realized it was the first time the two of them had exchanged severe words.

'Are you?'

'Yes!'

She held him more tightly.

'Let me tell you something. Your family came from Dorsoduro. They once had money. Prestige. Comfort. Hereabouts we've none and we've never known anything different. This is a hard part of the city and people relish it that way. Your family—'

'I know where we came from. I know what they think of me here.'

'Did you know your father was a Fascist?'

He struggled for an answer.

'No, he wasn't. Don't insult the dead.'

'The truth is never insulting. It's just the truth. Your father joined up back when everyone else did. When all the middle classes thought Il Duce would save them from the communists. He told me so himself and dammit I nearly walked straight out. Except he was a decent man. Just someone who got fooled along with the rest of them. He would never have wanted this nightmare but then . . . who did?'

As a family they'd always stayed away from politics. His father had ended the conversation, quite curtly, if talk over dinner strayed into that area. And this, it seems, was why. The Uccello were a once-affluent family who'd danced to Mussolini's tune. Along with so many others. That was one more reason why they never mixed with the locals in the terraces and tenements of Castello. Cramped hovels where, for many of the poor, Stalin, Marx and Gramsci and all the other gods of the left held more sway than any prayer or blessing Filippo Garzone could utter from the pulpit of San Pietro.

'I promised your mother, Paolo.' There were tears in her eyes. He'd never seen them before. 'I *promised* I'd take care of you if anything happened. I'll be damned if I'm going to lose another to this stupid war as well.' Her strong hands shook him and she nodded back at the rooms. 'Get those two out of here now.'

Of course she knew. How could he have thought otherwise?

'Who told you?'

'You think I need to be told? Don't risk your neck for strangers. Don't—'

'They're going to help us finish this work,' he broke in.

She was quiet for a moment. Then she nodded at the looms and the half-finished fabric there.

'You could kill us all for three pieces of velvet. You know that?'

'They help us,' he said. 'And then they're gone. The two of them are tired now. Tomorrow I need you to teach them.'

'Three pieces of velvet . . .' she whispered.

That night they ate mostly in silence. He got the impression the two of them had slept most of the day and spent the rest arguing. Neither would look at the other. Mika seemed restless, angry, unhappy to be cooped up in a backwater hidden away from the city. Vanni, crippled as he was by his wound, had little choice. All the same he appeared very different to his sister. Calm, thoughtful, funny at times. They cared for one another deeply, he guessed, though as an only child himself it was hard to untangle some of the obvious complexities between them. Perhaps Mika thought she was taking care of her brother, and he the same for her. And neither realized at all.

She went through the few books the Uccello had on their shelves and didn't approve of any. Foreign adventure stories mainly, about the world beyond Italy and some of the science fiction Paolo had loved growing up. *Around The World in Eighty Days. Twenty Thousand Leagues Under the Sea. The Time Machine.*

'Children's stories,' Mika said with a scowl. 'Is this all you've got?'

'I was a child,' he explained. 'If you want me to look for something else I can try. Just say what—'

'We'll live with what we've got,' Vanni interrupted. 'Don't go attracting attention. These books will do. I'll read them.'

'You said you wanted our help,' his sister added. 'You haven't asked for it.'

'You looked like you needed some rest.'

'We're rested. What do you want?'

He took a deep breath and said, 'I was hoping I could teach you to weave.'

Mika laughed out loud, then put a hand to her mouth.

'I'm sorry. I didn't mean to be rude. Us? Using those ancient contraptions you've got out there?'

'I apologize for my sister,' Vanni added with a sharp glance in her direction. 'Sometimes her manners are lacking.'

'I did say I was sorry!'

Vanni took her hand across the table.

'Mika. We're guests here. Paolo's risking his life. For strangers.'

'I know that, brother.' She didn't snatch her hand away. Instead she leaned over the table and kissed his cheek. Then, to Paolo's embarrassment, his. 'It's just that those things are so old . . .'

'They're the only machines that do the work,' Paolo pointed out. 'What else?'

'Let me try to explain.' Vanni did his best. Their family, he said, worked for a company Paolo had heard of. Olivetti, in Turin. Both mother and father had been engineers developing typewriters for the owner, Adriano Olivetti.

'We're born to be part of the modern world,' said Mika.

'Not that the modern world appreciates it at the moment,' her brother added with a shrug. 'Olivetti's fled to Switzerland. He's a Jew. Converted to Catholicism to keep Mussolini happy and his factory working. But a Jew all the same. Not all of us who worked for him were so lucky. Our parents included. If we hadn't been in Padua we'd have been with them.'

'Machines,' Mika pointed to the workshop. 'Modern machines. That's what's going to free us from the tyranny in the end.'

'Or so Stalin promises,' her brother muttered.

'When they're in the hands of the workers. Not slaves like we are now. Like that woman you've got out there.'

Her brother smiled.

'I hardly think young Paolo makes much of a kulak. Or a likely candidate for collectivization.'

'I don't know what you two are talking about,' he admitted. 'I haven't a clue.'

Vanni slapped his arm.

'Communism, chum. The one true faith. Or so we're told. We are its crusaders though . . .' He moved too quickly on the chair and winced. The leg had to hurt. 'At the moment we're in a sorry and depleted state, between battles.'

'Time's all we need,' Mika noted, and there was a hard tone back in her voice again. The anger was always there, Paolo thought. And the need to be active, to do something. 'History's on our side. It marches forward. We're its drumbeat, getting louder all the time.'

Vanni laughed. He almost looked like a school kid when he did that. Something of his good humour rubbed off on Paolo Uccello too, not that he expected it.

The visitor hobbled to his feet.

'A rather faint drumbeat at the moment. Show me your old machines, Paolo. I'll happily do what I can. We're in your debt and know it.'

'I do not weave. I do not sew or knit.' Mika picked up a book with a look of obvious disdain on her face. *The Shape of Things To Come*. 'Goodnight.'

Early the following morning Paolo Uccello walked to Gallo's in via Garibaldi, carrying his mother's old canvas shopping bag. Gabriele, the grocer, was a slight man with a comical moustache and a comb-over of thinning grey hair. He stood behind the counter in his white overall stained with flour, tapping his fingers nervously on the counter just as he had the day before when Paolo made his first nervous venture into the store.

'You want something for your friends from the mainland again?'

'I do. Thank you.'

Food for three, cigarettes, wine. All for the price of one. Filippo Garzone's organization – or perhaps Diamante's, he wasn't sure and didn't want to know – seemed to be working. The chap said little. Paolo had made sure that he waited for the place to be empty before he walked in.

Inside the paper bag for the bread there was a wad of notes. Paolo took them out, placed them on the counter, and said, 'I believe these got here by mistake.'

'I don't think so,' the grocer replied.

Paolo smiled, left the money there anyway and walked outside. As usual there was a bunch of locals, men mostly, at the bar of Greta's along the street. They watched him go, he felt sure. But that wasn't new. He was an Uccello and could always feel their eyes upon him as he went for a walk around their part of Castello, a middle-class intruder among the proletariat of the terraces.

By the time he got back Chiara and Vanni Artom were sitting at the Jacquard looms. She looked cross. He seemed deeply amused.

'We've met,' Chiara announced before Paolo could say a word.

'I must say,' Vanni added, 'your lady friend's a wonderful teacher. She was on her own. I didn't want her to be lonely. So, since we're due to be working together, I thought it best if I came and asked her some questions. Chiara explains everything so much better than you.'

'That's because she knows so much more than me,' Paolo replied and handed out a couple of *cornetti* for the three to break between them.

The night before he'd taken a lantern into the workshop and, under the dim light, showed Vanni Artom the basics of how to use the Jacquard. Just the simplest task, pushing the weft yarn with the beater, allowing the loom and the punch cards to arrange the thread and form the pattern without any extra work on the part of the operator. The hard part, the cutting and shaping of the soprarizzo he never mentioned. That was for Chiara.

Vanni kept clutching at his leg. How easy it was going to be for him to work hours on end . . . it was hard to guess. Mika had emerged from their bedroom and watched for a while, reluctantly and grumbling. Both listened as Paolo did his best to outline in a very rudimentary form the way the Jacquard worked. At one point when he explained the role of the punched cards in determining the pattern Mika had appeared quite interested. Their father, she said, had spoken of development on a similar system at Olivetti that might one day be used for automated calculating machines to do away with the drudgery of pen and paper and the abacus.

All the same, when he showed her that the job of weaving velvet was entirely manual – pushing the beater, preferably to the goldcrest rhythm he'd learned from his father – she'd lost interest and returned to bed.

'Enough cornetto,' Vanni announced, standing up and brushing the crumbs off his rough, torn country jacket. It wasn't warm in the workshop. The excess of conservatory glass made sure of that. There was still the slightest fragrance from the citrus trees outside which, with the briny tang of the lagoon nearby, made the place feel fresh and pleasant. Much worse could be found in Venice and in Mestre, his father had always said. Mills and factories where labourers slaved away in dark and cramped conditions for a pittance. Though now most of those were idle, waiting on what came next.

'You,' Chiara told Vanni, 'can take the spare loom in the middle.' She glanced at Paolo. 'It wasn't set up entirely correctly but I've seen to that. Do what I told you. The beater, nothing else. If a thread breaks I'll hear it. If you make a mistake, I'll hear it. If you slack or try to do something different—'

'You have excellent hearing, signora,' he said with a smile. 'I'm grateful to be your student.' He tipped a salute to Paolo. 'Grateful to be here. As is my sister even if she's not always good at showing it.'

'Less chat, more work,' Chiara replied, then rolled up her sleeves and went to the left-hand loom, the better to watch the apprentice as he got down to the job.

As the clatter of three looms began to beat a busy rhythm in the Giardino degli Angeli, two men met outside an old, genteel cafe on the campo by Giovanni e Paolo, the basilica older locals called Zanipolo. One was tall, with a shock of grey hair and a beak-like eagle nose. He wore a heavy black coat and stooped a little as if there were a weight upon his shoulders. The second was in the flowing black cape of a priest in winter. They greeted one another as if surprised, which they were not. Their caution was, perhaps, extreme. No one was likely to see a former surgeon in his sixties and a priest a decade and a half younger bump into one another by the equestrian statue of the bloodthirsty medieval warlord Bartolomeo Colleoni. Still, both felt the need to be careful. The assignation had been quietly organized after news of the safe arrival of Vanni and Mika Artom. Since then the men had heard only that Paolo Uccello had visited Gallo's shop in via Garibaldi and been given supplies for three as arranged. Cigarettes among the pasta, cans of vegetables and cheap wine from the barrel.

Garzone wondered if that was another curse he'd passed on to the rather sad and solitary Uccello trapped in his hideaway behind the walls of the Giardino degli Angeli: tobacco. He was little more than a lad. Still, there was more to care about than the state of his lungs.

Three months on from the arrival of the Germans, Venice was on edge. Everywhere locals felt frightened and resentful of the foreigners who strutted the streets in their unfamiliar uniforms as if they were the new masters and would never leave. Most Venetians loathed Mussolini. Some of the older residents dreamily longed for the days their great-grandparents might have remembered, when Venice was a state of its own, an independent republic, not part of a reunified Italy. Now Il Duce was captive to Hitler and the Crucchi were in charge, it was difficult to decide where one's national loyalties lay. With a king who'd fled Rome for the protection of those who'd invaded the country from the south and rained bombs on the industrial and military areas of terraferma day and night? Or to the Fascist dictator who'd got them into this mess in the first place and was now keeping his captive population tame through a more direct and personal form of terror?

Principally, Filippo Garzone judged from quiet conversations in the confessional, people came to the conclusion that the primary responsibility of every sensible family in the city was to oneself and one's relatives. If they had allegiances elsewhere, only those who knew him personally – partisans or the devout who quietly came to their aid – spoke frankly of them in the cold and airy depths of San Pietro di Castello.

Over the past year there'd been plenty – men mostly, but not always – who, in the quiet of his small wooden confessional, had admitted to assault, the smuggling of weapons, even, on occasion, murder, then listened in silence, waiting for some word of comfort. Not absolution. He could never offer that. But these were strange, unbelievable times. He couldn't always condemn them either.

Diamante's old workplace, in truth his own basilica, lay across the campo from the cafe where they sat down to drink their *macchiati* and eat pastries made thin and crumbly by the shortages of war. It was the hospital that spread out behind the façade of the former *scuola* of San Marco, the most beautiful entrance to a medical facility anywhere in the world, or so Diamante always claimed. None who saw it disagreed. Here he'd started work as a junior doctor in his twenties after medical school in Bologna. Here he'd worked diligently, seven days a week, nights too, caring for the sick, learning the complex administration of the medical facilities, some modern, some ancient, that ran all the way back to the waterfront with its views of San Michele and Murano to the north. Here, too, he'd risen to become a senior surgeon and administrator until the Racial Laws intervened and deprived him of his livelihood. A bachelor, Diamante had saved enough to survive, and still earned a little money treating Jewish patients in the city. Though mostly now he was occupied with other work.

'Is there any word on when your friends may be moving to more suitable quarters?' Garzone asked, dipping a dry and tasteless biscuit into his coffee.

'None. I apologize. Is that a problem?'

The priest frowned.

'Hard to know until it arises. If the pair are sensible and stay behind Uccello's walls, I don't see how they can be found. It's hard to think of a better hidey-hole. Few know about it. Even fewer think about it. The locals have never taken to the Uccello. So long as they stay out of sight. But men took them there. If there should be—'

'My friends are doing what they can, Filippo. We're all grateful for your assistance.'

'Huh.' He laughed at that. 'What have I done? Put a lonely young orphan in great danger, against his instincts, I think. He still smarts from the loss of his parents. He blames the very side your friends are fighting for over their deaths.'

Diamante stirred his empty cup.

'The Artoms are fighting for a cause, not the Americans. From what I hear I suspect they'd prefer to be liberated by the Russians much more than a bunch of Yanks.'

'Oh,' Garzone muttered. 'I don't believe you ever mentioned that.'

Diamante seemed puzzled.

'Would it have made a difference? If I'd said they were godless communists whose last wish is to return us to the kind of easy-going democracy a pair of old men like us can just about remember? Would you have said no?'

'Of course not. But I would like to have known.'

'I assume your young friend feels the same way. He took them in, didn't he? No going back from there. If he were fool enough to walk into Ca' Loretti and hand them over they'd still shoot him for harbouring them in the first place.'

'True,' Garzone admitted. 'And here we are, drinking coffee, chatting amiably as if it's back before the war and we might be engaged in a friendly argument over whether La Fenice deserves its status.'

'You're a theatre man. You always prefer the Goldoni.'

Back in the Thirties the two of them would come here for better coffee, better *biscotti*. Hour after hour they'd dissect the latest productions in the city, amateur critics both.

'There's opera now if you want it, Aldo. *La Traviata*, I believe. They'll sell you a ticket, surely. They always seem to like Jewish money even if they don't like Jews.'

'That's a little unfair. Since you're not an opera man you miss the nuances. They put on Boito's *Mefistofele* last month.'

'So I read. Was it good?'

'I don't know. I didn't go. It was a subtle slight to Il Duce and his enslavement to his new master, Hitler, I believe. I admire their courage but to risk the wrath of the Fascists over a libretto and a piece of music seems a little rash to me. This is a time to stay out of sight. Not flaunt oneself with the Crucchi and their whores in the boxes of La Fenice.'

'Understandable.' Garzone took a deep breath and told him the one piece of news he had. An anarchist from the Lido by the name of Tartaglino had been arrested by the SS and tortured. 'I heard they cut off his ears before they shot him. Did you know?'

'No,' Diamante confessed. 'I've never heard of this Tartaglino. Was he part of any network?'

'Not that I'm aware.' The priest ordered two more coffees and let the waiter go back to the counter before he continued. 'A strange kind of intellectual who lived on the Lido. An atheist. Or anarchist or something. An eccentric fellow with eccentric beliefs.

Lord knows why they picked on him. I doubt he had anything to tell them except a few bizarre theories about Gramsci or some other philosopher he admired. I wonder . . .'

He found it hard to say.

'You wonder what, Filippo?'

He stared his friend straight in the face.

'I wonder what I'd do in those circumstances. If they picked me up and took me into that dump of a municipal building where I used to go to plead mercy for a parishioner who couldn't pay their taxes. I wonder if they put me to the torture, whatever it may be, whether I'd truly have the courage to say nothing. Or betray everyone and everything to stop the pain. I'm a priest. I'm surrounded by images of martyrs wherever I go. But for the life of me I've no idea whether I would have the courage to be one myself.'

Diamante said nothing.

'I was hoping you'd have an opinion, Aldo.'

'My opinion is that no one knows. Not until it happens. Personally I believe I'd allow them to go so far, then talk. And tell them such rubbish that it would be of no use whatsoever. At which point either they'd kill me or discover it was rubbish and resume. After which perhaps I'd try to take my own life—'

'Which is a sin. For Catholics.'

'And giving the Nazis what they want isn't?'

He always won the arguments they had. That was one reason Filippo Garzone admired the man.

'You're braver than me. The Jews have always had to be. The things we've done to you. The things we're doing now, though God knows what they truly are . . .'

Diamante smiled, reached across the table and took the priest's hand.

'Now that *is* nonsense. I'm a surgeon, remember. I've seen inside more bodies than most men could ever imagine. How does it go? "Hath not a Jew hands? Are we not subject to the same diseases, healed by the same means? If you prick us, do we not bleed?" It works both ways. You and I are no different. And remember I'm not merely a secular Jew. I'm an atheist. I'm amazed you even talk to me.'

'I feel I should be doing something.'

'You have,' Diamante insisted. 'And now you should do nothing.

Very slowly. A month ago the Germans asked me to compile a register of the *qehillà*.'

It was a word Garzone had never heard.

'The what?'

'Qehillà. It's what we call the Jewish community. Those of us who live within the city of Venice, from Burano in the north to the city, to the Lido. Even a married couple who live in Malamocco and an old man in the rest home in Alberoni, would you believe? They're all my flock now since the Fascists decided I was to be its president. As an atheist this is rather new to me. Though on that subject . . .' He glanced out of the window at the hospital across the square. 'Deprived of my natural home I must say that the longer this goes on the more Jewish I begin to feel. It's odd. Perhaps I will ask a rabbi a few questions one day. If there are any left.'

The priest tried to think this through.

'They want you to compile a list?'

Diamante nodded.

'Of everyone. Not just the ghetto. Every last man, woman and child with Jewish blood in Venice and the islands.'

'That's impossible! We have what . . . a hundred thousand-odd people in this city! The obvious apart . . . who's to know who's Jewish or not? Unless they volunteer and you'd need to be an idiot to do that.'

Diamante stirred his empty coffee cup and slowly shook his head.

'It's not quite as hard as you think. Jews usually know who Jews are, even those who try to hide it. Relatives. Friends. People they went to school with. People they need to rely upon now they can't do much without the help of other Jews. It's not beyond the wit of man to find names. I gather the Germans are calling in assistance to make sure I do it right too. One of ours who's crossed the road.'

'No, surely . . .'

'The fellow's called Salvatore Bruno. From Turin originally. Though he sometimes goes under other names when pursuing his work. A notorious individual who's travelling Mussolini's small state pointing the finger right and left. Sometimes Bruno gains their confidence by pretending to be a partisan. Sometimes he drags them into a room where the Nazi torturers can do their work.

Whichever way, the end's the same. They go into a wagon, disappear, or simply die against a wall or on a hillside in the mountains. Then he gets his bounty. I'm told it's usually seven thousand lire a head. Given his success he must be a wealthy man by now. The bastard's on his way here, I gather. At some point very soon I'm to hand in my report for his approval.'

'And then what?'

Diamante looked around the room. They were the only ones there. No one could hear. It was more as if he didn't want to say the words.

'They round us all up, I imagine. Why else would they need a list? The end I don't know in any detail. Only the beginning.'

Garzone's voice almost failed him.

'Oh lord. What are we becoming?'

'What have we become already and never noticed?' his friend replied. 'People are getting the message already. I do wonder if perhaps the Black Brigades are spreading it deliberately through their informers. To get us to move. To expose ourselves. To panic. Already some are trying to flee to Switzerland. A few make it through, those with enough money and the right contacts to bribe. Any who get caught are robbed, then shot on the spot. I gather a few brave souls are trying to make their way south beyond the German lines. You could try and take a boat down the coast from Rimini and pray the coastal defences don't see you. Or the British or Americans blow you out of the water if you make it that far.'

Garzone clasped his hand.

'I'll speak to people I know. We can get you out of here.'

The old surgeon stared at him, shocked and jerked back his arm.

'Are you serious? This is my home. The only one I know. I was born here. If anyone were to deny me the privilege of dying here I should be very cross indeed. Besides, they made me their president.'

'The Fascists did that. The Nazis. What do you owe them? Nothing.'

'I'm not running. I can't—'

'I beg you.'

'Don't waste your time.'

Before the war their conversations could run for hours, covering everything from politics to football, opera to the latest exhibition in the Accademia. Now he could feel this one petering out by the second.

'How long will it take you to compile this list?'

Diamante laughed, then leaned forward with a conspiratorial wink.

'Oh. I finished that last week. Give me a job and I do it properly.'

'Do they know?'

'Of course not. Do I look a fool? There are a couple of hundred very visible Jews among us. Many of the ones I know of are elderly. Few with the money to bribe their way out of this here even if that were wise. How can they flee? Where to?' He leaned forward again to make the point. 'Listen to me. You see the difficulty you have in keeping two communist renegades out of their hands? A brother and sister used to subterfuge and fighting? How can I do that with a middle-aged baker and his wife, their children in tow? Or a widow in her eighties who can barely walk?'

Garzone hated the fact but he could see his point.

'Then what?'

'I told you. I do nothing. Slowly. I smile and apologize and say I will do better. And all the while I delay, offer excuses, give people the chance to try escape if they wish. More than anything we behave like the craven underlings they think us. One day – one glorious day – release will come. It must.'

'And how many of you will be left by then?'

It was a harsh question and he wished he'd never asked it. There was real pain on Aldo Diamante's face at that moment.

The awkward interlude was broken by loud voices at the bar. German, a language neither man understood much at all. Three men in dark suits appeared to be throwing questions at the frightened woman behind the counter. After her faltering answers they stayed silent for a moment. Then one pointed at the best bottle of grappa and bellowed, '*Drei!*'

Her hands shook as she served them brimming glasses, more generous than any paying local would ever get. She didn't dare ask them for money.

'One day,' Diamante repeated, then got up and walked smiling to the door, tipping his hat as he left.

* * *

The mist was gone. The sky above the glass roof of their conservatory workshop was wreathed in the cold, hard sun Paolo associated with the depths of winter, a time when Venice looked so beautiful that it might have been a painting. Once, before the war, his mother had taken him to an exhibition at the Accademia of work by an English artist, Turner, vague, shifting watercolours she loved so deeply she kept a print of one in the living room above the dining table. *Boats in Front of the Dogana and Santa Maria della Salute*. Painted just over a hundred years ago.

Paolo had liked it too but, being a picky child, had argued that there was something wrong with the view. It wasn't accurate. The buildings featured, the panorama, could never have looked the way Turner had portrayed them.

'Silly boy,' she'd scolded him. 'It's art. Not a photograph. Something that lives in your head. Not in front of your eyes. Use your imagination for once.'

Thinking back that must have been six or seven years before, just as Mussolini was tightening his grip on Italy, locking up his enemies, placing restrictions on the Jews. His mother and father had recently moved to Castello from Dorsoduro. Money was tight. They were laying off weavers and that wasn't something they enjoyed. And, it seems, they were Fascists too. That was when they began retreating into themselves, into the Giardino degli Angeli, withdrawing him from school, hiding behind their brick walls, struggling to make ends meet.

Soon they had only Chiara Vecchi to help them.

Imagination was a place he'd usually avoided. Particularly of late. There were corpses there, eyes open, looking at him.

He pushed the beater forward, moving the yarn, delivering the pattern set in the punch.

Si-dah-si-dah-si-dah-sichi-si-piu.

A minute or two in he caught Chiara's eye. She looked happier now. The newcomer had quickly found that rhythm too. So Paolo bent forward, smiled at him and was warmed by the sudden grin he got in return. Vanni Artom was different, quite unlike the Venetian men he met out in Castello. There was none of the need for money and stature, the battle to be tougher, stronger than anyone else. Vanni possessed something gentle, almost feminine in his soft eyes, lazy grin, the easy way he fell in with what others wanted. His dark hair was so long he looked like one of

Caravaggio's boys, fey and mysterious. Working the loom he had to struggle to push it back from time to time.

I could hold your arms and guide you, Paolo told himself.

Si-dah-si-dah-si-dah-sichi-si-piu.

That was an idea that came out of his imagination. One more reason why he tried to avoid that habit. So often it offered up thoughts and images and desires he didn't want. The others at school had noticed too, even when he was just eleven or so. It was one more reason he was glad to be out of there. One more reason perhaps why his parents liked to keep him hidden away in the Giardino degli Angeli, away from the harsh, cold world beyond its walls. He didn't *fit.*

Three Jacquards working at regular speed made quite a racket. They weren't to know that Mika Artom had watched them from the cracked-open door of the apartment. Then, when she was sure they were fully occupied with the work, gone to the back door, slunk out, found herself on the patio. There she soon found a way of escape round the brick wall, along the narrow stone edge all the way back into San Pietro.

A group of soldiers in grey German uniforms were gathered by the bridge, backs to her, staring at the white marble campanile of San Pietro, leaning slightly on its own by the side of the basilica.

Her heart started beating the way it always did when the Crucchi were around. Out of fear. Out of pure hate too.

She went the other way, into a web of alleys so winding and tangled she wondered if she'd ever find the other side.

Luca Alberti took a measured risk when he marched into Greta's grubby bar in Castello. A wasted adventure that hadn't produced a speck of useful information. So he went back to the old, tried ways of the job. Knocking on the doors of those he suspected were in league with the partisans and cowardly enough to talk. Taking his small band of informers to one side and reminding them that good tip-offs got them double their usual money, maybe even more. And if they came up with nothing useful then maybe he wouldn't pay. Maybe he'd stop turning a blind eye to their other shady work, smuggling, stealing, extorting money from shopkeepers in return for black market goods they couldn't get easily elsewhere.

Still it hadn't worked. If the Artoms were in the city then no one on his books seemed to have any knowledge of them.

Oberg appeared too distracted by other matters to moan much about the lack of progress, though his underlings, Sachs and Sander, made caustic comments from time to time when Alberti returned to Ca' Loretti empty-handed. He always smiled and said nothing in reply to their taunts. Sometimes he wondered whether it might not be worth staying to watch the fall of the city, whenever that came. He'd enjoy seeing that pair of loutish thugs put up against the wall. One reason he'd made that little speech in front of Trevisan in the dump in via Garibaldi was to push out an option. The idea that maybe he'd be open to playing both sides if the reward was there. In his heart Alberti remained a Venetian. He didn't mind the Fascists running the city. The Crucchi were a different matter. They were no more welcome than any of the invaders of old, the French and the Austrians.

When the British or the Americans finally crossed the single bridge that connected the city to terraferma, a reckoning was coming. Men like Rocco Trevisan and his comrades might be hailing them as liberators. But pretty soon they'd be after revenge against those they hated. When that came it would take the same form the Crucchi delivered now. A merciless beating, a quick trial if you were lucky, maybe a hanging or a firing squad out in the street.

If he played both sides he might avoid that. Not run off to a distant, foreign country after all. But that was a hell of a risk. A couple of weeks before a report had passed his desk about a wanted partisan near Bolzano. Nineteen years old, a monk until he took up with the fighters, he'd escaped a raid and run off into the hills. Spent days trekking the mountains trying to find friendly territory, only to turn up in some primitive remote village where the locals thought he was a German spy and shot him on the spot.

There wasn't much point in trying to convince Trevisan he was still a good guy at heart. That boat had sailed.

'Want another coffee?' the kid behind the counter in Marino asked.

'No. You didn't ask me how things are.'

The lad just blushed and looked scared.

'That's good, sonny,' Alberti said. 'You're learning. Keep your mouth shut. Do nothing. That way you just might get out of this shit alive.'

A boat had turned up at the jetty by Ca' Loretti, packed full of Germans. Uniforms, leather coats, smart caps, lots of medals. They loved their silverware and ribbons.

He watched them disembark with the clumsiness of people who hadn't grown up around boats. They then formed a square around a single individual. Alberti wondered if they'd found someone, a captive, some poor idiot who was going to be taken into the cells the worst of the Crucchi kept out back for torture. But no. This man was short, maybe thirty-five or so, swarthy. Flabby face and a nose that made Alberti think straight away, *You're either a Jew or doing a damned good impersonation of one.*

He wore an impeccable black overcoat that must have cost a fortune and a broad matching fedora with a wide brim and a shiny band in grey and silver. Everything about him spoke of money and power as the Germans marched the guy up the alley towards the sentries at the entrance.

Alberti stared as he went past. Faces were part of his job. Remembering them a skill he'd honed over the years. He'd seen that one before. On a report that had been sitting on Oberg's desk when the Germans were out of the room.

There was the sound of boots on cobbles from up the alley. It was a bunch of German grunts escorting someone into the building who didn't want to be there. Tall, stooped, dark-coated, long grey face.

Aldo Diamante. The man they'd put in charge of the city Jews.

He thought about the other face and the connection came up straight away. The photo had been on a report from Turin. He was the Jew hunter Oberg said was on his way. Salvatore Bruno.

'Shit,' he murmured, finishing his coffee. 'Something's up.'

It wasn't simply boredom that led Mika Artom to slip out of Paolo Uccello's home. There was something she'd been seeking ever since they nearly died with the rest of their cell as they sabotaged the railway line in the Vallagarina valley outside Rovereto. A cause. A need. A goal. The cold and plain apartment of a weaving family on the edge of Venice seemed a strange place to find it. But there the answer was.

She'd been rummaging through the living room while her brother and Chiara Vecchi worked the looms outside. The rattle and clatter they made along with Vanni's occasional raucous laughter covered up her rifling through the drawers, the desk and the cupboards.

To begin with, she felt it was nothing more than an idle, maybe shameful attempt to peer behind the shell of their reticent young host. She wasn't sure what she was looking for. A clue to what made him hide away from everything behind high walls, a ruined garden, a conservatory turned into a feeble kind of factory. Almost a small fortress against life outside. It wasn't the Crucchi he feared so much, she thought. It was the world, whatever it contained. The loss of his parents might explain it. But the Artoms had experienced more deaths than Paolo Uccello could imagine: family, friends, comrades in arms. Their loss fired her anger. The last thing she wanted was to closet herself away in a bare and draughty house at the edge of the lazy, lapping waters of the lagoon.

Money would be useful if they had to flee again suddenly. Not that she could find much of that beyond a few thousand lire stashed away in the desk drawer. A spare weapon? Just the thought made her laugh. So in the end she contented herself with poking around being nosy. A thief who'd no idea what she sought.

The desk was where his father had kept all his business papers, neatly stored in a grey cardboard box file labelled 'Sales' in the bottom drawer. There were perhaps forty documents there and the way the dates changed over the six years they covered demonstrated the failing health of the family trade. In the past four months there'd been only one inquiry from a potential customer. The city it came from immediately caught her eye: Turin. Then an address that made her blink and look at it twice to be sure. The Piazza delle Due Fontane. That took her straight back home and she felt her blood rising with all the memories. As a child, she and Vanni used to walk there with her parents until an oppressive block of white Fascist era buildings, all squares and oblongs, not the soft, worn stone of the old monuments she loved, rose from the dust of construction.

When the war came Mussolini's security men took over the offices, with Germans along for 'advice'. By now, or so she'd heard, the Gestapo occupied the entire square. It was from here the team that murdered their parents had emerged. She found it impossible to remember those cold, cruel marble blocks without seeing blood running down their façades. No one worked in Due Fontane without some connection to the Nazis.

And here was a letter sent from the place, commissioning work from Paolo Uccello's father. Three small banners for a presentation, all identical, all 'to be finished to the finest standards of the Venetian Republic of old and fit to be presented at a meeting of very important officers and citizens of the state'.

The name at the bottom made her shiver too: Salvatore Bruno. The Jew hunter. The man who'd sought out families across northern Italy and handed them over to the Germans to be shot or deported. Her own included.

The next letter, typed like all the others, began by saying the commission was to come from a new man, Ugo Leone. Signed by him too. Though it seemed obvious to her that the signature was the same. Why? Because Bruno was surely aware that his name was becoming well-known in partisan circles and to advertise his presence was only to invite trouble.

The most recent letter was brief and brought forward the deadline for delivery to the Hotel Gioconda by a few days, to the afternoon of December the fourth. The following Saturday. The message ended, too, with a clear and interesting threat.

> There will be great and important men in attendance, Uccello. I must advise you it would be perilous to your reputation if not your person if you were to disappoint them and me.

So the hated Bruno and a handful of his Nazi and Black Brigades friends were coming to Venice for some kind of celebration. Probably business too since the capture of his fellow Jews was something the avaricious Bruno never shrank from. The man had made himself wealthy on the blood of others. There'd been at least two attempts on his life already, both failures ending in the vicious murders of the partisans who tried to kill him.

Third time lucky, Mika Artom thought. But for that she'd need new friends. And if it meant betraying the promise they'd made to Paolo Uccello . . . well, that was war.

It was nearly four. The light was almost gone. She and Vanni had visited Venice twice with her parents in their teens, back when they had money and a semblance of freedom. But that had been to the tourist parts: San Marco, the Rialto, the Basilica and the Doge's Palace. They'd gone to the top of the campanile of San Giorgio Maggiore and stared out across the entire city and the lagoon. A lost summer's day, captured in the memory like a coloured postcard filed for another time.

They never came anywhere near this part of Castello. Still she had the vaguest of addresses in her head from talking to a couple of partisans from a Veneto cell who'd joined them in the safe house outside Padua for a while. Via Garibaldi. A long, broad street of shops and cafes, once a canal, running all the way down to the main waterfront and St. Mark's Basin.

Eventually, after many cul-de-sacs that ended in a stretch of black water, she emerged into something that looked, for the most part, like an ordinary city street. A few shoppers strolled along lugging bags. Back at the top, towards San Pietro, it had to be, a porter was pushing a trolley laden with wooden boxes, grunting as it bounced across the cobbles. A couple of German soldiers stood smoking by the iron gates that led to a small park, watching everyone and everything with an idle curiosity.

Don't slow down. Always seem busy. Never look back when they stare at you but never look down either. Appear normal, always.

They'd all learned that. You had to if you didn't want to get picked up and probably never come out alive.

The Venetians who'd spirited them out to the lagoon had talked of a cafe. A dump of a place near a static boat that sold vegetables by the water. Then they'd vanished back into the mountains to carry on fighting.

On a hunch she followed the porter with his boxes. He stopped by a grubby boat with a meagre selection of produce arranged for sale across the deck. Sure enough, there was a cafe to the side.

Mika went in and ordered a coffee. A bent old bird in a stained cotton apron stood behind the counter, a huge and battered pan of soup boiling away beside her. At the end of the bar sat a man and a woman, thirties, maybe early forties, both smoking, watching her much the way the Nazi grunts had out in the street. He seemed as hard as nails, gaunt, dark face, suspicious searching eyes. She had the shiniest red hair Mika Artom had ever seen and looked like she just came out of make-up for a movie.

There was a line the partisans in the mountains used when they tried to make contact in strange territory. She'd no idea if it would work here. No clue whether it had been compromised either, which always happened after a while.

'Signora,' the woman behind the counter said, putting a cup on the counter. 'You're a stranger here. I've not seen you before.'

'True.'

'Where are you from?' the man demanded, then screwed out his cigarette butt on the tiled floor.

'Turin. You?'

The woman with him was staring straight at her.

'What's someone from Turin doing here?' she asked.

'Sightseeing. Is this the place called Greta's?'

'What's it to you?' he asked.

'I thought I might find a friend here. That's all.'

Come out with it. You've got to.

Then the man along the bar got to his feet and what he said almost invited the words.

'You sound like you're lying.'

'No, sir. *Meglio una brutta verità che una bella bugia.*'

Better an ugly truth than a beautiful lie.

They moved quickly, him and the woman. Before she could say or do a thing he was behind her, blocking the way back to the door, opening his jacket so she could see the pistol on his hip.

She hadn't taken her own gun with her. Which was perhaps stupid. Or wise. You never knew till later.

The crone from the bar was in the shadows at the end, pushing open an old door painted glossy red.

'Move,' the man ordered, dragging her towards the dark. 'Move now.'

Hauptscharführer Oberg's office was crowded for once. Germans in uniform. Ones who outranked his boss judging by the ribbons and metal shining on their chests. Sachs and Sander were on their feet nodding vigorously as they spoke to some of the newcomers, creeps as always.

'Oh look,' Sachs cried as Alberti entered. 'Our little Venetian pet's arrived. Come. We're toasting one of your countrymen who does serve a purpose.'

'Whatever you say,' he replied with a quick smile.

The visiting Crucchi didn't even bother to give their names. Only the information that they'd come directly from headquarters in Salò and would soon be travelling on to Trieste.

The old doctor Diamante sat in the corner, grey-faced and

miserable, as if he'd just been told of a death. The other stranger Alberti had seen outside, the short Jewish-looking man in the good clothes, stood in the midst of the Germans, guffawing at their jokes, cradling an empty glass in his hand.

'Fill us up,' Sander ordered, nodding at the open wine bottles on his desk. 'You make a good waiter. Have a glass yourself.'

'Not when I'm working,' Alberti said and went round the small crowd, doing as he was told. The only one who paid him any attention was the Italian newcomer who looked him up and down and asked, 'Do I know you?'

'I don't think so.' He held out his hand and introduced himself. 'Used to be in the Carabinieri. Now I'm liaison with our friends here. Local. Speak Italian and Venetian which I trust makes me useful. You?'

'Salvatore Bruno. From Turin. You've heard of me no doubt.'

'Read about you too. Busy guy. Caught any Jews lately?'

Bruno tapped the side of his nose.

'More on the way. I promise.'

'We can talk about this later,' Oberg cut in. 'Not now.'

Alberti knew when he wasn't wanted. So he wandered over to Diamante who didn't have a glass at all or seem to want one.

'Are you alright, doctor?' he asked. 'Can I get you something?'

'Nothing you have to offer.'

It was the only time he'd ever heard the man sound even faintly rude.

'How do you know? If you don't ask.'

He said that quietly. The others were too interested in their drink and the kind of self-congratulatory chatter the Germans liked when they got good news.

'You can judge a man by the company he keeps. I heard you found the soldier who raped and murdered that poor woman the other day.'

'Not for me to talk about such things,' Alberti replied with a shrug. He waved the bottle and an empty glass. Diamante shook his head. 'You can see for yourself. I'm just the waiter here. Local help.' He bent down to make sure they weren't overheard. 'Those things I said. When they fished that woman out of the water. It was for their benefit. You understand that? Truth is . . .' Closer, he whispered in his ear. 'We're more engaged looking for partisans than Jews right now. If you people keep your heads down maybe you'll see it through.'

Diamante scowled, got to his feet, pushed him to one side and went and touched Oberg's sleeve.

'Do you really need me here?'

The German glanced at Salvatore Bruno who was listening intently and said, 'You understand what's required of you? As president of your community?'

'I understand what you're asking. I also understand it's impossible in the time you've given me. As I've said repeatedly.'

'Saturday, Diamante.' The Italian had winked at him then. 'I know it's the Sabbath. But you're no believer. Any more than me. Which is why we'll survive.' He tapped his fleshy nose again. A nervous habit, Alberti thought. A tic. This man was nowhere near as confident as he wished others to believe. 'Best know which side your bread is buttered. Our German friends are practical, not vindictive. They look after those who help them.'

Diamante gazed right at him with a jaded expression of distaste.

'There are hundreds of families here with some Jewish heritage. It's impossible to name them all in a week or two.'

Bruno stretched out his arms and grinned for the benefit of his audience.

'Sir, sir! Once you ran a busy hospital. Very efficiently I'm told. Just do your best, man. Give us what you have. On Saturday night we have a little party here. Bring me your list and we can enjoy a drink or two in the Gioconda. There will be entertainment. The ladies there—'

'I do not mix with whores,' Diamante snapped. Which was, Alberti thought, exactly what the man from Turin had wanted. 'A month or so. That's all I ask. Then I'll give you as good a list as anyone can provide.'

Oberg stepped between them.

'You don't have a month. Neither do I. Salò has issued orders.'

A flush came to Diamante's grey cheeks.

'Salò? What do I care of that? I'm no citizen of Mussolini's phoney republic. There are two Italys at the moment. I don't believe the one with a legitimate government and our monarch at its head has seen fit to demand a list of anyone.'

There was silence then. Alberti took the old man's arm.

'Come, doctor. You're tired. Upset. It's understandable. Let me take you home.'

'I can walk these streets without your help. You're the ones who need protection.'

Salvatore Bruno laughed in his face.

'Now that is a sign of impending decrepitude. Excuse my frankness.' That tap of the nose again. 'People tell me you seem a decent fellow. With some cooperation on your part, names, places, bank accounts . . . who knows?'

'Time to go,' Alberti said, and almost dragged Diamante to the door before the old man could say another word.

It was dark outside. The German guards were stamping their feet on the cobbles in the alley that led to the Grand Canal one way and the heart of San Marco the other. The water was high, close to flooding, backing up the drains down the alley. Most days the city didn't stink. This wasn't one of them.

'You're sure you don't want company? There are fools out there who think everyone that walks out of this building's their enemy.'

'I have no enemies.'

Alberti raised an eyebrow and looked back at the guards and the building looming above them.

'You're a clever man, Diamante. Much smarter than the likes of me. But there, I fear, you're wrong.'

'Plague is a disease. Human beings are infected by it. They are the symptoms, not the illness itself.'

'That's an intellectual argument. I'm not an intellectual. You won't find many among those Crucchi we just left either.'

'Some of the sick will die. In the end others will survive. Once we find the cure. And we will. That's what people do. Find another way to live.'

'Till it all comes round again.'

'It won't,' Diamante insisted. 'After this horror . . . it can't.'

Stubborn old fool, Alberti thought. The Jew hunter had offered him a way out. It might have been a lie but it was an offer all the same, and few of his kind were going to get that. Not when they'd been stripped of every last cent and piece of jewellery and property they owned.

'If you don't give them what they want they'll find it anyway. Then put you in a cattle truck along with the rest of them.'

Diamante's frown was short and bereft of feeling. A doctor's look perhaps, the kind they gave when a patient was beyond hope and need to know it.

'Why do you do this, Alberti?'

'As I keep telling people. Because someone must. It could be a lot worse than me. What I said when they dragged that woman out of the water . . . I didn't mean it.' He jabbed a finger at Ca' Loretti. 'If this bunch are happy or even halfway so then they're not out murdering people on the streets. You've got to keep them like that. Distracted. Feeling safe. That's good, isn't it? That's something.'

He didn't know why he was saying this. The old man had no real position in the city any more. He was just another Jew, probably as good as dead anyway. His opinion didn't matter one jot.

Diamante held out his hand. It was bony, wrinkled, but it was the hand of an artist too, sculpted, careful, controlled and in spite of his age didn't tremble. Alberti shook his cold fingers and wondered how often they'd delved inside a man or woman, looking for a tumour or some other kind of cancer, seeking a way to remove it, to save a life.

'That's for you to decide, Alberti. Your conscience if you have one.' He turned to head off down the shadows into the warren of streets on his long walk home to the ghetto. 'If you have a conscience you should listen to it sometimes. Men who don't will never fare well.'

'They'll kill you if you screw with them, old man.'

'We all die one day.' Aldo Diamante wrapped his thick coat more tightly around his chest. 'What matters is that others remember how and why we fell.' He touched his hat. 'Goodnight.'

There was another business behind Greta's bar: a small room used for hairdressing. Rocco Trevisan perched on the ledge by an old, cracked mirror, the grey background poking through the glass. Sara Vitale, the woman with him, sat by his side playing with a pair of sharp scissors.

They'd listened to her story which she told as succinctly and as accurately as she could. It was important to be frank with the details. Partisans were quick to pick up lies and liars didn't live long.

'Who brought you here?' the woman asked.

'Some men in a boat. Our friends in Padua found them.'

'Names?'

'I don't have them and if I had I wouldn't tell you.'

'Fair enough,' Trevisan said with a nod and offered her a cigarette. He watched as she lit it with shaking fingers. It was odd. She was never that scared when they went out to kill Germans or lay explosives along train lines. But these two strangers had a hardness and a determination about them she didn't care for. Maybe this wasn't a good idea at all. Maybe she should have listened to Vanni, stayed in the rundown apartment behind the weaving workshop the way she'd promised.

'Where are you staying now?' Vitale asked.

'That's another thing you don't need to know. I can come here and talk to you any time. Or somewhere else. I want to help.' She lit the cigarette and took a long lungful. 'I want to fight. To kill Crucchi. That's enough, isn't it?'

'And your brother?' Trevisan wondered. 'What about him?'

'He's wounded. He'd only slow us down.'

Which was true, up to a point. Vanni's leg was bad but it would mend in a month or two. All the same his spirit wasn't quite there. Perhaps it never had been, as much as hers anyway. They'd joined the cell in Padua in fury after hearing of the slaughter of their family back home. They knew they couldn't return to Turin until the Nazis and the Fascists were gone. They were Jews. The Black Brigades were hunting victims everywhere, Salvatore Bruno helping all he could, across the north from east to west. There seemed no alternative.

The wild, red anger in her head never abated. In truth it only grew, week by week as the fight seemed ever harder. Vanni lacked the same fire. Her younger brother didn't like the violence, the weapons, the grenades and bombs. He wanted everything to be over, done with, consigned to the past. Only then could he be back with his books, his professors and his arty friends, not hunting Crucchi out on the chill bare slopes of the Dolomites. She could see him hiding out among the looms in the Giardino degli Angeli, with the fey young stranger Paolo Uccello, barely more than a schoolboy, for as long as the war lasted if he had the chance.

'So it's just you?' Vitale asked with a sneer.

'I can fight. I know weapons. I know bombs. I'm not scared.'

'Only a fool's not scared,' Trevisan told her. 'You know what they do if they get you in Ca' Loretti? Pull your fingernails out. Rape you. Tear you to pieces.'

She almost laughed. Venice was a place apart, almost a holiday resort still, perched across a single bridge at the very edge of Italy. In Turin, in Milan, Verona, Padua, there was much worse going on.

'I'm not scared,' she repeated very slowly. 'Are you?'

They looked at one another and said nothing.

'When you have an operation I want to be part of it.'

'Nothing planned,' Trevisan said.

'What? In Padua they said you were busy here. Dedicated. Courageous—'

'We are!' His voice was loud and threatening. 'We're just . . . depleted.'

She waited. Finally the woman explained. One of the cell had gone freelance a few weeks before and murdered a German in an alley in San Marco. It was unplanned, unauthorized. The idiot had simply lost it when he saw the Nazi pestering a local woman. The reprisals had been swift and merciless. Ten local men slaughtered, four of them nothing to do with the partisans at all.

Trevisan scowled.

'We lost good soldiers because one idiot shot a drunk in the street. We're not scared. We just want . . . bigger fish in the net. They don't come here so much. Unless it's for the whores and the drink and the gambling in that hotel of theirs. We've tried putting people in there but they always get caught. They know the locals.'

In her pocket Mika had the letter she'd taken from Uccello's desk. The one that pointed to some kind of heavyweight Nazi and Black Brigades gathering in the Gioconda that coming Saturday. She put it on the table by the mirror.

'They intercepted this in Verona,' she said. 'Passed it on. That's why they wanted me to come here. To give it you.'

Trevisan snatched at it and the two of them read the commission from Turin.

'This is that queer kid's father,' Vitale said. 'The weaving family in San Pietro. They always said he was a Fascist.'

'The father's dead,' Mika insisted. 'Him and the mother got killed in an air raid in Verona. Some friends of ours recovered that from the papers they left behind.'

'"There will be great and important men in attendance."'

Trevisan waved the letter and smiled. 'I know what happened to the Uccello. Do you think we don't hear things? You're sure this is real?'

'I told you. It came from the cell in Verona. They had someone in the morgue who handled what was left of them. He found it. They wanted me to pass it on. They told me about this bar. For the love of God what else am I supposed to offer you?'

He was barely listening.

'The Gioconda,' Trevisan muttered. 'The shit that goes on there. Last time we tried to put a woman inside she wound up tied to a stake outside the back of Ca' Loretti. They cut her throat.'

'We all take risks.'

He sniffed.

'She was my niece.'

Sara Vitale stared at her. Then reached forward and took hold of Mika's dark, straggly hair.

She shrank back and said, 'I don't like being touched.'

'Best get used to it from now on,' Trevisan replied. 'Wait outside. Greta can get you a drink.'

The place was closed, the old woman sweeping up. Via Garibaldi was mostly dark, with only a few dim lights in the windows of apartments above the shuttered shops.

'Can I get a Negroni?' she asked, needing something strong. The kind of drink they'd enjoyed in Padua at student parties when someone had the money.

'A what?'

'Gin. Vermouth. Bitter.'

Greta slung something together from a bunch of bottles that had no labels. It didn't taste anything like it should but the heavy, alcoholic buzz was there and that was what she needed.

Twenty minutes or more she waited, struggling to try to start some conversation, failing. The woman seemed as good as deaf. Either that or she only heard what she wanted.

Maybe this was all a bad idea. Maybe she'd exposed them all, Vanni and the Uccello kid. Not that she'd given away a single clue about where they were hiding. But if these two wanted to follow her, or try to force her to find out more, they surely had the means.

Maybe Vanni was right and they should hide out for a while.

Find somewhere in the hills. Live like hermits or peasants. Try to find some kind of equilibrium where they could think things through, talk them through as well, the way they used to. The war and the threat from the Germans and Black Brigades didn't just make them fugitives. It banished all the things they took for granted: conversation, friendly argument, the need to find some kind of consensus about the road ahead. In a way she and Vanni were both closer to one another than ever. In another, it felt as if they'd never been further apart.

Then the red-painted door opened and she realized the time for second thoughts was over. Trevisan was there, holding a gun.

'Get back in here,' he ordered.

Mika did as she was told.

'Sit down,' Sara Vitale said.

She couldn't take her eyes off the weapon.

'*Sit down.*'

Mika Artom took the old metal chair in front of the hairdressing mirror.

'What's this?' Trevisan held it sideways.

'Walther P38, standard issue. Had one of my own once. Took it off a dead German. You?'

He glared at her.

'None of your business. Best handgun they've got. You got a weapon now?'

She reached into her jacket and took out the military knife she'd held to Paolo Uccello's throat the night they arrived.

'Some use that is against the Crucchi,' Trevisan said. He held out the weapon. 'Tell me if there's a shell in the chamber.'

'No. I can't see a pin.'

Vitale asked, 'How many rounds?'

'Eight. And one in the chamber.'

'Do you know how to take it to pieces?'

She shook her head.

'No. I always tried to kill another German when I needed a new one.'

Quick as a flash Trevisan turned the thing round and in a way she couldn't follow disassembled the slide and then the barrel. Then notched it all back together.

'Here.' He threw her the thing, then a pack of shells. 'Show me how to load the magazine.'

The moment she'd got the bullets in he snatched the weapon off her and pointed the barrel straight at her head.

'Now. Tell me where you're living. And who with?'

Mika looked straight at him, straight at the woman and said, 'Fuck you. I wouldn't tell the Crucchi. I won't tell you. They're my comrades. I don't give them up for anybody.'

Trevisan pointed to the pin. There was a shell in the magazine.

Mika shrugged, looked down at the floor for a moment, as if she was about to give in. That was enough. The red fire was rising and there was no stopping now. Trevisan hesitated. She flew at him, one knee to the groin, nails biting deep into his hands until he yelled. The weapon fell to the floor and she followed it, got her fingers round the butt, rolled once, rolled again, let the momentum help her to her feet, pointed the barrel straight at him.

Trevisan was sucking at his hand.

'Here.' She threw him the gun and he caught it in one. 'Kill me if you like. If you don't have the balls to take down Nazis you might as well.'

He looked at Sara Vitale.

Mika tapped a finger against her long, dark hair.

'Go on then.'

'Stay still,' Vitale barked, then grabbed at a pair of scissors and a bottle by the mirror.

'Why?'

'You talk too much,' Trevisan said, then came and placed his hands firmly on her shoulders.

He was bleeding where her teeth caught him. She felt good about that.

They worked through the day, barely stopping except for a drink and a piece of bread and dried-up ham, a chance to rest their weary arms. Mika never came out to see how things were going. Sleeping, Paolo guessed, and he was happy about that. Vanni seemed more relaxed when she wasn't around. So did he. The gun she'd held to his neck was hidden somewhere in his parents' room. He'd be happy if he never saw that again.

At six, exhaustion set in. Paolo told Chiara to go home and after a long argument she agreed. She'd overseen the two of them, watching everything they did, uttering a few sharp comments if something looked wrong.

By the end of the afternoon they'd made good progress. The pattern was well-established, the rampant golden lions, the contrasting scarlet background. It was the kind of bellicose design that still hung in rooms in the Doge's Palace, marking victories of the past. He couldn't imagine the Uccello producing something quite as forthright as this. The claws, the limbs, the upright roaring head of the lion lacked subtlety, deliberately so, he felt.

In his heart Paolo understood the commission had to be connected to the military. Turin had a reputation for being a hive of Fascists. They had the money for this kind of thing too. But if Vanni had guessed too he didn't say. The newcomer seemed happy to be learning the way of the loom. The gentle persistent rhythm of building the velvet, Chiara's careful, considerate tutelage when he went wrong, and her encouragement as more and more, and so quickly, he got the hang of the process. They would make the order in time if they kept up like this. He'd deliver it himself to the Hotel Gioconda that Saturday afternoon.

Then Father Filippo would come along and say it was time for the Artoms to move on to another safe house. They weren't supposed to be in the Giardino degli Angeli for long. He'd be on his own again. A little money but no work. Sitting in the desolate emptiness of his old home, missing his parents, waiting for some other challenge to find its way into his life.

He thought he'd miss Vanni Artom too, though this seemed a rapid, even rash, judgement to make so quickly. His talkative, thoughtful nature brought a warmth to the place that had been missing since his parents died in that firestorm in Verona.

When they were finished, he rushed to help Paolo tidy up some of the litter around the looms even though he limped with every step, wincing too from time to time. Then they returned to the apartment, for food and drink and rest. He needed the dressing on his wound changed. The blood was seeping through the torn sheet that passed as a bandage.

Vanni called out for his sister. No answer. Paolo watched him go into the bedroom, heard cursing in there, one voice only. When he came out he was red-faced and angry for once.

'She's gone,' he said.

'Where?'

'How would I know? She does what the hell she likes.'

It was strange. When they'd burst through the door, the Germans so close behind them, he'd never really felt fear. It was all so unreal. Now, though, he got a picture straight in his head, his mother and father lying in their coffins, wrecked bodies, battered faces past recognition. The war had been somewhere else when the three of them set to work on the looms, a different world beyond their walls. In that moment, Mika vanished who knew where, the bloody nightmare had wormed its way back into his life.

'Don't worry, Paolo. She won't betray us. Even if they caught her. She won't . . .'

'I don't understand why she left.'

Vanni was leaning on the table. It was obvious from his face he was in pain.

'She can't sit still. Not anymore. I do my best. Things haunt her. She can't let them go. I guess none of us can but at least you can try. In the hills . . .'

There was something he wanted to say even though it was a struggle.

'In the hills . . .' Paolo repeated.

'We were there to blow up the railway line, then get out. Mika, when she starts on something, there's no stopping her. It's like the danger makes her feel alive, I don't know. She pushed us all too hard. Took risks we didn't need. Just the two of us made it out of there. She feels guilty about that. We both do. Which only makes things worse for her. And I can't even bloody—'

He cried out and his leg gave way. Paolo had to take hold of him round the chest to stop him tumbling to the floor.

They stayed like that, so close it felt like an embrace, until Vanni smiled and said, 'If you could rip me a sheet . . . I can try and change it myself. I'm sorry I'm so useless.'

'You're not useless at all,' Paolo replied, easing him down on to a chair. 'You rescued me today. Without you I'd . . .' He was blushing. He could feel the heat in his cheeks. 'I'll do it.'

He went into his parents' room and found an old piece of cotton bedding by the corner, some strips torn off already, by them a tube of cream. Back at the table Vanni had removed his trousers and sat there in baggy underpants, eyes closed. Around his right calf fresh blood was seeping through the fabric.

'You shouldn't have been working so hard, standing so much,' Paolo said. 'You could have told me.'

'You said you needed help. We owe you that.'

He touched the dressing. It was stuck and there was more than blood there. Yellow pus too.

'You killed him? The German who did this?'

'Mika did. Stuck him with a knife afterwards too. Lots of times. She gets mad. Can't help herself.'

The first line of bandage came off, sticking to the inner section. Vanni whimpered, 'I'm really not very brave. Best you just tear it off quickly. She does.'

'Take a deep breath. My mother always said something like that.'

He ripped at the bandage. When it came away the wound looked worse than he'd expected. It was a deep slash into the muscle at the back of the leg. He understood why Vanni couldn't manage to deal with it himself. There was no way he could see what he was doing.

'Paolo. I can manage with the cream if you give it me.'

'No you can't.' The ointment was white and had that antiseptic smell he remembered from when he grazed himself as a kid. The tube was almost empty. 'We've got something like this in a cupboard. You can have it. This is pretty much gone.'

A dab on his finger and then he ran the ointment round the scabby wound. He stared at the purple skin, the gashed flesh, the thick yellow ooze around the edge. It looked worse than anything he'd seen on a crucifix of the dying Christ, set behind an altar.

Vanni's fingers ran through his hair and he said, 'You're a sight more gentle than my sister.'

He pulled his head away. Being touched like that felt wrong.

'I'm sorry, Paolo. I didn't mean . . . I didn't mean anything.'

'Take a deep breath again.'

He wrapped the clean sheet round the wound and the smears of cream. It wasn't going to hurt so much. He just didn't want to hear any more.

Silence filled the room. Then a wave broke against the rocks outside.

A series of deliberate knocks on the door made the two of them jump.

'It's alright,' Vanni said, getting up and taking the key from the kitchen table. 'It's her.'

He unlocked the door. The wind flew in and so did Mika Artom.

The hood was so far over her head Paolo didn't recognize her at first. There was a large, khaki, military-style holdall in her right hand.

'Where the hell have you been?' Vanni barked at her.

She laughed and dragged off her baggy hood. Mika's long dark hair was gone. Now she was a platinum blonde, the colour blowsy, cheap, straight out of a bottle, her hair styled in a bob like an old movie star.

You look like a whore, Paolo thought. One of the women of the night he'd sometimes see slipping between the colonnades of the Piazza San Marco, asking men if maybe they'd like to buy them a drink. Or just a straight walk to one of the flophouses behind San Lio.

Mika put down the bag and ran her fingers through her locks. A few strands of gaudy, fresh-cut hair fell to the floor.

'Sorry, brother. Did I interrupt something?'

Paolo got to his feet and handed over the rest of the tube of cream.

'I'll leave you two,' he said and went to his room.

An hour later Vanni Artom's heat and anger had subsided. There was no point. They were both in tears, seated on the old bed, his arm round her, Mika's around him. Vanni understood full well there was no way she could stop herself. It didn't matter how much he argued. It didn't matter, sometimes, that she knew herself what she was doing was wrong. Joining the partisans had changed them both, in different ways. It had made him more cautious, more wary of the peril around the corner. Mika simply wished to find its source, confront whatever was there, kill it, and to hell with the consequences.

She'd changed into an old woman's nightshift she'd found in the wardrobe. He was in a pair of ancient men's pyjamas.

'At the very least he deserves an explanation, love. We could get him killed.'

Mika wiped away the tears, stroked his hair and asked about the wound. Anything to change the subject.

'Paolo helped me change the dressing.'

She nudged him with her sharp elbow.

'I think he likes you. Haven't you noticed the way he keeps stealing a glance now and then?'

'We promised we wouldn't leave this place—'

'He's queer. Even if he doesn't know it. You do though.'

'This isn't important.'

She smiled.

'What? Hiding who you are from yourself? That doesn't matter?'

'Not right now.'

'Maybe not. Maybe it matters more than ever. You know . . . I never pushed it in Padua but there was that boy you used to hang around with. The one from Vicenza, philosophy or something.' She came close and nuzzled his cheek, delivered the softest, quickest of kisses. 'He always had a smell about him. Like violets.'

'Don't.'

'They'd kill you twice over even if you never did a thing. Jew and a homo.' She nodded at the door. 'Him just for the one.'

'Padua was a long time ago. You met Giulia—'

'Oh yes, I know. Giulia from Mantua. You had girlfriends too.' She punched his shoulder. 'Greedy boy. You turn whichever way you like. That's fine. I don't mind. We're beyond their stupid rules. So long as it doesn't get in the way of what matters.'

'What matters . . .'

In the bottom of the bag she'd brought he could see something wrapped in canvas. Khaki. It looked military and familiar.

'What's that?'

'I don't get to open it yet. They said not to. I'm just keeping it for them.'

'Did they? We said we wouldn't try to run anything. That we'd just hide. No weapons.'

He reached for the bag but she put a hand out and stopped him, took out a letter from a pouch on the side instead and thrust it into his hands.

'Time to wake up, brother. The banners you're making are for Salvatore Bruno. The Jew hunter. The one who helped kill Mum and Dad and all those others.'

'How—?'

'Read the letter, Vanni!' There was that sudden flash of anger. 'Just read it, will you?'

He could scarcely believe what was there.

'My God. Do you think Paolo realizes?'

A shake of her bright, shiny head.

'That kid doesn't know what day of the week it is. Besides, it doesn't say anything in there about the Fascists. I went through all this place's business correspondence while you were playing at being Ariadne. Bruno's name's on the first and an address in Due Fontane. Then everything else comes from someone who calls himself Ugo Leone.'

He closed his eyes, leaned back on the pillow and said, 'There's nothing we can do.'

'We can pass it on. I tracked down the cell in via Garibaldi. The one they told us about. We can trust them.'

Vanni rolled his eyes and wrapped his hands round his knees.

'Oh for pity's sake. How can you possibly know that?'

'I know! These are the people they told us about. I never let them know about this place! Don't look at me like that.'

'A week ago we nearly died. Maybe we should have. Maybe it should have been us up there in the mountains not—'

'This is war, brother.'

'Keep your voice down. I don't want him to hear.'

'No.' She played with her hair again. 'I guess you don't.'

'We're in Venice. We said we'd stay out of sight.'

'We fight. That's what we do. We fight and people die.'

'Soldiers die! Paolo's barely a boy.'

'We've lost younger than him.'

'Yes! Shepherd kids who didn't have a clue what they were getting into. He's no soldier. You can't—'

'I told you. They don't know where we live. I go to the place they've got. Nowhere else. That's the deal. I've compromised no one. I won't. I promise.'

'You promised you wouldn't set foot outside this place.'

She waved Bruno's letter in his face.

'Very good, Mika. There's two of us. Me, I can barely walk. What are we supposed to do about that?'

'Are you serious?' She shook her head. 'Salvatore Bruno's coming here on Saturday. A bunch of Nazis and Black Brigades with him. We know where they're going to be. In that hotel of theirs.' She touched her hair again and smiled. 'I got a job there. They took my picture. I get a fake ID card.' She tweaked his arm. 'I called myself Giulia. You know. After your Giulia. Giulia Grini. Start work there tomorrow. Serving drinks. Doing whatever the Crucchi want.'

Mika rolled off the bed, grabbed the holdall and lugged it on to the cupboard. His heart fell. The thing looked heavy.

'If you want to stay here with your boyfriend that's your choice.' She dragged something out of the bag, then pushed the thing under the bed. Whatever else was in the khaki canvas she didn't want him to see it.

Beaming, she held up in her hands a shiny evening dress, scarlet shot silk, worn, a little creased, but still elegant.

'What do you think?'

'I think you're crazy and you're going to get us all killed.'

Mika laughed, so freely, seemingly without a care. He loved her, of course, but that love was so close to pity when she was like this. It was as if the world outside the door, grim, dark and bloody, wasn't quite real.

'Not till Salvatore Bruno's gone,' she said, dancing round the room.

She turned on the light and started to sing a song. A cabaret number that was popular in Padua.

He liked the sound of her voice. Then a noise grew over it and Vanni Artom couldn't work out for a moment what it was.

The door burst open. Paolo stormed in, scared out of his wits, slapping the wall for the light switch.

He found it. Mika fell silent. Outside they heard the sound again. A motorboat, cruising the lagoon. The small and dusty side window on the room wasn't shuttered. A beam of pure white light pierced through at the corner.

'Down,' Paolo whispered and gestured with his arms.

All three of them fell to the floor, stayed there, breathless, silent, waiting as the spotlight ranged round the darkened room.

The voices were German again and nearer than before. Mika began to edge towards the bag she'd brought until Vanni's arm went out to stop her.

A good three or four minutes passed. Then one of the boatmen yelled something, the rattle of the motor went a few tones higher, and soon there was nothing beyond the window but darkness and the slow, relentless rhythm of the lagoon.

Still they waited. The Germans didn't come back. Paolo got up, went to the window and dragged the wooden shutters together.

'I should have thought of that,' he said. 'No one's lived in here for a while. If you leave the lights on they might notice.'

Silence. Finally Mika said, ‘I’m sorry, Paolo.’

‘You said you wouldn’t go out.’

‘I did. Something happened. It won’t involve you. No one will know we’re here. But I can’t . . .’ She put her arm round her brother again. ‘We can’t ignore it.’

PART THREE

The next day I ate breakfast alone again. Dad was out chasing contracts or girlfriends or both somewhere. Chiara turned up just before nine, told the maid what to do when it came to the cleaning, and fled when I tried to turn the conversation to the war.

Maurizio Scamozzi texted and asked if I wanted to go to San Nicolò to mess around on the beach. They were going to have a barbecue, go swimming, play football, whine about stupid interfering teachers. Maybe there'd be some girls around, he said, though that I doubted. And beer. What Maurizio promised and what he delivered were two things usually. I didn't like him and his circle much but if he'd asked me before I'd have gone along, out of idleness and boredom as much as anything. Now though . . .

I told him I was going to be busy for the rest of the week. It wasn't just the fact I'd promised Nonno Paolo I'd visit him and hear the next part of his story. What I'd read already was making me think harder, about myself, the past, who we were. I couldn't get the people and the places emerging page by page out of my mind. This wasn't an imaginary world, certainly not a fictional one. It was my real grandfather there, in a Venice that still existed beyond the door.

I had to see these places for myself. I needed to chase down the ghosts his words had brought to life. So I grabbed my favourite Nikon and went to look for them.

Ca' Loretti was in San Marco on the other side of the Grand Canal, close to the Giglio vaporetto stop. I would have walked but it was too hot, so I pushed my way on to the number one boat where, as usual, it was standing room only, crammed with tourists sweating in the humid lagoon heat.

Two streets from Giglio I found the place. One more tall canal-side building among many. The place looked exactly what it was: a slightly shabby office block that probably hadn't seen much more than a lick of paint in thirty years. The girl behind the desk glistened with sweat and looked as if she'd rather be at the beach, not trapped in a shabby blue uniform dealing with an inquisitive teenager. I told her: I wanted to talk to someone who could tell me what Ca' Loretti was like during the war.

'This was where the Crucchi were,' I added. 'The SS. Where they . . .'

She stared at me as if I was mad, then asked, 'Why aren't you at school?'

Through the large glass doors at the back I could see the courtyard. It was smaller than I imagined and full of pretty palms and raised flower beds, red and blue and yellow. The strange thing was I didn't find it hard to imagine tortured people here. Or that somewhere close to those pretty flowers the Nazis had tied people to a stake and shot them. That was one of the lessons I think he was trying to teach me: evil wasn't special. There was no need for extraordinary villains with scars and wicked, dark glints in their eyes. It was ordinary, mundane, a part of the city, a lurking virus within us all.

'It's for a project. This is where the Crucchi were,' I repeated.

'We don't do history tours. This is just a council office.'

'I know but . . .'

What could I do? Tell her of all the cruelty, the blood, the pain this place must once have seen?

'Never mind,' I grunted and went outside.

Here was the alley Aldo Diamante had walked. In many ways it might not have changed in half a century. These were the cobbles the old Jewish doctor had stepped on, along with the boots of so many German soldiers. This was the shade they would have been grateful for if it was summer. To my left there was still the jetty by the canal. A sleek, shiny water-taxi was there. A couple, a woman in a flowing white wedding dress, a man in a dark suit, stood on the wooden platform surrounded by a bustling crowd who applauded and cried at the sight of them. Their photographer was taking pictures, the flash setting off little beams of light that bounced across the water.

A waiter came out with a tray of glasses, spritz and champagne. Fifty-six years before, a group of Germans in uniform had disembarked here, marched into their headquarters guarding a Jew hunter called Salvatore Bruno, a name so hated by the partisans he changed it to Ugo Leone at times. I could almost see them as if they were here, alive and full of energy and rage. This, I felt, was what Nonno Paolo wanted, another reason he was giving me his story. He needed it to be mine now so that I might share his burden. He wanted me to be infected by something, though why, and just what it was, remained beyond my reach.

Halfway along the alley the bar was still called the Marino. Now it advertised expensive foreign cocktails, caviar and panini for a price no true Venetian would ever pay. I went inside and asked if there was a *barista* around called Beppe.

The waiter behind the counter was Chinese and looked as if he hadn't slept in days.

'Who Beppe?' he asked. 'Don't know no Beppe. When he work here?'

Half a century ago, before either of us was born.

'Doesn't . . . doesn't matter . . .' I stuttered.

'You wanna drink?'

I doubt I even answered.

Back at Giglio I took the number one to Giardini. Via Garibaldi was still a half-humble part of Castello back then, quiet, with local shops and market stalls, fruit and vegetables, fish, outside the iron gates near the old hero's monument. The statue was a local landmark: Garibaldi, the proud military statesman, bearded, with a cap, beneath him the lion of Venice, all set above a circular fountain where turtles basked in the weed-strewn pool at its base. At his back was a second figure, a stone infantryman, arms folded, rifle slung over his shoulder. A minute's walk away the Biennale was in full swing, smartly dressed crowds of art lovers heading for the international pavilions. All I could think of was a man called Luca Alberti dreaming he might have made an actor back when they were shooting films there during the war. Not a traitor, a tool of the Germans and the Black Brigades.

The statue of Garibaldi's guardian soldier seemed to be staring at all these foreigners chatting as they ambled to the gates, as if to say, 'You don't remember me, do you?'

Venetians love a ghost story. There was one about this place we got told as part of a history project at school. Reunification, the *Risorgimento*, that we did study. The later wars not so much. Originally the monument was just the old man, beard and cap and lion. But, after it was erected, people in the nearby streets began to report there was a phantom haunting the area, a ghost in military uniform jumping out, scaring people, demanding attention every night. The superstitious Castello locals decided he was a volunteer from the tenements who'd died during the campaign for reunification. The fellow was a bodyguard for Garibaldi who'd vowed he'd always protect him. So they paid for another statue at the old man's back and the ghost was never seen again.

Greta's bar seemed much the same, full of locals, cheap drink, cheap food, even a glossy red-painted door at the back. It was called something else now and the sullen chap behind the counter said he'd never heard of Greta, a man called Rocco Trevisan or a hairdresser who once worked there, Sara Vitale.

Taking pictures all the time, I walked across the wooden bridge into San Pietro. Smart speed boats lined the channel where the body of a murdered woman called Isabella Finzi was dragged from the grubby water. A girl with long hair was practising her guitar on the grass. Another bridge led me to the red-brick wall of the Giardino degli Angeli. There was an ugly, grey, metal gate at the entrance, shiny and new, temporary perhaps, a heavy padlock and chain keeping it secure. I wandered over the bridge anyway and poked the lens of my SLR through the bars. The place seemed abandoned, long grass with wrecked masonry poking out in places, fruit trees that looked as if they had gone wild, in the distance the cracked and dusty glass of the old conservatory, rising in three arches, a low stone building behind.

A black-clad figure like a priest or a doctor, Filippo Garzone or Aldo Diamante, lumbered into my viewfinder so quickly it made my heart jump. As I jerked back from the shock an engine sounded and I thought I might look up to see a German launch, a machine gun on its bows, edge across the distant line of water beyond the ruined watchtower. But no. It was simply a gardener in dark overalls, firing up his saw to work on the sprawling trees.

I needed a long moment to calm down after that. At least the place wasn't open. That meant I didn't need to find the courage to go beyond that iron gate.

Head a little woozy I went back to San Pietro and hopped on another vaporetto to the hospital.

* * *

He was waiting, more grey-faced than usual. His eyes, always so acute and inquisitive, seemed lazy, though they still caught me as I walked in with a bunch of flowers.

'Chrysanthemums? You buy them for the dead, Nico. Not the living.'

'Oh. Sorry.'

In my confused state after a morning spent between my city and his of old, I'd missed my stop, found myself at Fondamente Nove and bought a bunch without thinking from one of the florists that plied the trade to San Michele across the water.

'I'll call the nurse for a vase.'

She turned up, tut-tutting and shaking her head. I should have thought: they were the flowers for the cemetery. The coming November the first, *Ognissanti*, the Day of the Dead, I'd surely be with my father catching a boat to San Michele and placing a wreath of them on Nonno Paolo's grave.

'You've been taking pictures,' he said when we were alone.

My camera bag was on the floor. He never missed a thing.

'Yes,' I said, and added that Scamozzi had been trying to tempt me out to the beach.

'Don't let me stop you if that's what you want.'

'It's not. I want to be here. I want the rest of the story.'

'Ah.' He sounded a little down at that. 'I do hope I'm not upsetting you. That's not my intention.'

'What is?'

'Just . . . to pass something on that might be useful one day.'

I sat by the bed on a hard, metal hospital chair, staring again at the low, white-walled island across the water.

'I'll be there soon enough,' said the old, tired voice beside me.

'I don't want you there.'

'I must admit,' he added, 'I thought I might have enjoyed life a little longer. All those damned cigarettes. Should have given them up years ago. Promise me you'll never start.'

Naturally I kept quiet.

'Ah. I see I'm too late. How idiotic of me. When I was young, most lads were smoking when they were twelve or thirteen. I never had the opportunity. Very severe parents. Also they made me cough at first. It took some work.'

'Did he start that too? Vanni?'

'You have been reading carefully. Good. I'm flattered.'

'I never knew you could write.'

He laughed. Then coughed. Then laughed again.

'I can't. Not really. I just had one story to tell and that was it.' He tapped his chest and that made him croak once more. The wheeze that followed seemed to come from deep inside. 'There was never going to be anything else. Not real writing. I was too busy selling velvet for one thing. But a single story, if it's good enough . . . that'll do.'

'Would you have smoked if you'd never met them?'

He shrugged and said, 'Who's to know?'

'It's just that . . . the Artoms. That couple. They sound bad news.'

Grandpa waved his bony finger at me.

'Good news. Bad news. Mostly it's just news in the end. You should never judge a story till it's finished.'

When we stopped talking the room filled with all the hospital sounds I was beginning to recognize: the whirr of the air conditioning, the beep and buzz of monitors and machines, the tap-tap of footsteps outside along the corridor.

'Are there any more questions you want to ask, Nico?'

'Is it true? That you . . . what Mika said about you?'

He folded his arms, wrinkled his nose and asked, 'What in particular do you mean?'

He knew full well.

'Please. Stop playing games with me.'

'I'm not.'

'Is it true you and him . . . you fancied him?'

He nodded.

'Him being Vanni? A man?'

'Yes.' I hoped I didn't sound too annoyed at the way he'd dragged that out of me. 'That's what I mean.'

'Have you never felt an interest in another boy at school?'

'No!' I cried.

'You don't have to shout, lad. There's just the two of us in here. And I'd never tell.'

'No,' I said more gently. 'I never have. I never will. It's not . . . not me.'

'Ah.' He smiled. 'A young man who's certain about the future. Lucky fellow.'

'I mean . . . I know. I'm attracted to girls.'

'So was I. Even now . . . there are some pretty young fillies in this place. I flirt with them. What's an old man to do?'

'But—'

'I was shy when I was young to be honest. More fool me. There was an English poet who was once asked, towards the end of his life, if he had any regrets. He said yes. He'd never had enough sex. I understand what he meant.'

'I'm not sure we should be having this conversation.'

'Though it later turned out that same poet had what the English call "a little bit on the side". Writers, eh? Why shouldn't we be having this conversation?'

I was blushing and it wasn't even that hot.

'You're my grandfather.'

'Correct.'

'It's . . . weird.'

He seemed to find this terribly funny.

'Oh lord, Nico. If the fact a couple of men in extremis should get close to one another is . . . weird . . . I hate to think what you'll make of life later on. Unless you lead a dull one. I wouldn't wish you that.'

'I didn't need to know. I really didn't. I'm not even sure I believe a word of all this.'

'Sometimes stories are lies we tell ourselves in an effort to understand the truth.'

With that cryptic comment he turned to the side of the bed. His blue striped pyjamas rolled up his chest at that moment. His ribs stuck out like those on a starving child in Africa. There were the red scars of operations on his wrinkled chest. Just seeing them made me think of him changing the dressing on Vanni Artom more than half a century before. He'd got beneath my skin and that, I realized, was precisely his intent.

'Here.' He retrieved another envelope from the bedside cabinet and threw it on the sheets. 'Only two more episodes of this story after this. Unless you'd rather give up and spend your time with Maurizio Scamozzi.'

'I don't want to hang out with that little creep. I want to be here with you.'

He smiled, reached out and touched my hand.

'I'm glad of that. I only wish I had better words to tell you how much.'

The title was scrawled on the front. I recognized his spidery hand, the flowing letters and the way the ink from a fountain pen fell across the page.

'Things happen,' he said and he wasn't smiling any more. 'That's all I've got to say.'

TANGLES IN THE LOOM

The arrival of a group of senior German officers from Salò along with the Jew hunter Salvatore Bruno was the spark for an impromptu evening of even greater debauchery than usual in the upstairs ballroom of the Gioconda. It was important to be seen even if one did not much take part. Those missing would be noted.

Casino tables had come out for the occasion. Hauptscharführer Oberg had stayed for thirty minutes, smoking a series of small cigars, saying little, watching Bruno's party work their way from roulette wheels to cards, winning always, naturally. Then he pleaded work and returned to Ca' Loretti, happy to be out of the place.

Luca Alberti stayed. For two hours and a half, which was all he could take. He consumed nothing more than three glasses of Prosecco followed by the tiniest taste of grappa and steered well clear of the women who flocked around the Germans like flies smelling fresh meat. A humble Venetian collaborator was no match for these well-heeled visitors. The newcomers had more power and wealth about them than any of the locals and didn't mind showing it. Not just money but illicit items from the black market. Tobacco, drugs, jewellery, perfume and silk stockings were among the whispered gifts in return for a night between their sheets. In the city's impoverished wartime condition, he could hardly blame the floozies for trying their best. Most were from out of town though one he recognized, a pretty young woman from Cannaregio, a widow or separated, he couldn't remember, mother to three children, struggling to get by. She smiled more convincingly than the rest, worked harder in bed too as he'd discovered for himself the month before. But it was a cold and false kind of passion, driven by hardship, not the need for company. One night was enough to reveal that her affections came at a price his lowly police salary could never sustain.

Before the conflict the ballroom of the Gioconda was a place for rich foreigners in town for opera, theatre or art, civic events and fancy marriages. It was ornate to the boundaries of good taste, full of ormolu mirrors and gilt furniture, glittering Murano chandeliers dangling from a ceiling decorated with putti and swooping angels. The canal side seemed nothing but glass, a long line of floor-length windows that gave out on to a terrace over the small *rio* beneath. In summer the hotel laid tables outside for lunch and dinner, but November was too cold for that. It was a shame. Alberti liked that quiet, secluded spot where on occasion one heard the swish of a gondolier's oar and a snatch of song. No black wells leaked sewage into the waterway that ran straight into the Grand Canal, so the smell was as sweet as anywhere in the city centre.

Alberti was glad to get out of the place and go to bed, though the night was long and disturbed by all the familiar noises from neighbouring rooms.

That Friday morning he'd made sure to be at his desk on time. Oberg was there alone. Throughout Ca' Loretti Germans who'd indulged too much in the Gioconda the night before stood around sipping at coffee, complaining about the heads they'd got from rotten Venetian booze.

Sander turned up half an hour late, sat down, then suddenly excused himself and raced to the toilet, hand to mouth.

'He shouldn't drink so much,' Oberg announced without looking up from his papers. 'You too, Sachs. You're officers. On duty always. I don't want you lurching round stumbling drunk.'

Alberti reached for a pencil and began to sharpen it.

'I'm aware of my position, sir,' Sachs replied, looking hurt. 'I trust I did nothing to bring my comrades into disrepute.'

'If you had you wouldn't be here,' Oberg snapped.

'In all fairness,' Alberti cut in, 'the hooch they were serving last night was not the best.'

Sander lurched through the door wiping his mouth.

'Bad grappa is terrible on the stomach,' the Venetian added. 'This place smells a bit this morning too. Maybe someone's been putting something they shouldn't down the drains.'

Pale as a sheet, Sander glared at him as he sat down.

'Giovanni and Mika Artom,' Oberg said, looking at all three of them. 'The terrorists. Are we any closer to understanding if they're here?'

Alberti let the Germans stutter their way through that. They had their own sources in the city, informers they were unwilling to share, perhaps even with one another, certainly not with a local. All, it seemed, had been as short on news and intelligence as Alberti's own.

'Perhaps,' Sander said, 'they're not in Venice at all. All we heard was that they were on their way.'

Sachs added, 'Maybe they bumped into the wrong sort getting out. Those evil bastards will kill one another as readily as they'll murder us. They are Jews. Some of the commies hate Jews too.'

'But they're Jews *and* commies,' Alberti pointed out.

'So what?' Sander demanded.

Alberti shrugged.

'Maybe you're right. They never got here. For which we should be grateful.' He tapped the folder on his desk. The intelligence file on the pair. 'They seem quite . . . efficient.'

'Dammit.' Oberg looked positively furious. 'You should be giving me more than this. There's a string of atrocities that's followed the two of them all the way from Padua. From what we got out of their murderous peers the woman seems to be the leader. As violent a criminal as we're likely to face.'

'A woman?' Sander sniggered behind his hand. 'We're scared of a couple of Jews led by a woman?'

Oberg was always worrying at some problem, large or small. Alberti found his anxious state intriguing. The man seemed more agitated than usual.

He got to his feet, grabbed his coat and asked, 'What happens tomorrow?'

Oberg looked up from his papers and said, 'Tomorrow?'

'Bruno. Leone. Whatever we're supposed to call him. He told Aldo Diamante there was going to be a party.' He shrugged. 'If there's something, some aspect of security I should know about . . .'

Oberg hesitated for a moment and glanced at his fellow countrymen. There was clearly something here they knew, intelligence that had yet to be shared with a local menial.

'If you don't want to tell me, sir—' Alberti began.

'No,' Oberg interrupted. 'There's no reason you shouldn't be party to the information. We do trust you, Alberti.'

'I'm honoured.'

'Don't be. You've earned it.' Oberg looked him up and down. 'You know they'll kill you as readily as they'd murder one of us. These people. As far as they're concerned you're one of us.'

Alberti nodded.

'Then I'm honoured by that too.'

'On Sunday we begin to sweep the city,' Oberg went on. 'Not bands of Black Brigade thugs out for vengeance. There'll be soldiers. Ours. Raiding parties. For one week we focus on the Jewish problem and little else. Our orders are that by the end of the month every last Jew we can find must be in custody and ready to be shipped out. Salò is issuing the decree first thing in the morning. Everyone of Hebrew extraction will no longer be an Italian. They'll have no rights. Not under the law. No business here. All their property, their money will belong to the state. Tomorrow night there's a reception for all the senior officers. Black Brigades. Salvatore Bruno. We . . .' Oberg didn't like any of this and it was obvious. He was a soldier. He wanted to be fighting a war, not locking up civilians. 'We mark the occasion.'

There was silence then. Doubtless Mussolini needed the money. Alberti had heard rumours that in the camps in Germany and Poland they murdered Jews by their thousands while those who remained were employed stealing the gold from the teeth of their dead brothers and sisters to fill the Nazis' coffers. Perhaps it was inevitable such habits would one day find their way to Italy.

'It must be quite the party you've got planned.'

'I don't want this known,' Oberg said. 'Any of it. Not outside this room.'

Too late, chum, Alberti thought. The way the Germans boasted and gossiped with women they wished to impress, half of Venice probably understood something was afoot. Where and when too. That was why Oberg was so worried. Arrogance was a constant weakness of the Nazis, one they consistently refused to recognize. The partisans probably had got wind some further crackdown on the Jews was on the way too. Now they'd been given a target to aim at, a chance to get their vengeance in first.

The Gioconda. All dressed up for a glittering Saturday night with a guest list of top Nazis and Fascists. What a target.

He got his hat.

'That goes without saying, sir. Rest assured. If this murderous pair are here, I'll shake this city till they fall out of her pockets, straight into our lap.'

* * *

Late lunch in the Uccello house at the back of the Giardino degli Angeli. Half a tumbler each of Prosecco *spento*, white bread and dry *provolone* cheese from the shop in via Garibaldi, fetched by Paolo that morning in a brief, rushed excursion from home. Just the three of them. Chiara said she had to make a brief visit to a sick parishioner with food. Paolo suspected she hadn't taken to Mika Artom and simply didn't wish to be around.

Thanks to Vanni the work was now on schedule.

Mika only got out of bed when she heard them putting plates on the table. She sat next to her brother wearing a baggy black wool overcoat from his parents' wardrobe. It seemed odd and unnecessary. He'd lit the fire. The place wasn't so cold. This was practical as much as for comfort. It was impossible to work the Jacquard accurately if you were freezing and there was no room for mistakes.

He'd heard the two of them arguing into the small hours, shouts and shrieks, angry, accusing. For a while he'd hidden his head beneath the pillow hoping to drown them out. To drown out everything if he could find a way. His fears about harbouring two dangerous fugitives. His worries about delivering the strange commission the following day. His feelings too which were odd and conflicting, some disturbing, others pleasant in a way.

Vanni was nothing like the men he'd come in contact with over the years. He seemed gentle, intelligent, exotic somehow. In a different world, Paolo would have invited him to explore the city and see some of the sights he loved so much. Carpaccio's unfortunate dragons being slaughtered by a heartless Saint George in the scuola of the Schiavoni. Mantegna's tortured Saint Sebastian in Ca' D'Oro, naked except for a flimsy loincloth, his athletic body pierced by a thicket of arrows, wounds open and bleeding, face turned to heaven, a mysterious message written round a candle in the corner: *Nihil nisi divinum stabile est. Caetera fumus.* Nothing is stable if not divine. The rest is smoke.

A sight that had moved the young Paolo ever since his mother took him to see it as a boy. Most tourists flocked to the obvious places, the Rialto, San Marco, the Accademia, and missed the smaller, more intriguing sights of the city. Vanni Artom, he felt sure, would appreciate them just as he did.

If only there was the opportunity.

If only they could walk the streets together free of fear.

'We shouldn't eat in silence,' Mika Artom declared, breaking the awkward peace with a sweep of her arm. 'If you're mad at me out with it.' She pointed her lump of bread across the table. 'You too.'

'Mika,' Vanni said. 'I've said this a million times already. We promised we wouldn't leave the house.'

'No, no, no.' Her hair shone and waved as she spoke. He couldn't stop staring at it. She did seem a different woman. Attractive, sexual, even in his father's overcoat. 'I promised nothing.'

'We said—'

'Please,' Paolo begged them. 'No arguments. We have to go back to work. The commission . . .' The two of them shared glances he didn't understand. 'We have to finish the banners. I must deliver them. Then . . .'

'Then what?' Mika asked.

'I was told you wouldn't be here long.'

She grinned.

'My brother seems to like this place. He's taken to it. The loom.' Her smile grew broader. 'Taken to you, Paolo.'

Vanni tried to shut her up but it was impossible.

'And you like him too. This is good. He always has need of friends. Me, not so much. Still, I approve.'

'Father Filippo . . . the priest . . . he told me—'

'I'll be gone by Monday. At the latest. There. What Vanni does is up to him.'

'We'll both leave as soon as we can,' he said. 'The moment we hear there's somewhere to go. We're grateful for your courage in sheltering us here. I'm sorry if we haven't made that clear.'

Mika kept toying with her hair. Then she reached into the pocket of the overcoat and pulled out something Paolo hadn't seen since his mother was around. Lipstick and a small mirror. He watched, fascinated, as she pouted at the glass and ran the bright scarlet stain, as glossy as fresh oil paint, all around her mouth.

'Why are you doing this?' Paolo asked. 'Why change the way you look?'

Mika laughed at him.

'Silly boy. Why do you think? If they have a picture of me it won't be much use now, will it?' She reached out and touched her brother's long dark hair. 'I've met a friend who can do this for you too. Strawberry blonde maybe. Curls too. I think curls would look good. We'd be a pair of beauties.'

Vanni grunted and gulped at his coffee.

'What do you think, Paolo? What colour would suit him?'

'I think he's fine as he is. If you two stay out of sight here, like I was told, no one's going to know. Keep going outside—'

'I'm a fighter,' she interrupted. 'Even if my brother isn't. You can't do that inside a damned . . . damned greenhouse, playing around with a needle and thread.'

'What we do's a little more than that,' Vanni told her.

'Would you like me to move out now, Paolo?'

'No. That wouldn't be safe at all. Where would you go?'

The smile vanished. Her eyes darkened.

'People like us always have friends. Somewhere. It's just a matter of finding them. If you want me to try—'

'Mika!' Vanni's voice was loud and angry. 'We gave our word. We owe him that.'

'And what do we owe our dead parents? All those thousands of Jews getting shipped off to camps in Germany never to return? To our dead comrades we left in the hills? To unborn children who'll grow up under Mussolini's thumb if we let them?'

'Perhaps you owe them a duty to stay alive and one day make things better.' Paolo wasn't sure where that came from. Maybe it was the same inner outrage that had spoken up when they'd dragged the body of Isabella Finzi out of the canal across the way. A dangerous voice he realized. Had he kept quiet, then the Artoms would surely never have found their way to the Giardini degli Angeli.

Not, he thought, glancing at Vanni, that he regretted his interjection at all.

'I have a job to do,' Mika announced, getting to her feet and throwing off the heavy overcoat.

Beneath was a shimmering silk dress, almost the same scarlet as her lipstick, the front cut low to show off her breasts. The fabric hung loose on her. A poor fit, he thought. It was made for someone else. All the same, in the bleak, drab greyness of wartime Venice she surely stood out. No one wore clothes like this, not in any of the places he knew. It was unthinkable.

'Don't fret, young Paolo. Don't stare at me like I'm a whore.'

'So don't look like one,' her brother shot back.

She patted down the fabric, checked her face in the mirror once more, then dragged the baggy coat back on.

'I'll leave by the back. No one will see me. No one will know I come from your quiet little paradise. Nor will I be taken.'

Mika reached down to the floor, pulled up a large fabric handbag and slammed it on the table. It was old, battered, the kind of thing Chiara might once have owned and thrown away. Paolo's breath caught as she opened it up and retrieved a handgun, placed it on the table, stroked the butt with her fingers.

'If by chance the Crucchi do find me . . .' She picked up the weapon, held it in her fingers as if she loved the thing. 'You needn't worry.'

'Please . . .' Vanni was begging and from the sound of his voice it seemed clear he knew this was pointless. 'For once listen to me. We should stay inside.'

'Here?'

'Yes. Here.'

'Here is warm, brother. Here is comfortable. Here the Crucchi will never come. Or so you'd like to fool yourself. I can't. There's a world beyond these walls and every day those bastards drench it in our blood. War is where I belong. You too or so I thought. Still . . .' She glanced at Paolo. 'Go back to your needle and thread. Fool yourself that's all there is.'

The outside conservatory door opened and closed. They all heard it. Chiara Vecchi returning. It could be no one else. Only she had a spare key to the door by the bridge.

Mika shoved the pistol back in the bag, stood up and brushed the breadcrumbs off her chest.

'Ciao, boys,' she said. 'Behave now. And don't wait up.'

Not that Filippo Garzone would admit it to his flock, but the basilica of San Pietro di Castello he found unlovable. It was a leviathan of a building, the vast dome impressive, the rest not so much. Too large for the congregation of the tiny, half-deserted island on which it stood and, in winter, as chilly as the grave. Once, on paper at least, San Pietro had been the most important place of worship in Venice, the city's official cathedral, superior to the Doge's bejewelled San Marco posed gloriously on its piazza next to his palazzo. But the truth was that popes and kings and politicians much preferred San Marco in the very heart of Venice to distant, humble Castello. Early in the nineteenth century the basilica was toppled from its shaky place at the top of the church hierarchy and San Marco given the crown it had long worn in all but name.

The monied and the powerful then gathered all the more round the famous piazza, with its elegant cafes, its galleries and museums while the far reaches of Castello fell further into poverty and seclusion. Most of the city barely knew the place and, with a single Veronese canvas as its only noteworthy work of art, nor did visitors much either. Garzone would occasionally attempt to interest a passing sightseer in its more obscure attractions, among them the 'chair of Peter', supposedly used by the apostle when he preached in Syria. In truth it was a fetching piece of archaeological chicanery, for him at least. The remains of an Islamic funeral monument, with inscriptions from the Koran in Kufic script on the side, reworked to resemble a saintly throne. His enthusiasm rarely found favour with the occasional wandering tourist, most of whom were lost and seeking directions. Still, San Pietro's isolation helped the priest in the role he'd decided to pursue secretly and at no small risk to himself as the war wore on.

He was not a political man, certainly no communist like a few of his fellow priests who'd taken to the testament of Marx with enthusiasm of late. Still, he had a strong sense of both justice and service to his community, two attributes challenged by the Fascists when they came to power, and as good as dispatched altogether after Mussolini started his vile regime in Salò as a puppet of the Nazis.

Gradually over the years, as quiet men and women came to him for help, Garzone had positioned himself as a conduit, first for those who fell foul of the state, then lately for others, partisans, politicians, trade unionists who sought to oppose it. In his own mind he knew the war was, from Mussolini's point of view, unwinnable. It was only a matter of time before the Allied forces in the south took Rome, then moved to capture the rest of the country, with both the king and the official government by their side.

The question he wrestled with daily, sometimes in conversation with his good friend Diamante, was how a good man might approach such circumstances, what help, practical and moral, was appropriate when it was needed. Garzone had set himself some rules. For one thing he would never involve anyone else close to the church. As far as they knew he was a quiet man who, while out of tune with the political will of the day, saw his primary responsibility to be the pastoral care of his parishioners. There were two sound reasons for this. He'd no wish to involve others in actions which, if they became known to the Germans, would lead to immediate imprisonment, doubtless torture, and in all probability a violent death or dispatch to one of the camps.

The second was equally practical: in wartime Venice it was impossible to be certain who to trust. There were informers, paid for he felt sure. There were others who might send a man into Ca' Loretti too: idle gossipers, passing on a whisper, those with a grudge or seeking vengeance or simply individuals who wanted a quiet life and would inform, perhaps reluctantly, on any individual they thought a threat. Everyone suffered from the war in one way or another. At the same time they heard stories from terraferma, tales of aerial bombing by the Allies, reprisal raids by vicious gangs of Black Brigade thugs, rapacious profiteering and bloody black-market feuds. The city on the water was spared most of this since it lived at the edge of the conflict, a precious gilded prison too beautiful for the horrors Italy was seeing elsewhere.

There were occasions, it seemed, when the right decision was beyond a simple man like him. To act or do nothing? Both might end in bloodshed, for guilty and innocent alike. Under no circumstances would he allow church premises to be used for storing weapons or explosives. Nor would he listen to the ideas and certainly not the plans of the men and women who came into his confessional from time to time, desperate to talk to someone they could trust.

Sometimes he regarded himself as a coward. But mostly that Friday morning he thought of himself as a lonely, tired priest, freezing in his solitary office, wondering whether it would be sensible to see how the Uccello lad was faring or if he was best left alone with his fugitive visitors.

There was a familiar slam. The main church door. He knew that sound as well as he knew his own voice.

Perhaps a confession. An appointment for a baptism. A funeral. A wedding. Even in war the daily round of life and death, birth and renewal, went on.

He gathered his heavy priest's cloak around him and stepped out into the vast whale's belly of the nave. The place was gloomy, as always in winter, but something bright and vivacious seemed to lighten it. At first he thought it was birdsong. Then he realized: it was the chatter of children, light, high and excited.

There was a tall, distinguished figure with them wearing a familiar long winter coat.

Garzone was both pleased and wary. Aldo Diamante never visited without a reason.

'Children, children,' the man from the ghetto cried.

There were three of them, two girls who looked like twins, ten or so, and a quiet boy a few years younger. They had the pale complexion and straight dark hair he'd come to associate with some of the young Diamante brought to San Pietro from time to time.

Garzone strode out to meet them, shook the old doctor's hand, then greeted the newcomers.

'Your campanile's bent, sir,' one of the girls said with a grin.

It always amused visitors that the bell tower of San Pietro was both separate from the basilica itself, built in the grass campo by the side and leaned at a precipitous angle.

'Ah yes,' he replied. 'It used to live on the roof but one day a young lady of Castello passed by, stepped in some dog poop and cursed with such language that the campanile shrieked and jumped straight off, landing where you find it today.'

All three of them stared at him.

'Is that true, Uncle Aldo?' the other girl asked.

Diamante nodded.

'I was always told that when I was your age.'

'An alternative explanation,' Garzone added, 'is that the earth here is so soft and muddy an architect thought it best to build a tower on the ground rather than add to all' – he gestured at the vast dome – 'all this. After which it leaned somewhat. I prefer the first explanation. It's more fun.'

He kept smiling. It was hard. He could see the pain and fear in Diamante's eyes. In those of the young boy too.

'I take it you're going on holiday, children.'

They nodded at the priest.

'A mystery trip,' one of the girls said.

'I have some *caramelle* in my office. Please . . .' He gestured to the door. 'Enjoy them while I have a word with your uncle.'

'He's not really our uncle,' the boy said finally.

All the same they went and he showed them where the bag of sweets was.

Outside, back in the belly of the whale, Diamante looked more miserable than Garzone had ever seen him.

'When will you have someone pick them up, Aldo?'

'Eight or nine. A boat. There's a fishing family called—'

He grabbed the man's arm.

'Don't tell me. I mustn't know.'

Diamante shook his head as if to clear it.

'Of course not. What must I have been thinking? They're Adele Besso's children. You know her?'

'No. Sorry.'

'Her husband's been seized as a troublemaker. They'll come for the rest of the family soon. The mother insists she stays. She seems to hope she can help her husband. Dear God . . .'

Garzone made him sit on a pew.

'There's something happening,' the priest said. 'I can see it in your face.'

'I must produce this list! The names of every one of us in Venice. I've stalled and stalled but there's a . . . a beast in the city. A Jew hunter they use. One of ours. A traitor. My time's running out. I can't delay more than a few days. If I could save them all . . .'

'Tell me what I can do.'

'You can see these three safely on their way. After that.' He stood up and wrapped his coat tightly around himself. San Pietro seemed chillier than ever that morning. 'After that, who knows? The tide comes and I have nothing to sweep it back but a little broom.'

Diamante marched over to the door, flung it open and stared at the children with his fiercest of faces.

'Amos. Bianca. Anna. This is important. Father Filippo here's a good man, a patient man. You will not take advantage. No naughtiness. The three of you will stay here and do as he says. Don't set foot outside this place until the boat comes for you this evening. When that happens you get on it without a word. You hear me?'

Silence, then the boy asked, 'When will Mamma come and join us?'

Diamante coughed and for a moment the priest thought he might break.

'When she can.'

'But—'

'*When she can . . .*'

'I'll see you out, Aldo,' the priest said.

Just to be sure he locked the door behind him.

The day was turning the dull grey of winter when rain was around and mulling whether to turn to snow. Gulls scavenged the grubby shoreline where the body of Isabella Finzi had been hauled from the water. Diamante couldn't take his eyes off that spot either.

'The pair you've placed with the Uccello lad . . .'

'I cannot save them all,' Diamante murmured. 'I cannot.'

He looked lost and that was so unlike him.

'No, Aldo. We're only old men trying to do what we can. Let's go for a coffee soon. You need company.'

Diamante pushed his felt hat harder on to his grey locks and did his best to smile.

'You're a remarkable chap, Filippo. I envy your quiet certainties. I almost resent them to be honest. I wish I had your faith.'

'You have a faith of your own. A coffee. Tomorrow. When my guests are safely on their way. You have time, surely.'

Garzone wondered if he'd even heard. Diamante was staring at the crooked campanile rising out of the thin winter grass, looking as if it might topple over at any moment.

'The beast will soon be loose,' he murmured. 'They're good children. You'll have no problem there.'

The priest watched Aldo Diamante amble across the grass. There was another figure crossing over from the bridge by the Giardini degli Angeli. A young woman huddled against the cold in a shabby overcoat too big for her small frame. She had very bright blonde hair tucked beneath a black beret. An unusual sight for this part of Castello where women rarely made a show.

'The beast will soon be loose,' he whispered and wondered what Aldo Diamante meant by that.

No matter. Speculation was a luxury for times of peace not war. There were three small Jewish children inside his basilica. All to be kept safe and out of the way until the evening when men would emerge out of the dark, a small boat waiting by the jetty, ready to try take them God knows where.

He marched back inside, unlocked the door to his office, found them finishing the last of the caramels. Garzone never felt entirely comfortable around children unless they had parents to keep them in check.

'Gone,' one of the girls said, holding out the empty bag. 'Got any more?'

'No. Sorry.'

'Going to get some, Father?' asked the other one.

All the plans he had for the rest of that day – visiting the sick, the worried, the desperate, trying to spread what comfort he could – were now in ruins. These three mites could not be left on their own.

He clapped his hands. Teachers often did that and sometimes it even worked.

'I know. A game.'

'Football,' the first girl suggested. 'Outside.'

'No, young lady. I have no ball. I am too old to play. And outside is not a place to be.'

'Where's Mamma?' the lad asked and the priest realized he'd been waiting for that.

'She'll meet you on your holiday. Tonight a boat. Tomorrow . . .' He did his best to smile. 'Tomorrow . . . in a short while all will be well.'

They stared back at him and said nothing. He was a poor purveyor of fictions, he felt. Or perhaps these three had already developed a talent for spotting liars.

In the workshop of the Uccello the day passed at a steady pace, the awkward silence between the three of them broken only by the rattle and slap of busy looms, echoing the song of the goldcrests absent since late summer.

Si-dah-si-dah-si-dah-sichi-si-piu.

Vanni struggled with that at times. The vigilant Chiara, always listening, would stop what she was doing, walk over and instruct him with great patience on how to work the Jacquard correctly. He was quick to learn but distracted. The argument with his sister lingered, Paolo thought, along with some of her sly and calculating comments. As an only child he possessed no feel for what it might be like to grow up with a sibling. Particularly an older sister who seemed more forceful, more *male* in some ways, always the first to act and take decisions. The two cared for each other deeply. That was obvious. But they were so different, Mika hard, determined, unstoppable, Vanni cautious, thoughtful, always observant of others and what they thought.

Still, these were uncomfortable notions. What mattered was the work, the three lion banners in soprarizzo for the mysterious Ugo Leone who was expecting them the following afternoon.

By five they could continue no more. Chiara got up, stretched, yawned, reached for her coat and bag and asked where Mika was.

Neither of them answered.

She was a cheery woman usually, even in times like these. Not an optimist. That was impossible in the present state of affairs. But someone who did not let the privations of the city and the times interrupt her daily business: work and an endless round of parochial visits on behalf of her local priest. Before she left she gave Paolo a present: a bag of S-shaped *bussolai* biscuits, golden and crisp, that she'd baked herself. Since she came from Burano, where bussolai originated, she was, she always said, better at making them than any housewife unfortunate enough to hail from the city.

Vanni took one, bit into it and told her it was wonderful.

'Better dipped in a cup of coffee. Or wine. Or something stronger,' she said. 'Perhaps your sister would like one.'

'She's sleeping,' he said. 'Tired.'

Paolo didn't look at Chiara at that moment. He knew full well what she was thinking.

'You've a talent for the loom, Vanni,' she told him. 'Do you enjoy weaving?'

'Funnily enough . . . yes.' He looked at his fingers. There were blisters and red marks from the strain of the constant work. 'I never realized I could do anything with my hands.'

'You sound surprised.'

He smiled and said, 'I suppose I am. The Artoms were never supposed to be made for manual labour. That was for others.'

'You mean the workers?' Chiara said, shaking her head. 'I thought you were communists.'

'Who told you that?'

She shrugged her shoulders and said, 'There can't be anyone in Venice who hasn't heard the Germans are hunting high and low for two fugitive partisans. Jewish. Political. Someone could pick up a lot of money if they handed you in.'

Paolo felt bad seeing the sadness on her face. Chiara had worked so hard to look after him since his parents died. Now outsiders had arrived and threatened to tear down the walls of the sanctuary she'd tried to build.

'After we deliver the banners Vanni and his sister will move on,' he said, hoping this might cheer her.

'When?'

'That' – Vanni took another biscuit out of the bag and bit into it – 'would be telling. We'll go. We'll be thankful such generous, brave people helped us. Please . . .' He came forward and embraced her, kissed her on both cheeks. 'I'll do anything I can to protect your young friend here. Anything.'

Chiara retreated from his arms and brushed her elbow across her damp cheeks.

'Without you we never would have finished. Not in time. We can put this work to bed in the morning. Then I'll go over everything carefully, checking every thread. There are gilt boxes in the cellar and tissue paper so we can present them the way your father always did. No one else makes velvet like this in Venice. Perhaps they never shall after we've gone. It's important your customer feels he's getting his money's worth.'

He hadn't revealed much about the commission and, of course, she'd noticed.

'Thank you. As ever.'

'If you like I can deliver them,' she added. 'I know you don't like walking round the city. Especially places the Crucchi linger. A woman will be less conspicuous.'

The offer was tempting but all the same he said no: she'd done enough.

They watched her leave, a hunched figure passing through the garden and the ruins of the old palace. Chiara Vecchi was now the nearest to family he had.

'You've a good friend there,' Vanni said with a pat on his shoulder. 'A guardian angel.'

'I wish I could be the same for her.'

Vanni was staring at the complexities of the Jacquard, the myriad threads, the punch cards rigged to make the pattern. A job he'd only half-learned himself, one that perhaps Chiara Vecchi alone possessed with any skill in the city at that moment.

'What will you weave next?' he asked. 'After we've gone.'

'I don't know. So much to choose from. We need to find a customer first.'

'What kind of things?'

All the Artoms had seen was the commission for Ugo Leone's banners. It was a fraction of what the Uccello could make if they wished.

'Lots. I'll show you.'

Paolo turned off the weak electric lights and the two of them went back into the house. He grabbed an oil lamp and held it out until Vanni got the message and put a flame from his cigarette lighter to the wick. Then he went to the window by the lagoon, found the cellar door beneath the rug and pulled it open.

'Down here,' he said and they descended into the damp and gloom.

Luca Alberti was tired of rousting his informants. They knew nothing. If they did his combined threats and promises and money would surely have loosened some lips. All day he'd spent walking round the city, every one of the six *sestieri* that formed Venice, from Cannaregio to Castello, Dorsoduro to the back streets of Santa Croce and San Polo, even the few mean streets of San Marco where the partisans had some support. In return he had nothing to show but sore feet and an aching head from too much bad coffee.

Out of luck, out of ideas, he'd no great appetite to return to Ca' Loretti and the doleful stare Oberg reserved for those who'd failed him. Though mostly he didn't want to spend more time in the company of the man's dumb and unpleasant underlings. Sachs and Sander were the worst of the Nazis. At least their boss had the look of a man given a shit job and determined to do it out of duty. Those two enjoyed every minute, especially if it entailed dragging some local into one of the rooms downstairs, getting out their knuckledusters, their knives, their spikes and electric prods. Sander was responsible for putting a bath in one of the interrogation cells and liked to strip women naked, hold them underneath the water till they were nearly dead. Then do whatever he liked.

Alberti watched just the once and was determined he'd never witness that again. He was willing to yell and threaten and punch a confession out of someone if that's what it took to keep the Germans happy. More than that and it wasn't just distasteful but also pointless, a case of diminishing returns. He'd seen men and women he felt sure were innocent confess to all number of imaginary crimes out of fear and pain, then pick a name from the list of suspects they were offered, ignorant of whose fate they'd sealed, just desperate for the agony to stop.

The idiot Sachs had a saying: *In the end everyone talks*. Which they did. But the fool never realized that it never meant they spoke the truth.

Alberti found himself by the long stretch of the Cannaregio canal near the Tre Archi bridge, glum after failing to extract anything useful from a shoe repairman in the area who, from time to time, had passed on useful gossip. The ghetto was a few minutes' walk away. He had no informers there. The small Jewish community always looked at him and the Crucchi with fearful, hate-filled eyes. There were a few who'd take the opportunity to do him harm too, he didn't doubt. But for the most part they simply wished to be invisible as they had been before the war. Back in the Thirties a few had even joined the Fascist party believing that its support of middle-class businessmen against the threat of Communism meant Il Duce was on their side. Which was never true – the Racial Laws that came in at the end of the decade proved it. But Mussolini didn't have quite the hatred of everything Hebrew to match the despot in Berlin. It was only when he became Hitler's puppet that the round-ups and the murders had become routine and organized in earnest.

He checked his pistol, quite openly as he stood in the street, in case anyone was watching. Then he took one of the winding alleys that led to the tiny island called the Ghetto Nuovo where, around the small square of the campo, in cramped tenements rising five or six storeys high, the city's Jews had first been segregated four hundred years before.

Diamante lived on the third floor of a block overlooking a home for the elderly and frail, a place that had no call on a list for the likes of Salvatore Bruno. When the Nazis needed Jews to drag to cattle trucks that were, he suspected, already positioned at the station of Santa Lucia, they'd find thirty or forty easily here. It was the rest that was going to be difficult.

The old doctor answered the front door himself and stood there, seemingly amazed that Alberti had braved the ghetto at all.

'I was hoping we could talk.'

Alberti looked around. There were a few people walking the campo in heavy overcoats. None near. No one, he felt, so stupid they would try to gun down a servant of the Nazis in the midst of the ghetto. The reprisals in a place like this would be horrific.

'Well you'd better come in,' said Aldo Diamante.

His apartment was neat and clean, one room set aside for medical examinations, all white, with instruments and that antiseptic smell a man like Alberti, fearful of all doctors, loathed. He was glad Diamante led him somewhere at the front that looked more domestic. There was an old sofa, a dining table with fresh flowers, windows on to the campo and an ornate iron fireplace where logs burned furiously. At the end of the room was a large portrait in oils, a couple in middle age, probably from the turn of the century, with a young boy standing between them, what looked like a stethoscope in his hands. Next was a framed photo of a skinny fellow in his mid-twenties or so, Diamante he guessed, with a pretty woman posing by a gondola on the Grand Canal.

'Your family?'

'My mother and father. And me. I knew I wanted to be a doctor all along.'

'I never knew you were married.'

'We weren't. Natalia died when we were engaged. A boating accident visiting relatives in Rimini. She drowned along with her cousin.'

'I'm sorry to hear that.'

'It was forty years ago. I don't remember what her voice sounded like. Mostly I keep that photograph so I can still picture her in my head. She was a nurse in the hospital. A lot's happened since.'

'A lot to come. May I take a seat?'

Diamante stared at him the way he must have looked at a patient who refused his advice.

'Why? What do you want?'

'To talk. Is that a crime? Will your fellow citizens hate you for allowing a creature of the Crucchi through the door?'

'No. But I may hate myself.'

All the same he pulled a chair out from the dining table and gestured for Alberti to take it. The two of them sat opposite one another. The flowers were roses and had a strong and spicy scent which, with the heat of the fierce wood fire, made Alberti's head feel worse.

'What will they do with this list of mine? Tell the truth now. You're a Venetian. You owe me that.'

Alberti took a deep breath and thought, *Sometimes it made no difference*.

'I don't know. Maybe put it in a filing cabinet and mark it as something to be dealt with in due course. The Crucchi here are idle bastards. If they were real soldiers they'd be elsewhere, wouldn't they? Trying to kill Russians, the Americans, the British. Struggling to keep Greece under Hitler's thumb. We get the dregs, doctor. You must have noticed.'

Diamante didn't believe a word of that. It was obvious.

'Then why work for them?'

He groaned. So many times he was asked this question. There was only a single answer, not that anyone else appeared to understand it.

'I told you already.'

'I know. I'm not soft in the head. Your answer was unsatisfactory.'

He pulled back from the table. The room was far too hot. Perhaps that was a Jewish habit. He wasn't sure.

'It's the only answer I have. Most of them can't speak Italian let alone Venetian. They don't know their way around. They're too arrogant to admit it. There'll always be someone to help them. If it wasn't me it might be some murderous lunatic from the Black Brigades.'

Diamante nodded as if he was taking that seriously.

'So you're simply a former policeman doing his job.'

'Exactly.'

'Then why are you here?'

Alberti leaned forward and rested his elbows on the shiny table. There was a point to be made.

'To help. The Nazis have word two terrorists are hiding in the city somewhere. Communists from Turin. They've murdered many. Crucchi soldiers. Civilians. Brother and sister. Mika and Giovanni Artom.'

The old man grunted something he couldn't hear, then said, 'What about the bastard who murdered poor Isabella Finzi? Tell me about him.'

'Shot in the Arsenale this morning.'

It wasn't a good or convincing lie.

'Mika and Vanni Artom,' Alberti repeated. 'You've heard the names?'

'I'm a retired physician, now forced to be president of the community here. Why would I associate with people like that?'

'Because they're Jews.'

'Good God, man! I barely thought of myself as Jewish until some bigoted hack of Mussolini's went through the records and decided to lump me in with everyone else.'

And yet, Alberti said, he lived in the ghetto.

'I inherited the place from my father. It suits. I—'

There was a knock on the door. Gentle, timid. The two men stopped.

'Were you expecting someone?' Alberti asked.

'No.' Diamante got to his feet. 'Excuse me.'

The man moved quickly for his age. In an instant he was at the door, his back to the table, talking in low tones.

Perhaps this was a stupid idea. Alberti was alone, as good as on enemy territory. If they killed him here, inside . . . who'd know?

He took his gun out of his holster, held it in his lap, then turned to see.

Mika Artom had spent a tedious day in an upstairs bedroom above the bar in via Garibaldi, alone most of the time, the door locked, nothing to read but a week-old copy of the local paper. Lunch was stale bread and equally stale cheese served by a silent Greta. From the window she could see the street: one fish stall, one vegetable stand by the iron gates to the park by Garibaldi's statue. It was a cold misty day, not many people wandering the broad cobbled thoroughfare. There wasn't much food on the stalls either. Venice was suffering a mean, spare winter.

She regretted the argument that morning and its source which was, she knew all too well, an odd kind of jealousy. It wasn't hard to see the young Venetian was attracted to Vanni, even if he wasn't quite sure of it himself. This wasn't new. Men could be terribly uncertain of themselves at times. Giulia, the occasional girlfriend, was a quick-witted, pretty kid one year younger, someone Mika could have come to regard as a friend if the war hadn't intervened. Her parents were hard-line Fascists, wealthy too. The last thing they wanted was their precious daughter in love with a left-wing Jew.

The boys he hung around with were different and there she did feel something was wrong, couldn't stop herself even when she tried. They always turned quiet, almost sullen if she walked into the conversation. It was never going to be easy striking up a friendship. The university was a place where queers were tolerated. The city outside less so. One of Vanni's friends had been beaten up for hanging round a park near college, a place they liked to frequent. Now, with Mussolini under Hitler's thumb, they were on the wanted list too. It wasn't just Jews who got thrown into cattle trucks and herded off to God knows where and what. Gypsies, queers, political activists, followers of supposedly heretical Christian sects all faced internment as well.

Sex didn't interest her, except as a means to an end. There were bigger issues to deal with. So perhaps a shapeless, uncomfortable sense of pique had driven her out of the Giardino degli Angeli, just as much as her need to get back into the war. Vanni was better with people than she'd ever be. Perhaps she envied him the ease with which he could fall in and out of bed with anyone he liked.

'No time for that right now,' she whispered.

Downstairs a door banged.

Trevisan was with Sara Vitale, both of them shivering, complaining about the bitter cold and the chicory coffee Greta was serving while the Germans got to enjoy the real thing. Venetians were never far from a moan.

'Your hair looks good,' Vitale said, throwing her coat on to the bed before pulling a set of documents out of her bag. 'I should have charged you for that.'

'I'm going to earn it, aren't I?'

'You are,' Trevisan agreed, then withdrew some documents from his pocket. An entry pass for the Hotel Gioconda with her photo and her fake ID as Giulia Grini. It gave her occupation as waitress.

Mika still hadn't worked out this pair. Were they a couple? Maybe. But there was some rivalry there too. Trevisan was a handsome man, probably popular with women. Dark eyes, dark hair, narrow, cunning face and a quick smile when he felt like it. Forty maybe, a few years older than Vitale. Both had the lean and anxious look she'd come to recognize among partisans. It expressed both a need and a fear, and she understood both implicitly. To be an underground fighter required more than simple courage. You needed a reckless disregard for your own welfare, something that meant you never slept well, kept normal hours, normal relationships either. The last man she'd had was a mountain shepherd three months before out in the hills behind Verona. The idiot had thought he could talk himself through a roadblock. The Black Brigades tortured, then shot him by Lake Garda and dumped his body in the water along with the corpses of his two younger brothers, neither of whom knew a thing about his work with the partisans or his affair with a communist Jew from Turin.

She'd gone with him because it made sense. It bound the man to her and the physical satisfaction they got from grappling with one another in his barn was a diversion she'd appreciated at the time. He'd talked though, as she knew he would, so by the time they shot him she was fifty miles away trying to find shelter with a new cell, new comrades.

That was another reason every partisan had to be anxious. You could trust the man or woman next to you with your life so long as they were free. Once they were in the hands of the Crucchi or the Black Brigades anything might happen.

'We've got a porter at the back who'll let you in with these,' Trevisan said. 'Go there tonight. Work. Serve them drinks. Smile. Don't talk. Don't act too friendly. If you do one of them's going to make you go to his room and we don't want that.'

'I thought I was a waitress, not a whore.'

Vitale sniggered, a nervous, childish sound.

'You're Italian, love. Pretty now I've done something with your hair. We're all whores to them.'

'And if I needed you to be a whore for real,' Trevisan added, 'you would be.' He folded his arms. 'Wouldn't you?'

'For the cause,' she said, even though it sounded weak.

'The cause,' the woman repeated. 'We heard what happened in the mountains. One of those guys was cousin to someone we know from Murano. They said it was your fault.'

'It was,' she agreed. 'I fouled up.'

'Get scared?' Trevisan wondered.

'No. I don't. I thought I could rely on everyone to do what I asked. Ballarin? The Venetian was Ballarin?'

Vitale frowned.

'Maybe. Does it matter?'

'He was a good guy. Didn't follow orders. I'm sorry he got killed. Tell them that.'

'Women don't run operations when I'm around,' Trevisan said.

She wasn't going to rise to that bait.

'This is your game, friend. What do you want of me?'

'First, a dry run.' He pointed to the floor plan for the Hotel Gioconda that Vitale had unrolled. 'This is the ballroom the Crucchi use. Sometimes it's a casino. Tonight it's just a drinking den. Tomorrow . . . party time.'

He drew a finger across the map. She followed. The room seemed huge, with a balcony over a small canal described by hand-drawn wavy lines.

'What floor's it on?'

'First one up,' Vitale told her. 'You could spit at someone in a boat down there.'

Trevisan scowled.

'Yeah. Sometimes they do just that. Bastards. There's an old trade entrance through a water gate. Back from when the place was a private palace. They never use it. The Nazis probably don't even realize it's there.'

Tomorrow she was to watch through the balcony windows for a small boat to emerge from the city side, not the Grand Canal, around six in the evening. Once that stopped close to the back of the hotel she was to go to a service door at the edge of the room, unlock it and get out of there.

'Here,' he said and gave her a key. 'Let us in. We'll do the rest.'

She knew she was blushing, angry and struggling to keep it in.

'That's it? I unlock a door? That's all? I want a weapon. The bag you gave me . . .'

'I told you not to look inside.'

'I didn't. I just took out the dress like you asked. I assumed—'

'It's not all,' Vitale broke in. 'We haven't finished.'

She walked over to a drawer in the room and came back with something Mika recognized. An explosives timer.

'There's a grand piano at the left side of the room. Hardly ever used. They don't do music. Before you unlock the door, you're going to look under the cover of the piano. We're placing a little present for them in there. You'll see this. Set it for five minutes.

Unlock the door and get out of there. When we hear this thing go off we come in. If we hear nothing . . .'

'We know you fouled up,' Trevisan added.

'I could come with you.'

Vitale shook her head.

'Impossible. We only fight with people we know.'

So much didn't make sense. If they had someone who could plant a bomb surely they possessed the means to prime it? Someone who could unlock the door too?

'I don't get it. Why do you need me to do this?'

'Because we don't have a choice.' Trevisan shrugged his shoulders. 'We're damaged. This cell's leaky. I can't risk using anyone else. Only me and Sara here know you exist. And old Greta downstairs and she doesn't get which day of the week it is. That's the way it's going to stay. Set the bomb. Open the door. Run. Then we go in and kill more Nazis and the rest of those scum than anyone's ever seen round here.'

'And after?' she asked.

He hesitated for a moment, then recited, 'There's only one way in which the murderous death agonies of the old society and the bloody birth throes of the new can be shortened, simplified and concentrated, and that way is revolutionary terror.'

Trevisan smiled at her.

'You're one of us, aren't you? Done your reading? My old man used Marx for nursery stories.'

'I've been fighting. Too busy for books. The reprisals . . . ten Italians for every dead German—'

'OK. Let me give you a saying from another kind of religion. "The blood of the martyrs is the seed of the church." There will always be blood. There will always be martyrs. The church we raise afterwards will be ours. Even if some of us aren't there to enjoy it.'

He lit a cigarette, handed it to her.

'When I said after . . . I meant what happens to me and my brother?'

'We'll find a way to send you to terraferma,' Trevisan said. 'We've people in Verona who need volunteers. There'll be hell to pay here. We vanish. We regroup. We fight again. I don't want to be carrying a stranger when that's going on.'

'Here.' Vitale showed the timer. 'This is how you set it.'

'I know how to set it,' Mika told her. 'I've probably used these things more than anyone you know. I deserve better than this.'

Trevisan sighed and rolled his eyes.

'Don't be so stupid. Without you we can't get in there. I just don't want you around when the shooting starts. Too messy. Too uncertain.'

He reached out and touched her blonde hair for a moment.

'We need you, kid. Just for this. We need you to smile, stay anonymous and vanish.'

Sara Vitale waved away some of the cigarette smoke and spread her arms wide.

'Then . . . boom.'

Alberti found himself sweating in Aldo Diamante's tidy, old-fashioned apartment and it wasn't just the heat from his roaring fire.

His fingers tightened on the weapon on his lap. Then there was light, childish laughter and two kids ran into the room, straight up to the fireplace where they stood giggling, rubbing their hands together, chattering wildly.

'Do we get sweets, Uncle Aldo?'

A boy about eight and a girl around ten. Black coat, black trousers, white shirts. Dark hair, shiny. Pale faces and just looking at them Alberti thought to himself, *These are the kind they call Orthodox and if it wasn't for the times they'd be dressed different, wouldn't mind standing out at all.*

A woman followed. Alberti tucked the gun back in his holster.

She looked worried, stared at him, then Diamante and asked, 'Who is this?'

'Just a visitor,' Alberti said getting to his feet with a quick smile. 'To the doctor. I thought I had something wrong with me.'

'You do,' Diamante shot back at him. 'You know what it is as well.'

The kids kept crying out for sweets. Diamante found a jar by the window and let them dip in their hands. Their mother – it was obvious from the way she looked at them – seemed ready to weep.

Alberti stood his ground.

'You won't mind if I seek a second opinion? Especially when the malady is so subtle and easily misdiagnosed.'

Still nervous, the woman said they could come back later.

'No need,' Alberti told them. 'I'm leaving.'

Diamante saw him to the door, then tugged him outside so his visitors couldn't hear.

'You're a Venetian. They're innocents. Your fellow citizens. A brother and sister. Born here. Don't . . .'

'Don't what?'

'Don't do what the Nazis tell you for once.'

Alberti shook his head. He'd expected better than that.

'Who do you think I am? God?'

'I think you're an ordinary man in extraordinary circumstances.'

'I'm nothing more than a prison guard in the jail of the Crucchi's making. Just as much an inmate as you.'

'Not quite,' the old man muttered. Then he reached inside his jacket pocket and took out a fat wad of lire. 'Here. Take this. It's only money. I've no need of it.'

Alberti hesitated. He was used to getting bribes and, on occasion, bribing others himself. But only when he initiated the bargain.

'You offend me, Diamante.'

'I don't mean to. I apologize if I've got you wrong. You can only judge a man on what you see.'

'What you see is what I told you. One more prisoner in their jail.'

Diamante got closer until his face was so close Alberti could hear his ragged breath.

'I'm begging . . .'

'What power do you believe I have?'

'The power to look the other way. I saw your face. You know why they're here.'

Of course he did.

'Looking the other way gets you killed.' He stepped back. 'They shoot you for just thinking about it.'

Diamante stared at him and there was hatred in his eyes at that moment.

'I've lost count of how many men and women I've seen leave this world, Alberti. Through sickness. Through violence. Neglect. Do you honestly believe death frightens me?'

'It wasn't you I was talking about.'

'They want rid of the Jews. All of us who've lived here for

centuries. Tonight I hope to relieve them of a little of their burden if you let me. Two children. *Children.*'

'Not the mother?'

'No.' His voice went quieter, down almost to a whisper. 'Her parents are sickly. The Black Brigades made them move to the old people's home across the way and snatched their apartment. She insists she stays with them.'

Alberti couldn't stop himself.

'Then tell her she's a fool. Soon they're going to raid that place. They don't need a list for that. They've got that fellow of yours, Bruno, to help them.'

'No fellow of mine. You're closer to us than that creature.'

'No.' That was wrong. It had to be. 'I'm not.'

'I told your boss. I told Bruno. A week is what I need to finish the list. They can wait.'

'And in the meantime you smuggle out your little children? Like something out of a Bible story?'

Diamante closed his eyes and leaned against the wall. He looked ill, exhausted.

'I'm not a religious man, Alberti. Don't talk to me of Bibles. Take the money and look the other way. It's no use to me anyway.'

Alberti snatched the notes and stuffed them in his pocket. He wasn't sure why. It made him feel bad.

'You don't have a week.'

Diamante squinted as if he was struggling to believe this.

'No, no. They'll wait until I'm finished. You said it yourself. The Crucchi are fighting a war. They've better things to do than hunt down Jews. 'Finding these partisans you mentioned for one thing. You said they'd put it in a filing cabinet . . .'

'I lied! I'm paid to lie. Sometimes it's easier than telling the truth.'

Had he been a few years younger Diamante might have gone for him at that moment.

'You have the devil in you, man. Either that or you are him.'

Luca Alberti tried to laugh.

'No. I just want to live. I lied because in this world that's how we manage. Just once I break my rule.' He took out the money and waved it in Diamante's face. 'Tell yourself I did it for this if it makes you feel better. They're coming for you all on Sunday. They know that list of yours has to be as good as complete. Give it to them tomorrow or they'll tear this place apart, you too. Then they'll clean out the old folk like those in that home of yours across the way. Monday it'll be the schools. After that they can sweep up the rest, house by house. It's arranged. They're marking it with a party tomorrow night. There's some decree from Salò. All Jews will be stripped of their nationality throughout the republic. Their property and their money forfeit to the state or whichever Black Brigades bastard gets to them first. You'll be shipped off like cattle to those camps they talk about.' He shrugged. 'Sure, that Bruno fellow said he'd spare you. But he's a Jew catcher. A Jew himself. He knows that's not going to happen. They spare no one except the few who suck their cocks.'

'Like you.'

It wasn't a question.

'I'm not a Jew. A day is all you have, Diamante. Ship out what little ones you can. I risk my life telling you this. I don't expect gratitude but if you don't go quietly and they take you into Ca' Loretti for interrogation. Then . . .'

He didn't want to say it but the old man made him.

'Then what?'

'Then I'll claim the right to question you myself. They barely speak Italian anyway. Not a word of Venetian among them. You won't get out of there alive.'

Alberti put on his beret and found the light switch for the stairs. It was a humble enough tenement for a man like Aldo Diamante who could surely have afforded much better. Somewhere in this tangle of tall, storeyed buildings there were sumptuous synagogues full of gold and silver plate, or so rumour had it. The Jews had kept their places of worship hidden away for centuries in the belief that, if only they were segregated, the rest of the world would leave them alone.

The Nazis and the Black Brigades would descend on all those spoils in the days to come. He'd listened to Sachs and Sander talking. They wanted every last Jew wiped from the face of the earth and their hands on whatever riches they supposedly possessed. Not that Aldo Diamante's modest apartment seemed somewhere to look for treasure.

'A day,' he repeated and wandered down the stairs.

* * *

All the same he hung around, shivering in the shadows as a freezing night fog wound its way around the city, silvering the crooked cobbles of the ghetto, setting a frosty sheen on the wooden bridges that were the boundaries of the tiny Hebrew enclave.

He'd been foolish. Diamante might so easily give him up if he were seized for interrogation. Were Alberti to wait and follow the fugitive children he could uncover one of the escape routes the Jews used, a prize which Oberg might appreciate, though with the taciturn German it was always hard to tell.

Twenty minutes later the front door of Diamante's building opened and four figures came out, two adults, the boy, the girl. The woman was howling. He could hear her across the street. Then she kissed her children one by one, hugged them, held them, whispered something in their ear as Diamante watched. Probably another lie. *I'll see you again soon.* A lie she couldn't bear to tell herself.

Alberti wondered how many of his kind the old man had smuggled out this way. If these children made it across the lagoon to terraferma, then through the treacherous paths of the mountains into Switzerland in the hands of decent people, they'd be safe. Not that it was going to be easy, or cheap. And if the Black Brigades caught them on the way they'd be robbed, then killed like rabbits on the hillside, along with everyone with them.

He watched the mother cuddle them one last time, then wave as they set off for the bridge that led towards Castello. He'd never got on with his own son who was twelve or thirteen now, living with his mother across the water in Mestre. They were better off out of Venice anyway. Being the wife and son of a collaborator was risky. He didn't see why they should suffer too.

Castello. Probably the terraces behind via Garibaldi. Or, further on, the quiet, remote island of Sant'Elena where there were clear routes into the lagoon, places a skilled boatman might smuggle a couple of youngsters into the night.

It would have been so easy to follow them and maybe alert a guard along the way. They could take them all. Though Diamante would surely find a way to shop him then. All that talk about interrogating the man on his own was just boasting. The Crucchi would never have allowed him to be alone with any prisoner for long. Their trust went so far and no further.

In a minute Diamante and his two tiny wards were across the

bridge. The mother watched them every step of the way, dabbing at her face with a handkerchief.

'You're as good as dead,' he thought. 'And maybe you know it too.'

He walked back into San Marco, along the meandering streets that led behind the Rialto towards Ca' Loretti.

It was time for a drink.

Paolo hadn't spent much time in the cellar since his parents died in the bombing raid in Verona. Too many memories there and no practical need. Everything wrapped in oilcloths below was history and memories, neither of which he wished to approach just yet.

Still, Vanni seemed taken by the weaving and the looms. He was curious to know more about the Uccello and so, slowly, rediscovering so much for himself, seated at the cellar table, Paolo told him what he knew. How his grandfather Simone had discovered the Jacquards unused since Napoleon closed the old weaving school on Fondamenta San Lazzaro, then, with some commercial cunning, acquired them for a song along with all the old patterns and cards the school had owned. Here they were still, templates for velvet that had graced the Vatican, the Doge's Palace, royal castles in Russia, England and so many throughout the Habsburg Empire the record books had lost count.

'Show me more,' Vanni begged as they sat flicking through an encyclopaedia from the seventeenth century full of line drawings of machines: looms, creels, warpers and a series of trevettes, the blades used to cut the velvet's pile. Almost two hundred years old but these were recognizably the same kind of equipment they had been using out in the glasshouse that day.

'More what?'

'More of what you can do.'

Paolo returned to the stacked piles wrapped up against the wall, then sorted through them until he found his favourite. Collections of fabric samples, some assembled by his grandfather and father over the years, but one inherited from the school, dating back to a vanished weaving company that closed when Napoleon arrived.

It was a leather-bound volume with the name of a long-lost artisan, Giacomo Benedetti, imprinted in gold on the front and beneath a date: 1778. Just eight years before the fall of the republic after more than a millennium as an independent state. Dust and the remains of insects rose like a golden mist in the lamplight as he unhinged the bronze clasp on the cover and let the contents breathe for the first time in years.

Each page was a sample of fabric. There must have been fifty or more pieces there, the colours faded, some thread damaged by insects over the centuries, but each with a small sheet of paper sewn into the corner with the details of the pattern, the price, the thread used and the customer.

Vanni flicked through them, smiling like a kid who'd just found lost treasure. Paolo watched, pleased to see him so happy.

'Here,' he said, as his visitor went past one of the most interesting examples, a piece of velvet his father had first shown him when he was ten or so. It was an old-fashioned pattern, soprarizzo naturally, the pile all silk, the ground eighty per cent cotton and the rest gold thread. Muscular soldiers surrounded with semi-naked muses against the background of a garden composed of fantastic flowers and winding vines. 'Read the description.'

Vanni's smile grew broad with astonishment.

'Oh my God. Is this true?'

'Why wouldn't it be?'

The label gave a name for the pattern in French: *Liberté, égalité, fraternité*. The slogan of the French Republic and the revolution. The note said the customer was Benjamin Franklin, the first ambassador of the newly free United States to France and gave an address in Passy outside Paris.

Vanni stroked the pile. The colours were so weak it was impossible to imagine what it must have been like on Franklin's walls.

'I guess even revolutionaries love a little luxury from time to time,' he murmured. Then he ran his fingers over the velvet once more. 'It's like touching a ghost. A piece of history.'

'My father always said that too.'

Vanni looked at the pile of stored documents – books, patterns, cards – by the back wall. They ran to the low ceiling and stretched the width of the room.

'You've got so much here,' he said. 'So much beauty.'

Paolo laughed.

'What's so funny?'

'It's old. It's dead. Like this place. Like me. What can I do with this? I've no money. No one else but Chiara who knows how to make velvet the way they used to. Even if people wanted it.'

Vanni's hand fell on his knee.

'People will always want beauty, my friend. In ugly times they'll come to crave it even more. You've got a commission, haven't you?'

'Just the one.'

'Work is work, Paolo.' His hand hadn't moved. If anything it felt firmer. 'One day the war will be over and we can be ourselves again. Then you'll rebuild the House of Uccello. You'll get the right workers. The commissions will flood through the door. I see a great future for you. I wish I could be a part of that. I think I make a better weaver than a partisan. My sister would surely agree.'

Smiling, his head bowed, he came and whispered in Paolo's ear, so close his breath felt warm and welcome, 'Do you?'

Paolo retreated a little from his presence, closed the book, watched the dust motes rise as the ancient faded pieces of velvet went back where they belonged, obscurity and darkness.

'I'm sorry if I'm being forward,' Vanni said. 'If I . . . misread the signs.'

'No . . .'

'Occasionally I drift between men and women. Which means I'm three times damned. A Jew. A communist. A part-time queer. I know the first are none of your business. But I wondered if the reason you hid away here . . . perhaps . . .'

Beyond the tracery window there was a noise. A boat on the night lagoon. Vanni got the idea straight away and extinguished the lamp. They sat there in darkness waiting for the inevitable. But there was no white searchlight beam scanning the building, piercing the tiny tracery window, finding the damp brickwork of the back wall. No German voices.

An arm worked its way round Paolo's shoulders. Vanni's mouth came close to his ear and whispered, 'Maybe it's nothing. Stay still. Don't move. They won't find us. I promise.'

Paolo Uccello was remembering the fishermen's boats from before the war. Sometimes his father would hire one to take the family out for a picnic in the lagoon. They were the good days, back when they had a little money. Now he'd barely set foot outside Castello in months.

The searchlight vanished. The wash of the boat hit the rocks outside. They could hear the swell it made splashing noisily against the jetty.

'I'm sorry,' Vanni said again and withdrew his arm. 'I'm being presumptuous.'

Paolo lit a match and held it between the two of them, then said, 'I've never . . . Never been with a girl. Or a man. It didn't happen. It didn't feel right.'

Vanni nodded and there was a brief, wry smile.

'Ah. Well I went to university. It was hard not to get your hands dirty, as it were.' He leaned on the table, elbows against the wood, hands beneath his chin. 'Does it feel right now?'

The match burned down to his fingers. He cried and dropped it. Vanni took out his lighter and got the lamp going again.

He looked older, sadder sometimes now.

'We should go upstairs,' Paolo said.

'You can't run from your feelings. From what you are. It just follows you. Trust me. I know.'

'I'm scared. Your sister scares me. You too. In a different way.'

Vanni got to his feet and winced at the pain from the wound.

'We need to make the most of the time we have. It doesn't come round twice. I'm going to take a shower. If you want I'll come to your room. Maybe just to talk.' He held out his hand. 'If you don't then we shake as friends and I'll never mention this again.'

Vanni Artom's hand felt warm and gentle, not that of a warrior though Paolo believed he could feel the start of the hard skin that always came from labouring on the Jacquard loom.

The engine outside began to fade. It was headed for San Pietro and once again Paolo Uccello wondered about those words he'd spoken in haste as they dragged Isabella Finzi's sad and mangled body out of the grey water. One rash outburst and his life was changed.

'Well then,' Vanni held out his arms. 'Now I go upstairs. Will you help me, Paolo? With this stupid leg it's not easy getting up there on my own.'

The porter who let Mika Artom into the Hotel Gioconda looked scared as hell. She wondered if he was acting under duress. It wouldn't have been beyond Trevisan. Or her if she was running this cell. On occasion you had to be as hard on your allies as your enemy. There were times when conscience needed to take a back seat.

A skinny, sick-looking man who might have been close to retirement, he wore a dark, grubby uniform and the downtrodden look of a hotel lackey confined to the back of the house.

'Toni,' she said when she showed up at the staff entrance bang on eight as Trevisan had commanded. 'I'm the new girl.'

He looked her up and down, shook his head, glanced at her fake ID, then checked her bag.

'Shit. What kind of idiot are you? What's this?'

The gun. She took one everywhere when she was in the hills.

'I'm sorry—'

'Sorry? You got to go through the guards to get into the ball-room. You think they wouldn't notice this?'

He put the bag in a cupboard and said she could pick it up on her way out if she wanted. Then nodded at the stairs.

From what she'd heard the Gioconda had been one of the finest hotels in Venice until the Crucchi took over. Behind what she assumed to be a glorious façade it looked a dump. Peeling paint on the walls, cracked plaster, dust and cobwebs hanging from the ceiling of the staff quarters. The smells coming from the kitchen were good though. Wartime rationing didn't seem to stretch to the Nazis and their Fascist friends. Trevisan had told her: they had the pick of the fruits of the lagoon, from the vegetables on Sant'Erasmo to wild fowl shot around Torcello and Burano, the best of the fish and seafood landed in the south by the depleted fleet based in Chioggia.

'I said I'm sorry. Do I see you tomorrow?'

He grunted half a laugh.

'Not a chance. You make your own way in. The guy who's portering . . . he's a halfwit. Churchill could walk through that door and he wouldn't bat an eyelid.'

So you won't be here when the attack begins, she thought. Good timing.

'I could really use some food. It's cold.'

'No food.' He nodded at the stairs. 'Get up there and serve them drinks. You're on till eleven. Don't hang around one minute after. They'll think you're a whore.'

She took off her coat and her winter cap.

'Jesus, you look like a whore.'

'It's just a dress,' she said, then hung her coat on a hook above the cupboard with the gun and went upstairs.

Beyond the shabby corridors and functional rooms meant for staff the Gioconda was palatial. Tall ceilings, deep carpets, fine furniture, mirrors everywhere and Murano glass. The upstairs ballroom over the canal was vast, with a stage on the near wall, now covered in tables, and a smaller podium in the corner by the window where a grand piano sat, a cloth thrown over it to stop people putting their drinks straight on the polished wood.

To the side was a long bar where a cocktail waiter, a tall man, distinguished-looking in a white suit, marshalled a small team of six.

'You're the new one,' he said, looking her up and down, much the way the Germans, some in uniform, some in dark suits, did as she walked over to the counter.

'I am.'

'Name?'

'Giulia.'

He shrugged, uninterested. This one wasn't a part of Trevisan's cell, of that she felt sure.

'If you sleep with them it's five marks or fifty lire. Don't even touch anyone from the Black Brigades. They'll beat the hell out of you and kick you out of bed without paying a cent.'

'Thanks for the advice. Fifty lire for fucking the Crucchi?'

It was a stupid thing to say. The barman looked amused.

'Yeah. Like I said . . . it's money and that's more than you'll get from anyone else in here. Me included. The Germans own this place and seem to think they're worth it. Charge less and one of the other girls will scratch your eyes out.'

'I'm here to serve drinks. That's all. I go home at eleven.'

He blinked and said, 'Oh. We're recruiting from nunneries now. Times must be desperate. Here . . .' The glasses were sitting behind the bar already, half filled with Campari, ice, lemon and an olive. The guy popped open two bottles of Prosecco, then topped them up. 'They get as much spritz as they want for free. Wine too. If any of them ask for something stronger they got to pay. They know that but they might try it on.' He smiled, just for a second. 'They might try lots on with a poppet like you.'

She'd never served drinks before. It was harder than she expected, keeping the tray straight, wandering by the groups of chattering Germans and their tame Italians, letting them take what they wanted, ignoring the pinches and the caresses that came almost every minute, steeling herself to smile and say, no, she wasn't available, she had a sick mamma at home and needed to be back by eleven thirty at the latest to look after her.

Close up the Crucchi looked disappointingly ordinary. In the past she'd seen them almost as devils, not quite human. It was easier to think of them that way. She and her comrades were there to kill these scum before they got the chance to kill them. Yet the faces she smiled at as she wandered the room could have been men she saw on the rickety, rattling, old tram carriages back in Turin, some vile, some bored, some quite unremarkable. All of them, she felt sure, capable of murder and terror and cruelty. They had to be. They were Crucchi. And she was just as sure she could shoot them face to face and would given the chance.

The ones who were harder to read were the Italians who scrutinized her more carefully, listened to her speak, judged her accent – Piedmont, she couldn't hide it. Twice some fat, sweating, middle-aged man she took to be from the Black Brigades asked what a woman from across the country was doing in Venice. Working, she said. Looking after a sick mother who'd been married to a Venetian and lost him in the war.

A sour-faced thug in a black suit, rings on his fingers, a livid scar down his right cheek, asked for her papers and didn't like it much when she said they were downstairs in her bag. No way to carry them wearing a cocktail dress.

'What are you doing later?' he asked.

'I have to see my mother, sir. That's why I'm here. She's not well at all.'

He didn't push it. There were other women in the room, mostly more scantily dressed than she was. An awkward one wasn't worth the effort.

Time passed quickly when she taught herself not to think. Just go back and forth to the bar, get more scarlet tumblers of spritz and a few bowls of snacks, wander the room, make sure it didn't look like she was listening.

She was, of course, but even that was disappointing. There were perhaps thirty Germans in the place and a dozen or more Italians.

A few were chasing the women who were placed there like decorations, with nothing to do but talk and arrange where in the hotel they'd sleep that night, or so she guessed. Their conversation was dismal, about family and how much they missed home. About how the war was going to be won one day even if it didn't look so good at the moment. A couple of them even spoke of going to the opera.

The Crucchi weren't stupid, anything but. They'd never let slip a secret or a plan in a place like this.

Over the course of the evening she'd confirmed the layout of the place matched Trevisan's map. The staff door she was supposed to open was on the right-hand side of the room, barely visible, painted the same cream colour as the walls. Just a keyhole to say it was there, nothing more, not even a handle on the outside. The piano was by the opposite wall. There was no one clicking his fingers for a drink so she wandered over and took a good look at that. A Bechstein it said. Shiny but she wondered how long it was since the thing had been played.

A man wandered over while she was looking, came so close he made her jump and the one glass of spritz left tumbled to the floor, bounced off the carpet sending drink everywhere.

'Sorry, signora. I didn't mean to surprise you.'

He spoke Italian marked by the rough accent of Venice and was down on the floor picking up the empty glass before she could get there, wiping the drink into the carpet with the side of his shoe. With a wink he nodded at the sweep of his feet.

'A man trick for when you've spilled something. Do you play?'

'Play what?'

'The piano, of course. What do you think I meant?'

'I didn't hear you right. No. I wish I did. I'm sorry, I'll get you another drink.'

'I'd like that.'

When she came back, tray full again, he took two and laughed.

'I shouldn't say this, sir,' she told him, 'but you look like you've had enough already.'

'There isn't enough. There'll never be enough. Fetch me two more when these are empty.'

'No. You drink those and go home.'

He nodded at the ceiling.

'This is home. Want my room number?'

'I'm here to serve drinks. That's all.'

He placed one of the glasses back on the tray and held out his right hand.

'You look like you're new to this. Luca Alberti. Pleased to meet you. Room Four One Three.'

She didn't take his hand but she did say her name.

'Giulia? So what are you doing here . . . Giulia?'

'Working. My mamma's sick. I need the money.'

The way he said nothing made her wonder what he was thinking. Maybe he wasn't as drunk as he first looked.

'You sound like a local,' she added. 'But you live here?'

'Safest thing to do when you belong to the Crucchi. Bear that in mind. There's a bridge you cross sometimes and no turning back.' He touched the side of her head. 'I like your hair. That's new, isn't it? My wife used to dye her hair. Cost a packet.'

'A friend does it for free.'

'What's the real colour?'

She looked round. No one was watching them. They all felt safe in this place. It was obvious.

'I got to work.'

'I got to find Jews. Know any?'

'What?'

'Jews. Couple of partisans. Sorry, terrorists we're supposed to call them. On the run from Turin. Brother and sister. Like I said. Jews. Not that the Jews here say they know them. You think—'

Her face flushed and she yelled, 'What?'

He answered slowly as if she was stupid.

'I was asking if you'd heard anyone talking about a couple of Jews from out of town. Hiding somewhere probably. Don't think it's in the ghetto. Too obvious. I don't know—'

'What makes you think I hang around with Jews?'

'I didn't say—'

'I ought to slap you.'

'Just asking.'

She made sure she sounded furious, got louder so that people started to notice.

'Damn it.' She placed the tray on the piano, balled a fist. 'I will hit you.'

'Feel free, lady. Been a while.'

'No.' She dropped her hand. 'You're not worth it. People like you . . . Dead drunk when you should be working. The sooner we ship that filth out of the country the better. Il Duce should have been doing it years ago. Took Hitler to rescue him and put a spine in his back before we even started looking proper.'

Alberti grinned.

'For one so young and pretty you do have strong feelings.'

She jabbed a finger at her chest. The dress was low. All the men were looking.

'I'm a patriot. What are you?'

A German voice spoke up, bad Italian, struggling with the words.

'Alberti's just a servant.' The Nazi was in a grey uniform, young, narrow face, long nose, sardonic expression. Stank of booze too. 'Ignore him. He works for me.'

'I work for your boss, Sander. Both of us do. Let's not forget it.'

The German wasn't even listening.

'You're new?'

Sander was eyeing her with a look she knew too well.

'Just started.'

'You've got a good heart.' He reached out and stroked a finger down her breast. She didn't flinch. 'What are you doing later? I got a nice room. A comfortable bedmate.' He tapped his jacket. 'A little money too. But let's face it . . . here a little money goes a long way.'

'Later I'm going home.'

His face fell.

'You disappoint me. I hate that.'

'Sick mamma,' Alberti cut in. 'Loving daughter. Never get between the two, chum. You'll have to pick a new bedmate tonight.' He smiled right at her. 'This one looks too special. Aren't you . . . Giulia?'

She went back to the bar, sure she wasn't shaking. Sure.

The rest of the night went past so slowly she wondered if she'd really make it till eleven.

But make it she did and after that she went down the staff staircase, got her coat and the bag with the handgun, stumbled out into the cold and frosty night where the grey mist was so thick it was hard to see a few steps ahead.

Alberti had watched her leave, smiling, raised his glass as she vanished through the door.

He was just a man, maybe a lothario like the Nazi Sander. One who happened to be hunting her and Vanni.

That was all.

The boat was late. Aldo Diamante wondered if it had been caught by the Germans. San Pietro was so close to their patrols out of the Arsenale. Then there was the weather. The freezing fog had got thicker as he walked the children from the ghetto through the back streets of Castello out to Filippo Garzone's solitary basilica. It chilled him to the marrow and he had to keep feeding the kids caramels to stop them squawking. On a night like this most sane sailors would stay at home, even the vaporetti which were the principal form of transport around the city. All the same the men of Venice who worked the lagoon often seemed more happy on water than land. In peacetime he'd watched them work like slaves all week, then spend their spare time racing all their many different kind of *sandoli* rowing boats along the broad waterfront from Fondamente Nove across to the Lido. If anyone could find a way through this it was them.

And so they waited hour after hour in Filippo Garzone's office, beneath a simple painting of Jesus with little children, trying to pass the time. The priest knew songs and games and had a few jigsaw puzzles from the Sunday study group the basilica ran. Religious themes, of course, unfamiliar to the children of the ghetto, or so Diamante expected. But in truth these five kids were old enough to remember school days before they were segregated from their Christian peers. So there was a brief delight as they rediscovered tunes and pictures and stories they'd forgotten.

Garzone was heartened by their response and grinned at Diamante as they turned the pages of his books, marvelling at the pictures and the poems.

'See,' he said, leaving the children to it for a moment, 'nothing vanishes. It merely hides and waits.'

'True,' Diamante agreed and tried his best to match the forced joviality of his mood. It was so cold in the church he never took off his heavy winter coat. There was a satchel slung over his shoulder, one that had the logo of his old hospital on it and the winding serpents of Asclepius, the perennial symbol of medicine. It had once accompanied him on his rounds.

A distant church bell tolled eleven. San Pietro's own campanile had been silent for years for lack of money and support. The children were quiet by then, one of the girls fast asleep.

'If they're not here by midnight it's off,' Diamante said. 'Either they abandoned the attempt or the Germans caught them.'

Garzone nodded.

'In that case your little flock can stay with me. Here. If need be I'll try to find other places for them to stay. No one wants to see the young suffer.'

'I don't know,' Diamante replied. 'If I can't get them out tonight perhaps they would be best back home . . .'

The two of them fell silent. Diamante felt guilty toying with his old friend like this. They both knew he was trying to make the best of a desperate situation. For the life of him he couldn't think of anything else to say.

Then there was a rap on the door, so loud it made the two men jump and the sleeping child wake and start to cry.

Three men, bearded, wrapped in dark jackets, wool caps low over their skulls, stood outside, shivering, stamping their seafarer's boots on the hard stone.

'We came for cargo,' grunted the first one.

'And our money,' added the second, holding out his hand.

'Of course,' Diamante replied. 'We have both.'

Garzone watched with distaste as he retrieved an envelope from his coat and handed it over. A thick wad of notes, Reichsmarks, lire and even some American dollars. The second sailor counted them with his finger, licking it as he went. Then he nodded.

'Will you get them to Switzerland?' Diamante asked.

'That's the plan,' the lead one replied. 'Are any sick? Or awkward?'

'They're good obedient children,' Garzone cut in. 'They think they're going on holiday and their family will join them later. Please don't disabuse them of that idea.'

The priest had heard stories about Jew smugglers, a few in confession. Some were honest partisans seeking to do good. Others were simply black marketeers looking for a bigger profit than they might get from tobacco, drugs or drink. A few, the rumours said, were thugs and murderers who took their money and either handed over their charges to the Black Brigades or killed them and dumped their bodies in the northern marshes where they'd never be found. There was, of course, no way of telling. The men who worked the lagoon, fishing, carrying cargo, legal or illicit, running errands between the islands, were a tough breed who never said much, good or bad. Diamante's contacts must have made this arrangement. He could only hope they'd done their job.

'Bring them,' the first man said. 'Make sure they're wrapped up well. It's cold out there.'

'There are five now,' Diamante said.

The boatmen just stared at him. Diamante's glance told Garzone there was another conversation to be had here and he would not be party to it. So the priest went back inside, found scarves and gloves, too big but all he had, did his best to smile and tell them all was well.

'Time for your holiday, little ones. Your boat's here. Now . . . Be good. Do as the sailors say. You've a long journey ahead. An interesting one. Across the water. Into the mountains. In a few days you'll be in Switzerland, a marvellous country. There are cow bells and cheese and trains and skiing.'

'Have you been?' the young boy asked.

'No. But I've heard much.'

He took the hand of the smallest girl. She'd started to cry and he didn't want to know why.

Outside the fog seemed as thick as he'd ever seen it. He couldn't begin to imagine what kind of vessel might make its way safely through such an impenetrable night. Before he could introduce the children, the first boatman smiled at the crying girl, pulled a small doll out of his pocket, bent down in front of her and said, 'Will you look after her?'

The thing looked ancient. She took it anyway.

'It was my daughter's,' the man went on.

The girl asked, 'What's her name?'

'The doll? She's called Carina. Little darling.'

'I meant your daughter.'

The smile on his face hardened.

'Her name doesn't matter anymore. Come.' He took her hand. 'Time to go.'

The two men watched them vanish into the fog. After a while an engine sounded, then faded away to nothing.

'I think they must be good, honest fellows,' Garzone said. 'The way he dealt with that child.'

'They thought they were picking up three. Not five.'

'You paid them though, didn't you?'

'That I did.'

Diamante kept staring at the opaque night as if there were answers out there, hiding, waiting to be found.

'Will you have more . . . cargo for me to deal with tomorrow?'

'No.' He took out his woollen cap and pulled it over his ears. 'There's no one left to fetch them. No time.'

'Aldo.' He took his old friend's arm. 'We're here. We live. We breathe. There's always time until we abandon it or God offers us another choice.'

Diamante shook his head and, just for a second, laughed.

'Ah, yes. God. You reminded me. I have something I would like you to keep. In your care.' He shrugged his medical bag off his shoulders. 'Please.'

The priest shook his head as he watched in the faint light of the doorway. There was more money, in three envelopes, lire, Deutschmark and British pounds. Then, before he could object, Diamante retrieved a leather jewel case and handed it over.

'You don't need to open it.'

'Don't I?' Garzone replied and did.

Several necklaces, two with what looked like genuine pearls. Brooches. A man's wristwatch, a Swiss brand that he believed to be expensive. And two rings, one plain gold, one set with a diamond.

'This is a wedding ring,' Garzone said. 'And perhaps an engagement one too.'

'My mother's,' Diamante told him. 'Keep them safe. If something should happen to me use all this as you see fit.'

The priest tried to hand it all back.

'I'm more than happy to help with your children. Don't make me feel like a pawnbroker too.'

Diamante stepped away and shook his head.

'For pity's sake, Aldo, we don't give up now!'

'Who said I'm giving up? I have a home full of old junk. Mine. My parents'. Their parents' too. If the Germans come I'd rather the few precious things among it went to my neighbours, not my enemies. That's all. Safekeeping, old friend.' He held out his hand. 'Safekeeping. There's duty and bravery in those who take on that task. Not that they often hear our thanks.'

There was, Garzone understood, no point in arguing. He felt tired and terribly depressed.

'Have you spoken to anyone?' he asked. 'One of your priests?'

Diamante seemed amused.

'Not about spiritual matters, I'm afraid. Those I leave to more intelligent men than me.'

'Then . . . may we meet in our usual place tomorrow? It's my time to buy the coffee and biscotti. I would like that. Perhaps the weather will be better. We can toast our five small friends on their way to new lives in Switzerland.'

Diamante turned and grimaced at the foul night. His mind, it seemed, was elsewhere.

Finally he smiled at Garzone and said, 'That's a splendid idea. Ten o'clock would suit?'

'Ten o'clock.'

'For once I'll break my morning rule and have a grappa too. You're a brave man, Garzone. I'm astonished you don't seem to realize.'

'Ha! I'm custodian of a church few visit and a flock who mainly keep themselves to themselves. I do what I can. I had children in my care today. I heard their laughter from time to time. Their young voices. They reminded me of why I'm here. Even a priest needs that from time to time.'

'Those two other . . . visitors you kindly placed in the house of your friend. Have you heard from them?'

Garzone sighed.

'Not a word. You?'

'No.' He tapped his cap. 'It's late. We must stop thinking we can save everyone.'

'Perhaps,' the priest agreed. 'But we should never stop thinking we must try.'

The old doctor nodded, tipped his hat, then vanished into the shifting, formless night.

Wreathed in the dense swirling cloud that had descended on the city, with only a torch to guide her down streets where lamps were rare and feeble, Mika Artom struggled to find her way home. There was no curfew in force as there was in other cities. It was one more way in which Venice seemed to hope it was above the war. Besides, any control on movement would have been meaningless on an evening such as this. There was no straightforward path anywhere, only winding alleys, low arches that led to dead ends by sluggish canals, tall palazzi and apartment blocks lit by a few candles and the odd electric light.

Along the way she'd somehow found herself passing La Fenice where the last of the concert crowd was making its way out into the cold, damp night, all in fine clothes, chattering, wondering whether to go home or find a late-night bar. As if times were normal and the conflict that created two warring versions of Italy didn't exist.

Then, lost, trying to guess the way, she'd stumbled across a bridge into the broad open square of Campo Santa Maria Formosa. A group of German soldiers huddled by the church, smoking under a waxy yellow street lamp by the stone face of a hideous monster, eyeing the few locals passing in the night. One spotted her – a woman always attracted attention – and called out.

The gun was in her bag. She had no idea how to get back to San Pietro. No choice but to obey.

Shivering, looking scared, in part because it was expected, she walked over, took out her papers, explained, in slow, clear Italian, that she'd just come from working for the crowd at the Gioconda and had the staff ID to prove it.

He raised his eyebrows at that and asked, 'You're one of the girls?'

'I'm a waitress,' she said as severely as she dared. 'My mother's ill. I have to work. I got called back to look after her. I don't know my way. This place . . . It's so easy to get lost.'

He handed back the papers and said with a sneer, 'All those bastards in the Gioconda. They think they're on holiday. They think they can whore and booze and eat themselves stupid while the likes of us go fight their war for them.'

'Hey, Günther!' one of soldiers called. 'We're not fighting here either.'

'Soon enough,' he replied. 'Where are you trying to go?'

Don't tell him exactly, she thought.

'Castello. Via Garibaldi.'

He pointed across the campo. She could just make out a bridge.

'Cross over there and keep going that way. In the end you get to the water. Turn left past the Arsenale and keep on walking.'

'I know it from there. Thanks. You're very kind.'

He smiled and there was a glint in his eye.

'Maybe they'll let the underlings into the Gioconda one day. I'll see you there. You can be grateful.'

'I serve drinks. That's all.'

A few minutes later she found the broad waterfront of the Riva degli Schiavoni, then crossed the bridge by the Arsenale canal. There were soldiers everywhere near the military base inside the old naval compound. Twice more she had to show her papers and once got propositioned by a slovenly drunk in uniform. But the ID card for the Gioconda worked a kind of magic and none of them asked to see in her bag. It seemed a woman who mixed with officers and high-ranking Fascists in that place carried a little weight.

Free of the last man, she turned into the wide mouth of via Garibaldi, hurried up the street, past Greta's closed bar, found her way into the warren of lanes that led towards San Pietro.

It was almost midnight by the time she wandered across the green by the basilica, the campanile looking strange and yet more crooked in the dim, strange light of a single lamp burning through the fog.

The hidden path into the apartment of the Giardino degli Angeli was precarious enough when she could see clearly. In the grey shroud that had fallen on the city she had to take care with every footstep as she edged along the wall of the garden, out to the platform by the lagoon, then worked her way to the stairs and finally, breathless, chilled to the bone, rapped lightly on the door. Twice rapidly, three times slowly. The signal she and Vanni had agreed when they first began to run with the partisans.

A while she waited, then the door opened. Vanni, still in his day clothes, his face cold and furious.

'Thanks,' she said and slipped in, went straight for the bottle of grappa by the sink, poured herself a sizeable shot, gulped it down.

There was an atmosphere in the place. She could feel it. Paolo Uccello was sitting at the table, staring at her. The bedroom door was open. She saw what was on the bed, swore, marched in there.

On the sheets the bag was open. They'd rifled through the canvas holdall that Trevisan had given her, with strict orders not to look inside. She had, of course; not that she'd let on to Vanni. Now the contents were spread out over the thin cotton coverlet.

Two handguns, four packs of shells. Three stick grenades. All German in origin, all capable of putting anyone caught with them in front of a firing squad. She could understand why Trevisan would leap at the opportunity to hide them elsewhere even if he'd no intention of asking her to use them. A safe house for weapons was always useful.

The two men came in behind her.

'Vanni. I asked you not to look.'

'He didn't,' Paolo said. 'It was me.'

She glanced at the two of them, a knowing smile on her face. 'What were you doing in here?'

'I live here.' The Venetian finally seemed to have found his spine. 'This is my parents' bedroom. I was told you'd stay inside. Keep out of sight.'

She tucked the weapons back into the holdall, then hid the bag back in the wardrobe where she'd left it.

'Mika. Are you listening?'

'Yes, Paolo. I am.' Don't get mad, she told herself. This was not the time. 'No one knows we're here. I wouldn't tell the people I'm working with where we live. They didn't follow me. I checked. I know you want to keep out of this. I know you want to hide and pretend nothing bad's happening outside—'

'No.' Vanni went and stood next to him. She wondered what had gone on while she was out. The Uccello kid had hardly set foot in the bedroom since they'd turned up. It was almost as if he was scared of bumping into his parents' ghosts. 'You should have told us.'

'I didn't know what was inside that bag, honestly. I think this is just somewhere they want to keep them hidden. Don't worry. I'm not going to use them.'

'What *are* you going to do?' her brother asked.

She thought about the right answer.

'Tomorrow. There's some kind of party in that hotel of theirs. A ceremony. I don't know what or why. Maybe those banners you're weaving are something to do with it. Maybe . . .'

The two men glanced at one another.

'What time are you supposed to hand them over?' she asked.

Paolo said, 'I'm going there at four.'

'Good.' She nodded. 'Don't hang around. They've got something planned for later. I'm just lookout. From the inside. That's all.'

Mika walked up to them, took her brother's hand, then Paolo Uccello's. Joined the three of them, fingers linked together.

'Listen to me. Please. I want us out of here just as much as you. The deal is I work lookout. Then afterwards they're going to fix us a boat and smuggle us to terraferma. We'll be gone.' She turned to Paolo. 'Well I will anyway. If my brother wants to stay here and do needlework—'

'Don't be funny,' Vanni snapped. 'When? When do we get out?'

She shrugged and said, 'Sunday, I guess. They didn't say. Bigger things on their mind. Look . . .' She squeezed their cold hands. 'All I have to do is be a waitress. I open a door. I let them in. Then I leave. They don't trust me to do more than that. They won't help us if I won't help them. It's the only way.'

She looked down at Vanni's leg.

'I need to change your dressing.'

'No you don't,' Paolo said. 'I did it. You were late. He needed it.'

A smile, then: 'What Vanni needs Vanni gets. Don't worry. I won't do anything to bring the war over those walls and disturb your peaceful little angels.'

She bit her lip and wondered whether any of this worked. It was hard to believe Paolo would betray them. He surely knew if he did the Germans would still turn on him for hiding them in the first place. If she found out he was trying then . . .

Then she'd kill him. There'd be no choice.

'Goodnight,' he said and left.

Vanni took off his trousers and sat on the bed. The dressing on his leg was clean and fresh. No blood. Paolo Uccello had delicate fingers, she guessed. It was needed for the work he did.

'You know you're going to have to keep him sweet, brother, don't you? Just for one more day.'

'What the hell's that supposed to mean?'

She sat next to him, stroked his long, dark hair. On the run he hadn't shaved. Soon he'd have a full beard. That would be useful. When they were arrested briefly in Padua the photographs the Crucchi took pictured him clean-shaven.

'Whatever you like.' Mika kissed his bristly cheek. 'He's sweet on you. Keep him that way and he'll do anything you ask.'

Vanni glared at her.

'You can be a real bitch sometimes, you know. Are you telling the truth? About what they want? Us getting out of here?'

'Yes! For God's sake . . . why would I make any of this up?'

Maybe he believed her.

'Are you going to leave with me?' Mika asked. 'Or stay here? With him?'

'I can't walk. I can't fight. I'm sick of the whole thing.'

She laughed and said, 'And I'm not?'

'No.' The look in his eyes was sharp and accusing. 'I think you like it. The risk. The danger. The idea you might kill someone. Or get killed yourself. I think it makes you forgive yourself for when we screwed up in the mountains. I think it makes you feel alive.'

'Now there,' she said and jabbed a finger at his chest, 'you couldn't be more wrong.'

Aldo Diamante had always lived in the ghetto. There'd never seemed a reason to be anywhere else. He knew its history, naturally. That was something you learned at school. How the small island known as the Ghetto Novo was instituted in the early sixteenth century as a place where the city's Ashkenazim were forced to live, confined there at night, the bridges policed by guards, and made to wear red hats or yellow belts if they entered the city at large during the day. How different groups of Jews – Italian, Levantine, Sephardic – formed separate communities there, each with its hidden synagogue built within the high tenement walls.

His own family hailed from Toledo in Spain and arrived in Venice in the 1550s via Amsterdam, or so his father always claimed. Not that the Diamanti deemed this of importance. Jewish they might be but secular too. The young Aldo was shown the Spanish synagogue, naturally, but primarily as a curiosity, an example of a superstitious rite to be respected if not observed. His father had been a professor of political economics at the city university, Ca' Foscari, under the patronage of Luigi Luzzatti, a wealthy Jewish intellectual who'd travelled from being a revolutionary expelled by the Austrians during their occupation of the city to holding senior political offices after the creation of the new, liberated Italy.

Luzzatti had briefly been prime minister of this reunited country little more than thirty years before. A Jew like him now could not teach, could not work freely with his fellow gentile citizens, could not even have his name in the phone book. Soon, when the Black Brigades began to sweep the cities and the countryside for yet more Jews, he would be confined to a cattle truck and dispatched to a distant camp in a foreign country, probably never to return.

Though it occurred also to Diamante that a wealthy Venetian like Luzzatti would doubtless have departed long before, to Switzerland, England or America. Money gave a man choices denied those of meaner status.

The room was stifling hot thanks to the roaring log fire. He got up from his old armchair and walked over to the desk by the window. Outside a single street lamp cast its waxy yellow beam over the cobbles of the square.

Ghetto.

The name came from the Venetian for foundry, the original purpose of the small island tucked away in the midst of the city.

Growing up the word possessed little in the way of evil connotation, particularly in the Diamante household where science and logic ruled and he was schooled to look to the future, never the past. It was primarily a historical term for the place, a prison once but the world had grown up, begun to understand itself better. History was there to inform the present but never dictate it. This collection of tall buildings and teeming apartments stood as a monument to a persecution that belonged to different, more primitive times. Venice, freed from Austrian rule and part of a new, energetic, ambitious nation, had learned its lesson.

Until the late Thirties it never occurred to Diamante that the bad old days might return. Then Mussolini began to find it convenient to mimic Hitler's prejudices, to bring the salute and the jackboot to the fore of national life. Along came the Racial Laws of 1938, but even then life was harsh, not unbearable. The punishment for being Jewish was discrimination, not yet outright persecution. It was only after the dictator's fall and his ascent to a puppet throne, the strings pulled from Berlin, that the truth began to dawn. The old evil was rising, perhaps to become something more harsh and cruel than anything the Jews of Venice and elsewhere had encountered before.

In this new northern republic of Italy he and his kind were no longer simply to be shunned. They were to be the targets of a virulent form of hatred where logic and plain humanity had no place. As a medical man he always looked for analogies. The one that came to him was that these were all symptoms of a pathological illness that came and went. A pestilence that men hoped science would someday cure, like polio or malaria. Though no one would know if the treatment had truly worked and banished the disease forever, or whether it might return one day, different, changed, more resilient to the treatments and potions than before. There was a depressing thought. Even when Hitler was defeated – and he would be – perhaps the conditions that created him and his kind in the first place were part of the genetic make-up of humanity. A propensity for barbarism that was a flaw in the blood, one that might hide for decades, centuries even, but never be annihilated.

Diamante picked up the folder marked in his spiky doctor's handwriting 'Qehillà'. Most of the names he'd had on file for weeks. There were now nearly three hundred there, women, children, men, all with addresses, occupations, ages. Some he'd left off deliberately hoping that might save them, or provide the chance to escape. Though lately he'd come to think this was wishful thinking. If they were still in Venice now there was no opportunity to vanish. The prison doors were slamming shut. In spite of the optimism of his good Christian friend Filippo Garzone, he'd no idea if or when they might open again, and who would be left to emerge from the ruins once that occurred.

He wished he could write the priest a letter. There was so much to say. An apology that they would not enjoy another leisurely coffee in Rosa Salva. Thanks for their long, interesting and rewarding friendship. A regret that they would never again visit La Fenice for the opera, not that he believed the priest was a fan. He simply enjoyed the company and to indulge a friend. Then, inevitably, shame on Diamante's part that he'd gone along with the Crucchi at all, agreeing under pressure to be president of the qehillà after the rabbi who'd held the position had been forced out. Finally, some expression, however faint, of hope that one day a new and optimistic light might dawn over Italy, with it the kind of freedom and intellectual honesty he'd foolishly taken for granted.

The trouble was he felt certain the Germans would surely find any such message and pounce on the quiet, decent Catholic hidden away in his vast and empty basilica on San Pietro, praying for the day the Republic of Salò might fall. Diamante had, in his own mind at least, been careful not to incriminate any of those around him. Though if the Nazis and their torturers locked him in a room and began to work with their needles and pincers and all their devilish cruelties he could not, he knew, guarantee that silence would continue.

What man could? Filippo Garzone? He was unsure and there were those two fugitive partisans from Turin to consider, along with the young Paolo Uccello, one more innocent enmeshed in the schemes of others, perhaps against his will, trapped by a single outburst as he watched the body of a murdered woman dragged from the cold lagoon.

Of all the reasons to take the course he planned, the idea he might betray those around him was uppermost in his mind.

Aldo Diamante smiled as his finger ran down the names on the pages, families, children, mothers he knew and had treated over the years in Giovanni e Paolo. Now he couldn't set foot past its glorious, historic doors, once the entrance to the religious society known as a scuola that worshipped next to the basilica of the same name. At least, as he'd told everyone repeatedly, he'd worked in the most beautiful hospital in the world. Not many men could say that. Nor any Jew perhaps for many years to come.

He went to the fireplace and, one by one, placed the sheets of the qehillà list on the flames, watched them shrivel, turn dark, then, as he poked the ashes, vanish up the chimney where they'd disappear into the dense winter fog.

It took longer than he thought. There was a community in these pages, alive, vibrant, full of laughter and generosity, as deserving of life as any other. He placed each sheet on the burning logs and watched it blacken and fold in the flames. A part of him wished he'd paid some attention to the rabbis. They surely had words to say for a desperate time like this. But prayer was never the Diamante way, even now.

The last piece of paper had only five names on it, a happy, middle-class family on the Lido, not far from the Grand Hôtel des Bains where a German author, much admired, once wrote a novella called *Der Tod in Venedig*. Death in Venice. Diamante had read it as a student and found the story quite depressing. No one, he believed, should die of cholera in the twentieth century.

That, at least, he found amusing. It was the fond thought of a young man, naive, fired by the daydream that the world might be made a better place, if only one discovered the means, the rules, the treatments and the procedures. If only science and logic replaced superstition and ignorance.

When the final sooty flake of paper had disappeared up the chimney Diamante shuffled to the desk, picked up his old leather medical bag and sat with it on his lap next to the busy, licking flames. He'd contacts still at the hospital, brave nurses and doctors who provided him with the means – drugs, medical instruments – to carry on his work in the ghetto, with Jewish patients alone.

A supply of morphine was essential, naturally.

He took out his favourite syringe, one he'd owned for a decade or more, made in Vienna, the glass clear and well-marked, the needle as sharp as the day he'd bought it.

Out of habit he picked up the bottle of bleach and water he always used to disinfect the thing before he used it.

He was still shaking his head at that last pointless act as he dragged his favourite armchair across the room until it faced his two most beloved belongings, the photograph of himself with Natalia on a gondola close to Vivaldi's old church, La Pietà, taken forty or so years before. And the portrait of his parents, the twelve-year-old Aldo standing between them, a stethoscope in his hands, a future already decided.

There'd been so much love over the years. In spite of everything, Mussolini, the Germans, he felt he'd been lucky.

So many people to remember too, all the many shades of humanity a curious city like Venice had to offer.

He reached out and pulled the photo album from the shelf by the fire.

Aldo Diamante was smiling at all those familiar faces when finally he found the vein.

PART FOUR

For once my father was there at the table when I came down to breakfast. It was nearly nine, early for me when there was no school, late for him. He looked up from his coffee and a plate filled with the crumbs of a cornetto from his favourite place, Tonello.

'When do you go back to class, Nico?'

'I think . . . Monday. Sorry about all this, Dad.'

'Not me you need to say sorry to, is it? The poor kid you beat up.'

'I didn't beat him up. That was Scamozzi. I know I should have tried to stop him. It won't happen again.'

He scowled.

'Scamozzi. I can't believe you hang around with scum like that. You know his family were Fascists during the war?' He grimaced, as if a bad memory had returned. 'Given half the chance they'd go that way again.'

'Someone said we were Fascists once.'

His face lit up with fury and that was rare.

'Who said that?'

'Some kid. I don't remember. Not Grandpa. His father.'

'Tell them not to be so stupid.'

'What did we do?'

'I wasn't even born. Why ask me?'

'I know. But—'

'We survived. That's enough, isn't it? Plenty didn't.'

I tried the line about writing a school project and explained I'd wanted to talk to Chiara about what happened back then but she wasn't interested. He listened, eyes wide, clearly amazed I was even considering such a thing. When I stuttered to a halt he asked, 'Why on earth would you want to do that?'

'I thought it might be interesting.'

'No one wants to talk about it.'

'That's why I thought it might be interesting.'

Then came the short lecture. Italy had swallowed the lies of the tyrant Mussolini. Il Duce had become the toy of Hitler. The country was divided and stayed like that in a way long after the war was over while different political factions fought for control.

'When I was your age people were thinking maybe the Russians would come and we'd go commie. We had the Years of Lead and terrorism, idiots on both sides, bombs in the street. That's all over, thank goodness. People don't want to talk about the past. What's the point? It's nearly a new century, for pity's sake.'

'Don't we learn? Isn't that what history's for?'

'Not that history. You don't learn anything from insanity. Now . . .' He got up from the table and checked his watch. 'We're both going to visit your grandfather. I've got a plane to catch afterwards. Won't be back for a few days. Don't get into trouble.'

This time it wasn't a girlfriend but a meeting in London. Something to do with banks. I'd been planning on going round to the camera shop to see if my films were back from the day before. It seemed that would have to wait. All the same when we arrived at the hospital he wanted to talk to Nonno Paolo on his own for a while.

I sat outside the room staring at the lagoon and the walls of San Michele, unable to stop myself wondering how long it would be before we were both seated on a black funeral boat headed out there, a coffin inside covered in wreaths.

They were together for a good forty minutes. I could see them through the glass, talking, animated too. Perhaps it was an argument. Then Dad got up and walked out of the room and said it was my turn.

'That's your future settled anyway,' he added.

'What's going on? I don't . . .'

I couldn't say anything else. He'd closed his eyes and the pain there was so obvious I didn't know what to do. Dad had kept his emotions hidden, from me anyway, all that summer. Now I realized how raw and agonizing it was for him too. I felt an idiot for not trying to see things from his perspective. That's being a kid, I guess. You just don't notice.

He blinked, was fighting back the tears. So I hugged him and he did cry then so I joined in.

'Nonno Paolo's been thinking things through,' he said when

he'd got back some of his composure. 'There are going to be some changes. It's one reason I've been away so much lately.'

He came out with the news. Grandpa had negotiated for the House of Uccello to be taken over by a giant multinational conglomerate. We were to move from being an independent upmarket producer of fine fabrics for those with money to burn to being a *brand*, our name on everything from sweatshirts to trainers, with franchised stores across the world.

'If others can do it I suppose . . .' Dad shrugged. 'Congratulations, Nico. We're about to enter the world of the idle rich.'

'We don't have to if you don't want. Surely?'

He shook his head.

'It's either that or leave me to run the company.' He nodded back at the window. 'He doesn't think I'm capable.'

'Nonno Paolo's sick. Maybe he's not thinking straight.'

He put down his case and stared right at me.

'It's his body that's failing. Not his mind.'

'I mean it, Dad. It doesn't need to happen now, does it?'

'Do you honestly believe this is my idea?' His voice was breaking. I'd never seen him this bad, not even when Mum left us. 'Do you think I'd be catching a plane this very day if he hadn't told me to?'

That had never occurred to me.

'Stay around for a few days, Dad. He needs you here. I do too.'

'I can't! He's been working on this for almost a year. It has to be done now. He says so. He's right. He usually is. I'm not the man he is. No one is. All the work he's put in could fall apart when he goes. He's already taken soundings. The shareholders want this. They don't think I can run the company the way he does. It has to be fixed. In a day or two I'll be back.'

A day or two.

'I don't want to be stuck here on my own anymore.'

He patted my shoulder, hugged me, kissed my cheek.

'Don't worry. You'll cope. The Uccello are good at that. We're going to sell our name. Put it on whatever others choose for us. And after that we're all secure for life.' He spotted the clock on the wall. 'Damn. I'm late. Keep him company, Nico. I have to see the lawyers in London.' He touched my shoulder and smiled. 'I'm sorry I've been distracted of late. Grandpa's illness. All this uncertainty about the company. When it's over we'll have more time for one another. I promise.'

'I'm sorry I just . . . sat back and watched.'

He looked surprised by that.

'You didn't. He told me you've been coming here every day. He's loved that. He says he's never felt closer to you. But . . .' Dad wagged a finger and I saw Nonno Paolo in him just then. 'Steer clear of that little bastard Scamozzi. All you'll get hanging round evil little creeps like that is trouble.'

When I walked into his room straight away he asked how Dad was. There was no easy answer. This wasn't just about the company. They were going through the final steps of saying goodbye to one another. I couldn't imagine what that was like. I still can't.

'Dad doesn't know about any of this, does he?' I said. 'What happened in the war? You? The partisans? Not a single thing?'

He waved a skinny grey hand. His face seemed bloodless. He seemed to be fading by the day.

'You won't understand yet but there was no point.'

'Didn't he ever ask?'

'No. Thank God. Don't you see, Nico? People forget the pain so quickly. We're built like that. If we weren't we'd never achieve a thing. When he was your age no one wanted to hear about the horrors their parents had lived through, any more than we wanted to trouble them with our past. The truth is war's almost boring when you live through it. The dark creeps up on you like a summer night. It's there before you realize. No guns, no explosions, to begin with. No one bleeds. It all seems rather unreal. And then . . .'

There was another coughing fit. When he finally got his breath back he said, 'I know I usually begin by asking you for questions. Not today. I want to know. What do you make of these people? These characters in this story?'

'I like them. Some of them.'

He said, eyes wide, 'Really?'

'Most. Even Alberti. He doesn't seem a bad man at heart.'

'Good and bad. Black and white. We all want to file people and events into categories. Doesn't matter we live in a world that's mostly a lot of different shades of grey.'

It had to be said.

'I don't like Artom.'

'Which one?'

'Vanni, of course. I warmed to Mika. She seems trouble but she's brave. She's up to something. It may be something bad. I don't know yet. But she can't stop herself. She seems . . . genuine.'

'But foolhardy too. Surely.'

'I think . . . I think foolhardy's a part of being brave. If you weren't you wouldn't dream of doing those things.'

His voice lowered a tone and he said, 'What's wrong with her brother?'

I guess I was blushing.

'You know what's wrong.'

'No, I don't. Tell me.'

I leaned forward and touched his bed clothes. They were so white, so pressed, so stiff they felt like a shroud, or how I imagined one.

'He's leading you on. He's using you. Your . . . feelings. Also he's sitting there doing nothing, hiding out from the Germans while his sister risks her neck.'

Nonno Paolo looked out of the window for a moment and I wondered if there was a tear in his eye.

'Without Vanni we'd never have met Salvatore Bruno's deadline. Who knows what would have happened then?'

'Perhaps. But just sitting there at a loom . . .'

'Standing, actually. He was wounded. The man could barely walk.'

I kept quiet.

'Go on,' he urged. 'Out with it.'

With folded arms and a deliberate pout I said, 'No. I know what you want me to ask and I won't. Sorry. The point I'm trying to make . . .'

He was laughing. At me. At himself.

'The point I'm trying to make is . . . will you stop that?'

He couldn't. There were tears in his eyes. A strange, unexpected, unwanted moment of hysteria gripped us both.

'Please . . . will you cut that out?' I begged.

'Sorry. Sorry . . . I don't get much amusement in here. And your face . . .'

'I thought it seemed obvious he was using you. That's all. You said Mika begged him to . . . to keep you sweet.' A thought struck me. 'Did he tell you that?'

'Ah.' He leaned back on his pillow, happy it seemed. 'You're asking yourself the obvious question. How could I know the content of conversations I was never party to?'

It hadn't really occurred to me until then. Perhaps because his story had begun to get to me.

'How can you?'

He sighed.

'I can't. I can still guess. And people tell you things. You remember them. Perhaps not precisely but that doesn't really matter. A story can be true even if some of the details are . . . inexact.'

'You mean made up?'

I got a severe glance for that.

'I thought I'd said this already. We write our own lives, Nico. If we don't the danger is we let someone else write them for us.'

'Did you imagine you loved him?'

There. I couldn't stop myself.

He took my hand and gave me a rather indulgent look at that moment. The sort a parent offers a child who's said something stupid.

'You do keep wanting to jump to the end of the story.'

'You can tell me that much, surely.'

He thought for a moment and I realized this was a question that perhaps had gone unanswered in his own head.

'The two of us were close. How much is our affair alone.'

'What?' I was offended. 'You're the one who's put all this in my head. Now you tell me it's none of my business!'

'Oh.' He squeezed my fingers and his eyes glazed over. 'There's a reason I write about these things, not speak of them. You'll come to appreciate it, I hope. These were unreal times and both of us lived quite unreal lives. Don't judge me . . . don't judge *us* by how things stand today.' He blinked and a sudden glassy tear rolled slowly down his wrinkled cheek. 'How I have loved watching my awkward, confused grandson grow over the years.' He wiped his face with the sleeve of his pyjama top, closed his eyes, looked so old, so tired, so weak. 'And now I make him miserable.'

'I really don't want you to die, Grandad . . . You're only seventy, seventy . . .'

He bent his head and gave me a familiar mock cross schoolteacher look.

'You don't know how old I am? I imagine you'll forget my birthday next.'

'No.' It came back. 'It's September the thirteenth. You're seventy-four.'

There was a little shrug of his skinny, withered shoulders.

'If you say so. I stopped counting long ago. The years . . . fade after a while. The whole damned business of growing old is a nuisance. So much left to do. To say. To tell. Look in the drawer.'

There were, I saw, only two envelopes left, sliding over each other.

'Read in order. It's important. Just the one.'

I didn't move.

'Dad says we're selling the company.'

'*Merging* the company. Putting it on a firm footing for the future. A man of my time always wants to pass on something better than he inherited.'

'You've done that ten times over, Grandad.'

'Not on my own. I had good people to help me. Like dear Chiara. I owe them all the chance of some continuity. Things can sometimes fall apart so fast. I've witnessed it. I'm sorry if your father's upset. He knows it's for the best.'

'You should have told him. About the Artoms. About the Giardini degli Angeli. I know it might have been embarrassing. What with Vanni and—'

'Not again, boy! This is your burden, no one else's. Now off with you. There's lots to read.'

TRAITORS

Saturday. The banners would be delivered to a man called Ugo Leone in the Hotel Gioconda. Some kind of partisan attack would occur that evening. Then, in a day or two, Vanni and Mika would vanish. This strange week, the most unsettling since he'd lost his parents, would come to some kind of close.

Paolo Uccello got up early that morning and walked the familiar path to the shop in via Garibaldi, bought bread and pastries, cheese and bottled water. The grocer looked terrified when he arrived but he didn't put money in the bag any more. The shelves were mostly empty. Everyone needed food but many were fishing for it in the lagoon or living off old stores of flour and pasta while growing yeast for bread out of the air in jars. Gabriele Gallo probably had more need of cash than him at that moment. And soon the commission would be delivered, with it the welcome fee for its completion. Then he'd spend money with the timid old shopkeeper for real.

'In a day or two,' Paolo said, 'I'll only need enough for one. I'll pay too. If you have a good Prosecco. I'd like to give a friend of mine a gift. She's call—'

'Don't tell me names,' Gallo interrupted. 'What kind of fool are you?'

'She's just a friend.'

'These people . . . they say they're patriots . . . they come and ask you these things and you say yes before you've even thought about it. Like that with you?'

He picked up the bag. The cornetti looked pale and underdone. He wasn't going to complain.

'I've been a fool,' the shopkeeper went on. 'Next time they come asking you say no. I'm going to. Don't care how hard they try. I got a daughter. Cripple. Can't walk. Can't do anything. A wife who can't cope on her own. If the Crucchi take me God knows what happens to them. You think they'll look after the two of them, these so-called patriots? If the Nazis shoot me?'

'I . . .' Paolo wished he'd never started the conversation. 'They're good people. I'm sure.'

'You're an infant,' Gallo snapped and stared at him with the coldest of expressions. 'What do you know?'

'Thanks.' Paolo lifted up the bag and tried to smile. 'I'm grateful.'

'You're as big a fool as me, boy,' the grocer told him, then picked up a fatty piece of ham, sniffed it and placed the meat on the slicer.

It was the smoke that drew them to the door of Diamante's block. Any number of three-hundred-year-old fireplaces ran to the chimneys on top of his ghetto building. But half the apartments were now empty – the owners interned, vanished, or in hiding. Of the rest a couple couldn't even afford fuel. The city firemen from the depot near Ca' Foscari went door to door, sniffing, scared the grey plume emerging from the top of the building might herald something worse than a simple flue where the soot had caught. The prospect of fire among the city's cramped, narrow houses, many of them half-timber, had terrified Venice for centuries. It was one reason the council demanded the truncated cone pots be used on roofs everywhere in the hope they'd disperse sparks more efficiently.

Ten minutes after they arrived, Bargato, the senior duty man, hammered on Diamante's locked door. No answer but there was a smell coming from inside, one every fireman recognized. He told them to break it down. Stumbling through, the men were met with a grey-black haze billowing around the room like the lagoon fog that had enshrouded it the night before. The source was obvious. A lively log fire set in a metal surround, feeding into what had to be a half-blocked chimney. Bargato had trained for this, years and years of practice. Two blasts from the chemical extinguishers and it was nothing but sizzling embers and the men could start to wave their hands around, trying to clear the air enough to take off their masks.

He went to the windows over the campo and threw them open. The wind caught and swirled the smoke around, sending it outside into the bright, chilly day.

Down in the square a woman stood holding the hands of two children, staring up at the window.

'Is the doctor in?' she cried and sounded desperate.

'Not now, signora,' he answered.

'I need to see him, sir.'

He took off his mask. Most of the men had too. His eyes stung from the smoke but he could breathe.

'I said . . . not now.'

There was a commotion behind him and someone swore.

Bargato left the window and went to look. They were all Venetians. Working for the fire service was a good job. Posts handed down from generation to generation, reliable, well-paid. Some of the time they didn't even get to smell smoke but dealt with sunken boats or elderly people too sick to get out of their attic homes.

The rest of the team had gathered at the far end of the room, grouped around what looked like a large armchair set beneath a painting that covered most of the wall. He walked over and found himself for a moment caught by the people depicted on the canvas, so well they might have been alive even through a thin film of soot. At the back stood a distinguished man in his fifties or sixties, silver hair, silver beard. He wore a severe dark suit, a watch chain in his waistcoat and had his left arm around the shoulders of a shorter woman, dark-haired, younger, smiling, in a rich purple velvet dress. Between them, their hands on his shoulders, was a young and very serious-looking boy of twelve or thirteen, eyes wide and intelligent, staring straight out of the painting, in his hands a stethoscope.

The oldest man in the fire department, Moro, a part-timer from Giudecca, was weeping.

'Cut that out,' Bargato ordered.

'Diamante,' Moro cried, pointing at the picture. 'His old man. His mother. The boy. He was always going to be a doctor. I remember him coming to school with his little medical bag and listening to our chests back when I was little. When the Jews could go to the same class as us. Twenty years later he was treating my little Marta when she had the scarlet fever. Maybe saved her life.' Moro took one step forward and pointed at the child in the painting. 'He always looked like he was examining you. Aldo. Poor Aldo.'

He reached out and touched something Bargato hadn't noticed. The sight of it made him jump back and, for a moment, he thought he might throw up. His fingers had found the dry and sooty hair of a man seated in the winged armchair. It must have been dragged in front of the picture. No one would sit with their face up to the wall like that. He didn't seem to be looking at the painting, more at an old photograph of a young man and a pretty woman posing by a gondola.

Aldo Diamante had died in his customary pinstripe suit, head back, mouth open, eyes too. He looked like people did when they were asphyxiated by fire but untouched by the flames. A layer of grey soot sat on his narrow, intelligent face which seemed fixed in an expression of surprise. Something was in the dead man's lap. Bargato reached down and took it from his stiff fingers. A photo album. Life in the ghetto from the looks of it. Decades and decades. Photos of the hospital too, pretty nurses, doctors, all lined up in white uniforms, standing by the waterfront on the Fondamente Nove, ambulance boats in the background, a large cross in a white circle on each.

'Dead Jew,' one of the men grunted. 'That didn't happen by accident. Important Jew too. Someone had better tell the Crucchi.' He laughed and said, 'Know a funny fact my dad once told me?'

'Show some respect,' Moro spat at him.

'Dead Jews don't get no respect. My old man said in the old days they used to take them out in coffins same way as us. Out by the canal at San Pietro. Locals there . . . if they knew it was a Jew they'd stand on the bridge and spit as the boat went past.' He looked down at the stiff corpse in the chair and chuckled. 'He reckoned the *ebrei* had to pay for their own little canal round the Arsenale just so's they could get their dead out without us gobbing on them. Maybe this bloke—'

Moro felled the man with a single blow and left him sprawling on the floor.

'Enough of that,' Bargato barked. 'We make this place safe. I'll call them. There's got to be a telephone here.'

'He's a Jew, boss,' someone said. 'They took their phones away, didn't they?'

He left them there and went outside.

The woman was still out in the campo with her kids. Bargato told her to make herself scarce and quick. Soon there'd be Germans and soldiers. She didn't move.

'The doctor . . .'

'The doctor's dead, love. He won't be helping you now.'

She started to cry. The kids, two boys, maybe six and ten, looked embarrassed.

'Please,' he begged. 'I've got to bring them in.'

The nearest working telephone he could find was in a cafe by the Cannaregio canal.

The German he got put through to was called Sachs. He didn't sound happy at all.

Forty minutes later they were there, Alberti, head hurting from the worst hangover in ages, lurking in the shadows, trying to still the voices in his head.

He'd liked Aldo Diamante even if the old Jew seemed to loathe him in return. The man had that stolid Venetian determination about him that came from growing up in a city where everyone lived cheek to jowl, fought for work, battled against the hard lagoon, freezing in winter, steamy in summer. Waiter or vaporetto hand, accountant or cook, the men and women of Venice knew they lived apart from terraferma and were proud of that fact, set on defending it. A quiet, inner stubbornness was the mark of them all and Diamante wore that like a badge.

Then the Fascists came along and, for a while, lulled people into thinking they were just another bunch of politicians. Slowly, bit by bit, life turned harder. Finally, and perhaps it was inevitable because this was the course unconsciously they'd chosen, the city fell under the thumb of Hitler. So Venice was back to being occupied by foreigners, Austrians and Germans. Diamante, being an intelligent, observant man, must have understood what was happening all along, watched, planned, did his best to think matters through. Alberti, a paid hand for the state, whatever the state might be, was in no such position. His marriage had disintegrated, his kid hated being the son of a turncoat cop. His job kept shifting ever further from simple police work to that of a political enforcer. The change was so subtle he'd never really noticed until the Germans arrived that September and, after checking out his loyalty, Oberg had offered him a room in the Gioconda. One way, perhaps, to keep alive even if it didn't help him sleep at night.

The sullen German was there watching as Sander and Sachs went through Diamante's apartment, pulling out drawers, scattering the contents everywhere. Clothes mostly, more photo albums, some musical documents which seemed to be *libretti* for operas. A couple of uniform Nazi grunts lurked by the door, rifles over their shoulders, complaining about the smell of smoke.

And Salvatore Bruno, the slick-dressed Jew from Turin strode around the room, gazing at the pictures on the wall, stepping daintily about the corpse still slumped in a chair in front of the family portrait.

Alberti had the cop's habit of judging people very quickly. Bruno wore a smart, well-pressed suit beneath a dark-blue wool coat. His face was always animated, narrow, bloodless, with a toothbrush moustache that wasn't far off that of Hitler's though paler in colour and far from full. The rest was shaved so perfectly he must have taken great care himself, or risked his neck with a barber – something Alberti himself would never dream of doing. And then his shoes. They were always a sign, Alberti thought. A working man chose something practical, hard-wearing and rarely polished. Bruno had on black brogues, so shiny they glittered.

Most of all though, Alberti believed he found the man when he looked in his eyes. They were anxious, forever flicking round the room for encouragement or a sign of suspicion. Then, when he met the gaze of another, glancing quickly away.

Salvatore Bruno wished the Crucchi to believe him a convert, a Jew who'd seen the light about the perverse and wicked nature of his tribe. But he wasn't an idiot. He surely knew that a Jew was a Jew and when his usefulness expired, as it must one day, there'd be a reckoning. In that respect the two of them were not so dissimilar. Alberti regarded the inevitability of that fate with a degree of acceptance and no small amount of innate cunning. The Jew from Turin was clearly terrified beneath the shaky outward portrayal of certainty and confidence in the Nazis and the Black Brigades around him. He knew there was no possibility of escape.

'There,' Bruno said in a hurt, weak voice. 'There's your list, Oberg.'

He was at the fireplace, toe of his shiny brogue poking through the ashes that lay in front of the smouldering logs.

Alberti had seen the remains of burned paper the moment he walked in but never bothered to mention them. It was obvious what had happened. They could find out for themselves.

'You mean he burnt it?' the German asked. 'After going to all that trouble to put those names together? Alberti!'

He joined them and looked down at the blackened flecks of paper on the hearth.

'Did you have any idea this was in his head? When you spoke to him?'

Sachs and Sander were watching avidly, waiting for him to make a mistake.

'None at all. I thought he was going to bring them to us today, just like he said. Though if I may speak freely . . .'

'Do so.'

He nodded at Bruno.

'This fellow pushed him pretty hard. Diamante was a man of substance here. He ran the hospital. The whole city looked up to him. You treated him like he was one more craven Jew so frightened he'd bend over and show you his Hebrew arse. Well . . .' He cast a glance at the figure slumped in the chair in front of the painting. Someone ought to put a sheet over the man at least but it didn't look as if it was going to happen. 'How wrong can you get?'

'We can still . . . we can still round up p-plenty,' Bruno stuttered. 'I can do it. I can sniff Jews out anywhere.'

Sachs and Sander had started rootling through the drawers of Diamante's desk. One of them had found a fob watch, old, battered, probably worthless, and was dangling it in the light from the window. The place would be plundered before the morning was out. Not that anyone was going to want the painting of the Diamante family in their prime.

'We can start with the old people's home across the way,' Bruno added, desperate to offer something.

'There's only a handful left there,' Alberti said. 'Most got cleared out to the infirmary on the Lido weeks ago.'

'It won't be empty,' the man from Turin insisted. 'They're Jews. They're not going to turn down a free bed and food. If—'

'I've got better things to do than this,' Oberg interrupted. 'Enjoy the reception this evening, Signor Bruno.'

The uniforms had got in on the act of looking for something to steal. One of them was going through Diamante's old black leather medical bag, holding up instruments and bottles, asking his mate what they were.

Alberti couldn't take any more.

'If you want me to check the home across the way, boss . . .'

'No need,' Oberg replied.

'They'll want to bury the old man today if they can. Jews always do it quick. If you let them get on with it they'll be too busy to worry about us.'

Oberg nodded at the door and told him to wait outside.

He was glad to get out of the smoky stale air of Diamante's apartment. In the chilly sunlight of the campo people were watching from doorways. Furtive, hidden, scared. They knew Diamante's death was the start of something, not the end of it.

Across the square a familiar figure in black was shuffling out of the *sotoportego* that led into the ghetto from the east. There was a priest's zucchetto cap on his head as he bent into the winter wind. Alberti took one look, then hurried over to stop him.

'Garzone. *Garzone*.' He grabbed hold of him in the shadows before the man could go further. 'What the hell are you doing here?'

The priest glared at him.

'Am I to seek the permission before I can walk around my own city now?'

'I ask this for your own sake. Things are happening.'

'I was due to meet my friend Diamante. He didn't show. I'm worried. So I came to see—'

'Too late. He's dead.'

Garzone's mouth fell open and his hand went to his priest's cap.

'I don't believe it.'

'The firemen found him in his apartment, full of smoke, this morning. There's a syringe on the floor—'

The man in black's face flushed and he shook his fist. Alberti looked and wondered if he'd ever done that before.

'No. You bastards killed him. I've known Aldo Diamante nearly twenty years. He'd never do such a thing.'

Alberti groaned. This was going to be hard.

'He was supposed to deliver a list. The names of all the Jews.' Something flickered in Garzone's eyes and Alberti thought, *I hope the Crucchi never take this fool in because he'd blab everything in an instant.* 'But then, I see, you knew that. He burned the list he'd been preparing, then took some kind of overdose. I imagine he wanted to make sure they couldn't take him into Ca' Loretti, to that little room of theirs and . . .'

There was no need to say more.

'Christ.' Garzone crossed himself and slumped back against the stained brick wall of the underground passage that led back to the bridge, to the city beyond, to some kind of safety. 'Why?'

'I imagine he saw no other way out.'

He took hold of the man and turned him round, pushed him back into the deeper shadows.

Garzone dug in his heels and glared at him. There were tears in his eyes.

'I just lost a dear friend because of crooks like you. I want to see him. I want to mourn when they bury him.'

'No, you don't. You don't want to be around this place at all. It only gets worse from now on. If you know any Jews out there tell them to hide—'

'Hide where, Alberti? This is where they live. All that surrounds us is sea and sky.'

'Go, you fool! Leave while you can.'

Back in the campo the uniforms had emerged from the apartment. They were carrying bags and cases, things they'd stolen. Diamante's corpse they'd leave to the Jews. That, to them, was nothing.

'I pity you,' Garzone said, tears clear and deep in his eyes, of anger as much as grief, Alberti felt sure. 'I pity you and one day I must find it in my heart to forgive you too.'

He turned then and walked back towards the end of the sotoportego. A patch of brightness beyond the realm of the Jews. Alberti watched him cross the bridge, waited to make sure he didn't turn back.

A minute he stayed there. By the time he returned to the campo the soldiers were in the old people's home on the far side of the square. A couple of them were dragging out a sick-looking man in a wheelchair.

In the window of an apartment opposite a young lad, thirteen, maybe a year or two more, around the age of his own son, was staring in his direction.

The kid raised a toy gun and fired an imaginary bullet straight across the square.

'You before me, sonny,' Alberti muttered as he strode over to join the troops. 'You before me.'

* * *

By the time Paolo Uccello got back to the Giardini degli Angeli, Chiara and Vanni were hard at work. The basic work on the commission would be as good as done before midday. The final task of cutting and finishing them he'd leave to Chiara. But by one at the latest they'd be ready.

Now that the banners were real, not punch holes on cards or drawings on paper, it was easier to see them for what they were: rampant lions, furious gaping mouths, militaristic boasts. Paolo had guessed all along these were for the Nazis or the Fascists. Why else would they be delivered to Ca' Loretti? Now they were something he could look at closely and touch he despised the things and wished his father had never sought the job, however much they'd needed it. Once you took their money they believed you were theirs. Perhaps, Paolo thought, they were right.

The day was bright for now, the sky with the wash of winter blue, the horizon smeared with the promise of fog. Chiara had baked a simple lemon cake to celebrate. Around ten they took a short break. Mika came and joined them as they ate outside the conservatory in the winter sun, away from the breeze, feeling the warmth on their faces.

This felt like the lull before the storm, but it was welcome in any case. The last few days had been anxious, full of doubts and thoughts he hadn't wanted to entertain. About the future. About who he was and how he felt when Vanni was around. Love and sex were never discussed while his parents were there. It was as if matters like that occurred out of nowhere, like the weather, and were accepted much the same. He assumed the day would come when he'd marry, have children, introduce them into the workings of the Uccello family of weavers. Though how that might happen, and whether it was something he really wanted, he'd never much considered. Until that week. Now he knew he didn't see any of it in his future at all. He was different and they'd known all along.

Vanni and Mika made small talk, chatting about their childhood in Turin. It seemed a very different kind of upbringing to the sort most received in Venice: liberal, carefree, outgoing. Their father had taken them to Paris once, a city that enchanted them. Paolo had only once travelled across the bridge to terraferma, on the train to Verona as part of a school trip. The city on the water was a world in itself, a universe in some way. There never was the need to look elsewhere, except for work and money and that was always left to his parents. While for Chiara, who'd grown up in the island village of Burano, the bustle and noise of Venice was, she said, quite enough. She'd never set foot outside the lagoon in her life, nor wanted to.

As they packed away the food and the Artoms returned to the house Chiara took him to one side.

'People are asking questions, Paolo.'

Chiara didn't look scared. It was hard even to imagine that. But she did seem puzzled.

'What people?'

'Well. One anyway. An ignorant old bastard I take food to for the church. He was one of Il Duce's foot soldiers back before the war. Crippled now. Seems to think he can fight his corner from bed. Asking around. Poking his nose in.'

'What did he say?'

She stared straight at him.

'That the Crucchi and the police are out looking for two young Jewish terrorists hiding out somewhere. Brother and sister. The man's been hurt in the leg. They're going to shoot them and anyone who hides them.'

'Oh . . .'

She waited. He got up and went to his loom, the one at the far end.

Chiara wandered over.

'When I get paid this afternoon,' Paolo said, checking the tautness of the thread. 'I'll come straight round and give you half the money.'

'I'm an employee. I get a wage. Not half.'

'I'm the boss. What I say goes.'

She kept quiet and gave him the kind of look he used to get from his mother. One that said, Don't argue.

'Please,' he begged.

'I don't need your money. I've got family on Burano. They can feed me. You've got no one.'

'I want you to stay away from here. Go back home maybe. Be with your people.'

'You think you're going to be with him?'

No. He didn't. Mika and Vanni Artom were like the migrating birds who passed through the garden, headed north or south depending on the season. Perhaps they were unsure of their destination but they surely knew it was elsewhere.

'I doubt that. Chiara . . . I'm grateful for everything you've done. I don't need looking after anymore.'

'So you seem to think,' she said, checking over her own loom.

Then they went to work.

Soon the glasshouse rang to the familiar rhythm of the goldcrest's song.

Si-dah-si-dah-si-dah-sichi-si-piu.

Vanni had picked up the ways of the Jacquard loom faster than anyone Paolo had ever seen. By eleven the three banners were finished on the looms. Then Chiara took out her scissors and an eyeglass, told them to get out of her way while she set about checking each thread, cutting and mending as needed.

Mika came out with rough hacked local bread, cheese and ham, and placed it on the frail wooden table in the garden. He wondered why they were eating pork. But then he knew nothing of Jews, all the different kinds. Perhaps the two of them only thought of themselves as Jewish in terms of their oppression, not so much their identity. It was hard to tell and he didn't wish to ask.

Chiara picked up her panino and said, 'You make good food, young lady.'

'Thank you, signora. You're very kind.'

She smiled then, easily, freely and he saw a different person, the one Mika Artom would have been if it wasn't for war. Ordinary, happy, nothing special though perhaps that was a kind of special in itself. A young woman looking towards the future with bright and optimistic eyes. A job in a hospital. Or a country doctor going on her rounds in a little Fiat car. Somehow he knew that was never going to happen. She probably did too.

'Have you finished?' Mika asked. 'The three of you? Is it done?'

Chiara went back into the house and returned carrying three gilt boxes from the cellar. The words 'Uccello, Fine Weavers, Venice' were stencilled in silver on the top. When she removed the lids and the wrapping they could see the banners, red and gold, swaddled in tissue and folded very precisely.

'They're beautiful,' Vanni observed and no one said a word as Chiara folded them back into their paper wrapping.

'They're for a Fascist,' she said as she replaced the lids. 'I know you're taking them to Ca' Loretti, Paolo. Who else could it be for?'

It was, he said as calmly as he could, a commission. One his parents had died winning. Not that there was any relevance to that. It was only a way of trying to shut her up.

'Things,' said Mika, patting the lid of the nearest, 'may be beautiful and ugly at the same time. Sometimes the beauty lies in what they are and sometimes the ugliness in who owns them. Half the art in Italy was bought by the purses of monsters and tyrants.' She tapped the box. 'I suppose we need to learn to appreciate the object, not the owner.'

'I don't like it,' Paolo said. 'I don't like the way it looks. The way it . . . crows. Like them. Like we're under their thumb.'

'But we are,' Chiara said. 'Best not forget it.' She checked her watch. 'If you've finished with me I need to go. Mouths to feed. Prayers to say.'

Mika came over and kissed her on the cheek. Chiara smiled at her and said, 'I wish we'd met in different times. Happier ones. I never talked to anyone from Turin before. I bet you've got more stories—'

'Plenty,' Vanni replied as his sister rushed inside for some reason.

They waited. She emerged with the grappa bottle and four small glasses and poured a toast on the tabletop next to the cardboard boxes for the banners.

'To us,' she said, beaming. 'All of us. To meeting here after the war's over. When the Germans are gone. When Italy's a better place and all of us can just . . . live our lives.'

'To us,' Chiara repeated, then tipped hers back in one go. People from Burano didn't like to linger.

No one could think of a thing to say after that.

Two o'clock in Ca' Loretti. Gulls cawed and clamoured beyond the windows but there was no sound from the downstairs interrogation cells, no one in the small garden where the paving stones so often ran with blood and the red-brick wall bore innumerable bullet marks from executions. Business at the hub of the intelligence and security forces who held the reins of Venice was at a halt.

This was supposed to be the great day. The moment the heads

of German units across the north got together with the leading lights of the Black Brigades and marked the coming capture of every last Jew in Venice. The final sign that the once-independent republic was truly a part of Hitler's empire, a new colony of Berlin stretching from the Adriatic to the Ligurian and, in the occupied north, the Tyrrhenian seas. That, Alberti believed, was the real point of the glittering reception planned for the ballroom of the Gioconda that evening. Every last semblance of resistance, of identity, would be surrendered there. The uneasy atmosphere that had gripped the city ever since the Crucchi took control the previous September would give way to total submission. The hotels and ballrooms, the theatres and opera house, the bordellos and the beach resorts along the Lido, now belonged to the Nazis. If Hitler had his way they always would, part of a German empire that embraced the whole of Europe.

A small chorus had been press-ganged from the local choirs to sing Fascist anthems, German, Italian, Venetian. From what the kitchen staff of the Gioconda said the food would be grander, richer than anything even the wealthiest of Venetians had seen for years. Some of it, he was told, came in the self-same goods wagons from France via Milan that would be used for transporting captured Jews back to the camps in the north.

Yet Diamante's suicide had cast a shadow over the day, as the old doctor had surely wanted. It was easy enough rounding up Jews who still chose to live in the ghetto. The rest were scattered throughout the city and the Lido, often anonymous, invisible among their gentile neighbours. News of the coming declaration from Salò was leaking out all over the north. Some areas had begun the round-up already. In Ferrara a convoy of wagons, packed to the gills with families seized overnight, was on its way to Milan. Venice, as always, seemed slow to catch up. A mere seventeen pensioners had been seized from the old people's home in the ghetto that morning, then herded into a warehouse near the station. All their papers, money and possessions went into the hands of the Black Brigades, supposedly for examination and storage, but still it seemed small beer.

Sachs and Sander marched round angrily cursing Jews, Venetians, foreigners everywhere, swearing, when Oberg was out of the room, that they wished they'd been posted somewhere that had a backbone, not the delicate, old whore of the Adriatic that deemed itself too precious and too proud to face the task in hand. This was all bluster, naturally. Neither of them had shone when in the field, which was precisely why they'd been dispatched to the less-demanding role of security in Venice.

Alberti watched all this in silence. On the way back from Diamante's he'd stopped by the Marino bar and got a couple of shots of grappa from Beppe, the terrified kid behind the counter. A part of him wanted to stay half-drunk most of the time. It felt better that way. Unlike some, he was a man that booze made less talkative, more thoughtful. More inclined to watch and wait to see what the Crucchi and their creatures would do next.

Oberg marched back in carrying a folder of papers. Sachs and Sander fell silent. Their courage didn't extend to arguing with the boss. Salvatore Bruno followed, a peacock, all false smiles and camaraderie.

'The terrorists from Turin. The Artoms,' Oberg said, stopping by Alberti's desk. 'The ones you've been hunting with no success.'

'Sir.'

'Have you received any information to indicate they're here?'

'None whatsoever.' He was expecting this interrogation so he pulled out a list of all the calls he'd made, the informants he'd threatened. 'I'm out of options. Sorry.'

'Not very good, are you?' Bruno noted with a sarcastic grin.

Watch your tongue, Alberti thought to himself.

'I've worked this city as a cop for fifteen years, friend. One thing I've learned in all that time is that if Venice wants to hide something it's damned good at it. Back when we ran this place on our own maybe I could have got people to talk. Now . . . it's not so easy.'

'Excuses,' Bruno muttered.

'No. Realities. Maybe they're not even here. There are a lot of other places to hide. Treviso. The marshes. In San Donà pretty much half the town's turned partisan from what I hear. The Artoms are Jews. You're the hunter. You go find them.'

'Perhaps I will,' Bruno said with a smile.

Alberti realized he didn't simply dislike this man. He hated him. There was something cruel and sinister about him, a darkness that could only come from fear.

'Sir,' he said, looking at Oberg, puzzled. Something had gone on here, something he didn't know about. 'Give me my orders.

Tell me what you want me to do. I can keep on asking but I'm beating up all the same people. Unless someone else has leads we can work on . . .' He shrugged. 'We're kind of stuck. I don't think any of those ancients we pulled out of the home this morning have got any tales to tell.'

'Do you have any idea who we're hosting here tonight?' Oberg asked.

'No.' It was a stupid question. 'No one's told me. It's all been cooked up above my head. I'm not psychic. This job would be a sight easier if I was.'

And there, he thought, was the grappa rising. Too fast, too snappy, without a second thought.

'Pretty much every senior officer, German and Italian, from the Veneto will be in the Gioconda tonight,' Oberg went on. 'We will have a ceremony.' He nodded at Bruno. 'A bond will be sealed. Between you. Between us. Between our helpful friend here.'

'Good,' Alberti said with a nod. 'Do you believe they know? The partisans?'

Oberg didn't take his eyes off him when he asked, 'What do you think?'

'I think you should assume so. You can't bring in all this . . . stuff. The food. The singers. The staff who are going to work that room. You can't do it without people working out something big's going on. Venice knows a lot about throwing parties. Fair bit about gate-crashing them too.' He folded his arms and leaned on the desk. 'If you want me to take a look at the security . . .'

Sander laughed at that and so, on cue, did Sachs.

Salvatore Bruno loomed over him, smirking in his sharp suit.

'Is there something I should know?' Alberti asked.

'No.' The Jew tapped his shoulder. 'It's taken care of.' He sniffed very visibly. 'Don't hit the booze too hard, pal. You need a clear straight head. We've a memorable night to come.'

Time to leave for the Gioconda. Vanni had insisted he change clothes, from his rough work jacket and old trousers into a suit he picked for Paolo from the wardrobe. Dark, a little tight now, made by a tailor in San Marco two years before. The last time he'd worn it was for his parents' funeral in Mestre. He stood stiff and a little embarrassed as Vanni chose a shirt, went into the kitchen to iron it, then a silk tie from his father's collection.

'When you collect money you must be smart,' Vanni said, examining him up close as he put the tie on. 'Especially with Fascists. They like their clothes. They like their uniforms.'

'It's just money.'

'Money's good, friend. Money's something we all need.'

'You look the part,' Mika said from the door. 'How about me?'

She was back in the scarlet dress, hair perfect, powder on her face, red lipstick again. From his mother's bedside drawer she said.

'Very nice,' her brother said. 'And—'

He stopped. There was a bell attached to the distant bridge door by a pulley on a nearby tree. Now it was ringing.

'We'll make ourselves scarce,' Vanni said. 'Come on.'

He grabbed his sister's hand, moved aside the carpet, opened the trap door, then the two of them raced down the steps. Paolo covered it after them. It was a good hiding place, as the priest Garzone had spotted. So few people in Venice had cellars. The city was built on mud and timber.

The bell sounded again.

'Coming,' Paolo yelled across the garden, then got his coat and the three gilt cardboard boxes.

Standing in front of the locked door, puzzled, a little frightened, Paolo wondered, Maybe he should have carried a gun, not cardboard and rich velvet. One of the weapons that was still in the bag in his parents' old bedroom.

It couldn't be that hard to use one. Vanni would show him. Mika certainly. But there wasn't time and as he stood on the wooden steps and asked who was there he realized there was no need either.

'Paolo, Paolo. It's me. Father Filippo.' The priest sounded breathless and desperate. 'For pity's sake let me in. I . . . I'm on my own. It's safe.'

He hammered on the door again. Paolo opened it.

Filippo Garzone was one of the most placid men he'd ever met but at that moment he looked quite distraught.

'We need to speak. It's vital—'

'I have to go.' It was almost three thirty. He'd walk to the Gioconda. It would take a while. 'I have to see the Germans.'

Garzone took off his priest's cap and ruffled his grey hair. 'We'll talk along the way.'

It was getting dark already. Another thin winter mist had begun to roll in wisps along the street that led back into Castello proper. As always there were gulls, and from somewhere the sound of a boat engine, muffled by the weather, echoing off the terraces that wound down all the way to via Garibaldi. A sewage boat must have emptied a pozzo nero nearby. It was one of those rare moments when Venice stank of shit and piss.

The priest put a hand to his shoulder and stopped him at a corner by the lane back into the city.

'Aldo Diamante's dead,' he said, staring at his feet. 'My good friend killed himself last night.'

'Oh lord,' Paolo said and walked on down the lane, to think, to get away from the stench.

Garzone followed, took his arm, made him stop again.

'Listen to me, Paolo. I owe you an apology. I should never have involved you in these schemes.'

'It's done. I've no regrets.'

'Of course you haven't!' Garzone sounded angry for once, not himself at all. 'You're young. You can't imagine any of this will touch you.'

'I lost my parents, Father. I can imagine that very easily.'

'I'm sorry. I didn't mean . . .'

'You're upset. Go home. I've work to do. I must deliver—'

'He surely killed himself for fear of what he'd say if they took him in! You understand?'

Diamante seemed a brave and serious man. It was hard to imagine him breaking and Paolo said so.

'No one knows what they'd do,' the priest shot back. 'No one. Not him. Not me. Do . . . you . . . understand? You need to get that pair out of there. I thought Diamante would arrange it. They came through him. I've no idea how. Or through whom. I have no one to turn to, Paolo. No one. Do you appreciate what I'm saying? You have to get them out of there.'

'They'll leave of their own accord.'

He started walking again, mind whirring as Garzone kept up, his priest's robes flapping wildly like crow wings. It was hard to believe Diamante was gone. The man was a figurehead beyond the ghetto, someone half of Venice had come to know through his work in the hospital. Harder still to believe he could kill himself.

'I still don't understand why—'

'They're coming for them. The Jews. Then they come for the rest of us. Anyone who disobeys. Who says a wrong word, looks the wrong way. The worst times are ahead. *You must get them out of there.*'

'And after that?'

Garzone put a hand to his shoulder and stopped him so abruptly the golden boxes almost tumbled from his arms.

'I shouldn't say this. I wouldn't if it weren't important. After the Jews they will look for the gypsies. The communists.' He gazed straight into Paolo's face. 'The homosexuals. Anyone who's different. I've known you a while. I've watched you. I talked to your mother—'

'About what?'

'About . . . you. There's nothing to be ashamed of. Whatever people say. Some of my fellow clerics in the church too and they, of all people, should know better. God made us in his own image. Every last one of us.' He laughed, or tried to. 'The Vatican would throw me out of San Pietro if they heard that, even though a good number of the men there are made the same way.'

'I don't know what you mean.'

Garzone threw back his head and uttered the mildest of curses.

'I can see it, Paolo. If I can see it others can too. There's a reason you hide away behind your little army of stone angels and it's not just because your parents are gone. You know it too.' He reached out and touched Paolo Uccello's cheek. It might have been Vanni at that moment. 'Don't think you're a freak of nature. Or alone. I was young once. A student at the divinity school in Padua, before I was ordained. There was someone there. A young man from outside Vicenza. He was . . . not destined to be a priest. If I'd followed my own heart and stayed with him neither was I. So I made the choice. Though I didn't make it in ignorance of both the pleasure and the pain I left behind. You're not alone. However much it feels that way.'

'What happened to him?' Paolo asked. 'Your friend?'

'He was the son of a farmer. He married his neighbour's daughter and the last I heard they had eight children, a sprawling estate and made some of the best illicit grappa a man might ever taste.'

'He got married?'

'Happily. We're complex creatures, son. We reflect a complex world and, I don't doubt, a complex heaven when we get there. But this present state of affairs is run by those who would simplify things. You. Me. The places we know and love.' He came closer and his voice grew stern. 'They will simplify it by removing everything they fail to understand, everyone who doesn't fit their picture of how this world should be. You must do as I say. Get that pair safely out of there. Stay out of sight as much as you can. Use Chiara Vecchi as your window into the city outside. And wait.'

'You mean . . . like a coward?'

'The ranks of the martyrs are brimming already, son. You've no need to add another corpse to the pile.'

He didn't know what to say. Father Filippo had always been one for stories. He'd listened to a fair few himself back in the days when they first moved to their outpost by San Pietro and his parents went to church for a while to try, in vain it turned out, to become a part of the community there. It was possible this was one more parable to add to the list, a fable meant to reassure, not to be taken literally. Though perhaps, now he thought about it, he was one of the reasons they'd retreated behind the walls of their little fortress home. There'd been a silence in the Uccello family for years, one none of them wished to mention.

I talked to your mother . . .

'You did as I asked when you took those two in. Do as I beg you now, please. See them gone, then hide till the day it's safe to come out.'

'When will that be, then? When?'

It was a cruel question, an unnecessary and unanswerable one.

'I fear I made you grow up, young man,' the priest said in a sad and wavering voice. 'I fear I dragged you into a world for which you're not ready.'

Paolo tapped the cardboard boxes.

'I have business to transact, Father. Goods to deliver. Thank you for your thoughts. Good day.'

A line of German soldiers was checking everyone going into the Gioconda. The name of Uccello was on a list, though it was his father's, so it took a long explanation to a hatchet-faced officer before he was allowed past, and that only after they'd rifled through the cardboard boxes and patted him down.

The unsmiling receptionist behind the front desk looked at him and shook his head. There was no one staying in the hotel called Ugo Leone.

'I have an order,' Paolo insisted, placing the boxes on the counter. 'Three ceremonial banners in velvet. I was asked to bring them here.'

A group of singers had begun rehearsing on one side of the cavernous room, going through the music they'd been given. Staff in bellboy uniforms were busily moving tables up the staircase. A gigantic Nazi flag fluttered from the balcony alongside a large portrait of Hitler; next to it a smaller one of Mussolini. The place had the kind of bustle that always made him feel uncomfortable and out of place. Then, alongside the preparations for some kind of event, there was the military. The ground floor was swarming with German soldiers, all in uniform, all armed.

He told the receptionist, 'They're for the event. Someone from Turin ordered them.'

'Turin,' the man muttered and got on the phone.

Twenty minutes later a tall, gaudy individual, maybe forty, slick suit, pale face, prominent eyes, a small moustache, greasy combed-back hair, marched down the stairs.

'Signor Leone?' Paolo asked.

No reply. The man just picked up the boxes and unwrapped the banners from the tissue inside. Then he walked back to examine them beneath the glaring light of a sprawling Murano chandelier.

'Who are you?' the fellow demanded.

'My name is Paolo Uccello. Someone, I don't know who, contracted with my father to produce these banners. I was asked to bring them here. For Leone.'

'Leone's not around. I'll take them.'

He didn't move.

'The contract stipulated a final payment on delivery. Today, sir. Twenty thousand lire.'

The man stared at him.

'Do you have a signed contract with you?'

That had never occurred to him.

'My father had a letter of commission. He was killed on the

way back from agreeing it in Verona. Along with my mother. An American air raid.'

'I'm sorry to hear that.' He didn't sound concerned at all. 'A letter means nothing. Was there a contract, signed by both parties?'

'I . . . I assumed Signor Leone was a man of his word. We make fine velvet. By hand. It's time-consuming. Expensive by its nature. The price agreed was a very fair one. To be frank we did this at a loss.' He hesitated, then added, 'Though the Uccello are true patriots so we make no complaint about that.'

The fellow held the banners up to the light again. They were beautifully made but all the same Paolo wished them gone. There were too many connections, to his late parents, to Vanni and his sister. The scarlet looked like blood in the bright chandelier lights and the lions cut ever more violent, aggressive figures.

'If we could settle up, sir . . .'

'Lot of money for three little bath towels.'

He didn't rise to the bait. It was obvious where this was going. His father had always dealt with business. He knew how to haggle, how to argue, how to handle someone who tried to get out of a deal. That happened all the time in Venice. Life seemed to be one long act of bargaining. But it was a talent he never allowed Paolo to share. Weaving, the ways of the Jacquard, the goldcrest rhythm, the art of the loom. That was what his parents pushed at him. Never the practical ways of commerce.

'I can fetch the letter. It's a document that would stand up in court. The law—'

The man laughed. He had sharp, wolfish teeth, very white.

'The law? What kind of fool are you? We are the law. The Germans. The Black Brigades.' He tapped his chest. 'Me.'

'The law says I'm owed.' Paolo reached out for the pieces of velvet. 'Pay me and they're yours. If not . . .'

The fellow threw the banners into one of the open boxes on the floor.

'You haven't got two cents to rub together, have you? Still, you walk in here. Try to screw the likes of me—'

'It's honest work. No one else in the city could make these things for you. No one. We need to be paid.'

The man called over one of the bellboys and told him to pack the banners back into their three boxes and take two upstairs to the guest rooms of a pair of visitors. Paolo barely caught their names. One sounded German and came with a long military title. The second was Italian, a count by the sound of it, aristocracy.

'This . . .' He pointed to the last box. 'Put in the cloakroom. I'll pick it up later.'

'*Si*, Signor Bruno,' the man replied and walked off with all three.

Paolo looked straight at him and said, 'Bruno . . . I've heard of you. The Jew who hunts Jews.'

'Who told you that?'

'I read it in the paper.'

'I'm a servant of the state. I love my country.' Bruno reached into his wallet and took out some notes. 'There you go.'

'That's not enough.'

'Five thousand, sonny. All you're going to get. Take it or leave it.'

'My parents died working to get you those banners.'

He laughed and Paolo realized that, while he'd never in his life hit someone, maybe that could change.

'What's that got to do with me, you little idiot? I didn't kill them. Your old man knew we were never going to pay his stupid price. Guess you never got his business nous, huh?' He brandished the money in Paolo's face. 'Take it and crawl back into your hole. We' – he tapped his chest – 'run this city. Little people need to learn to do as you're told.'

Don't get mad, he thought. At least not too much. And don't be a fool either.

'*Grazie*,' he said and slowly took the notes. 'I wish you well, sir, and your celebrations.'

There was a bar across the way. It was probably somewhere else the Crucchi hung out. Just then he didn't care.

He walked in and asked for a *caffè corretto*, with sambuca, not grappa, the kind his mother ordered when he was a kid and she'd stop by the pastry shop on the way home from school. There was a first time for everything, he guessed. It was rare for him even to enter a cafe, unknown since they died. He'd always felt people were looking at him, thinking they saw something out of place.

A man in a long winter coat did just that. He walked over and Paolo recognized him: the Venetian with the German soldiers when they fished Isabella Finzi out of the water. Alberti. The cop Chiara had warned him about. The one who'd delivered the little lecture about Jews. Maybe he'd heard fateful Paolo's outburst too.

'I know you, kid.'

'I'm not a kid. I came in here for coffee not a conversation.'

He pulled out a warrant for the National Republican Guard.

Paolo sighed and showed him his ID.

'I didn't ask for that, did I?'

'Saving you the trouble.'

'Castello. Calle Largo Rosa. Number 3475. Where the hell is that?'

Addresses in Venice confused everyone, including people who lived there. A number meant little.

'Back of the Arsenale going towards Crosera.'

'What are you doing here, Paolo?'

'Delivering something I was asked for. They seem to be having a party.'

'They're always having a party. The Crucchi. At our expense.'

Maybe the cop had been drinking. Or he was inviting Paolo to speak out of turn. Something wasn't right. He was trying to work out some way out of there when Alberti's attention drifted to the window.

Paolo's breath caught. Bright blonde hair, lurid lipstick, his father's old winter coat open so you could see the shiny red dress beneath, Mika was walking towards the entrance of the Gioconda. She had a swagger about her, a common, look-at-me swing, the kind loose women used in the movies.

'Know that one, do you?'

'No.'

'Then why are you staring?'

'She's pretty. That's why you're looking, isn't it?'

The cop nodded at the door and grabbed his hat.

'If you know what's good for you get out of here. No place for the innocent.'

He was going after Mika. It seemed clear.

'Wait a moment,' Paolo said, grabbing his sleeve, something the man didn't like.

'What?'

'I heard you were looking for someone. Two Jews on the run.'

Alberti nodded.

Mika was at the door of the hotel, talking to the soldiers, showing them some kind of pass.

'Can't be anyone in Venice who doesn't know that.'

'Is there a reward?'

The cop took off his hat. He wasn't looking at Mika any more.

'Maybe. You get to stay alive. That's some kind of reward, isn't it?'

'I've done nothing wrong, mister. No need to threaten me. It's just that . . . if there's money in it I could ask around. Castello. People don't give things away for free.'

He was checking the hotel again. Paolo grabbed his sleeve and said, trying to sound tough, not that it was easy, 'Are you listening to me or what?'

Alberti batted his hand away.

'I don't know what I'm listening to.'

'I just got ripped off for fifteen thousand lire by one of those bastards over there!'

'What?' The cop, at least, sounded interested.

'They hired us for a job. Twenty thousand lire. When I turn up with the goods some creep gives me five and tells me to get out of there.'

'Guess you were out of your depth then, sonny.'

Mika had vanished inside the Gioconda. Paolo was sweating hard under his winter clothes. He'd never done anything like this. It felt odd. Both good and bad. Maybe this was the excitement she got from fighting with the partisans. If it was, perhaps he could understand why she couldn't sit still inside his remote little prison at the edge of the lagoon.

'Tell me there's good money finding your Jews and I'll ask around. If it's one more free gift to you and your Crucchi friends you can go screw yourself.'

Alberti laughed.

'My, my, boy. Maybe you do have a spine after all.' He patted Paolo on the shoulder. 'Tell me how I can find those terrorists and I'll see you get back all that money twice over.' The pat turned into a punch. 'Screw around with me and we'll be going into Ca' Loretti for a little chat.'

Paolo finished his coffee, then raised the little cup in a toast.

'Deal,' he said.

* * *

Twenty minutes it took him to get to Chiara's apartment. She argued when he forced half Bruno's paltry cash on her, swore at the man for cheating them out of what they were owed.

He didn't listen. Nor did he mention he'd spoken to Father Garzone. And certainly not the cop, Alberti.

Her face was puffy, her eyes red. It took him a moment to realize she'd been crying; it seemed such a strange thing for Chiara to do.

Putting that thought out of his head Paolo said, 'Please. Go home to Burano for a while. I'll be fine here. Honest. There's no work. We can both use a little time to ourselves.'

'And what will you do?'

He shook his head at that.

'Go back to being a recluse, I imagine.'

'You have that pair with you.'

'Not for long.'

She kissed him on both cheeks. The clammy salt dampness of her tears smeared against his skin.

'The man, Paolo. He's nice. Nice is dangerous sometimes.'

'I delivered the banners. It's all fine. My visitors will be gone tomorrow or the day after. They have to be. The priest says the Crucchi are coming for all the Jews.'

'They were coming for your friends anyway. They're partisans. Not just Jews. Oh . . .'

She tore herself away from him, screwed her eyes tight shut, balled her fists in sudden fury. Her first-floor apartment was too hot. The atmosphere was wrong. The place was small but it had the hallmark of a couple about it. There were photos of her husband on the mantelpiece, in uniform, smiling for the camera, ready to go to war.

'The poor doctor's dead. The Jew,' she said. 'He killed himself.'

'I know. I met Garzone. The priest told me.'

'Why do you think a man like Aldo Diamante did that?'

He had an idea. He didn't want to say it. So she did.

'Because he feared being seized, Paolo. Because he was afraid that if they took him into that place of theirs and began torturing him, he'd give them all the names he knew. The partisans. The cells. The priest.' She paused, then added, 'You.'

'He would never have done that.'

Chiara glared at him.

'No? You really think that? If they were to take me in, Garzone, you . . . which one of us could promise our lips would stay sealed?'

'It's a question of courage,' he suggested and heard the doubt in his own voice.

'That's the child in you talking. He's still there, whatever you think.' She let go and glanced at the photo of her husband over the fireplace. 'I've had enough of death. I've lost my own and so have you. Maybe I'll go to Burano in a day or two. There's a little hut we have on the marsh for hunting the ducks. Just me. It will do till times change.'

He didn't say a word.

'Paolo. I know you. The way your mother knew you. I know the kind of boy you are. We all do—'

'I'm not a boy . . .'

She gripped him again and her pale face shone in the weak electric light.

'*I know you.* This isn't your fight. Keep out of this, I beg you. Stay inside your little home. Be invisible. Be safe. Do what the rest of us will. We didn't start this war. Let others end it.'

He took her in his arms and kissed her damp cheeks.

She begged him then, 'Promise me! No more partisans. In a week or two I'll come back. We'll find some work. Here' – she held out the money – 'you've more need of this than me. I've got family. You . . . you . . .'

Chiara didn't want to go on.

'I've nothing, you mean? No one?'

'You've always got me. One day this nightmare will end. The two of us will walk round Venice and never have to look behind us. We'll sit behind those looms and listen to the birds sing.'

'It's winter,' he pointed out. 'There are no birds now.'

He didn't take the money, hard as she pressed him.

Outside the night mist was getting thicker, snaking down the narrow streets, rolling over the leaden, sluggish ribbons of water that ran between them.

Ten minutes and he was home.

Trevisan had picked three volunteers from the brigade. Two fishermen and Tosi, a welder from the Arsenale yards. Tosi had a limp and one eye. Not ideal but there hadn't been many takers for the job. Mostly the partisans worked on guerrilla tactics. Hit and run on individual targets. Sabotage on transport lines. The theft of guns and ammunition. Stealing into some grand Nazi and Black Brigade banquet and letting loose with automatic weapons was the most ambitious attack they'd ever attempted. The risks matched the potential rewards. They knew the back-waters of Venice as well as most men could map the roads around their home. If they managed to escape the Gioconda alive, they could find their way back to the boat, speed down the little channels, pick up fuel from a drop point near Sant'Alvise in Cannaregio and be across the water, to terraferma and safety before dawn. After that they'd head north and try to find the partisan cells around San Donà and safety.

There'd be repercussions. Terrible reprisals. Depending on the officer in charge, and how personally offended he felt by any partisan attack, the Germans might kill ten locals for every one of theirs who died. Sometimes fifty. On occasion in France, he'd heard they'd wiped out entire villages, all the kids, women, men, didn't matter how old they were, then razed their homes, their shops, their farms, their church down to the ground. He couldn't imagine what they might do in Venice. Wipe out an entire community maybe? Pick out civilians in the street and mow them down?

He doubted that. Since they'd occupied the city the previous September he'd come to think the local Crucchi were the weaker sort. Officers not thought fit for the hard and dangerous graft of fighting on the lines to the south. The city had become a kind of playground for them, a place they could retreat to recuperate and build their strength afresh. Oberg, the head of the Gestapo unit chasing partisans and Jews, was reputed to be a former school master, intellectual, quiet, unwilling to visit the bars and brothels most of his fellow countrymen seemed to love so much. The man had been wounded in action south of Rome so maybe wasn't a coward unlike some of the weaklings around him. All the same he would respond and, as Trevisan had said to Mika Artom, this was all for the good. A revolution could not be won without the spilling of blood. That of the innocent was the most precious of all. The men of Venice were hardy creatures, used to the cold winter lagoon and the fierce heat of summer. Kill their loved ones and you dug your own grave.

'Hey Rocco,' Tosi, cried. 'We got enough fuel?'

They were moored in the Rio San Francesco della Vigna, close to the colonnade of the convent attached to the church of the same name. It was as quiet a part of Castello as he could find. A friendly local who worked in the convent had agreed to hide four automatic rifles, three German stick grenades and a case of ammunition in one of the garden outbuildings. Tosi and the fishermen had picked them up that afternoon and ferried them to the steps by the canal in canvas bags. Now they sat in the back of the blue commercial boat Trevisan used for ferrying goods around the city.

'Yes. We have.'

'You're sure?'

Tosi was a good welder. He knew nothing about the lagoon and the craft that plied it.

'He's sure,' one of the fishermen cried.

The weapons were at the back, under a grey tarpaulin, covered by old fish boxes from the Rialto. If anyone saw them they'd assume they were one more transport craft delivering around the city. Or that was the plan.

'This old wreck's going to take us all the way to Campalto afterwards?' Tosi asked.

There must have been a service in the convent. An organ was playing and with it the slow, haunting chorus of a hymn.

'It is,' Trevisan said. 'We can get there. Crossing the water's the last thing we've got to worry about. You know how to use the rifle? How to throw a grenade?'

The welder laughed.

'No problem there, mate. I been watching these bastards on the range in the Arsenale. A couple of them let me have a pop at the targets.'

'You two are fine with this?'

The fishermen nodded. Like all their kind they didn't say much. Just got on with the job. The pair were frequent hunters out in the northern marshes in winter. They both knew firearms well. In truth he had a lot more faith in them than the mouthy Tosi with his limp and one good eye.

It was a twenty-minute walk to the Gioconda. The way by boat was far more circuitous, through a winding thread of narrow canals, most of them chosen so they went nowhere near the Crucchi guard posts and, for a large part of the journey, were overlooked by houses, not streets or open *campi*. Forty minutes to an hour it would take. Then, close to the hotel, they'd stop by the cover of a dead end *ramo*, edge slowly out so that Mika Artom might see the familiar hull from the bright lights of the terraces where the Germans and the Fascists drank and ate and planned their evening's whoring.

'What are we waiting for?' Tosi asked.

Trevisan groaned. He wondered how many times he needed to tell the fellow.

'We're waiting on his woman,' one of the fishermen said. 'Don't you listen?'

'She's not my woman,' Trevisan muttered. 'She's not anybody's woman. Only her own.'

The welder laughed.

'Well, she's late like a woman, isn't she? How long are we supposed to hang around here?'

Almost half an hour. When she turned up she was dressed like a man: black trousers, black seaman's jacket, shiny red hair almost completely covered up by a dark woollen cap.

'What happened?' he asked as the others got on the boat.

'Had to talk down Greta. She was getting worried.' Sara Vitale glanced at one of the fishermen. 'You know he's her nephew?'

'No. I didn't.'

'I had to tell her there was nothing to worry about.'

He scoffed at that and said, 'No. Nothing at all.' Then he took her by the arms and said, 'You're sure about this? You're sure you want to come? We can manage with four . . .'

Her eyes flared with a sudden anger.

'I told you I'm coming. And no, you can't manage without me. If I don't stay by the boat there's just three of you to go in and kill the damned Crucchi. Three's not enough. I wait. You shoot as many as you can. Then you go back down the steps like we said. I meet you on the private jetty. We go. Wherever. We just go.'

He nodded, then he embraced her, kissed her cheek which was cold and damp in the misty night air. Trevisan was uncomfortable with emotion.

'I never told anyone this before. You're the only woman who's ever meant a thing to me.'

She laughed.

'Jesus Christ. You must have led a boring life.'

He didn't know what to say.

She ran a single finger down his cheek, kissed him quickly on the lips, stroked his groin.

'The thought of killing Crucchi always makes me want you,' she whispered, amused at the way the others were watching them. 'When we get to Campalto . . .'

The engine of the boat interrupted the night.

'Put your cock away, Rocco, huh?' Tosi the welder cried. 'Are we doing this or what?'

She brushed her fingers against him once again.

'Sure,' he murmured but by then Sara Vitale was heading towards the boat.

The event was dubbed a celebration of eternal Italian–German friendship, a slogan repeated on gaudy hangings in the reception of the Gioconda where Nazi flags hung next to the black banner of the Fascists with its wooden rod and bound axe. There were portraits of Hitler everywhere, ones of Mussolini too, always smaller. Some of the visitors were men Alberti had never seen in his life. Italians from Salò. Nazis from as far away as Berlin.

Alongside the besuited civilians, Gestapo and Black Brigades he guessed, were the uniforms, grey mostly, SS, with a scattering of blue field army soldiers and a handful in brown. The last must have been among the few in the Afrika Korps to escape the shameful surrender across the Mediterranean at the start of the year, now redeployed to Italy to face the enemy once more.

Then there were the women. All young, all attractive in silk dresses and pearls. Whores every last one of them, he didn't doubt. Shipped in from Trieste, Milan, Paris maybe since he'd heard a couple talking French. They flitted round the room, smoking, drinking, looking nervous as they were perused by the men with the bored languor of those who knew they could pick and choose as they wished. Bought like cattle they couldn't say no. By Monday they'd be on the train to the next hotel, another brief interlude in a stranger's bed. The Jews weren't the only ones the Crucchi kept captive.

Some senior Nazi from Berlin had opened proceedings with a long and boring speech in German, his voice so high-pitched and nasal Alberti fought the urge to laugh. His own grasp of the Crucchi's tongue was good but all the same he struggled at times to follow the fellow's squeaky accent. Like everyone in the room he got the message. It was the kind of thing the Nazis said all the time. How the campaign to retake the south was progressing splendidly and soon would push the Americans and the British back into the sea, bloody and beaten. Then would come vengeance for the traitors left behind, one so harsh it would seal control of Italy for Mussolini – and by implication the Germans – forever. The Thousand Year Reich would stretch from the Baltic to the Mediterranean, from England to Asia. Those who'd turned against Il Duce in the summer coup in Rome would feel the harshness of its justice, and no one, not king, not his cabinet, would be spared.

The German was indulging in fantasy. Alberti knew it and perhaps the fellow did too. Whatever lies the fascist press was forced to carry, people had radios. They'd heard another side of the story from foreign stations like the BBC, all heralding the steady progress the Allies were making as they fought their way north and calling on those trapped on the wrong side to be patient and support the partisans. Much of that was propaganda too but it was more muted, spoke of setbacks as well as successes, and carried with it the hard, dull feel of truth.

More than that there was the word on the street. Italy had been cut in two but that didn't stop people travelling and speaking across the dangerous divide. Italian soldiers trapped with Mussolini in the north had begun to defect to the Allies and take up arms against the Nazis. Either that or they vanished into the countryside and the mountains to find the resistance fighters, usually taking their weapons with them as a gift. It was a dangerous game. The Crucchi and the Black Brigades shot any deserters they found and their families too at times. Even if those fleeing Mussolini's side escaped the German patrols, they could still face execution by suspicious partisans, or an accidental ambush on the way to the British or American lines.

All of this was, for the moment, forgotten in Venice, the louche old lady of the lagoon, where food and drink and liberal sex allowed the men who ran the Republic of Salò to believe they were briefly free of the cares of war.

Alberti leaned against the wall by the balcony doors, apart, alone, watching them. Oberg was silent and uncomfortable among his superiors; Sachs and Sander sucking up to senior officers who'd turned up from Milan. The German finished his speech, nodded, made the Hitler salute, watched as he got a forest of raised arms in return, and left the stage. There was a brief interlude, then different voices rang through the ballroom of the Gioconda, clear and perfect, Italian and Venetian through and through. The quartet hired for the evening, two men and two women singing in harmony without accompaniment by the unused piano, still covered in a white sheet, now with a candelabra, silver and gilt, placed on top.

They were local. Alberti knew that from overhearing them talking among themselves in the cloakroom before the event. Not one of them wanted to be in the hotel singing the songs the Fascists had given them. Old folk tunes rearranged with new words about patriotism and love of country, war and strength and determination. One song he knew from his school days. It was an old marching rally from the battles that took place to reunite Italy the century before. Strange, he thought, how the sentiments of old seemed to work in the context of now, in the heart of a ballroom bristling with occupying foreigners, Italians who'd become their slaves, of whores and camp followers, men and women who were watching the idea of Italy as an independent nation state vanish before their eyes.

Perhaps like him, like the singers on the stage, they had no choice. History moved on at its own pace, forced and controlled by others. You swam with the tide or you drowned in it, forgotten, lost. Like the Jews these Crucchi would be picking up over the coming days. Diamante's sacrifice was in vain, a delaying tactic, nothing more. All he'd done was place a minor obstacle in the path of the Nazi's squads of bully boys. They possessed an unshakable sense of right and might in the face of anyone foolish enough to oppose them. The wise Jews, the ones with money and contacts, had fled already, like the kids he saw being handed over to the old surgeon the night before, just as Diamante was planning his own death.

Maybe, Alberti thought, he should have noticed something different in the man's manner when he accosted him in his apartment. When Diamante had begged him for help. And what had been his reply.

I'm nothing more than a prison guard in the jail of the Crucchi's making. Just as much an inmate as you.

Which was true enough. He'd warned Diamante what would happen if the old man found himself in Ca' Loretti facing interrogation.

Then I'll claim the right to question you myself. They barely speak Italian anyway. Not a word of Venetian among them. You won't get out of there alive.

It was all irrelevant now, though the thought that his warning might have tipped the man over the edge into killing himself nagged Luca Alberti all the same.

The bitter night wind was creeping through the cracks in the glass. Alberti opened the door, stepped outside and lit a cigarette. In this part of San Marco the electricity was good, the lights were mostly on. A vaporetto cruised down the Grand Canal at the end of the little *rio* on which the Gioconda stood. Back before the war there'd been plenty going on hereabouts. Maybe a party in the piazza outside Florian's, someone playing jazz on a piano there alongside a trumpeter, a black saxophonist trying to make a living a long way from his American home.

And he'd have a wife and a kid in their plain but comfortable apartment in Cannaregio. Not a small room in a hotel full of foreigners and their fancy women, all paid for in Reichsmarks and Italian blood. The marriage had been fine until the world started to turn dark around them. Not perfect. But they got on, and his kid didn't hate him too much for being a cop.

How different life was just a few years on. How changed some people would be after this night was over too.

A figure caught his attention. It was the blonde-haired woman he'd spoken to the night before. The same one who'd caught the attention of the scared-looking kid he'd approached in the cafe earlier.

She's pretty. That's why you're looking, isn't it?

He was good at remembering what people said and how they said it. Good at being a cop back when that was what he did for a living.

The Uccello kid had been there when they dragged the crazy Jewish woman out of the water in San Pietro on Tuesday. There was something about him that made Alberti wonder if he was the kind to stare at a pretty woman at all. Venice wasn't troubled by the homos among its people. They were everywhere. A good few gondoliers weren't above the odd affair with perfumed foreign men swanning it through the city, so long as they had money. Not that those assignations happened any more.

Queers were on the Fascists' lists too. Not as high up as the Jews, but close.

The woman was a waitress, someone new in the Gioconda. Someone different too, and it wasn't just her blonde hair and interesting, intelligent face that drew his attention. Was it possible that the Uccello kid had been trying to stop him talking to her before she got into the Gioconda?

He just didn't know. All the same there was something odd there. Alberti threw his cigarette over the balcony down the narrow canal below. Something was happening. The blonde was moving through the crowd with her tray of drinks, not zig-zagging casually the way waitresses were supposed to do on these occasions. She had someone in her sights.

It was the Jew hunter, Bruno, smart as ever in his dark suit, greasy hair combed back, looking as haughty and pompous as usual. She strode straight through the crowd and handed him a cocktail, all the time wearing the kind of broad, inviting smile that said, *Just ask and who knows?*

A waitress. Not a whore. A woman who said she couldn't be bought, or so she'd insisted the night before when he spoke to her, though that was when he was half-drunk. Not a quarter way there like now.

Alberti thought of the way he was trained, the things he'd learned. Then he pulled out his pocketbook. The descriptions of all those he was chasing were written there. Some brief. Some detailed.

There was a photo. Of course she wouldn't look like that now. The height, the build, the accent. Some things never changed. But there was a clear resemblance.

The last place anyone expected they'd be looking for a fugitive Jewish partisan was in the very heart of the Nazis' lair. All the same, if Oberg ever got to know how a half-drunk Alberti missed all this he'd be lucky to escape with his job and maybe his life.

'Jesus,' he murmured, shaking his head when he thought this through. 'I just got taken for a ride by a stinking teenager.'

Mika waited until Salvatore Bruno was on his own before she approached him, tray in hand, and said, 'Want another?'

'I've got one.' He looked her up and down and the briefest smile crossed his face. 'But thanks for the offer.'

'They pay me to hand out booze. I'm doing what they ask.'

'You're not from round here. You talk like—'

'I talk like all kind of things. My dad was a bum. Worked the railways. We lived all over the place for years. Milan. Genoa. Verona.' She frowned. 'Had nearly a year in Rome which was good but then he came and got a docker's job in Mestre. Off work now. Got hit by a truck.'

'Oh.'

'Sorry. I didn't mean to bore you.'

He was a sly-faced man with a waxy pale complexion. This close she felt she knew that kind of northern Jew. Quiet, usually in business, middle-class, doubtless secular. Much like her own family in many ways. People who thought the coming cataclysm would never touch their lives. When she was a teenager and the Racial Laws came in she'd had a terrible argument with her father. Accused him of all manner of unfair traits. Being treacherous to his own, more motivated by self-interest than a sense of justice, cruel and heartless and unfeeling.

None of which, she now understood, was true. He was simply doing what many middle-class Jews like him did during the late 1930s. Going along with the general mood and hoping that would be enough to enable them to prosper until times changed and a more moderate, relaxed kind of politician came to hold the reins in Rome. If there was a fault in her father it was a common one at that time. He was too slow and reluctant to accept the wind was turning cold and harsh and soon would shift from Germany and Austria to the south. Too trusting, too believing in the natural goodness of everyday men and women, to accept that the day would come when the horrors of the Nazis – pogroms and internment camps – would find their way across the Alps to their quiet, comfortable, sensible bourgeois home.

Bruno finished his martini, placed the empty glass on her tray and took a flute of sparkling Franciacorta in its place. The Black Brigades refused to serve champagne. Mostly they loathed the French. So the best Italy could offer, pricier than the local Veneto Prosecco, was flowing freely that night. Beneath his arm was one of the gilt boxes Chiara Vecchi had found for the banners the three of them had woven on the Jacquard looms.

'You don't look like a soldier.'

'I'm not. Shouldn't you be busy?'

'I can stop talking if you like.'

He got the message. She wasn't just there to hand out free drinks, not if someone wanted it.

'No. Don't.'

'So what do you do, mister?'

'Find things.' He frowned and she wondered, *Was this too much?* Was she getting too close? It was a quarter to six. She'd soon start to make her way to the balcony. When she saw Trevisan's boat come down the side canal, she'd stroll casually over to the piano and drop her tray. They'd stare for a while, then look away. She'd get slowly to her feet, raise the sheet on the grand piano, find the timer. Prime it, walk to the door, unlock it.

And flee.

She so much wanted more than that. If she had a gun right now she'd think to hell with bombs and partisans outside and put it right up to Salvatore Bruno's temple, then blow his head off. Stand there, laughing, while the Crucchi gathered round.

But all she had was a tray of drinks and a few dishes of biscuits. Nothing she could use to kill the man who'd hunted Jews all across northern Italy, given up his own to torture and death.

'What kind of things?' she asked.

'Things that get me money.' His eyes glazed over for a moment. 'I got a wife and kid back in Salò. They need looking after.'

'You love your wife?'

He looked affronted by the question.

'Of course.'

'But she's not here.'

'She wouldn't like it. We . . . um . . .' It was coming, the excuse. She could feel it. 'We kind of drifted apart. She doesn't like what I do.' He grimaced. 'Some of the time I don't either. But a man does what he must.'

'A woman too,' she said.

'What else do you do?'

'Now that' – she leaned up and whispered in his ear, close enough that he'd smell her, feel the heat of her breath – 'is a conversation for another time and place. I don't perform in hotel bedrooms. Not for anybody. Not for any price.'

'I'm not staying here,' he whispered back. 'With all these . . .' He was a little worse for wear. 'All these . . . Crucchi.'

'Oh.'

She waited.

He pulled out a little pad and a pen and she wondered how many names he'd scribbled down there, how many men and women, children, he'd dispatched this way.

'Here. They gave me a dump of an apartment down near the opera house. I work for them. I kind of . . .' He hesitated and for the briefest moment she wondered if she felt sorry for this man. 'I don't really belong here.' Bruno put the half-finished glass on the tray. 'I'm going. I'm tired. I'll be here for a day or two.' A wan smile, then he put a finger out and moved a strand of her blonde hair away from her cheek. 'If you'd like to earn some money tomorrow . . .'

'What's that?' she asked, pointing at the golden box. 'They can't think bad of you if they give you presents.'

He snorted.

'It was my present to them.' He opened the box and displayed the banner. The scarlet silk and the golden lion. It shone with the newness of the fabric. The whole thing, stretched out as he let it roll to the floor, was barely the length of an arm. All that effort for this. 'To mark the eternal friendship between the Germans and our wonderful republic. Something that will last forever. Two for them. One for me. To remember. It's important to remember some things . . .' His eyes were glassy. He looked drunk, tearful. 'You've got to—'

'I've spent too long talking to you.'

'Salvatore. Call me that. And you . . .?'

The clock was approaching six. She needed to be on the balcony.

'Giulia. A pair of legs paid to serve you drinks. Maybe I'll come round and visit you. Then you can see the rest. If you've got the money.'

She didn't wait for an answer. Bruno was bundling the banner back into the box. She went and served a couple of Germans standing by the pillars next to the long balcony windows and watched him shuffle out of the room. No one looked. No one spoke to him or seemed to notice. Whatever function he'd served had been met. The man wanted out of there, to go back to the place the Germans had organized for him. A lonely traitor waiting on tomorrow.

Watch for the boat.

Head for the piano.

Drop the tray.

Arm the bomb.

Then cross the room and unlock the side door so others could do their job.

She hated the idea she wouldn't be a part of it. But there was no way. Attacks like this depended on timing, organization and swift execution.

Just do as you were told. Go back to the Giardino degli Angeli and Paolo Uccello, a man Vanni was toying with she hoped. Keeping quiet the way he knew best.

She glanced around, left the Germans, moved behind the curtain.

Thin mist swirled down the canal.

Six o'clock almost. No sign of a boat.

She hoped to God they wouldn't be late. The head waiter kept an eye on all the women working the room. He was a hard bastard and wanted labour for his money.

A sound startled her. Footsteps and the closing stink of a stale cigarette wafting past the pillar that hid her from the room.

Then the terrace door opened.

'Mika Artom,' said a voice she half-recognized. 'Come outside. We need to talk.'

Vanni was half-dozing on the bed in his parents' room when Paolo got back. He was in his underpants and a heavy woollen fisherman's jumper he must have found in the wardrobe. The wound on his leg was uncovered. It looked raw and bleeding again. At some stage they'd surely have to find a real doctor.

Paolo took one look, then got some water and a fresh bandage, told him to sit up on the bed and let him try to clean it.

Vanni tried to shrug it off.

'Don't be so concerned. My sister knows her stuff. Sometimes things need to get worse before they get better.'

He wiped down the cut as best he could, placed some gauze over the bloody slash, then wound the bandage round his leg. A gentle hand fell on his hair as he worked. Vanni made the odd quiet moan as he worked to tighten the fabric.

'I'm trying not to hurt you.'

'Same here.'

When it was done Vanni leaned back on the bed, against the wall and closed his eyes.

'Are you feverish?' Paolo asked.

'Probably not. Did you get your money?'

'Some of it. The bastard never intended to pay what he'd promised. But . . .'

Vanni looked at him and asked for a drink. Wine. Grappa. Something strong.

'Why?' Paolo wondered. 'Is that wise?'

'There's no such thing as wise these days.'

He went into the kitchen and came back with two small tumblers of amber-coloured grappa, the best they had, a bottle his father kept for special occasions: birthdays, Christmas, holidays. There was no easy way to break the news.

Vanni gulped half his glass down in one.

Paolo said, 'I'm sorry to tell you this. I heard while I was out from the priest.'

Straight away his eyes flashed with interest and a glimmer of fear.

'Heard what?'

'They're coming for all the Jews. Tomorrow. All of you. Diamante was meant to give them a list last night. He killed himself and burned all the documents he had. It might hold them up for a little while. It won't stop them.'

Vanni lay there silent, then asked, 'Did you know him? The doctor?'

'Not really. He seemed a good man. Did you ever meet him?'

'Of course not. That's the way these things work. The less anyone knows the better. That way . . .'

He didn't go on.

'That way you have little to tell if the Germans find you.'

He smiled.

'You do learn fast. We live in the shadows. It's safer there.'

'When you go . . . will you take me with you?'

Vanni looked as if he was trying to stifle a laugh, then asked, 'Why?'

'Because I want to be with you . . . I want to fight the Crucchi. I hate them.'

'Hating them's no use.'

'What do you mean?'

'What I said. If you hate them you treat them as people. Fear them by all means. But never give them identities. Never think of them as men. Or women. See them the way they see us. Me.

A Jew. As a man who sometimes loves other men. A creature less than human. Unworthy of life.'

'I don't know—'

'To them I'm no better than an animal. Vermin. A pest to be eradicated. As they must be to me. Not hate. Hate's an emotion and emotions get you killed.'

'Then,' Paolo said, raising a glass, 'that's how I'll feel.'

'Get me the bag from the wardrobe.'

He fetched it and Vanni zipped open the canvas holdall and took out a pistol. The barrel was black, the stock dark-brown wood.

'The partisans gave Mika all this for safekeeping. Know what I have in my hands?'

'A gun.'

'Very good. A gun,' Vanni said and withdrew a shiny magazine from the depths of the bag. 'A Luger Zero Eight. Old. They have better weapons than this now but we use what we can steal. Show me how to use it.'

Paolo laughed, embarrassed.

'I don't know. You have to teach me. Didn't someone teach you?'

'Yes. And they cut off his balls and hanged him from a tree not long after.'

From a side pocket in the bag he pulled out a pale green card with an image of Mussolini in a military helmet and the words beneath, '*Fascio di combattimento*'.

'What's this, Paolo?'

'I don't know.'

'A membership card for the Fascists. With a bit of luck it can get you past one of the bastards asking for papers on a train. What's this?'

Another piece of paper. It seemed to be an identity card from France with a fuzzy picture of Vanni on it and the name 'Pierre Goulet'.

'French papers. Fake.'

'Correct. And this?'

Another document. Italian this time. Another photo of Vanni.

'Your real papers. Your real ID.'

'True.'

'Why keep them? They'd give you away.'

Vanni laughed.

'Yes, if the Crucchi saw them. What happens when I get out of here? When I try to find the cell I'm meant to join? They need proof, don't they? Without it they might shoot me for a spy.'

'I hadn't thought of that.'

'Obviously. Also . . .' He tapped his chest, the woolly jumper of Paolo's father. 'You always have to remember who you are. I am me. Giovanni Artom. If you let them steal that there's nothing left to fight for.'

'I can do all this. I can learn. You can teach me.'

'You mean on the road? When we're running? Tomorrow, perhaps? The day after?' He hesitated, then added, 'With Mika too?'

That hadn't occurred to him. She seemed the boss. The one he'd have to convince.

'If you give me a chance . . .'

'The chance to die alongside a couple of wanted Jews.'

Vanni reached out and touched his hair for a moment. Paolo shivered but he didn't retreat. He thought perhaps he'd touch him again but instead Vanni grabbed the Luger and said, 'Watch.'

It happened so quickly he couldn't follow. Vanni flicked open a box of shells with his thumb, packed shells into the magazine, jammed it into the stock, flicked a lever somewhere, held the pistol high in his right arm and fired.

Plaster rained down on them from the ceiling, like a sudden shower of artificial hail.

'Sorry for the damage,' he said, sweeping the pieces off the bed. 'When the war's over, send me the bill.'

He took out the magazine and with quick fingers expelled every shell on to the bed sheets, then handed over the pistol.

'Now you.'

But he hadn't followed what had happened. It was all too fast, too far away from everything he understood. The workings of the Jacquard loom, the fabric, the scissors, the complex processes of weaving . . . these he knew by heart. Not as well as Chiara who could do the job with her eyes closed almost. But a weapon . . .

His shaking fingers found the bullets, then the magazine. Part of the thing was so hot he yelled and it fell from his fingers, then rattled on the floor. The shells followed, tinkling like notes from a child's music box as they met the tiles.

Paolo gave up, put the pistol on the sheets and said, 'Give me a chance.'

'You don't get a chance. You learn or you die. We all have talents, love. Fighting's not one of yours.' He grimaced. 'It's not one of mine either but I can fake it. Not you. My sister on the other hand . . .'

'When will she be back?'

'I've no idea.'

'Did she tell the truth? When she said she was just a lookout? She made it sound like nothing.'

Vanni shuffled up in bed and came to sit beside him.

'I hope so. I really do. We'll leave the moment we can. I don't want to put you in danger any more. It's not right. You don't deserve it. You're too . . . decent to be spoiled by the likes of us.'

'I don't want to be *decent*.'

'I don't want to be a lousy Jew partisan with a limp. Sometimes we don't get choices. Be yourself, Paolo. Not who you think anyone else wants you to be.'

He reached out and touched his hair again, slow fingers moving against his scalp. It reminded Paolo of his mother, doing much the same when he was a child, tearful over being bullied and teased at school. Getting called names he didn't understand. Or perhaps he simply pretended not to because the accusation behind them – that he'd been born abnormal somehow, wrong, damaged, unworthy of life – was something he didn't wish to contemplate.

'You shouldn't touch me like that.'

'Why? Don't you like it?'

'No.'

His eyes were dark and gentle, with a depth to them that made Paolo think perhaps he saw things that others missed.

'You don't sound so sure. What about this?'

He didn't move away. He didn't want to.

'We're just skin and blood and flesh,' Vanni whispered close to his ear. 'Here for a little while, then gone. Why waste such precious minutes?'

A boat engine sounded outside and not long after the angry squawk of a gull. There was a momentary flash of a searchlight but it was distant and soon vanished. A gusty winter wind rattled the shutters on the kitchen windows. The sharp salt air, cold as ice, seeped through the rotting window frames of the secluded house on the edge of the lagoon.

Bullets shifted and rattled between his toes on the cold tile floor, their metallic ringing silenced soon by the shedding of his clothes.

When they fell together on the old sheets his mind lost itself in places he'd always wanted to go but never found the courage. Then came a sigh, a gasp of pain, the sound of creaking bed springs, a rhythmic noise he'd listened to from time to time in his room across the hall.

Skin and blood and flesh. And heat.

Paolo gave in and when he did he thought of nothing but the two of them, locked together in a place where there was no war at all.

Rocco Trevisan's father had rowed the *traghetto* ferry across the Grand Canal between Santa Maria del Giglio and Salute until he decided the hard labour merited more than the few lire he got for taking locals across for a fraction of the price of a gondola. After that he borrowed enough money to buy a small delivery boat, moving everything from fresh food to furniture, picking up work by word of mouth, building a reputation, winning round all the mothers because his toddler son joined him on the water as soon as he could walk, wearing a little jerkin embroidered with the slogan *Trevisan Padre e Trevisan Figlio*.

Father and son. His mother died when he was seven. After that the two of them were inseparable, out on the water constantly, for work, for leisure, for activity, both legal and not. The young Trevisan had competed in regattas with his father rowing fancy historic boats like the *mascareta* and the *puparìn*. He'd accompanied his old man on hunting expeditions in the remote wild stretches of the northern lagoon in a borrowed *s'ciopon*, taking pot shots at winter wildfowl with the gigantic *spingarda* shotgun mounted in the bows. When he grew older and stronger he'd helped lug boxes of artichokes and greens in Sant'Erasmo and the two of them had ferried them to the Rialto market. At night, too, they might be found in the backwaters of the city, delivering contraband tobacco and alcohol down dark alleys to men whose name he never knew.

The life of a Venetian boatman was harsh. In his fifties his father, never a man to complain, began to struggle with the oars. It took a while for the teenage Trevisan to realize he was getting old and weary, weak and affected by years of strenuous labour.

One June night in his late teens he'd said he had to visit an old friend at college in Padua. His father never asked how a working-class kid from the mean terraces of Castello knew anyone at university. Maybe he guessed what was coming.

Rocco Trevisan headed inland on a train from Santa Lucia station but not for friendship. In six days spent sleeping in parks, avoiding the cops and pretty much everyone else, he managed to rob three rich students who were stinking drunk after a graduation celebration, two with the laurel wreaths still round their necks. Then a couple of traders he'd worked out were walking down the street with their takings for the bank. If he'd been caught he'd have gone down for five years or more, robbery and assault. His father would have been heartbroken.

But that never came to pass. He returned home with enough money to buy a new boat with an outboard, one that his father could manage from the tiller while Rocco did the lifting and heaving. When his old man asked where he'd got the money he simply said he'd borrowed it from a friend. Rocco Trevisan had discovered a talent for lying, for staying out of sight, hiding in the back streets that ran off from via Garibaldi out towards the Biennale gardens where the Fascists were now making their terrible movies. When war arrived all the lines became blurred. What was legal. What was acceptable. What was worth paying dues to Il Duce for and what contraband might be sold on without the cops finding out.

His father was an early member of the communist cell in Castello that caught fire after the Russian Revolution. His son grew up listening to his old man read Marx and Engels, hearing the same message over and over again.

Nothing changes without pain. The warriors of today are the heroes of tomorrow. Their deaths, their blood will bring about a better Italy one day, a country allied to its true friend in Russia, distant Stalin, who from time to time fed money into the coffers of those who followed his creed.

Adolfo Trevisan died in the bleak winter of 1941, broken by decades of grinding, physical labour. After that his son's communist faith evolved from simple hatred into a desperate craving for action, a blind vengeance against the uncaring world around him. He'd smuggled arms, robbed stores, though only ones that favoured the Fascists. From time to time he'd ferried men and women he didn't know in and out of the city. Jews too, though only for a price with them. They were Jews. They could afford it.

All the while he'd been careful to maintain the outward appearance of an ordinary, industrious boatman, ready to transport a table or a consignment of winter vegetables around the city for a price most deemed fair. It probably didn't fool the cops. Certainly not a sly local like Luca Alberti. But Trevisan was smart enough and quick enough to stay out of their grasp and make some money on the side. Maybe it was for the cash that, five months before, a newcomer called Sara Vitale walked into Greta's and chose him, the quiet, surly one. She'd been a servant in one of the palaces of the Grand Canal, kicked out of her job when the Black Brigades came and seized the property for their own. Within a few weeks she'd come to share his bed, but only when she felt like it.

He couldn't stop thinking of the past, his father, all the times they'd spent on the dark waters of the city and the open silver stretches of the lagoon. Maybe it was that thing they talked about: how your life flashed in front of you before the end. Or perhaps he was simply having second thoughts. Sara Vitale had brought something into his life he'd never expected, maybe never deserved. A kind of hope that gave him strength. He didn't want to lose that. He didn't want to lose her. The way he'd arranged this attack she, at least, ought to survive.

The sturdy motorboat he'd bought for his father edged along one of the narrow channels that wound through San Marco like the veins and arteries of a living creature. Trevisan had taken the tiller. No one knew this narrow, serpentine waterway better. A couple of minutes away from the hotel they turned a sharp left into the final *rio*, ducking as they went beneath a narrow stone bridge between two private houses. The water was high that night. Maybe there'd be flooding in San Marco. As a child he'd watched fascinated as the lagoon bubbled up through the drains in via Garibaldi, rising until it lapped at the doors of the shops and bars, forcing everyone to pull out their boots and sandbag their homes.

The Crucchi didn't know Venice the way he did. If his team could get in and out of the Nazis' hotel, job done, find their way back to the boat, they'd make it to Campalto. Maybe not all five of them but there were only two who really mattered.

'Rocco,' she whispered as she came back to join him in the stern.

'What?'

'It's my turn. Remember? The tiller.'

She folded her arms, took off her wool hat and let her hair flow down around her shoulders. Her face shone in the wan light of a near-full moon. Wispy mist kept drifting in and out of the city like smoke from a giant's cigarette. It was a perfect night to escape. Campalto would be easy. They'd make it.

He rolled down the throttle, got up and handed her the tiller, waited till her fingers closed on the grip. The canal here was no more than five metres wide. Hitting the wall either side would be so easy and a giveaway for any watching German guards.

'When we pass that window cut the engine,' Trevisan told her.

'Sure.'

The three men ahead reached down and found their weapons. Trevisan's was already waiting in the well of the boat, along with the stick grenades they had, a present from a cell on terraferma in return for the ferrying of some men.

'Take us into the landing by the hotel garden.'

'I know that too, Rocco. We went through all this, didn't we?' She was whispering now so only he could hear. 'You sound nervous. Don't. It's bad for the troops.'

'Thank you.'

As if he needed that. He touched her hair. She recoiled, smiled.

'Later.'

'Campalto.' He smiled back. 'We'll open a bottle.'

They were almost there. She killed the throttle. Silent but for the gentle slap of water against the hull, the boat drifted in towards the weed-covered steps by the side of the Gioconda's walled garden. The ledge was wide enough for two men and led all the way to the floor beneath the ballroom. Then there was the door the woman inside would open for them.

He could see it all in his head, had played it out time and time again.

The jetty was a minute away. Mika Artom would see them any moment, head for the piano, set the timer on the bomb. They'd lurk by the bottom door. When they heard the explosion . . . then they'd attack.

'Wait no more than fifteen minutes,' he said, watching the stone stairs loom up at them in the darkness. The lights of the ballroom were brighter than usual. They glittered on the black water making them more visible than he'd expected. Music and voices drifted down from above. The Crucchi sounded happy.

'I said—'

'I heard you, Rocco,' she replied, then stroked his cheek just for a moment as the boat drifted steadily towards the steps.

It was bitterly cold on the Gioconda terrace. She shivered, then he said her name again, placed his empty glass on her tray, folded his arms and looked outside at the black canal.

She couldn't find the words.

'You know that name?'

It was the Venetian she'd seen the night before. When she broke the glass and he picked up the pieces.

Luca Alberti. Pleased to meet you. Room Four One Three.

He didn't seem so drunk any more.

'I didn't hear what you said,' she told him. 'I thought you were asking for a drink.'

'Mika Artom. Jew from Turin.'

'No, mister. I don't mix with Jews. I told you.'

'Giulia. Is that right?'

'Yes.' She couldn't stop glancing towards the canal. They had to be approaching soon. 'I don't know—'

'The terrorists I told you about. A woman about your age. A brother Giovanni. He's wounded. But then again she was training to be a doctor so maybe he's alright.'

He came close and felt the sleeve of her silk dress. Frost was forming on the balustrade like icing sugar scattered across a cake. She didn't want to stay there long. Just see Trevisan's boat and . . .

'I don't know any—'

'You sound like you're from somewhere near there now I think about it. Being a . . . a patriot, like you said. I thought I'd ask.' He stared straight at her. 'Mika Artom. Twenty-three. Jew.' He laughed. 'But you know . . . an Italian Jew. Don't think she's got a hook nose and the makings of a beard. The only photo we have . . .'

He pulled it out of his pocket. The picture the police took when they rounded her up in Padua. Long, dark hair, no make-up. Face surly and full of anger.

'Don't know her,' she said, glancing at it, heart in mouth.

'Oh well.' He put the picture back in his pocket. 'Doesn't matter. She'll be dead soon. See . . .' He put a finger to his mouth and came close, spoke in a whisper, both of them out of sight from the crowd in the ballroom, blocked by the pillar. 'I can tell you this because I know you're one of us. The people she got mixed up with here . . . the cell. Seems the Germans got intelligence inside. They know what these scum are up to. Right now.' Alberti glanced over the balcony. 'Any minute. Bad time to be a partisan. There was this old Jew, Aldo Diamante. You probably never heard of him but he was mixed up with them.'

'How?'

He frowned.

'Who knows? Irrelevant now. The old guy killed himself last night before we could take him. It's all falling apart for those bastards. Just gets worse from here.'

She felt cold. She felt lost.

'What do you mean?'

He blinked.

'You want the details?'

She didn't answer.

'Fine.' He took a glass from her tray and raised the flute of Franciacorta in a toast. 'I understand. These bastards . . . I guess they knew we had our champion Jew hunter and lots of big guys in town from Salò.' He pointed through the glass, into the room. The piano covered by a sheet. 'They were planning to put a bomb in that thing. Then, when it went off, this Artom woman was going to let in some guys with guns.' Another look at the canal glinting in the lights from the hotel. 'She's got guts. I'll say that for her. Wanted Jew walking straight into the Nazi lion's jaws.'

He shrugged.

'And?' she asked.

'Woman's as good as dead. They got forewarned. The Crucchi picked up the idiot trying to plant the thing. Someone's probably pulling out his fingernails back in Ca' Loretti. Come tomorrow they . . . we . . . we'll have the whole gang rounded up in front of a firing squad. Or hanging from trees in the park by Harry's Bar. Depends how big a piece of theatre they want.'

He downed the wine in one and winced.

'I know this shit they drink costs a fortune. But me? I'd rather have a Prosecco. It's real. It's local. It's ours.' He ran a finger down her bare arm. 'I like what's ours. I'd like to keep it.'

The last time she was in Greta's she'd stolen a short, sharp-pointed kitchen knife while the old woman wasn't looking. It was tucked into a satin sash beneath the waistband of the dress, right alongside the key they'd given her for the side door down to the canal. An awkward place, the two hard lumps of metal sat against her middle. She couldn't sit down. Couldn't move too easily. To get to either she'd need to hitch up her skirt, unseen, somehow.

'Don't touch me,' she said and wondered, if she stabbed him now, if she got him to the balcony edge and pushed him over, would that solve a thing? Trevisan and his team would be warned off. She'd be dead or worse, taken prisoner, in minutes.

There was the distant ring of a man's voice somewhere below. She couldn't make out the words. It wasn't from the hotel patio by the water. Had to be someone on the canal. Then she saw the bows of Trevisan's boat as it edged in silence along the narrow *rio*, engine off, gliding through the wispy evening mist towards the Gioconda. At the front, erect and stiff and still, stood four men like sentries, something in their arms, all ready to move.

'I wouldn't go near that piano,' Alberti said. 'Anyone who does well . . . you know the Germans. They do leap to conclusions and never mind if they have to sweep up the blood and bits afterwards.'

Did he know who she was and was trying to warn her?

Or was he just a dumb local cop, half-drunk and talking too much?

The photo was her but a different Mika Artom. Not just in looks; the hair, the make-up, the student clothes so different to the blowsy evening dress Sara Vitale had provided, along with a change of hair style and colour.

'What are you thinking?' he asked.

'I'm wondering why you're telling me all this.'

'Because you're a patriot, Giulia.' The way he spoke her name had an edge to it. 'I like patriots. I'd hate to see them hurt unnecessarily.' He stroked her arm again and smiled and she was sure then: he knew. 'We need more of their kind. Not less.'

She edged forward and glanced back into the room. Six or seven German soldiers in grey uniforms were milling at the back close to the piano. There were more than she remembered when she came out on to the balcony.

'Maybe they don't have a clue what she looks like now. She could have . . . I don't know.' He squinted at her. 'Changed her hair or something. But if she's dumb enough to go and lift the sheets on that thing . . .' He pointed into the ballroom. 'See for yourself.'

One of the tall Germans, a civilian in a dark suit, had taken to the podium and was waving people towards the balcony, laughing as he spoke.

'Seems to me there's a show starting,' Alberti added, finishing half his drink, then throwing the rest over the balustrade. 'A German show. I doubt it's my kind of thing.' One last time he touched her arm. 'Or yours.'

Trevisan was the first up the greasy, slippery steps, rifle slapping over his shoulder, free hand out to help those who followed. Boatmen knew how treacherous the weed-strewn stones of Venice could be, how easily the unwary slipped on the green steps and found themselves immersed in the noisome city waters.

The door that led up to the ballroom of the Gioconda was maybe twenty metres along the narrow stone ledge. They stood beneath the spreading branches of an orange tree tumbling over from the hotel garden. Rotten fruit spattered the pavement. Pigeons rustled and cooed through the leaves. His mind wasn't working right. He thought they sounded scared.

'When's that damned thing going off?' Tosi grumbled.

'When she gets there.'

'You know this woman, Rocco? I heard she was someone new.'

'We don't have anyone else we could put in that room. She's fine. She's good.' He leaned over and whispered in his ear, 'She's a beauty too. The Crucchi will be eating out of her hand.'

'Trying to get into her pants more likely,' Tosi said and spat in the canal.

Trevisan sighed. He'd known these men most of his life. But they'd never been thieves, never robbed a bank, never fled from the police and hid out until it was safe and they could pretend they were just ordinary Venetians, going about their business. Every one of them lacked his guile, the gift for vanishing into the darkness when danger came your way. He was telling the truth when he said he didn't have any choice but to put the woman from Turin into the Gioconda. Any more than he had any alternative when it came to picking these three and Sara Vitale for one desperate strike against the Germans.

'When *is* that damned bomb going off?' one of the fishermen asked. 'What are we waiting for?'

He walked back to the boat. Sara Vitale was at the tiller, ready to start the engine when they needed it.

Along the pavement there was a new light. The side door was open. No one there. Just a way in.

'Maybe the bomb didn't work,' Sara Vitale said. 'She's got the door open. Take the grenades. Get up there. Throw them in. Shoot a few of the bastards. Doesn't matter how many get killed. We're making a point.' She tapped the tiller. 'As soon as I hear the shooting stop I'll take this thing outside. You come back down. We can be in Campalto before sunrise.' She reached out and touched his sleeve. 'If you know the way.'

'I could lead you there blind,' he replied.

Maybe they could abandon the whole idea. There should have been a bomb.

No time to think. What was there to debate anyway?

'Just do it, Rocco, will you?'

'I will,' he said and reached over, kissed her cold cheek.

The soldiers by the piano looked bored, as if they'd given up. Mika shoved against the mass of bodies flocking to the balcony. The men there – they were all men – stood around grinning, full of anticipation. No one took any notice of a waitress in a scarlet silk dress. No one saw her put the tray on one of the tables, carefully because the hidden knife from Greta's kitchen bit into her if she bent over too much.

There was just one German who wasn't headed for the door. The tall, smirking one who'd tried to persuade her to come to his room.

Herr Sander.

She glanced at the side exit and her fingers automatically stroked the key hidden away beneath her billowing dress.

The door was already open. German soldiers toting rifles lounged at the entrance, blocking it, idle. Waiting.

No chance of warning Trevisan from there.

No way of doing a thing from the balcony.

And the piano.

Alberti was telling the truth. She just knew it. There was no bomb. No signal for the men outside to strike. Just a trap, one that would soon ensnare her if she didn't find some way to escape.

She strode over to the far side of the room, found the broad double staircase down to the ground floor, didn't look back, didn't move quickly or slowly, just walked the way a woman might if she wanted to head to the bathroom.

The lobby was empty save for a couple of uniformed guards lounging by the long mirrors, looking annoyed as hell that they couldn't take part in the show. Behind the front desk a man and woman in black stood stiff and scared. They knew something was happening.

There was a pair of double doors to the canal side of the building. She opened them and slid through. Tables ran across the room in a geometric pattern. In the dim lights of the ceiling she could see cups and plates and cutlery laid out on every one.

On the right-hand wall was another long portrait of Hitler. On the left the same of Mussolini.

She walked towards the windows and peered out. Trevisan's boat was to the left of the terrace jetty, bobbing on the dark water. At the helm, standing, was a figure she recognized: Sara Vitale, her face illuminated by the light falling from above. No one else on board.

Mika stared at the woman beyond the windows. Vitale noticed her the way people sometimes did when they were being watched. She turned, stared back, wide-eyed, scared. Something else there too and for an instant it looked like shame. To the right, there were men on the terrace too, a group of them approaching the door she was supposed to open but couldn't get near.

'Trevisan!' she yelled and hammered on the glass. 'Go back, man! The Crucchi know! They know—'

They must have been too far away to hear. She pushed through the tables to get closer, was about to hammer on the glass again when footsteps sounded from behind and a hard punch sent Mika Artom sprawling to the floor. The stink of booze and bad breath all around her. Sander. The German who'd been watching her all along.

'First,' he said, tearing at her flimsy dress, 'we fight. And then we fuck.'

His hands were strong and grasping at her thighs, his Italian rough and hard to grasp. She reached for the knife in her belt, got her fingers on the hilt.

Another punch. She cried out in pain. Then again and the blade spilled from her fingers, vanished rattling across the polished wooden floor.

Trevisan led, that was his way. Grenade in left hand, rifle in the right, breath short, eyes sharp, thinking about the stairs ahead and what might lie beyond them. His three comrades followed behind in silence. They were just a few short steps from the side entrance when they heard doors open and a sudden burst of sound coming from above.

Maybe something else too. A shout. A fist banging on glass. He wasn't sure so he held up a hand and made the men wait on the damp stone terrace.

It wasn't hard to picture what had happened. Someone had opened the doors to the ballroom terrace above them and people had flooded through. There was a surge of jovial chatter, the clink of glasses, a few bursts of laughter. German. He couldn't understand a word. It sounded like a party.

'Those bastards won't be so happy when they see us,' Tosi said nudging his elbow.

'Shut up, for God's sake,' Trevisan hissed at him. 'We get in. We get out. We do it quick. Don't matter how many we kill. Just a few . . .'

'Didn't come here for a few,' Tosi spat back at them.

But Trevisan wasn't even thinking of the brief and bloody attack on the banquet. His mind was on what came after.

Campalto. Across the water. He barely knew the place. Didn't much like terraferma. Didn't enjoy the thought he'd be leaving others to suffer the consequences of their actions. The ones the Crucchi were bound to pick on would doubtless be small people. Someone who'd offered to store a few weapons. Passed on titbits of information. Maybe even just muttered an imprecation against Mussolini and his Nazi masters in a bar. But his little team were warriors and warriors were needed. It was one of the ironies of partisan warfare that the paucity of their numbers meant that their lives were more precious to the cause than those of the innocent.

He never liked that idea though he accepted its logic.

'Are we going to do this or what?' Tosi asked with another nudge of his elbow.

Two things happened then, both unexpected.

He heard the familiar sound of his boat engine coming to life behind them and when he turned he saw Sara Vitale, reversing the craft back into the city.

Then, before he could speak, he was holding up his eyes to try to shield them against a series of bright blinding white lights that burst into life across the water, aimed straight at them.

It took a moment for his sight to adjust. When they did his heart froze just like the breath inside him. A line of soldiers, four or five machine guns on mounts, floodlights by their sides, ranged along the opposite bank, picking them out like wild geese against a bright summer sky.

'Sara,' he murmured, puzzled, as he glanced again up the narrow waterway. The old blue boat he'd bought for his father through robbing and crookery, was vanishing beneath the bridge on the corner.

A gull squawked somewhere and a small flock of pigeons clattered up towards the velvet sky.

The crowd on the balcony above them had gone quiet.

An expectant silence had fallen upon the little canal by the side of the Hotel Gioconda. Even Tosi couldn't think of a thing to say.

Trevisan flipped the pin on the grenade and lifted his arm to lob it skywards, somewhere in the direction of the Crucchi across the channel.

But then the night was torn apart by fire and the deafening mechanical rattle of machine guns.

Overhead distant cheers. Behind the shattering of glass.

The first shell took him in the chest. The second the throat.

His fingers lost their grip on the grenade which tumbled down towards the black canal and exploded there with a deadly roar.

Dank water rose like a filthy fountain under the explosion's power, fell all around. The four men shook and danced like the rag dolls of an angry child as the gunfire bit.

The lagoon was in his mouth and so was blood. The taste of Venice, acrid salt and human waste, choking Rocco Trevisan as he fell gagging into the black mirror of the water that closed around him like an icy shroud.

* * *

Lights flared outside through the hotel breakfast room, piercing the dark with darting, incandescent beams. After the sudden burst of engine noise – Vitale reversing to safety she felt sure – the laughter and the sound of the crowd above had subsided. The tumult that followed was so loud and violent it seemed an unseen monster had torn apart the world. It took Mika a moment to realize what it was: the metal chatter of automatic gunfire ringing out in an insane chorus, followed by the screams and cries of dying men. As she scrambled on the floor, fighting the German's arms around her, stray shots tore through the windows of the downstairs room sending shards of glass everywhere, chinking off the tidy plates and cups and cutlery across the tables.

The man called Sander was undeterred. He was drunk, determined, but strong. Stronger than she could ever be.

Mika rolled beneath a table to face him. He hadn't seen the knife. She felt sure of that. But the thing had scuttled across the polished wooden floor. She didn't know where. Couldn't guess.

His hands went out, dragged her back into the space between the tables, slid between her legs and forced them open. Desperate fingers grappled at her stockings, tore them to shreds, fought to work on her pants.

Outside the shooting had stopped. There was that strange silence again. Then cheering from above, a roar, a toast. The performance was over. That one anyway.

The German had the shiny military belt they all wore. One side a pistol in its holster. On the other a brown leather hanger with a dagger held there by a buckle.

He was drunk. He was desperate for her so she reached out for his groin and touched the stump through the prickly military fabric of his trousers.

A laugh, a smile, a groan and he tried to push her head down, said something that sounded like '*mund*'.

Mouth, she thought. That must have been it.

'*Ja*,' she said and bent forward, just enough to put her right hand on his waist.

He made a happy sound.

The blade came out of the leather easily. Straight away she got both hands on the haft, held the bright length of sharp steel inches away from his throat, waiting for the moment, wanting him to see.

Sander opened his eyes and gasped. His right hand drew back

for a punch. Before he could get there she jabbed the point hard above his Adam's apple, jabbed again, worked it side by side. Blood, warm and sticky joined them. An animal sound, half gurgle, half surprise, came out of his throat. Another strike, stabbing, carving sideways ended that.

Mika clambered to her feet, pulled off her torn stockings. Stripped him of his uniform jacket, trying to keep the blood off her, not that it was easy. She was a mess, covered in gore, scarlet dress ripped from the waist down. Sander lay face down on the wooden floor, not moving.

She reversed the German's jacket until it looked like an ordinary men's coat. Then stuffed the gun into the pocket, put on the jacket and headed for the door.

The glittering foyer of the Gioconda was empty save for the receptionists, the same man and woman behind the front desk. Drink and happy chatter drifted down the broad staircase from upstairs. The Crucchi had made their kill. It was party time and there, perhaps, lay her only opportunity.

The receptionist came out from behind the counter. Mika took out her gun, waved it at him, couldn't think of a word to say.

'Get out of here quick,' he said. 'They're all upstairs getting drunk. If—'

'Guards,' she demanded. 'Where are they?'

'At the end of the street. There's an alley before on the left. Take that.'

'And then?'

'For God's sake go,' the woman behind the counter screamed. 'They'll kill us all.'

'Here,' the man said and handed her a small torch.

It was pitch black outside. In her head she could see Trevisan and the others dead on the hotel terrace, their bloodied, shattered corpses getting kicked around by gleeful Nazi soldiers.

The cell had been broken all along. She knew that the moment she saw Sara Vitale's guilty face through the window. Aldo Diamante, the man whose contacts had brought them to Venice, was dead. There was no good news, no salvation anywhere that she could think of. She needed Vanni, his calm and common sense to balance out her own impetuous nature.

More than anything though she wanted to be back behind the safety of the shattered statues in the Giardino degli Angeli.

The alley was where the hotel man said. It was barely wide enough for one person. In her haste and panic she kept bumping off the grubby walls, damp with wisps of lagoon mist.

Mika Artom lurched ahead, hand on the gun in Sander's jacket always, trying to find her way through the endless night.

It took the best part of two hours. Time spent dodging down narrow lanes, hiding under any sotoportego she could find. There weren't so many soldiers about and the ones that were on duty hung around the usual places. The campi, the bars and cafes they felt comfortable, the approaches to their barracks in the Arsenale.

Somehow she managed to align herself with the waterfront, avoiding the broad waterside terrace that led from San Marco out to Giardini, mirroring its path along the spider's web of streets behind.

Head down she walked through the shadows on the dark side of via Garibaldi. Greta's bar was closed for once, four German troops standing outside smoking, chatting. There was no light on and Mika wondered what the old woman there had to tell. Very little she imagined. Not that it would stop the Crucchi trying.

Soon she was in the warren of streets at the end, aiming towards San Pietro. One more bridge to the island with its basilica, another to the left, that slippery walk along the rock ledge and then she could rap on the door.

Close to that final bridge she nearly faltered. Across the bare grass, beyond the crooked bell tower of the basilica leaning on its own, a squad of troops was busy beating down the door of a small terraced house. If they hadn't been so focused on causing mayhem there, yelling in harsh German for someone to come out, they might have seen her slipping across the last narrow waterway before home. Even as she edged along the wall she was surely visible if they cast a torch that way. All she could do was try her best to keep a footing under the silver moonlight seeping through the winter mist.

Then she turned the corner, exhausted, damp with sweat and blood. Out of sight at last.

She tapped out the pattern they'd agreed. It took a minute or so, then Vanni was there.

Paolo sat at the kitchen table in striped pyjamas that looked as if they belonged on a kid. Vanni was in pants and a vest, all he normally wore at night.

They stared at her, horrified.

'My God?' her brother asked. 'What the hell have you done?'

She walked up to the mirror by the bedroom they used and looked at herself. Took out Sander's pistol and slung the grey uniform jacket on the floor.

Her dress was little more than scarlet strips from the waist down. She was covered in blood, from her throat to her legs, and some of it, she knew, was hers. A bruised eye. A cut cheek.

'What have you done?' Vanni asked again, then came and put his arms around her.

Mika started to shake. To choke down a sob. To try to force herself to think.

'They were waiting for us. They knew.'

Paolo's face turned white.

'Someone might have followed you here.'

'No one followed me here,' she barked back at him. 'Do I look like an idiot?'

'Mika . . .' Vanni kept his arms around her. 'You're bleeding.'

'Not my blood. Not much of it. I killed one of them.' She held up a finger and glared at him. 'One.'

She dragged off the remains of the dress Vitale had given her, ran her bloody fingers through the fake blonde hair wondering how quickly she could get rid of that as well. Stood in front of them, bra, grubby pants, caked blood running up and down her legs like daubs from a bad painter.

Then she threw off the last of her clothes and looked at herself naked, not minding that they saw. There was nothing left for her to reveal.

'I need to wash this dirty Crucchi shit off me now,' she said. 'You got a towel?'

Filippo Garzone sat in the silent belly of his church, not the most attractive in Venice but there was so many to choose from. San Pietro was his so naturally he loved it as one might love the runt of a litter. It was only natural the soldiers would look for him first in his small terraced house next to the basilica. Where else? That was where he'd lived ever since he'd moved from Vicenza. Perhaps it was difficult for the Germans to understand that, on a black night when the soul was tested, a man of God would wish to be closer to his altar than his bed.

Come they would though. He'd guessed that from the moment he'd learned about Aldo Diamante's suicide. The whispers he'd heard that evening, round-ups beginning throughout the tenements of Castello and an aborted attack on the Crucchi in their beloved hotel-cum-brothel, only made him more sure. Garzone was no partisan. In truth politics puzzled him since he failed to understand why, when it came to matters of life and death, temporal issues should take precedence over the spiritual. But someone, somewhere, perhaps under duress, would mention his name. Reveal him as a sympathetic ear for those whom the Germans wished dead. A whisper was all that was needed.

There were no regrets. He'd served his flock, be they Fascist, one of the rare religious communists among them or, more often, an ordinary citizen frightened and puzzled by the predicament in which he or she found themselves. Anyone who came and asked him to listen deserved to be heard, whatever reasons took them to that wooden booth in San Pietro. To be brought closer to God too if that was only possible.

It was just such a conversation the Monday before, later shared quietly with Diamante, that had led him to hear a rumour that two Jewish partisans from Turin were seeking sanctuary from the Nazis. Diamante, a man much like himself, detached but concerned, knew much more already, and had come to the conclusion there was nowhere safe where he could hide the pair. The Nazis were already starting to look at the city's Jews with greedy, expectant eyes. To place wanted fugitives in their threatened midst would only enhance the risk for all. Then the two of them together heard that unexpected outburst from Paolo Uccello as men dragged the body of the unfortunate Isabella Finzi from the icy lagoon. The young man's words meant an equitable solution seemed to suggest itself, hiding the pair with the solitary weaver living like a church mouse in his tiny home tucked away at the perimeter of San Pietro.

It was a mistake, on both their parts. The likelihood was always that the Crucchi would keep harassing and torturing those they suspected until the fugitives and those who'd helped them were exposed. He'd never walked close to their grim headquarters in Ca' Loretti but he'd heard enough tales from there. Of screams from the downstairs cells. Of shots ringing out in the courtyard, before them, on occasion, the defiant shouts of those about to die.

Did that mean he was wrong to involve the innocent young Paolo in the schemes of others more worldly? Which was best? The right decision made for the wrong reasons? Or the wrong for the right? What, in the end, was the difference in any case? In the end we were all dead, corpses in the arms of God awaiting resurrection. He'd cautioned his parishioners time and time again to be patient. To await the moment – inevitable surely, he always said – when the forces of freedom triumphed from the south and Hitler, Mussolini and the vileness that came with them were banished to grim chapters in history books yet to be written.

Mute, private opposition to the horrors around you was the wisest course of action. One that might save your life and that of your family even if it left a whisper at the back of the head, a cruel and hurtful voice that spoke of cowardice while others made the most painful sacrifices.

Thinking of all this in the pews of San Pietro, head bowed like any other parishioner before the altar, he opened his Latin bible, the one he'd owned since he was a teenager in then peaceful Vicenza, and found the page he wanted, scanning it under the waxy light of a single oil lamp. A suitable section. Matthew 26:36. The Agony in the Garden of Gethsemane, Jesus awaiting his fate after the Last Supper, knowing he would be betrayed and that his cruel death was only days away.

Matthew, always. For some reason he preferred this to Luke, perhaps because, being a physician, the latter felt moved to record Jesus sweating tears of blood as he prayed. Garzone was a man for feelings and emotions, never physical detail. They seemed needless.

Since the Germans flooded into Venice and seized control the previous September, he'd reread Matthew's version frequently. It seemed apposite. Part of his calling as a priest, his principal role in life perhaps, was to persuade the men and women and children of his flock that God was real and the blood of Jesus still flowed through them at the Holy Mass just as it once ran through the veins of Christ in Jerusalem almost two thousand years before. Some, perhaps most, regarded this as a fairy tale, a gilding of the lily that was the Catholicism they'd grown up with, as much a certain part of their lives as the vast expanse of the lagoon and the changing of the seasons.

Yet now, finally, Garzone believed he was beginning to see this part of Christ's story in true relief. Waiting for the Crucchi it almost felt as if Jesus himself had somehow made his way to the modest streets of Castello, was walking among the cobblestones and mean terraces, casting his gaze into the eyes of his weary and frightened parishioners. Into the face of his priest too.

And saying to them . . . *I understand my child for once I was afraid as well.*

In the smoky yellow lamplight Garzone's finger ran down the flimsy page until he found the line.

Pater mi, si possibile est, transeat a me calix iste.

My father, if it's possible, let this cup pass from me.

The cup being misery, death, pain, all the horrors the fallen world of man might deliver.

Then, three verses later, came the acceptance of his coming crucifixion.

Pater mi, si non potest hic calix transire nisi bibam illum, fiat voluntas tua.

My Father, if it is not possible for this cup to pass from me unless I drink it . . . thy will be done.

Fiat voluntas tua.

God's will. The greatest mystery of all. At the seminary when he was young, long before the war, they'd been visited by a travelling choir from distant Wales, not Catholics at all but no one minded because they had such beautiful voices. They'd sung a gorgeous hymn that had stayed with him, especially the opening words which a friend had translated from the English and Garzone, ever careful, had noted down in his diary, with a vow to remember them.

Immortal, invisible, God only wise,

In light inaccessible, hid from our eyes . . .

So much was veiled from the living, invisible because the frail and the fearful, and he was both, wished it to remain unseen.

Now that self-imposed ignorance was coming to an end. His finger stayed on Matthew's words and, as if by a kind of magic, the refrain of that old hymn returned from the depths of his memory and rang through his head, all those sweet foreign voices in lovely harmony. Filippo Garzone closed his eyes and smiled. He was a priest and had spent his entire adult life ministering to others. In all that time he had, perhaps, come to believe the Lord's will applied more to them than the man, the weak, imperfect man, through whom God spoke.

This deep and inner reverie was broken by a loud and violent sound at the back of the nave. Voices, harsh, threatening. German. Then the door was slammed open and the frantic beams of torches began to break through the quiet dark.

I never lock it, Garzone said to himself, amused. Why must they make such a racket? This is a church and a church is always open.

There should have been a prayer. He always found one of those when a parishioner demanded it, for happy times, baptism and births and marriages. For sad too, sickness, death, the diurnal turn of the world from light to tragedy and, after a while, back again.

But no words came. Only those still ringing in his head.

Fiat voluntas tua.

Immortal, invisible, God only wise.

He was murmuring them as a rifle butt stabbed into his shoulder. Once. Then again.

'I am ready,' Garzone said, raising his hands as he got to his feet. 'I am ready, and for what ensues I forgive you.'

Though he doubted they understood a word.

PART FIVE

I stayed up reading into the early hours, barely hearing the traffic on the Grand Canal fading to the odd night vaporetto and water taxi. The following morning there was a message from school. With only one more week to come before the summer break they'd decided the miscreants currently under suspension could stay away for that as well. Which meant I was now on my own for months, trapped in the lagoon, waiting on a dying grandfather and the strange story he was revealing to me piece by piece.

I didn't realize how much that was starting to unnerve me until I had to walk across the city to the hospital. That day I decided to cross by the Scalzi bridge and go through the Ghetto in Cannaregio, a part of Venice I barely knew. There were a few tourists in the campo, milling round waiting on the Jewish Museum to open. Opposite what must have been the building where Aldo Diamante lived and died was a large, municipal-looking block bearing iron lettering which read 'Casa Israelitica di Riposo'. The nursing home from which the unfortunate Jewish pensioners had been dragged by German soldiers. It wasn't hard to work out where Luca Alberti had stood watching them after he spoke to the priest, Garzone. It was under the sotoportego that ran out of the ghetto to the south east. So I went there, stood where he did. In the unseasonal June heat it was impossible to imagine a cold December day fifty-six years before, the screams and cries of the unfortunate, the hammer of Nazi boots on the cobbles. Now the few trees in the square were in leaf, visitors meandered round licking at their ice creams, a couple of kids played football against the old wellhead in the middle.

Somehow this only made the story in my head more real, more unnerving. I wanted to go up to them and shout, Don't you know what happened here? Can't you feel the traces of all that misery? There were old people around too, locals, I could tell from the dark, unfashionable clothes they wore as they sat on benches reading newspapers or simply enjoying the sun. A few might have been children during the German occupation. Perhaps they saw their own grandparents hauled out of their homes, forced into cattle trucks at Santa Lucia station, headed for the extermination camps in Germany and beyond.

I found myself shivering and close to tears. People were starting to look at me, perhaps the way they'd looked at a young Paolo Uccello, thinking . . . what's wrong with that one? Is he *normal*?

All the same there was still one place that troubled me more, somewhere I had yet to dare to enter. The Giardini degli Angeli itself. When I pushed Chiara she told me it was now a temporary exhibition space for the Biennale which explained the work I saw going on there. As a local I could walk in pretty much any weekday afternoon for free.

Not yet, I thought as I left the high tenement blocks of the ghetto and found the long stretch of the Misericordia canal that would, in fifteen minutes or so and by a circuitous route, take me to Diamante's old hospital of Giovanni e Paolo.

A trio of musicians, electric piano, bass and drums, was practising on a long barge by one of the popular Misericordia bars. A young girl pressed a flyer for a concert into my hand. Another time I might have thought of trying to come back that night. The place was popular. Kids I knew from school used to turn up there and hang out, drink beer, try to pick up girls. I took her leaflet, then pushed it into the nearest bin. More and more I felt I was walking through two cities at the same time. The Venice I'd grown up in. The different, darker, violent city that Nonno Paolo had known when he wasn't much older than me.

Half-dreaming I stumbled over the bridge into the campo of Giovanni e Paolo. Across the square was the cafe of Rosa Salva, somewhere Nonno Paolo used to take me for pastries and ice cream when I was tiny. Now, I knew, the very place a doomed Aldo Diamante and Garzone used to visit too. Was that why Grandpa liked it so much? Was he trying to keep in touch with those memories too while I stuffed my face with pastries and ice cream?

I wandered over to the front window, almost expecting to see them there, peering out at me, an expression on their faces that said, What took you?

Instead there was a gaggle of middle-aged women in blowsy floral dresses, a foreign party I imagined, tucking into cakes and coffee. People on holiday, trapped in the present, oblivious to the past.

One more part of the story, Nonno Paolo said. Then we're done.

'Say it,' he ordered.

'Say what?'

'Whatever's on your mind. Your face is what the English call an open book, Nico. Which is both a blessing and a curse. There's something there you want to get out.'

He looked more frail. His cheeks were an ashy shade of grey and his eyes had lost their usual bright and lively sparkle.

'I don't like him. Vanni Artom.'

'Because he's Jewish?'

'No!'

'Are you sure? Because he liked other men from time to time?'

There we were again. I could feel my face flushing once more.

'It's not that.'

He shook his head and asked, 'Then what?'

'He took advantage of you. He made you do those things to distract you from Mika. From the danger he'd put you in.'

I knew straight away I'd got that wrong.

'Didn't he?' I added.

'In the brief time the two of us were together we didn't do a thing we didn't want. You can't imagine what it was like then. We were living day to day. Hour by hour if I'm honest. Trapped in that place. Thrown together. Frightened. Desperate. As I said . . . curious. If you could count your life in days what would you look for?'

'Love,' I said because I thought it was the answer he wanted. That made my cheeks flush hotter too.

'Exactly. And love comes in many forms.'

He reached for the bedside cabinet and I saw how much the effort drained him.

'Let me,' I said and opened the drawer.

One more envelope. I took it out and noted the title, one that filled me with dread.

'Oh, poor Nico,' he said, shutting the drawer with a shaky, skeletal hand. 'I'm so sorry. Perhaps I'm being cruel, giving you this unwanted gift. A boy of fifteen. With Venice to himself. You could be out there, enjoying yourself. Feeling your young blood run through your veins. I'm not so ancient I forget what that was like.'

'We started this story together. We'll finish it together.'

'Even if it upsets you? Endings do that sometimes. This isn't a fairy story. It's real life. Messy. Such a thing lacks the symmetry of the tales you read in a book.' His eyes were glassy. 'Sometimes matters linger. Some things never go away.'

'I think I can cope, thank you very much.'

'You're not just putting on a brave face?'

'Does it look like it?'

He smiled and said, 'Only you know that.'

'I'm fine. You tell a good story. I can't stop now anyway. I'm hooked. It's as if I'm seeing these people on the streets. Diamante. The priest. Poor Mika.'

'Poor Mika . . .' he whispered.

I didn't know what to say. There was that awkward silence between us, one neither knew how to break.

Finally he tapped the envelope.

'Go read now. Come back tomorrow and tell me what you think.'

Then I kissed him, quickly, tenderly on both whiskery cheeks. He looked surprised. Shocked even.

'I do so hope I haven't made a terrible mistake.' His voice was breaking and there were tears in his weary eyes. 'It's hard to know sometimes what's right, what's wrong. Not till the die's cast and by then it's too damned late.' He patted my hand. I was ready to cry too. 'Time to go, dear grandson. This old man's story needs to run its course.'

BLOOD ON THE STREETS

Sunday morning, just before seven. Paolo couldn't face the Artoms. So he stole quietly out of the front door, stepped through the garden, past the rotting oranges and lemons and the dead eyes of the fallen angels, out through the door in the wall, across the little bridge into San Pietro.

Venice in December was always cold, today more so than ever. The sky had cleared overnight. A thin covering of sparkling frost sat on the cobbles and the bridges. There were icicles hanging from the runoff water on the boats moored in the dockyards to the south of the island and the smaller craft that lined the Rio Sant'Anna as it led to via Garibaldi. Fewer people than usual. Perhaps he'd come out a little early. Gallo, the timid, scared shop-keeper, might not even be open. He'd have to wait, maybe buy himself a coffee in Greta's. It felt good to be out of the house. Good to be away from Vanni and Mika. He'd no idea how they might escape now. How Mika might keep her promise to get them out of Venice.

As he strode towards the commercial part of the street a figure dashed out from the shadows of a sotoportego and dragged him into the dark.

A woman, sturdy, shaking in a black coat, a woollen hat pulled low over her ears.

'Come here . . .' she begged. 'We need to talk.'

Chiara looked terrified, so much it took him a moment to recognize who she was.

'Listen to me for once, Paolo. The Germans are everywhere. They've seized the priest, Garzone. They're taking people in for no good reason at all. Someone got killed last night. One of theirs.'

'Some of ours too,' he said and she stared hard at him for that.

'The priest never meant for you to become involved. You were supposed to hide them. Nothing more.'

'I am involved. We all are.'

She shook his jacket.

'Did you hear me? One of theirs is dead. They'll shoot ten of ours, maybe more, to get their vengeance. You must convince that pair to give themselves up and save some innocents.'

His face flushed.

'I can't do that. You know I can't.'

'Then tell them to go!'

'Go where?'

'Wherever! They're not your responsibility.'

'They're my guests.'

She closed her eyes for a moment.

'If you don't get rid of them you'll end up standing in front of the firing squad by their side.'

That thought had already crossed his mind.

'Then I'd die like a soldier.'

'But you're not a soldier, are you?' she cried. 'Come with me. Walk where I walk.'

Filippo Garzone spent the night alone in a small room on the ground floor of Ca' Loretti. There was a single window high in the wall, a table and two chairs. The walls were bare apart from a two-year-old poster for a Fascist meeting in Mestre. Once it must have been the office of some minor council official. He'd been in the building before the war when Mussolini's bureaucrats used it as their base though for what he couldn't remember. Probably asking for some impoverished local to be excused their taxes or begging for repairs to the rough streets around San Pietro. Life back then had been filled with such mundanities. How they were missed now.

There was no food, no water. But no handcuffs either and the Germans hadn't beaten him. Judging by the shrieks and shouts from the neighbouring rooms that was soon to come. Yet still he found it impossible to pray. His head was full of memories. Old ones, growing up in Vicenza with his loving, gentle parents. Later, finding his feet at the seminary. Coming to Venice and marvelling at the city, its richness, the peculiar nature of its inhabitants, cold and suspicious at first, filled with a genuine selfless warmth, most anyway, once he got to know them.

Then Mussolini's harsh, dictatorial rule – which many never minded so much until, by slow but steady degrees, the cruelty and the bitterness came, both never Italian traits. The Jews were picked on. Dissenting voices were exiled to the far south to work in the countryside, among people they didn't know. Fear crept through streets and factories, schools and hospitals. Loud, discordant voices – which Italians took for granted since everyone loved an argument – fell silent. People were waiting, wondering. Then it came, war. It seemed to him now an inevitability, like a change in the season, winter following autumn. Before anyone was ready, men who would otherwise have fished the lagoon or carried bags for wealthy foreigners appeared in military uniforms and vanished amidst forced cheering, to front lines in Africa and beyond. A good number never returned. Those who did were utterly changed.

Some aspects of this new Italy were amorphous and affected the nation as a whole. Others were small and personal and hurt like a pebble in the shoe or a scabby wound that refused to heal. Such as bullying a young and innocent man, an orphan, almost a boy still, barely able to look after himself, persuading him to accept two fugitive partisans into his isolated, lonely home. Though he wasn't sure the Paolo Uccello he met the day before, determined, unwilling to look him in the eye, was that same fellow. Sometimes it took a lifetime for people to change. On occasion, in extraordinary circumstances, it could happen in a week, a day, an hour.

He would not, he swore, offer up Uccello and those two Jews. Whatever they did to him. When Diamante and he had spoken in the cafe outside Zanipolo both had wondered what torture might do to a man. Garzone, someone who hated pain and suffering in himself as much as others, feared he'd fail, however hard he thought about all those revered martyrs whose deaths lined the walls of every church he'd ever visited. They went to heaven with an angel standing over them, holding out a palm leaf to welcome their holy deaths. But that was the pretty picture the Church wished to paint for its flock. There were no angels around Ca' Loretti. The palms he'd seen in the courtyard as they dragged him inside were mean and scrubby things. Among them stood stakes hammered between the cobbles with the obvious marks of bullets scarring the sooty brickwork behind.

'I will give up no one,' Filippo Garzone said out loud as the door opened. 'Hear me now. Whatever you do. *I will give up no one.*'

'*Buon giorno*,' replied a man with a familiar Venetian voice.

Luca Alberti walked in on his own, closed the door behind him, took a seat at the table. He pulled out a pack of cigarettes and lit one.

'You might have offered me a smoke,' the priest said.

'Do you know how much these things cost?'

'No. I . . . don't use them. I thought you might wish to be polite.'

Alberti appeared troubled. Not just on edge the way he always seemed when there were Germans around listening to his every word. Garzone felt he was good at looking into men's eyes. You didn't always work out what was wrong there. But at least you recognized the signs.

'I always hated church,' Alberti said. 'Too hot in summer. Too cold in winter. Damned sermons going on forever and never making any sense.'

'I doubt I'll be giving any more, will I?'

He leaned forward, blew smoke across the table.

'We've only got a few minutes, Father. Then they're in here. Do as I say and you might get out of this place alive.'

Sleep hadn't been easy for Mika Artom. Or her brother who kept wriggling and sighing beside her on the bed. Maybe an hour or two was the most she got and they were interrupted by dreadful, vivid memories. The lout Sander grabbing at her. The way he'd bled. The noise he made as he died.

Out in the mountains, patrolling with the partisans on their raids, she'd killed three Germans and one Italian, wounded a few more. But always from a distance. It was safer that way. The one time they got close on that last abortive mission Vanni had picked up the injury from a soldier's bayonet. Getting close was more than dangerous too. You saw their eyes. You were aware for a moment of the spark of humanity inside them, however dim.

Was it there in the German? Maybe somewhere. But the war was raging through her blood, hot and angry and vengeful. Trevisan and his comrades were being ripped to pieces by machine-gun fire outside the Gioconda. The raid had been betrayed by a woman the dead all trusted. The German would have raped her, then handed her straight over for interrogation once he was done. After that the inevitable. There was no choice. She didn't regret a thing. Still the images, the sounds, the hard brutality came back to taunt her. And the simple fact she'd wanted that, enjoyed every second.

From the bed, propped against the pillow, hands behind his head, Vanni watched her dress: the clothes she came in. Old shirt, wool jacket, mountain trousers with pockets for weapons, a knife, ammunition. The compass she'd used out in the wilds was still there. As if she needed one now. Everything looked poor, worn, a little dirty and it felt right too. This was who she was. Not a pretend-whore in a scarlet dress. Had she the opportunity she'd have found some way to wash the blonde dye out of her hair. But time was running out. So she found her old wool cap, then Sander's gun, checked the magazine: six shells.

'Mika. Is there any point in me asking what you're going to do?'

'You can always ask.'

'I did.'

She came and sat next to him, smiled, put a hand to his leg. The livid redness was going down but slowly.

'When will I be able to walk? Normally?'

'A few weeks. Hide out somewhere with your friend. This isn't your time. It's mine.'

His eyes had that sheen she hated to see. There was a gentleness inside him Mika tried so hard to ignore at times. But it was impossible. For him the battle was intellectual. Something he'd prefer to wage with words, not weapons. In that way they were so unlike.

'It's not safe here,' he said. 'Someone's bound to talk. Maybe they have already.'

'Then . . . find somewhere else.'

'You're my sister. I want you with me. With us.'

Mika raised an eyebrow.

'Us? I barely know him. He's a kid.'

'I think maybe we robbed him of that. There's a strength in him. A decency. You've seen it.'

'Decency gets you killed.' She gripped his arm. 'Look. I have to go. You hide here. Steal a boat when it's dark. There's plenty round the corner. Go out to the islands and find a cabin somewhere. Just the two of you. Steal. Live off the land. Be patient.'

'Why can't you wait too?'

'Because . . .' It was a good question and deserved a better answer. 'Because there's something I need to do.'

Her hands came away. She retrieved the gun from the pocket of her trousers, looked at it, put the thing away.

'I know where Salvatore Bruno may be right now.'

He said nothing.

'Did you hear me, Vanni? The man who betrayed us. So many innocents. Our family. The man who's going to send so many more to their deaths.'

'I heard.'

'I think I can find him. If I can then I can kill him.'

He rolled his legs off the bed and sat on the sheets, trying to hide the pain.

'Let me come with you.'

'You're in no fit state.'

'I can handle a gun.'

'Oh, for Christ's sake don't be so stupid! Look at you. I don't have time for an invalid. I don't . . .'

She stopped. That was enough.

'And if I could walk—'

'Then I still wouldn't want you. This is one man. It doesn't need an army. He's my prize. I've earned him. I'm not prepared to share.'

He hobbled off the sheets, grimacing as his feet hit the cold tiles.

Mika came and held him, head against his bare chest, for once struggling for the right words.

'We were happy in Turin,' he murmured into her hair.

They were, she thought. Mum and Dad, three kids. A good school though she sometimes had to take on a few of the older boys when they began picking on Vanni because he was a Jew. The darkness was always there, waiting to fall.

'They stole that from us too,' she whispered close up, enjoying the warmth of him, that fuggy brother smell he had.

'Mika. We're still family even if it's just the two of us. We can steal that boat together. Paolo can come along if he wants. If not . . . I'm with you. You're my sister. My blood.' He pushed her back from him, took her by the shoulders. 'We can do this. Together. We have to . . .'

She smiled. She kissed his cheek, brushed against him and knew he'd feel her tears.

It took a while but then she said, 'Stop making this so hard.'

For once he sounded cross.

'I want to. I have to.'

'I know where I can find Salvatore Bruno. The Jew hunter. The one who killed Mum and Dad. And all the others.'

He sighed.

'And if he ends up killing you.'

'He won't. I saw him last night. He's just a creep. A spy. A traitor. Not a soldier.'

'You don't need to do this—'

'God, Vanni! What are you saying? Of course I've got to do it. Who else is there? If I don't he leaves here, goes back to tracking us down and handing us over to the Nazis. Who else? Please . . .' She was crying freely and she wished she wasn't. 'Don't tell me I shouldn't do it. Send me out of here with your blessing.'

'And if I do that . . . you'll come back. We'll find that boat together.'

She wiped her face.

'Yes. I promise. We'll sail away. Somewhere they'll never find us. You, me, Paolo. The three of us can wait things out. See what happens.'

Vanni Artom kept quiet. His face wasn't made for misery. Any more than he was made for war.

'You're my kid brother,' she said. 'I'll always come back to look after you.'

Funny, she thought, how easy it was for two people so close to one another to lie with such glib and shallow ease. And both know it.

She kissed him and asked, 'Where's he now?'

'I don't know. I heard him go out. For food I think. He's been gone a long time. I'm worried.'

'You worry enough for all of us. Stay here. I'll be back. We'll survive this. Just like we got through everything before.'

He followed her into the kitchen and opened the door on to the rock ledge.

The winter sun was so low and harsh it hurt his eyes.

'You look like the old Mika,' he said. 'The one we left in the mountains. You look . . . happy.'

That got a grin and she made a pretend gun with her hand, mouthed a pretend shot, blew away pretend smoke from the barrel like a cowboy in one of the films they used to watch in the cinema in Turin as kids. Until the Jews weren't allowed past the door.

'Happier still in a little while,' she told him as she left.

* * *

It was the kind of winter day Paolo's mother used to love. Washed out colours, sparkling light. Venice in the guise of a daydream painted by that English artist she so admired, Turner. Though grey clouds were gathering, starting to build from the mainland, tumbling down from the Dolomites. Snow was on the way, probably soon.

Chiara made him stay to her right as they walked down the broad street, on the opposite side to Greta's cafe. The bar was normally full of locals at this time of morning, busily downing coffee and cheap grappa. Now German soldiers lounged by the door cradling their weapons while others, men in dark suits, crowded inside.

'Don't make it obvious you're looking,' she ordered. 'Keep walking.'

There were more soldiers outside Gallo's shop and the sharp, high screams of a woman wailing. Chiara took him into the alley opposite so they could watch unseen. The cries, he guessed, were coming from the man's wife who stood outside shrieking at the Germans. Then the little grocer came out, arms behind his back, mouth bleeding, head down, pushed into the street by a couple of Crucchi troops.

They could hear his wife's voice over the stamp of boots.

'He's done nothing. Signori. *Signori*. He's a good man. A loving father. He's done nothing.'

Paolo thought, Doing nothing's the same as doing something in times like this. There was no place to hide. No way of pretending you were innocent when they came for you. Garzone had simply begged him to pass on food and money to Paolo every time he came into the shop.

'Gallo doesn't know who I am,' he whispered. 'He doesn't know where I live. Garzone arranged things that way.'

'I told you,' she shot back. 'The priest's in their hands too.'

One of the soldiers fetched Gallo a hefty smack in the back with the butt of his rifle. The wife screamed again and got knocked to the ground. A group of locals had emerged from the alleys that led to the meaner terraces near the abandoned Biennale gardens. A few were throwing insults at the Crucchi. Most simply watched.

Chiara swore then, a vile, local curse. One he'd never heard before.

'You never should have taken that pair in.'

'My father never should have agreed to make those banners for a bunch of Fascists. But he did. And we made them. You and me. And Vanni. We got paid too.'

It was rare for them to share such cross words.

'I came out for food,' he added. 'Where's safe?'

'There's a question.'

'You can help me or I can do this myself.'

She said there was a place in the Campo Vittorio on Sant'Elena, the last island along, beyond the Biennale. It was too dangerous to go the other way, by the Arsenale which was crawling with Crucchi troops.

'You want me to come with you?'

Across the street soldiers were dragging filing cabinets from Gallo's store. A bunch of locals had surrounded the grocer's wife to stop the others hitting her. The woman was red-faced on the ground, beating the frozen cobbles with her bloody hands. One of the troops raised his rifle, pointed it straight at her. A man in a fisherman's jacket walked right in front to get in the way. A standoff. After a brief shouted argument a couple of women hauled the wife off the ground, took her in their arms and walked her down the street.

'Sant'Elena's too far,' he said. 'I'm going home. We can . . . we can make do till it's safe.' He corrected himself. 'Safer.'

'Paolo. Please, listen to me now . . .' In his head he could see her teaching Vanni the ways of the Jacquard loom like this. 'I told your mother I'd look after you. If anything happened to them. I promised . . .'

'So you said. A million times. You did look after me. When I needed it.'

In the damp, malodorous shadows of the hidden alley they embraced.

He was about to step back into via Garibaldi when she pulled him to her.

'This way,' she said, pointing into the darkness. 'I can take you home and none will see.'

Ten minutes later, along a circuitous route he felt sure he could never find again, they emerged close to the Rio di San Daniele by the Arsenale's eastern edge. Two minutes from home. He embraced her again, said something about how she shouldn't worry. They would survive this somehow. They'd see the war through.

'Are you taking the boat to Burano?' he asked.

'Soon.'

He wasn't going to get a straight answer to that one. So they said goodbye and he walked back to the little wooden bridge, unlocked the door, closed it securely behind him as always, and walked through the garden.

Vanni sat at the kitchen table picking sardines out of a can with a fork.

'Where is she? Where's Mika?' Paolo asked.

'You should know my sister by now.' He lumbered to his feet. Blood was dripping through the fabric of his pyjama trousers again. 'I couldn't stop her. I tried.' He grimaced. Whether it was pain from the wound or the memory Paolo couldn't guess. 'Dammit. Ah . . .'

There was a long groan as he tried to walk for the door.

'I have to get out of here.'

'Vanni. You can't. You're in no fit state.'

'Then you can help me. Or stay here. Either way I have to . . .'

Lurching for his jacket, he stumbled, fell to the floor, straight on to the stricken leg.

Paolo pulled him to his feet.

'You've got to stop this now.' The two of them were as close as the night before. 'Stay here. With me.'

'Tonight she says she'll come back and we can go and steal a boat somewhere.'

'Then that's what we'll do.'

'You think?' Vanni laughed, just a little. 'Mika lies. She tells people what they want to hear. Then does what she feels like anyway.'

'I know,' Paolo said and held him. Found the courage to kiss his cheek, hold his hair. 'But maybe she'll come back. Give it a little time. I was . . . indulging you.'

'A little time may be all we have.'

'Then let's use it.'

But he withdrew from Paolo's close embrace, limped towards the coats that hung by the back door.

'I need to see beyond your garden of angels. I need to see the light. The sky.' Vanni rapped on the window and looked at the weather. A few soft and gentle flakes had begun to fall. 'The snow. I love the snow.'

* * *

'A few minutes.' Garzone shook his head and frowned. 'You want me to beg for my life in a few minutes?'

Alberti glared at him.

'I don't need to do this. I could have let them come straight in.'

Garzone didn't doubt that was true. But the man must have had his reasons.

'I won't tell them you talked to me. Don't worry. I won't say you tipped me off.'

Alberti stubbed his cigarette in the tin ashtray on the desk, lit another, laughed and shook his head.

'What's so funny?' Garzone wondered.

'You. I already wrote down that I spoke to you. Kindly. You're a priest. I was trying to work out what you knew. Thinking maybe I could get you on our side—'

'That's not true and you know it.'

Alberti threw up his hands in despair.

'Jesus Christ! Why do I bother? None of this is about what's true. It's about what they want to believe. Outside the Gioconda they ambushed some idiot partisans last night. Watched and cheered, threw a party. Then that Jewish girl ruined it. They were supposed to grab her too. But they were too busy enjoying the show. She killed one of theirs and now she's gone.' He swore under his breath. 'Nasty little thug called Sander. Did us all a favour.'

'Every life has meaning. Even that of a nasty little thug.'

'You're not in the pulpit now, Father. Give it up. Sander would have come in here, cut your throat and laughed while you bled to death on the floor. Done it often enough. Any minute now his boss Oberg's walking through the door. He's a half-decent man for a German. Give him something and he might let you out of here.'

Garzone kept quiet.

'Are you even listening? The Crucchi shot four Venetians last night. Some fools who thought they could be heroes. The Jew, Mika Artom. She killed one of theirs. You know that name . . .?'

'No. I don't.'

That brought a smile to Alberti's face.

'Good, I believe you. Or else you're a pretty decent liar for a priest. Either way I'm impressed.'

'I don't care what you believe.'

'Believe this. They lost one of theirs. When that happens there's a calculation. How many locals got to die to make up for it? How many of our lives make up for one of theirs? There will be reprisals. As sure as the acqua alta comes when you least want it. For that they need names. You're a good guy. A decent guy. A *scared* guy who got pushed into helping them out.'

'Did I?'

Alberti sighed and closed his eyes for a second, exasperated.

'I know you saw Diamante. I know you and the old Jew were close.'

Garzone reached over, took one of Alberti's cigarettes, lit it, coughed, then coughed some more and stubbed the thing out.

'I thought you didn't smoke.'

'I don't. Bad for your chest. Still, what does that matter now? Do you sleep well?'

'No,' Alberti said with a shrug. 'I don't.'

'Do you go to confession?'

The man's eyes looked sad and weary, not quite dead. Not quite.

'I'm not the religious sort. If you'd seen what I have maybe you wouldn't either.'

'Or perhaps I'd believe even more.'

Alberti was silent for a moment.

'We don't have time for this. *You* don't have time.'

What came next was surprisingly easy to say. Somewhere along the way, in the company of the grunting troops who'd dragged him through the midnight streets, a corner had been turned in Garzone's head. All lives were journeys. He'd said that from the pulpit often enough. They had a single destination too, the grave.

'I've all the time the Lord allows,' he said. 'As have you. We're not so different.'

'I told them you were a friend of Diamante's. That you spoke to him not long before he cheated them of their list.' He ground his cigarette into the tin tray. 'Not that it matters any more. They'll round those Jews up anyway.'

'Why are you telling me this?'

'Because I'm going to give you the names you offer them. Not the Artoms. You know nothing about them. They were Diamante's. But there were those among your flock who confessed to working with the terrorists.'

'The confessional is sacred—'

'I'm trying to help! These names. Remember them. Rocco Trevisan. Adolfo Tosi. Gabriele Gallo . . .'

'The grocer? He wouldn't harm a fly. I won't—'

'Greta Morino.'

'Greta? The poor woman runs a tiny little bar. Why would I give them her name?'

The man opposite him winced.

'Christ, this is hard.' He leaned forward and jabbed a tobacco-stained finger in Garzone's direction. 'Listen and try to get this into your thick head. All the names I just gave you. They're either dead already or somewhere else in this dump as good as. They're not leaving. You still might.'

There were voices outside the corridor. Alberti glanced anxiously at the door.

'Oberg's coming. You're going to give them those names.'

'I don't know any names.'

'That doesn't matter! Say these people mentioned something that made your ears prick up when they were in church. They don't think you're a partisan. Just a fool who got taken in by all that shit.'

Garzone nodded.

'And if I do this you think they'll let me go?'

'Maybe. Give them nothing except your preaching and you're dead. One more corpse on my conscience.'

'Poor man! So this is for you? Not me at all?'

Mad all of a sudden Alberti reached over the table, grabbed the collar of his black jacket, pulled him close.

'Listen to me, you old fool. There's not a damned thing you can say or do that's going to keep them alive. The only one you might save is yourself.'

The door crashed open. Three people marched in. Dark suits, severe faces. The one in front, a hatchet-faced man who looked like the boss, Oberg he guessed, said something in rapid German.

Alberti swiped his hand round Garzone's face and the shock of the blow made the priest whimper, more in surprise than pain.

'This one's going to talk,' the Venetian said and slapped him hard again. 'Not that I think he's got much to tell.'

He got out of the chair and let Oberg take it. The other two lounged at the back, staring right at Garzone. From a neighbouring room came the sound of someone screaming. A woman, the priest guessed, though it was hard to tell. Greta Morino was pushing seventy and more than a little soft in the head. If it was her she wouldn't even know why she was there.

'Want me to stay?' Alberti asked.

'You speak their language,' Oberg replied. 'My Italian is somewhat rusty.' Not as bad as he made out, Alberti thought. 'Of course you're going to stay.'

'I have nothing to tell you,' the priest said before they could ask a thing. 'Except Aldo Diamante was my friend. A good man. Honest. A saint to everyone he met. We talked. Of the time when Venice was free. When men and women could walk the streets without fear. That's all.'

In German, Alberti said, 'He's a church man. He hung around with Jews.' Then, in Italian, he barked, 'Tell them what you told me, Garzone.'

The priest shook his head and said, 'And what exactly was that?'

'Rocco Trevisan came to you in confession and told you he was thinking of planning violent acts. So did that thug Tosi—'

'They're both dead,' Oberg snapped.

'What about Gallo and the bar woman?' Alberti demanded, staring hard into Garzone's face. 'You know them.'

'They are not of my flock. I believe the church of San Giuseppe is closer for them. As far as I'm aware—'

'If a man tells a priest he has murderous thoughts,' Oberg cut in, his Italian clear and exact, 'then we should know of it.'

'What happens in confession is for my ears alone, sir. Never yours.'

Alberti stepped forward, struck him hard around the face, then followed up with a couple of punches. Blood began to leak from Garzone's nostrils. His right eye was closed, bruised and cut above the brow. Still he said nothing, just stared at the desk, waiting for the next blow.

'We're wasting our time with this one,' Alberti said. 'He's not got the guts or the wit to do any harm. Let's kick him out of here. I'll watch to see who comes calling from his flock. If there's anything to be found there . . .'

Oberg lit a cigarette and sat back in the chair.

'Ah, but Alberti. You lost a colleague last night. I know you and Sander were not the best of friends but all the same. A woman terrorist we should have apprehended murdered him. On our own premises. One German victim. Ten locals must pay.' He shrugged. 'Think yourselves lucky. If this were Milan or Bologna there'd be twenty, thirty of them. I'm being generous.'

'He's a priest,' Alberti said. 'Popular. It will cause . . . offence.'

'All the more reason he should stand alongside the rest.' Oberg closed his eyes for a second, thinking as a spiral of grey smoke curled around him. 'I want an execution with meaning. Somewhere public. A place they'll remember.' He thought of something and pointed across the table at Garzone, dabbing at his bleeding nose. 'That square outside the church of his. Bring the others. They're all from around there. All known. They have that curious bell tower standing on its own . . .'

'A practical decision,' Garzone cut in with a smile. 'Had my predecessors attached it to the church then the whole building might have sunk deep into the sand.'

'How very interesting,' Oberg replied. 'White marble from what I remember. We'll stand them in front of that. The blood will show.' He glanced at Alberti. 'If you'd tracked down that damned pair of Jews in the first place none of this would have happened.'

'I am aware of that, sir . . .'

'Good.' The German glanced at the burly pair next to him, then nodded at Garzone. 'Bind his arms and get the rest. We'll march them through the streets, a squad all round.' He glanced at his watch. 'Make sure there's a crowd. At noon we shoot them all and their families can watch. After that we send troops house-to-house searching for that pair of Jews. They must be there somewhere. I want every last tenement searched and turned over till we find them.'

'You break a butterfly upon a wheel,' the priest said, looking up at him from the table.

'There are no butterflies in winter,' Oberg replied. 'Spring and summer are a long way off and for you they'll never come. Take him now. Don't rough him up any more. Don't do anything else to the rest of them. This . . .' He blinked and for a moment looked as if he might have second thoughts. 'This is a demonstration of our strength. Our determination. Not our cruelty.'

Garzone looked up from the table and burst out laughing.

'Poor man. To assign all this to your duty.' He struggled to his feet and held out his hands. 'I am ready, sir. Are you?'

The address Salvatore Bruno had scribbled on his pad was for a ground-floor apartment on the Fondamenta Fenice, a short street that ran behind the opera house by the side of a narrow canal. It was a monied part of the city, well away from the rundown terraces of Castello. A little enclave of luxury, with fine shops not far away, restaurants where liveried waiters in white jackets with gold braid were serving late breakfasts to clients who looked a little worse for wear from the previous evening.

The tributary to the Grand Canal where Trevisan and his fellow partisans had been betrayed by Sara Vitale, then slaughtered theatrically by German machine guns was only a few blocks away. But the Fondamenta Fenice appeared somewhere the war had yet to reach.

Well-off looking locals shuffled along, the women in fur coats, a couple carrying small dogs, heads held high, noses in the air since there was the remnant stench of an emptied pozzo nero nearby. Accompanying most of them, often arm in arm, were men in the uniform black of the affluent Venetian male in winter, heavy wool coats all the way down to the ankles, homburg hats, shiny leather gloves. As Mika Artom stopped by the corner, wondering how to proceed, a pair, elderly, meandered across the low bridge to Fenice, talking loudly about the opera and how much they were looking forward to seeing a coming performance.

Somewhere in the bulky concert hall across the narrow water a rehearsal had begun. The strains of an orchestra drifted out into the frosty day, accompanied by a lone female voice straining at an aria. This rich and comfortable couple stopped and smiled at the sound. She stayed where she was by the foot of the small bridge, determined they'd see her, about to speak. But the woman caught her with a shocked glance and the man muttered something about being in a hurry. The two of them dashed off towards San Marco, huddled together as if she were some kind of threat.

'I'm not a bloody beggar,' Mika yelled at them as they retreated into the shadows of a nearby sotoportego. 'I didn't want anything.'

Just a word or two. Some acknowledgement that the pain the rest of the world was sharing was visible to them too. They'd had this argument in Padua, so many times with students there. Pretty much none of them sided with the Fascists and the Black Brigades, or if they did, refused to acknowledge it. But most were reluctant to become involved, to act, to fight. She understood this wasn't simply cowardice, though that played its part. There was a mood abroad, one that called for patience in the face of horror. The Americans and the British were coming. Whatever the lying fascist newspapers and radio stations claimed, Hitler and Mussolini were losing the war. One day it would be over. They knew the brave had to die to make that happen. They just wanted the brave to be someone else.

In the meantime snatch squads seized Jews, young and old, dragged them from their homes, harried them in the street. Sealed them in railway trucks made for cargo, sent them off to foreign countries, unknown ends. Or, in the case of her parents, gunned them down in a drab field outside the city after making them dig their own graves. Italy was a jail and so many of its prisoners kept doffing their caps to the warders. It was insulting. It was just plain *wrong*. That last thought more than any dogged her, night and day, burned in her head, demanded she do something. It was why she'd ignored Vanni's pleas to stay safe inside his comfortable little nest in the Giardino degli Angeli. Why she sought out Trevisan and the band of partisans in via Garibaldi, in spite of the risk.

Why she'd agreed to their plan to murder as many Crucchi as they could in the ballroom of the Gioconda. Only to be betrayed.

Maybe Sara Vitale's treachery had saved her life. That and the intervention by the sad-eyed Venetian collaborator who'd tipped her off. Not that this mattered. She'd felt bad after the failed raid in the mountains. That was her fault too. Now her attempt to make amends had failed as well. The death of one lecherous drunken German wasn't enough. Maybe nothing ever would be.

In the dark of the sotoportego, three doors along from the door to Bruno's apartment, Mika Artom waited, thinking she might force her way in when someone came or went. Church bells rang somewhere, marking the hour. Still no one appeared. The gun weighed heavily in her pocket. Six shells. Enough for one Jew hunter.

The sky, so bright when she'd left by the back door of the apartment, had grown dull as she strode, head down through the streets. Now it was a miserable shade of grey. Wispy flakes of snow had started to fall, fluttering down like tiny white feathers, settling on the white marble bridge to the opera house, disturbing the few passers-by who brushed them crossly from their sleeves and jackets.

Deep winter was descending on Venice, bitter and icy, with a hard breeze rolling down from the mountains where she and Vanni and their little band of partisans had stumbled as they sought Germans to kill, railway lines to sabotage, weapons and ammunition to steal.

There was no going back. Not much going forward either.

A girl of maybe fifteen or sixteen was marching briskly along the pavement from the west. In her arms was a bundle of laundry. A lot of it. She had a sheet of paper in her right hand and kept glancing at it, then the numbers on the doors.

The snow kept getting heavier by the minute, the flakes fatter.

When the kid came to a halt in front of the block, Mika stepped out, walked over, said in as strident a voice as she could manage, 'You've come with laundry for Signor Bruno? Finally.'

She was young, nervous, a little frightened maybe.

'The Germans in the Gioconda sent me with fresh sheets. I don't know who for.'

'It's for the gentleman from Turin. The one the Crucchi love so much they put him here.' Mika held out her hands for the laundry and said, 'Let me in. I'll do it.'

The girl didn't move.

'This is my job. Why would you want to do it for me?'

A smile, then: 'Because Bruno ordered a morning whore as well. Unless you want that position as well.' She touched the laundry. 'But if you'd like to join us I'm sure he won't mind. He likes them young.'

Her face was like thunder. She thrust the sheets into Mika's hand.

'You go sleep with a traitor. Not me.'

'Now that . . .' Mika wanted to hug her, to scream at her too. 'That is just the kind of thing you don't say at times like this.' The sheets were still warm from the laundry. 'Open the door.'

Without another word she did.

The hallway was dark. It took a while for the girl to find the light.

'Which is it?' Mika asked.

'There's only one on the ground floor. Didn't they tell you?'

'Whores.' She nodded back at the world outside, where the snow was starting to fall steadily like a winter blanket. 'We're good at one thing only. Now get out of here. Don't say you saw me.'

'I didn't,' the kid said and slammed the heavy slab of wood behind her as she left.

Mika dropped the laundry, took out the gun, stood outside the door, listened.

Voices. A man and a woman. Laughter. The squeak of a bed. She waited for that to stop, then rapped hard on the door with the butt of the pistol and yelled, 'Laundry from the Gioconda, Signor Bruno.'

'Leave it outside,' a woman's voice yelled back.

Sara Vitale. It sounded like her. Two in one, Mika thought.

'Can't do that. They won't let me. People steal things. Please let me in. I'll just leave it on the floor. It won't take long.'

Not long at all.

The door opened a crack. Red hair, the glint of lazy, sated eyes.

She kicked at the wood, as hard she could, forced the thing open, slamming the edge straight into the face of the figure behind.

The gun.

One shot, stray, unaimed, stupid.

It missed of course.

Sara Vitale was moving sideways, quick as a scuttling rat.

The apartment was little more than a studio, poorly lit. The only light came from near the bed, where Bruno lay naked on top of the sheets, head back on the pillow, a look of surprise and anger on his face.

A second shot.

It hit him straight in the gut and he began screaming.

Something flashed in the dim light, a curse followed, a woman's voice. Then, in her left side, came the fiercest pain Mika Artom had ever felt, a sharp blade biting deep until it hammered into bone.

It took the best part of an hour to get Vanni dressed and out into the open air. He could barely walk more than a few steps at one time. Paolo had found a scarf of his father's, thick wool and a Scottish tartan, and told him to wrap it round his face. Underneath a fisherman's cap he was surely unrecognizable even if there were

Germans or their agents out on their streets with a description. The greater risk was a sudden stop and search. The only papers Vanni had were his own and the counterfeit French ID in the name of Pierre Goulet, one he thought compromised, too risky to use. So, after a short and intense argument, Paolo gave him his own card and told him to use it if questioned. He, in the meantime, would plead stupidity for leaving his ID at home. Any Italian collaborator accompanying the Crucchi patrols would recognize him as a local from his accent. It wasn't a rare event and usually the soldiers were too busy or lazy to bother with anything but a reprimand.

'Where do you want to go?' he asked as he unlocked the gated door to the bridge.

'Anywhere. Somewhere I can sit and breathe. A cafe. I need a beer.'

'The nearest bar's a long walk from here. It's been shut by the Germans. They've taken the woman who ran it.'

'Then the one after that.'

'Christ, Vanni.' He was leaning on the bridge post, out of breath, a dark stain on his trousers where the wound had begun to bleed again. 'You won't get there. You can't help Mika. Not like this.'

He didn't answer, just looked up and down the alley. To the left was the larger bridge to San Pietro where the marble campanile, stranded on its own in a patch of grass in front of the church, was half obscured by swirling clouds of snow, spiralling along its length in the icy breeze. To the right the narrow way led to the broader street which wound down towards via Garibaldi.

'Let's go back inside,' Paolo begged.

A group of men and women were gathered by the corner, gossiping, looking worried.

'No,' said Vanni as he hobbled over the steps.

'Twelve o'clock,' a dishevelled old man in a thick seaman's jacket was saying, shaking his head, balling his fist as he spoke. 'Twelve o'clock and they're advertising it like it's a circus or something. Sweet Jesus. They murdered Rocco and the others last night. Now this.'

There was a middle-aged woman in the heart of the crowd. It took a moment for Paolo to recognize her. Gallo's wife, from the grocer's shop. Her face was red, tears streamed down her cheeks.

A woman of similar age and looks, a sister perhaps, had her arm round her shoulders.

'My Gabriele never did nothing wrong,' the wife cried, voice cracking. 'Never harmed anyone. Let all of you run up debts when you had nothing.'

'That damned priest got him into this,' said the woman with her. 'Garzone. He was in cahoots with the Jews. If it wasn't for him . . .'

'They took the priest as well,' the old man barked back. 'Leave him out of this. He's a man of God who'd never turn away a soul in need.'

'The Jews . . .' the woman retorted, furious.

'They haven't harmed anyone. Aldo Diamante's dead, the best doctor we ever had. The Germans are putting the rest in cattle trucks at Santa Lucia! For the love of Jesus—'

'They're Jews! It's not our god, Beppe.'

The old fellow turned on her and snarled, 'These are men and women I grew up with. Venetians. Like us. Blame the bastards who are murdering them. Not their victims. I just told you. Last night they shot Rocco Trevisan. That fool Tosi too. Two others . . . I don't even know their names. The Crucchi did this. Not the Jews.'

'If they'd stayed at home Rocco wouldn't be dead,' she cried. 'If Garzone hadn't got Gabriele in his fool scheme he'd still be behind his counter, serving us all like he always did.'

He threw his hands in the air and yelled something about giving up. Then turned to go.

Vanni stopped him and asked what was happening.

The fellow eyed him up and down sharply.

'And who wants to know? You don't sound like you're from round here.'

'I'm an Italian, friend. Maybe I knew someone who got caught up in that shit at the Gioconda last night.'

He scowled.

'In that case you'll be dead soon too.'

'The priest,' Paolo cut in. 'The grocer Gallo. I know them.'

The old man shook his head and looked close to tears.

'One of theirs got killed last night. Which means someone has to pay. They're going to parade them through the city. Through San Marco. Along the waterfront. All the way up via Garibaldi. Going to make sure we all see. We all know.' He wiped away the soft snow from his creased forehead and nodded at the pale white pillar of the campanile ahead in the eddying white cloud. 'Then they're going to line them up against that thing and shoot the poor bastards. Nine men. Poor Greta from the bar. All because some woman from out of town killed one of theirs last night.' He pulled his old fisherman's jacket tight round him. 'Ten of ours dead for a single stinking German and it wasn't even us that murdered the bastard. One of them a priest too. Christ . . .'

'I need to be there,' Vanni murmured.

The man peered at him.

'Why? That's what they want. To put us all in the fear of them. A crowd of wailing women getting pushed back by their bloody soldiers. While the rest line up those poor buggers against the tower. Who the hell wants to watch that?'

'Garzone's my friend,' Paolo cut in. 'I want him to see me. I don't want him to feel alone.'

'Dying's best done on your own these days,' the man said. 'You don't need an audience. It's coming for us all soon enough.'

Vanni took his arm.

'Twelve o'clock? You're sure?'

'That's what they're telling everyone. They're Crucchi. I imagine they'll get there on time.'

Salvatore Bruno was writhing and squealing on the bed, mired in his own blood.

She couldn't think for a moment. The pain was that bad.

Then Sara Vitale, half-naked in a flimsy nightdress, was coming at her again, a knife in her right hand.

Mika ducked, still clutching at her side. The blade stabbed into a crack between door and frame and stuck.

'You stabbed me, bitch,' she said, then kneed Vitale hard in the groin. Which maybe hurt her even more.

The woman staggered back. Mika was between her and the knife now. No getting it. Not so long as she could stay conscious and the sharp, bright pain of the wound in her side made that easier somehow.

'You gave Trevisan and the other to the Crucchi.'

Vitale was trying to think of some way to come back at her.

'You were screwing this louse all along and Trevisan never knew. You—'

'We lost!' Vitale shrieked. 'Can't you see that? We lost. Nothing left to fight for.'

'There's always something . . .' Blood was starting to trickle down her waist. She could feel its warmth and the way it was coagulating on her skin. 'We win in the end. That's how history works. Even if we're not the ones there to see it . . .'

Vitale laughed at her. She looked crazy.

'You sound like Rocco. All the crap he'd swallowed from the books his old man pushed at him. Like they were the bible or something.' She took a step closer. 'Dead means dead. Always dead. Dead means others get to come along, step in your shoes and enjoy the life you should have had. I don't want anyone in my shoes. I'm owed better.'

'You're owed,' Mika said as she raised the gun. The man on the bed was getting louder. She needed to deal with that.

Vitale stood up straight, hands on bare hips, gazed right at her.

'Doesn't matter. They're going to shoot you all. Last night they were rounding up people. Names they'd heard of.'

'Names you gave them?'

She shrugged and the shoulder of her flimsy nightdress fell off. There were bruises on her shoulder, bite marks by the look of it. Bruno maybe wasn't the kindest of lovers.

'I told you. Dead is dead. It doesn't matter. Can't believe they were so stupid they didn't pick you up in the Gioconda.'

'Of course it matters.'

'They're going to search every last house in Castello till they find you. And your brother. Then they're going to tear you apart in Ca' Loretti, tie you to a stake in that yard out back. They were going to do that to me when they found me.'

'But you turned?'

'Yes. I turned. No more fighting. No more dreams. No more Marx and Gramsci.' She leaned forward, eyes blazing. 'Dead . . . is . . . dead. Unless you run. You want to know where? I can show you. You and your brother if he's still alive . . .' She glanced at the bed. 'We need to finish that bastard. You don't think I came here willingly, do you? I was part of the prize.'

One brief moment of hesitation. That was all it took. Vitale saw her chance, lunged for the weapon. Mika was quick enough to fall back, slam against the wall, cold and sweaty fingers wrestling with the gun.

The first shot went somewhere into the woman's left thigh. Then, as she fell screaming and thrashing to the floor the second caught her in her head.

Mika stumbled away, got to the bed, put her hands down to stop herself falling on the naked, bleeding man there.

'Don't shoot me,' Bruno begged. 'I got a wife and kids.'

Four shells down. Two left. There was more ammunition in the store Trevisan had her hide in Uccello's little house. A better handgun too and she'd stupidly left it there. Instead she took the dead German's weapon for no more reason than it felt right. None of this was thought through the way they'd planned raids with her vanished partisan band in the mountains. From the moment she'd woken that morning the day and her hunger had dragged her along, one direction, one aim only. What happened along the way. That was the only thing that mattered.

'I won't shoot you,' Mika said getting up and going to the door. 'I can't afford to.'

She retrieved the knife from the wood and tried to think of the bruises on Sara Vitale. Tried to summon up some excuse for the brutality she was about to wreak on the dying man on the bed, his guts half out.

Soon she could hear the rhythmic rattle of her own breath, panting from the pain and the work, almost obliterating his screams.

The church bells kept ringing as Garzone and the nine other condemned prisoners lined up outside Ca' Loretti. Perhaps that was another order from the Germans, following Oberg's demands. Make a performance of this. A piece of bloody, public theatre. Looking at the rest of them shivering in the steadily falling snow the priest felt he'd got off lightly. Most bore signs of beating. One, a man he didn't know, had a bloody mouth and no teeth. It looked as if someone else was missing an ear since there was blood leaking out from beneath a ragged white bandage, and the fellow kept feeling at his head tentatively as he trembled, barely able to stand in the bitter cold. A squad of troops had gathered around them, all in deep winter gear. They looked ready for battle in Russia, not a march through the streets of the old lady of the Adriatic, all the way from San Marco to San Pietro, one aim only on their minds.

Luca Alberti stood outside the cafe opposite smoking a cigarette, sipping at a cup of coffee. He caught Garzone's attention and the two men's eyes stayed locked on one another for a few seconds. The priest wondered what that meant. Probably Alberti saying, *Don't blame me. I tried.*

He wished he could have told him, I know you did but you were wasting your time. There would be no angels, no outstretched arm with a martyr's palm leaf beckoning him to heaven. No need of any of that either. He was the priest of San Pietro, a servant of Venice. These people were among the city's flock, strangers, residents of other parishes, it didn't matter. If a man of God was asked to accompany them on that final journey it was impossible to refuse.

Greta Morino was too old to walk far. So they'd found her a wheelchair and told Gallo to push her. The grocer, his face bruised and cut about, did his best as he guided her across the cobbles trying to fend off the questions she kept asking as they set off for the Piazza San Marco.

What's happening?

Where are we going?

What did I do wrong?

She kept on asking as the doomed and sorry band was marched through the narrow streets, watched from windows by silent, resentful faces, until they stepped beneath the arches of the Correr museum, out into the grand piazza itself.

There were faces behind the windows of Florian's, visitors, Germans perhaps, enjoying the coffee and pastries. No sign of life in the great basilica which he loved, after a fashion, though he preferred the modest plainness of San Pietro, more in keeping with his parish, to its baroque grandeur of glittering gold mosaics.

No lights in the Doge's Palace as they moved along in this strange formation, choreographed to the stamp of the soldiers' heavy boots.

They'd been ordered not to talk. Not to try to make contact with any of the locals who'd now joined the procession, silent but casting hateful glares at the troops. All the same the noise of the marching men was loud enough for Gallo to nudge him as he pushed Greta along. The old woman had given up on her bleating and seemed almost asleep.

'Father?'

'Gabriele.'

'Forgive me. I gave them your name.'

'Ah.'

'They made me. They beat me. They said they'd let me go.'

'The Devil knows how to tempt. When did they pick you up?'

'This morning.'

'Well, they took me last night in my church. So you've nothing to feel guilty about.'

The word jogged something in the old woman. She started singing fragments of an old folk song, one in Veneto, not Italian. A rambling tale about a young man meeting Satan one night while out fishing in the lagoon. Selling his soul for nothing more than a catch good enough to win the hand of a young woman he admired. She'd forgotten everything but the first two verses. As they approached the rise of the Arsenale bridge, the crowd behind now numbering perhaps a hundred or more, she gave up and started to weep.

The bells kept tolling. More modest ones now, in smaller campanili, their tones fainter, higher, more gentle.

'Don't cry, Greta,' Garzone said, putting a hand to her damp and greasy grey hair. 'Don't cry . . .'

'Where are we going, Father?'

'Home,' he said. 'Home for good.'

She went quiet. Gallo tugged at his arm again.

'Forgive me. Even if they knew still I should never have told them your name. They hurt me.' He spat on the cobbles. 'I was stupid enough to believe them.'

Garzone took the handles of the wheelchair and helped the two of them along.

'The ways of others led us here, Gabriele. We're a part of their scheme. Not the cause of it.'

They struggled over the last bridge before via Garibaldi. He turned and took one last look at Saint Mark's Basin. Steady snow obscured the view across to San Giorgio Maggiore. Above the soft bells sounding he could hear the cries of gulls and the engines of a few boats on the water. Four pairs of cormorants sat on the wooden piles by the nearest jetty, like hunched black hooks, witnesses to everything.

Home, he said to himself again as they entered a street so familiar he took the place for granted. Now he tried to take in every last detail. The ornate iron lamp posts. The flagpole where a swastika hung in place of the golden winged lion of Venice.

There was such delicate intricacy here, the lace-like tracery of the Gothic arch windows on the bank by the corner, the plaque on the wall that said it had once been home to the Cabots, father Giovanni, son Sebastian, who, more than four centuries before, mapped and explored much of North America. Almost every building in the street had some characteristic of its own, like a feature on a unique face. A trio of funnel chimneys, a carved balustrade, a piece of sculpture stolen from an ancient site. He wondered how he could have missed them all across the years.

It took a moment for him to realize the bells had ceased their peals. There was a crowd, three deep along one side of the street, truculent, unruly.

'Bastards! Crucchi bastards!'

The high, sharp cry from a bunch outside the closed doors of Greta's door took him out of his reverie.

'She's an old woman,' someone else yelled. 'A simpleton. Is that the best you can do? Kill the sick and the Jews.'

Oberg, leading the group up front, barked an order to one of his underlings. Boots stomped on the ground as they came to a halt. Greta Morino's scared, arrhythmic sobbing was for a moment the only sound Garzone heard. Then the officer ordered a couple of soldiers to peel off and seize whoever was yelling at them. As soon as they realized what was happening men and women, young and old, maybe forty or more of them, many he recognized, shuffled together to make it impossible for the Germans to find one voice among so many.

'Last night one of yours murdered a German officer. A man doing his duty,' Oberg bellowed in rough Italian. 'You know the consequences. I could shoot you all. Every one of you if I wished.'

Garzone pushed forward to the front of the group of prisoners.

'Signor,' he said in his loud, melodious voice, the one he used for sermons from his beloved pulpit. 'If you need to blame anyone, let it be us. Not them. Take us where you wish. Do what you want. You . . .' His voice was breaking. 'You can't kill everyone in the world. In my heart I don't believe any man would wish this.'

Alberti rushed up to the German and whispered in his ear. Every eye in the crowd was on the Venetian cop then. Garzone thought, If this mob had the chance to tear anyone apart it would be you first. You before the Crucchi. Which might not have been so fair. Though nothing was these days, nor would be till the war was over.

'The officer said you must be quiet, all of you,' Alberti cried. 'If you wish to say farewell to these criminals, then you may do so in San Pietro. In silence only. Those who disobey will be taken for questioning.'

'One day we'll come for traitors like you, Luca Alberti,' someone bellowed from the back of the mob.

A soldier moved forward to find him. Alberti put out a hand.

'I know that, friend. And I know what I'll say.'

He turned and looked at Garzone.

'Father. They're your people. Make them see sense. Don't let this get worse than it is.'

For a moment the priest was lost for words.

Then he said, half-amused, 'They barely listen to me from the pulpit, Alberti. Why ask for a sermon now?'

The Venetian pushed through the group of prisoners and stood in front of him.

'Because they know you. They'll listen. They won't forget you. I'll make sure of that.'

'I wonder,' Garzone answered with a sigh. There was a cliché uttered at funerals constantly. One he'd said himself from time to time. *We'll remember you. Never will you be forgotten.* It seemed an empty promise in truth but one that had to be made.

'Very well.' He stepped forward. They let him through to the edge of the platoon where he peered round the grey shoulders of the uniformed troops.

'Let us go, friends,' he said in the same clear, calm voice he used in the vast empty belly of his basilica. 'We're the ones the Lord is calling. Not you. Not now. Just us . . .'

Just us . . .

Mika Artom stood shivering in the midst of the crowd in via Garibaldi, listening to the last words Filippo Garzone would speak to his flock. It wasn't just the bitter weather. She'd been bleeding all the way from La Fenice, trying to hide the fact when she found the crowd gathering around the Germans' marching party of the condemned, holding her side as hard as she could to stem the flow.

People round her were weeping, with grief, with impotent fury. There had to be eighty or more armed German troops in the squad marching their victims along the street. Almost as many locals watching them, spitting pointless insults and pleas in their direction.

The German officer's words stung like acid on the aching wound at her waist.

The idea that Sander was doing his duty. What? Trying to rape a woman before taking her prisoner.

Something else hurt too. This condemned party, nine men, one woman in a wheelchair, Greta, were going to die because of her. Had she slipped out of the Gioconda the night before, then tried to escape somehow with Vanni, none of this would be happening.

The blood of the martyrs is the seed of the Church.

That was what Trevisan had said, some aphorism straight from the bible she'd never read.

She did know his other maxim though.

There's only one way in which the murderous death agonies of the old society and the bloody birth throes of the new can be shortened, simplified and concentrated, and that way is revolutionary terror.

Marx. A man who never fought a war. Never put his life on the line. She had, willingly. These people, a priest, a shopkeeper, an elderly woman who ran a bar, and seven others she didn't recognize, had simply been caught up in the wash of blood rippling out from her fury in the Gioconda.

Perhaps Paolo Uccello, the curious young man her brother seemed so taken with, would be a victim of her rashness, Vanni too. She could have done as she'd promised: stayed in the Giardino degli Angeli, out of sight, meek and obedient. Waiting on a boat to take them out to safety. Except that was not to her taste and even now, feeling the wound in her side make her weaker by the moment, she knew she didn't regret a single thing.

The standoff ended the way it had to. The crowd fell into quiet resentment then, when the Germans began to march towards San Pietro, a good number vanished into the alleys that ran both sides of the broad street, shaking their heads. She couldn't blame them. Only the hardened few, relatives, friends, partisans too she suspected, would wish to witness a firing squad.

When she began following, in the middle of the smaller group, she realized the weather had changed once more. The snow was no longer lighter. It was falling like a slow, thick blanket, settling on the cobbles, making them so treacherous a few of the elderly were slipping as they struggled to keep up with the troops.

By the time they crossed the bridge to the island she was feeling light-headed. It was a strange sensation, half floating, half feeling she might sink down to the ground any moment. The day was a swirl of white, broken by the stamp of feet, the grey uniforms, the moans and cries of the dwindling group of civilians following this miserable party to its end.

There were bells again. A simple chime, coming from up ahead.

'Piero!' a woman cried when the stamp of boots came to a halt. 'I love you.'

They'd stopped at the modest campo in front of the basilica of San Pietro, the troops assembled in front of the stump of the bell tower, rising on its own from the bare winter ground.

A voice came back to answer her, a man's, high-pitched and full of agony. His words were lost in the blizzard sweeping round them.

Mika nearly fainted. Loss of blood she guessed. It was dripping right through her waistband. When she glanced down she noticed she'd been leaving a faint pink stain on the snowy ground, like the trail of a wounded snail.

Another party was just visible through the soft white cloud around them. A crowd by the other bridge, the one that led to Uccello's tiny sanctuary. Maybe twenty or thirty people there.

The German officer barked something she didn't understand though she got the idea. The crowd were pushed back. The line of prisoners was made to stand at the foot of the campanile, no blindfolds, no time for that. The priest helped Greta Morino out of her wheelchair, put an arm round her shoulders, kissed her once on the cheek.

Another barked order and a group of soldiers formed a row in front of the campanile. Garzone crossed himself. Someone behind her was weeping uncontrollably.

The handgun was deep in Mika's trouser pocket. Two shells left. One would be enough.

'Please,' she said, shoving, half-falling through the crowd. The officer in charge stood at one end of the squad ready to give the order. 'Please . . .'

There couldn't have been more than five or six steps to go before she got to her target, when she heard a familiar voice.

'Mika! *Mika!*'

Oh Christ, dear brother, she thought. Not now.

'*Mika!*'

Vanni was holding on to the parapet of the wooden bridge across to San Pietro, struggling to stay upright, trying to see through the swirling snow, Paolo by his side, supporting him. A small crowd of locals shuffled nervously between them and the soldiers round the campanile. The firing squad line-up was almost ready.

With the snow and the emotion and the crowd, some silent, some wailing, others muttering curses, it was difficult to see. Still, Vanni had spotted her, a slight figure pushing to the front of the crowd behind the soldiers, head down, stumbling much like her brother. She looked hurt, determined, lost.

'I should have brought a weapon,' he muttered, trying to take a few steps forward. 'I should have . . .'

'Look at the soldiers,' Paolo whispered in his ear. 'Look how many. Do you want to die?'

'Maybe. Who cares?'

Paolo put his arms round him, held him close. The two men stayed in that embrace, briefly stared at by the locals around them.

'I care.'

'Why?'

'Because I do,' was all Paolo could say.

'Then stop caring. I'm not worth it. I'm not going anywhere now. This road ends here.'

He put his head up and yelled some foul-mouthed abuse at the Germans, so loud, words so vile people looked at him as if he was crazy.

Across the campo Mika finally pushed through, glanced their way for a second, perhaps hearing her brother's voice.

'Oh God, Mika. *Mika* . . .' Vanni cried.

A face among the Germans turned on them and Paolo felt the cold more than ever. The man's hard and searching eyes fell on him. It was the Venetian he'd first seen when they fished Isabella Finzi out of the water just a few steps away. The cop Alberti, the collaborator who'd questioned him when he saw Mika outside the Gioconda the previous day.

'We need to go.' He tried to pull Vanni back. 'There's nothing you can do. We need to get out of here—'

The tall, officious-looking German in command of the troops, shouted out an order. With a slap of wood and a stamp of boots the rifles rose up to the men's shoulders.

There was a single toll of a bell.

A cruel whipping wind sent a sudden blast of snow swirling round them.

'I need to see . . .' Vanni murmured, dragging his bad leg forward, trying to walk. 'I need . . .'

Oberg looked down the line of men at the foot of the strange, lone bell tower. The priest's eyes were closed, his lips moving, his right arm round the old woman who leaned against him, face pale and still as stone. The others simply stood against the cold marble, staring glassy-eyed at the line of rifles aimed their way. As the snow accumulated on their bent shoulders and bowed heads they looked more like statues than flesh and blood.

'Can we just get on with this?' Sachs moaned. 'I'm freezing my balls off out here.'

Oberg had signed off many executions but never a mass killing like this. There was a crowd to witness it. Two, he now saw, one behind the troops, a second by the wooden bridge back towards the Arsenale. If they watched and understood this was the price of insurrection, then perhaps there'd be peace in Venice, if only for a little while.

'Allow them a moment to say their prayers,' Oberg replied. 'I'll give the order when I'm ready. Have no—'

Voices rippled through the crowd as it parted to let someone through.

'If that lot start trouble we need to shoot them too,' Sachs said and sounded nervous.

'I doubt that will be necessary. I very much . . .'

From what he could see it was just one person causing trouble.

Head down, coming his way.

It was the cop in him that made Alberti the first to see what was happening. Mika Artom. The same woman he'd warned off in the Gioconda, stumbling through the crowd, gun in hand, lurching towards the firing squad.

Quick decisions. She was a good way from him, and the idiot Germans behind the squad were too focussed on what was happening in front.

He yelled at them to turn round, but in his anxious panic it was Venetian, not even Italian. Words they'd never understand.

The woman was through the crowd by then. Limping. He thought it was her brother who was supposed to be wounded.

There was a gun in her hand, held low as she shoved her way through the grey uniforms, almost there, close by where Oberg and Sachs stood next to one another to the side of the monument, looking at the forlorn line of figures waiting on the rifles and the call to fire.

She raised her arm. There was the dull sound of a shot being fired. One of the troops in front of her fell to the ground, shrieking, clutching his side.

Then she was through, Ernst Oberg turning to face her, shocked, as if he couldn't believe this.

'Stop,' Alberti yelled.

Thinking as he did . . . too late.

It was a single dull explosion. Puny. Nothing like a barrage of rifles. At first Oberg felt as if someone had punched him. He looked down at his chest. Saw, to his astonishment a dark stain growing there, leaking through the thick fabric of his grey wool military coat. He put his gloved fingers to it out of curiosity and stared in bemusement at the sticky blood they found.

'What . . .'

The words wouldn't come. There was no breath inside him, only a damp and painful ache. He found himself falling backwards, staring at the snowy sky.

'Shoot the prisoners!' Sachs was yelling, high and hysterical. 'Shoot them now. Kill any in the crowd who turn on you.'

The staccato rattle of rifle fire filled the air, then screams and shrieks and from somewhere the strangest sound to fill Oberg's mind.

A bell it sounded like but that was impossible. He'd ordered them all to be silent after a single toll to mark the moment the squad took up position.

All the same something was ringing in his ears, getting louder all the time, rising like the wash of the lagoon in angry acqua alta.

Before he knew it Ernst Oberg was on the ground, blood seeping out of his flapping mouth, watching the polished leather boots and the grubby snow-stained cobbles stamp all round him.

* * *

The firing squad was mowing down the prisoners by the bell tower. The other soldiers had turned to face the milling mob. Alberti stepped straight through, found Mika Artom gasping over Oberg's stricken body.

He shot her in the back without a word. She shrieked, the weapon fell from her fingers. Her hat came off, showing the blonde hair underneath as she fell to the icy cobbles and lay there floundering, bleeding, gasping. Sachs rushed up and put a second shot through her skull.

Garzone and the other prisoners were on the ground, a couple still moving. Sachs muttered a curse, then walked round with a handgun and casually finished each with a bullet to the head.

'Jesus . . .' Alberti muttered, looking at the mess. Oberg on the ground, the life going out of his grey eyes. Sachs in a panic, rudderless, not knowing what to do.

The crowd was torn between panic and some suicidal form of vengeance. So Alberti put his gun in the air, fired two more rounds and yelled at them.

'Go home now! All of you! There's enough dead here to fill a fucking cemetery. You need more?' Another shot vanished into the steady white cloud of snow whipping round the bloodstained ground by the campanile. '*Go home now!*'

There was a long moment of silence and he wondered, If they did turn on the Germans, who'd win? Some battles weren't so much about the weapons as the emotion. There was plenty of that here.

'He was a priest,' someone yelled. 'Greta an old woman.'

'I know,' Alberti cried back. 'And now they're gone. You want to join them?'

Sachs barked an order. Half the firing squad turned and faced the crowd, rifles raised.

Alberti walked off and took hold of his sleeve, snarled in his face, 'It's a long way home and they know these streets better than you. Hold them off.'

The German snatched a glance at Oberg on the ground, blood spilling out of his mouth, his chest, pooling on the snowy cobbles.

'She shot him,' Alberti said, pointing at the body of Mika Artom. 'It looks like the woman they saw leaving the Gioconda last night. Now she's dead. Leave it.'

Sachs barked at the soldiers to hold their fire. The mob were falling back. Scared, angry, vengeful, but nothing they could do about it. Not then.

'I'm in charge here,' the German snapped at him. 'Not you.'

'Sure, boss,' he said and made a quick salute.

Then that same voice came over everything again, high and pained and full of grief.

'Mika. *Mika* . . .'

They were still by the bridge back towards the Arsenale. The kid with the delivery for the hotel he'd seen watching the Artom woman as she went inside the Gioconda. Someone with him. Leaning, limping as the other one held him back.

'You deal with this,' he told the German. 'Give me some men. I got one of your terrorists dead in front of you. Now I'll bring you the other.'

Two more shots sent a couple of unseen birds flapping into the snowy sky. It was a second soldier going through the bodies, making sure they were all dead.

'Did you hear me?' Alberti demanded.

'Take who you want. I'll manage things here.'

The pair were vanishing over the other side of the bridge, the local with his arm round the brother, helping him hobble along. Then they were gone towards the warren of alleys that led west. No great problem, Alberti thought. Wherever they hoped to hide it couldn't be far.

'You,' he said to the nearest soldier. 'Pick six men who can shoot straight and follow me.'

Paolo had to drag him most of the way. Vanni Artom was weeping, spitting pointless curses into the wintry air. Blood drenched the lower half of his trouser leg as the heavy wooden door to the Giardino degli Angeli slammed behind them. Then Paolo locked it and threw the rusty iron security arm across into its clasp.

'Think that's going to stop them?' Vanni asked, leaning against the wall. His face was pale and streaked with snow and tears. 'Do you?'

'It'll give us a little time.'

'Guns.' Vanni lumbered off towards the house. 'I want a weapon. I'll show you if you want.' He glanced back and there was a sudden look of guilt on his face. 'I'm sorry. I never meant . . .'

Paolo caught up and put his arm around him before he could

fall to the freezing ground. They made their awkward way past the looms into the shadows of the house.

Vanni struggled into the kitchen and stood by the table, hands on the top to support himself, and nodded at the back door.

'There, Paolo. Go now. You don't need to be here. It's me they want. The Jew. The partisan. Not you.' He came and hugged him. 'Go, brother. You are my brother. I want you to live. Go out that door, steal a boat, or run and just keep running. I'll make such a noise here, put up such a fight—'

'This is my home. It's the only place I know.'

Vanni shook him, hard, eyes wide with anger.

'Then find another one. Go and live, for God's sake. It's not your war. It never was. We never should have brought this to your door.'

He shook his head.

'Don't say that. You brought life. You brought . . . colour. Where there was nothing.' Paolo kissed him on the cheek, a tender kiss, that of a lover. 'Until you I was barely alive.'

'Then . . .' There were tears in Vanni's eyes. 'Then I murder you too.'

Paolo pulled himself free of their tangle of arms and walked towards the back window.

'I hid all the guns downstairs in the cellar. It seemed safer.'

'I never saw you do that. When—?'

'When you were sleeping. We can use them. Together.'

He rolled back the carpet, lifted the hidden trap door, gave Vanni the torch from the table by the sink.

'Quick now. You first.' He was walking worse than ever. 'If you can manage.'

'I can get down. You'll need to help me up. When they come . . .'

'When they come we fight.'

There was a long moment of silence, then Vanni nodded and hobbled down the steep and narrow wooden staircase, gripping the banister, shining the torch beam ahead of him.

Paolo stayed where he was and watched every step until he reached the bottom.

There was hardly any light from the tracery window. The beam of the torch flashed round through the dark.

'Where are they?' Vanni cried. 'I see nothing here but the table and your things. Where—'

'Forgive me,' Paolo called down the steps.

He slammed the trap door shut and kicked the carpet over the tiles. In his parents' bedroom he found Vanni's ID in the drawer next to the bedside table. The picture was old, bleached out, stained by muddy water or maybe old blood. The monochrome face of a young man at a camera, no expression, no life. He could barely recognize it as the Vanni Artom he knew at all.

Paolo tucked it in his pocket, then went to the wardrobe. The weapons were still there. He'd never moved them.

A handgun. The one with the wooden butt. He remembered how quickly Vanni had put it to work. A couple of attempts were needed but pretty soon he had shells in the magazine.

When he returned to the kitchen Vanni was yelling from the cellar, mad as hell, though the floor and the distance muffled the sound a little.

He stamped on the carpet, hard, and called out, 'Trust me. Be quiet. Wait here. Listen. Do nothing until you hear a friendly voice. It may be a while.'

'What the hell are you doing, Paolo?'

His voice sounded hurt and troubled, like that of a child.

'The only thing I can think of. Please. Trust me. Stay quiet.'

There was a grunt and then no noise. He wouldn't find it easy to climb those steep steps on his own and the trap door was too heavy to open from below. Paolo's father said the cellar was much used when smuggling was rife in San Pietro. It was somewhere to hide . . . and stay invisible to the world above.

Paolo went to the kitchen drawer, took out a large knife, his mother's favourite for cooking, sat down at the chair and breathed deeply. Pain was something he'd always hated. In his heart he felt he'd been a coward all his life, in the doctor's surgery, at the dentist, at school when one of the other kids was bullying him.

But that was before, when he was young. He felt the sharp edge, steeled himself, then stabbed the point hard into his right leg. The pain was terrible for a moment, and the blood came quick and free. When he felt he could bear trying to walk he got up, lurched over to the sink, washed the knife and placed it back in the drawer. There was a rag there. He wiped away the blood from the wound and examined it in the light from the window. It was fresh and livid, half a finger long and deep. The best he could manage. It would have to do.

By the time he hobbled to the front of the house it was obvious the Germans had worked out where they'd fled. There were distant voices, shouts beyond the wall, sounding over the broken statues.

Paolo struggled to the first loom along, Chiara's, his father's before that, and pulled a stool to the side. The template was still set for Salvatore Bruno's banner. There was silk left to make maybe another ten centimetres or more. He touched the old wood, remembered the lessons he'd had over the years. Made the thing work one last time, then repeated to himself the little refrain he'd learned, from his parents and the summer birds darting across the garden, tiny beads of colour.

Si-dah-si-dah-si-dah-sichi-si-piu.

Shots. He looked outside and they were firing at the wooden door. Then boots kicked a way through. German soldiers. The Venetian cop with them too. The one who shot Mika, now looking for his second trophy.

Past the frosty glass of the conservatory they began advancing through the fruit trees, crouched low, expecting attack, a sight he found amusing. The cop stayed to one side, his face as immobile as the stone features of the shattered statues.

He got up from the Jacquard loom, stroked its threads as if playing the last notes on a lyre, walked to the door and stood there, a ghostly figure behind the murky glass.

Si-dah-si-dah-si-dah-sichi-si-piu.

The whispered words just came.

A second later they started shooting. A couple of bullets flew through the old conservatory windows, ringing around the looms, ricocheting off the back wall. Then more.

Si-dah-si-dah-si-dah-sichi-si-piu.

The sporadic gunfire turned into a volley, getting closer, quicker.

Glass fragments flew all around him as, beyond the windows, dark shapes approached.

He tried to think of a prayer but there was none. There were no words any more. Only a single deed.

Paolo Uccello held the gun away from him, fingers in reverse around the guard, opened his eyes wide, stared straight down the little circle of the barrel and, with a thumb that didn't shake, pressed the trigger.

PART SIX

There was no way I could sleep after I read that last chapter of Nonno Paolo's bleak and bloody tale.

To make things worse the camera shop had delivered the prints from my film. All the story's locations sat in front of me at the breakfast table, sharp, inviting, real. He kept a small library of local history books. I was able to find photos of the city fifty, a hundred years ago too, along with some paintings as far back as Canaletto. It shouldn't have been a surprise but so many of them were unchanged over the centuries. Little figures, sometimes painted, sometimes black and white in old photos, scurried across the cobbles. Generation upon generation of dead Venetians. I was starting to think my head might soon burst under all the strain.

Chiara turned up to check on the house. Again, I begged her to tell me what had happened in the Giardino degli Angeli during the war. She looked at me alarmed and asked if I was feeling well. Didn't ask why I wanted to know. Didn't tell me anything either, just that she needed to speak to my father about my state of mind. I pleaded, I started to cry. So did she and that only made matters worse. She kissed me, hugged me, then went for her bag and jacket. Nonno Paolo was, she said, a good man and that was all there was to know. Before I could blurt out another question she announced she was going to stay with a relative on Burano for a while, just as she had a lifetime before.

The idea of getting into the Giardino degli Angeli still nagged, partly because I wasn't sure I dared. If I waited till the afternoon I could probably get inside our old patch of land by San Pietro. Maybe if I crossed that wooden bridge, stepped through the doors the Germans had broken down with their gunfire and boots, walked through the conservatory, past three dusty Jacquard looms, into the little house . . . there I'd see a bloodied Mika, Vanni and the man I'd assumed to be my grandfather, Paolo Uccello.

Alive. Dead. I didn't know.

What was the difference? I was beginning to feel I was part of someone else's dream. A dark and secret history that was somehow meant to be shared with me alone. Until I was able to sit down with Nonno Paolo and ask him what, exactly, had come to pass I'd never understand.

After Chiara left I called Dad in England. A woman answered the phone and said he wasn't there. After that I don't remember how I got to the hospital at all, whether it was on foot or I took a boat. But I made it, wondering if Chiara was right and perhaps I was ill, and went up to the reception desk just before ten as usual.

It was the same woman I'd seen all week. Middle-aged, kindly, a little officious in the way hospital people are.

'I've come to see Grandpa,' I said and showed her my ID. 'It's OK. I know the way by now.'

She put out a hand as if to say stay there, reached for the phone, then started talking to someone so quietly I couldn't hear.

When she finished, I said again, 'I can find my own way, thank you.'

'I'm sorry, Nico,' the woman said. 'We all are. He was a lovely man. We called your father in England during the night to tell him. He's flying back right now.'

Hours vanished, stuck in an overheated waiting room, no one talking to me. Why? Death was for grown-ups and I was just an embarrassed kid waiting to be told what to do, how to feel. At the end of the afternoon my father arrived, bleary-eyed, and asked straight away if I'd gone in to see him.

Of course not. I'd got enough corpses in my head already.

He was soon in tears. So was I. We found ourselves clinging to one another again for the second time that week and I can still, after all these years, feel the mournful sense of agony and loss we shared. Now there was an adult on the premises a doctor came in and offered his condolences and all the kind of talk I guess you get on these occasions. A nurse brought us coffee we barely touched. There were papers my father had to deal with, forms to be signed. Nonno Paolo had suffered a heart attack around midnight. It was so sudden he was gone by the time the medical staff were alerted by the cardiac monitor. They'd done their best to revive him but it was impossible. He'd been very weak in any case. The end wasn't far away and it seemed he passed away quickly and peacefully, in no pain. Perhaps even in his sleep, not that anyone was to know. So many of the deaths that were still in my head were public, violent, witnessed out in the open. Yet, after a life more eventful than anyone might have guessed, Nonno Paolo had slipped away quietly and no one even noticed until he was gone. Somehow this sounded like the man I was only now coming to know.

Dad left the room and made some calls. To Mum in England, who'd always got on well with him. To Chiara. To a funeral service too, I imagine, since that trip across the water to San Michele, in a shiny black barge, all of us dressed in mourning suits, needed to be arranged. All the practicalities were beyond me. Beyond Dad too, I think. He looked drained by everything. None of this should have been a shock. Still, it was. A dreadful one for us all. A gaping wound had opened in our lives and just then I couldn't imagine how it might ever possibly heal.

I sat in that waiting room staring out at the silvery lagoon and the cemetery island with its white fortress walls, the boats running along the waterfront from Cannaregio to the left, past Fondamente Nove, the hospital, then on to the Arsenale and San Pietro. Past the Giardini degli Angeli too, of course, a place that now, more than ever, filled me with a bleak kind of dread.

By six in the evening it seemed the calls and the paperwork were done. A more senior doctor came in and repeated much of the detail his younger colleague had given us. Hospitals seemed to like to tell you the same thing over and over again, not that it made any difference.

Then the man looked at me and said, 'Would you like to see him too?'

'No,' I said straight off.

'It's alright,' the doctor said. 'I understand.'

I doubt that, I thought.

Dad got to his feet.

'Wait here, Nico. I need to. One more time. Stay here. I won't be long.'

When he was gone a nurse I recognized, one who'd been there a lot around Nonno Paolo, came in and closed the door behind her. She checked through the glass partition to make sure we were alone.

'How are you doing?' she asked as she took the chair next to mine.

'I don't know.'

She touched my hand and smiled.

'We never do. I see people pass away here all the time. It doesn't matter how much you know it's coming. The end always comes as a shock. If you want I can find a priest—'

'I don't need a priest.'

I hoped I hadn't said that too abruptly. She sounded a kind and thoughtful woman. There was an envelope in her hands.

'Yesterday, after you left, he asked for me. He wrote this for you. He said I was to pass it on if anything happened. I gather you two were talking. There was something he was worried about. Worried he wouldn't have the time to tell you. They know sometimes. Doesn't matter what we see or don't see on our monitors. They know.'

She waved the envelope. There was his handwriting on the front.

To my beloved grandson, Nico.

Just an ordinary envelope. A single sheet of paper by the looks of it. And something else inside. Small, metal. It felt like a key.

'Thanks.'

'He said it was for you alone. Not your father. He wasn't to know.' She smiled, then shrugged. 'He made me promise.'

'He's . . . he was very persuasive when he wanted to be.'

'He said it was a gift. Not that you might know it for years. Your grandfather was a charming man. I'm sure you miss him.'

I waved the envelope, tried to smile and thanked her. Then stuffed it into my jacket.

An hour later we walked home. Dad talked about the funeral and how now was a time for the family to be together. As we crossed the Rialto, he told me the deal was done in London the previous evening, hours, it seemed, before Nonno Paolo died. The House of Uccello had become part of some giant American corporation. A *brand*. That was what he'd wanted. We weren't just rich. We'd never need to worry about money again – not that we had in my lifetime anyway. And we were free, both of us. Free to choose whatever path we felt like in the years to come.

To mark the moment we ate in Grandfather's favourite restaurant behind the fish market: oysters and turbot and saffron panna cotta. I barely tasted a thing and stuck to Coke while Dad finished his bottle of Pinot Grigio. Angelo, the ancient waiter who'd served us for as long as I could remember, burst into tears when we told him. So did many people over the days to come. Nonno Paolo wasn't just a fixture for me.

Back in my room in the palazzo, Dad downstairs making calls all round the world, about the funeral, about the change in the business too, I opened the letter.

A small, old, silver key fell out. Accompanying it was a short note in a hand so shaky I could feel he was close to death when he wrote it. And that he must have known it too.

> Nico
>
> I told you that last chapter was the final piece in the strange jigsaw of my life. I regret to say, for once, I lied. There are more pieces to this tale and you need to see them in order to fully understand it. Use this key and open the locked drawer at the bottom of my desk in the mansard. There you'll see why I was unable to pass this final part of the story on to you here in hospital.
>
> If you're reading this rather than have me tell you in person it means I'm gone. Death comes to us all. Weep and mourn a little but not too much. You have a life of your own to make. Look back for a little while and then look resolutely forward.
>
> Know that I love you and your father both, my dear grandson in particular because there's something in your manner, quiet, thoughtful, curious, sensitive, fragile at times too, that I recognize and admire. It's because I love and trust you I've passed this burden on. Not that you may appreciate this now. Perhaps you resent me for marring your teenage summer with this tale of blood and madness.
>
> If so I apologize, but sometimes pain is necessary. It reminds us we're alive.
>
> Enough of cryptic mysteries. They will reveal themselves as they see fit.
>
> Farewell, dear Nico. Your bright and affectionate presence has lightened the weight of these recent years. I am only sorry we ran out of time. But then we always do.
>
> Your loving grandfather.

The first thing I thought was: you didn't sign your name.

Nearly midnight, after more tears and shared memories with Dad, a large grappa for him, a tiny one for me, I went to my room.

When the place was silent I sneaked upstairs to Nonno Paolo's mansard study.

A part of me was desperate to see what was in that drawer.

Another part feared it more than anything.

I remember there was something happening across the way. One of the bigger palazzi on the Grand Canal was holding a party. There was music, so loud it drowned out the passing boats. Or perhaps that's just my head getting things wrong. I was pretty shaken by then, and shaken people do stupid things. Like looking into drawers when they're in no fit state to handle what they might contain.

Nonno Paolo's typewriter was still on the desk. The place had his smell about it, dust, old age, a fragrant kind of antiquated cologne. And the faint fustiness of damp that always hung around the Colombina, the price of living in a building that stood on ancient timber driven into yet more ancient mud.

I read his note again, then placed it next to the typewriter. The little key was fiddly. Perhaps that bottom drawer hadn't been opened in ages. Maybe it wouldn't work at all and then I'd have an excuse. I could walk away, try to forget about everything, find some way to flush his story from my head and return to normal, whatever normal was. Right then I wasn't sure.

Third try it turned.

There was another envelope in there, much like the ones he'd been giving me in the hospital only older. Nothing written on the front. Right above it, crushing the paper into the corner, was a grey metal pistol that looked military, as if it might have come from the war. Crammed alongside was a gilt box, faded, dusty, on the top in silver stencil the words: *Uccello, Fine Weavers, Venice.*

It took a while for my fumbling fingers to prise open the lid. There was a reason that was so hard. A stain, dark, dry and old, ran from whatever it contained right up to the plain cardboard inside the top, like an accidental seal.

I picked up the thing inside before I'd even realized what it was: a piece of old soprarizzo velvet, the colours mute and dull. Still I could see the pattern and it was much like the ones his words had formed in my head. Angry winged lions, rampant with gaping furious mouths. This was one of the banners Paolo Uccello, Vanni Artom and Chiara Vecchi had woven that bleak winter week fifty-six years before, now cut in two down the middle, the tear marked by dangling threads.

I dropped it straight away. It wasn't hard to make out that much of it had once been soaked in blood.

Not caring if Dad heard or not I went back to my room, got all the other envelopes he'd given me, returned to his study, threw them in the drawer with the others, the gilt and silver box with its vile contents, the gun, wishing all along I wasn't cursing him in my head.

Enough, I thought, and turned the key. Then I went to the window, opened it, stared at the gleaming water, the lights across the canal, listened to the party music filling the tiny enclosed universe of Venice, a place I knew I had to flee.

The note, the last thing he'd ever written, I balled up and threw out of the open window. The little key to his secrets followed, vanishing over the moonlit water.

I don't remember much after that, not until we buried him.

It was a sultry summer morning. We stood in the middle of a gleaming black launch as it navigated the choppy waters across to San Michele, me, Mum and Dad, arms linked, together for the first time in years. Chiara was there too, weeping enough for the rest of us. The coffin was covered with flowers, as was the roof of the boat. A small crowd, employees, city officials, old family friends, stood on the waterfront at Fondamente Nove to watch us leave. Nonno Paolo had paid for a burial plot in advance, not that any of us knew the details until after. Since the cemetery island was overcrowded we'd been granted a lease on a grave for ten years or so. After that Grandad's remains would be moved into a metal box and reburied in a small wall compartment he'd reserved a few plots away.

After the funeral I didn't talk much. Mum told Dad she was worried about me. Chiara probably said the same. He knew something was wrong but he'd no idea how to deal with it. Any more than me. Finally two weeks after the funeral, when I turned down one more invitation to go out to the beach in a family outing to Alberoni, the two of us sat down together at the breakfast table. He wanted a talk.

Everything Dad said made sense. How it was natural to mourn when you lost a relative you loved. How that same relative would want you to end that grief after a while, pick up the pieces and get on with your life. I couldn't argue with a thing. After all Nonno Paolo had used pretty much the same words in that letter he left for me in hospital. Still, I could hardly tell Dad why I'd retreated into the miserable, puzzled state I was in. To do that I'd have to go back into the mansard study, show him a wartime gun, a bloodied piece of fabric, and read the last chapter of Nonno Paolo's grim and violent story.

I couldn't face it so I lied. Venice was too small, too stifling, I said. I was coming up to sixteen. I needed to grow, to escape, to see more of the world than I could manage from my bedroom in the Colombina with its view of nothing but a stretch of sluggish water and a line of very old buildings.

Being Dad, of course, he listened.

A week later I was packing my bags. I never could have guessed it would be two decades before I'd look through that window again.

Where did all those years go? Into running mainly.

First I went to an international school in Oxford where I learned English and French and pretty soon the name of every pub along the Iffley Road. Oxford suited me, the bustle, the loudness of the city that seemed to drown out everything else. When my time at school was done I managed to get a place at a business college there, with the help of Dad's money, naturally. It's amazing how you can stretch out a university education when someone else is paying. Oxford would occupy almost eight years of my life before finally I left.

We corresponded through email and phone calls and met from time to time at the villa he'd bought himself in Sicily, usually with his latest girlfriend in tow. At regular intervals Dad would ask me if I'd like to spend some time in our office in Santa Croce, now a branch office of the conglomerate that owned the House of Uccello. After I kept coming up with any number of excuses why I didn't want to return home he finally asked why I seemed to hate the place. Whether it was him or something else. I said it wasn't complicated. Venice was for old people and tourists. I needed to live somewhere different, somewhere I could breathe.

Why did I never tell him the truth? For one thing I felt it would have been a betrayal. Nonno Paolo gave me his story. He could have told Dad, but he held back everything. There had to be a reason, not that I understood what it could possibly be. Then there was Chiara and the fear in her face whenever I'd raised the subject of the war. I'd no idea what she wanted to keep buried. Perhaps I'd no right to be told and Nonno Paolo no right to tell it either. Given her obvious disquiet I couldn't possibly risk hurting someone who'd been so selflessly kind to three generations of Uccello men over fifty or more years.

She died, something of a legend on the island of Burano, at the age of ninety-two, seven years after Nonno Paolo, just as I was finishing one more module in Oxford. I did come back for her crowded lagoon funeral, but only because it was on her island home. I went there directly by water taxi from Marco Polo airport, stayed in a local hotel, and left without ever seeing an inch of the Grand Canal. Dad and I ate a sad funeral supper in a restaurant he loved, the Gatto Nero, afterwards: *risotto di gò*, goby fish fresh from mud cooked with rice, the dish the place was famous for. It was the taste of home: simple, rich, full of the fragrance of the lagoon. I still couldn't wait to get straight back to the airport the next morning.

There was another reason I kept quiet. If I talked I'd have to confess just how much Nonno Paolo's story had haunted me over the years, and still did. Pieces of his narrative would pop into my head, unwanted, and refuse to leave. The Turner painting so admired by Paolo Uccello's art-loving mother, the boats in front of the Dogana and Salute, came to be something of an obsession for a good six months after I discovered the original was in the Tate in London. As soon as I read that I caught the first bus I could to see it. Six or seven times over the coming months I went back to stare at the thing again. As the young Paolo had pointed out, it was a fabrication. This was the Venice I knew but not quite as it was in real life. The artist had shifted the perspective, moved entire buildings, rebuilt the city to suit his own imagination.

Did the artist twist real life deliberately to achieve some effect? Or was it just accident, a scene misremembered? The first, surely. Turner, I found out, kept detailed preliminary sketches for much of his work, some of which were in the same gallery. It was obvious he must have hired a boat, sat in the lagoon, looked at the scene in front of him *and decided to change it*. Just the kind of trick Nonno Paolo might have played with his story too. Was he really saying that he wasn't the son of the original Uccello family at all? That the original Paolo had sacrificed his life to save a wounded Jewish partisan from Turin, a man he loved called Giovanni Artom? How could that be true? How would he – and Chiara – keep such a secret for five and a half decades? What, in pursuit of the picture he wanted to paint, had he changed? And how much of it was the truth re-arranged, how much pure invention?

There were, of course, no answers. Only further questions the more I tried to unpick the tangle of threads I had at my disposal. Of course the locked drawer in the mansard might offer me the final part of the story, but I wasn't ready to face that.

To Dad's exasperation I decided my future now lay with the visual arts, not commerce. With his support I went to Paris, bought a lot of expensive camera equipment and determined to be a photographer. Almost four years of trying everything, fashion, landscape, news, left me dependent as ever on his support. For one brief, insane moment I even considered flying out to Lebanon to see if I could work my way into Syria to try to document the civil war there. When I mentioned that on the phone it was one of the few times he lost his temper. He caught the next plane and gave me a brisk lecture. Entering a perilous war zone was, he said very forcefully over a suitably lavish dinner near Les Halles, one crazy idea of mine he would never bankroll.

Not that it mattered. A Parisian cameraman I half-knew had gone ahead of me. Five weeks later, as I hung around Dad's Sicilian villa trying to bring him round to the idea, it was all on the news. Pierre had been kidnapped and very publicly murdered by his captors. I couldn't look at the hideous videos. Besides, in my heart I knew why the idea of seeing war close up intrigued me, and it was nothing to do with Syria at all. I wanted to witness how closely real life matched the images I had of the Artoms' final bloody days in Venice, pictures I couldn't get out of my head. It was the challenge of the Turner painting again. I was trying to match what was in my head against what I knew to be real.

Not long after Paris I ran out of excuses. I couldn't face another bout of education or endless rounds of trying to sell my quite average photographic skills. I gave in to his appeals. Dad found me a position in London working for the European corporate headquarters of the conglomerate that now owned the House of Uccello. Nothing too onerous. Anyone could have done it, and for half the salary they were paying me. To begin with I was checking on consignments, talking to customers and suppliers, trying to see where things were going wrong and put them right. Long hours, no great social life, a flat in a new block in Docklands not far from the office.

I liked London, though after that strange referendum set the English apart from the rest of us in Europe I found life as a foreigner changed somewhat. Not so much in the capital – half of us there were from other countries. But when I had to visit depots in the regions I began to feel uneasy. One time, on a train to East Anglia, I took a call from our Bologna office, in Italian naturally. I didn't notice the angry looks I was getting from the surly individual opposite until I'd finished and he spat out, 'You lot can all fuck off home now. Brexit. That's what we voted for. Best you get gone.'

If it hadn't been for one of my fellow passengers stepping in it could easily have come to blows.

I tried to stay in the city as much as I could after that. Even there you only had to follow the news to understand something was changing, and it wasn't good.

Bored with chasing couriers, I talked my way into the publication section in marketing and started to work on the production of brochures and catalogues for the many different brands we owned. It was work I took to for once, and I like to think I was good at it. One time Dad came over he admired a book about industrial design we'd produced for a Swedish subsidiary. Why not pillage the archives of the House of Uccello and produce a lavish volume about all our historic velvet patterns too?

It was a good idea. But still nothing was going to drag me back to meet Nonno Paolo's ghosts. Until, one June morning in 2019, almost twenty years to the day he died, I got a call I'd dreaded for so long.

'Nico.' Dad sounded strange, almost frail, which was unusual. He always seemed the healthiest of men. 'I'm calling you from the bloody hospital. I can't believe it. I know you're not going to like this but I need you here.'

'Where's here?'

'Where do you think? Please. Come home. If only for a little while. I know you hate this place but it's important. Your old father's never asked much of you over the years.'

This was a downright lie. I was now thirty-five years old and in all that time he'd never asked for a thing, while I just kept on taking and taking.

'What's wrong?'

'Can't talk on the phone. I took the liberty of having a word with your boss. You're free to go. Come quick, please. Right now.'

One day later I was back. He was in Giovanni e Paolo. The hospital didn't seem much different as I stepped through that familiar entrance for the first time in twenty years. It still looked more a façade for an art gallery than a medical facility. The same woman could have been behind the front desk for all I knew.

Dad was in a private room one floor up from where Nonno Paolo died. Across the lagoon San Michele shimmered in the distance just as it had before. I couldn't stop looking at those distant white castellated walls as I walked in.

Half-moon spectacles on, reading a copy of the *Financial Times*, he beamed at me as I came through the door. I'd seen him in Sicily the Christmas before with his then squeeze, a Croatian woman who was twenty years his junior and extraordinarily beautiful.

'Sit,' he said, patting the chair at the side of the bed.

'How are you?' I asked, my heart in my mouth. 'What's wrong?'

'Who said anything's wrong?'

'I thought you were sick.'

'What made you think that?'

A little voice inside me wanted to shriek.

'You're in hospital, Dad. You said it was urgent.'

'Oh that's just a little thing. A hernia. A few days and I'm out of here. Nothing to worry about.'

'You scared the living hell out of me!'

He did the Dad thing he always tried when he'd got something wrong. Said oops and looked theatrically guilty.

Finally, it seemed to occur to him that perhaps I might have got a different message from his call.

'I'm sorry. I didn't mean to worry you. It's just that events are moving very quickly and there are things you can't leave to a phone call.' He reached out, touched my hand, smiled and said, 'It's good to see you. It always is.'

'I'm glad you're not sick. I was worried.'

'Especially good to see you here.' He gestured at the window, still largely oblivious to the fact he'd put the wind up me. 'Home.'

'London's my home now.'

'Too noisy that place. Besides, after this Brexit nonsense you'll have to beg for a work permit or something, won't you?'

I shrugged and said nothing.

'I never did understand why you took against Venice. I thought . . .'

When he didn't finish I said, 'You thought what?'

'I thought it was me. Your mother leaving like that. Me and women.'

I laughed. This was so ridiculous.

'No. It was never you. Where's Marina?'

'Gone back to Dubrovnik.' He frowned. 'They never stay. You must have noticed. They like my money. Me . . . I'm not so interesting. How about . . . how about you? That lovely Irish girl, Mary? I liked her.'

'Her name was Morag. She was Scottish.'

'Yes. That one. Lovely girl.'

'So you said. I'm in between relationships at the moment.'

'Well! We've something in common there.'

'I'm sorry it didn't work out, Dad.'

'Don't be. I'm used to it. Look . . .' He gestured at the window. 'I know this wasn't the most exciting of places when you were growing up. No cars. No bikes. No fun. A city for old people, not the young.'

'It wasn't just that,' I murmured, not that he was listening.

'It's all very different now. We're really international. Part of the world. Just listen to the accents on the streets.'

'They're tourists.'

'Not all of them. Plenty live here. Work here. You can fly anywhere from the airport. New York. Tokyo. Broadband and Wi-Fi and phones and all that nonsense. We've got the lot.'

'What is it you want?'

There was a slyness about him. That, at least, he'd inherited from Nonno Paolo. He hesitated for a moment, then broke the news that had summoned me to his bedside, heart in mouth, thinking he might be on his last legs, which clearly couldn't be further from the truth.

The House of Uccello, it seemed, was about to be coughed up by its US parent. The conglomerate was slimming down and had come to the conclusion an upmarket Italian fabric and clothing business no longer fitted its corporate profile. My father had negotiated the buyback of the company. We were to be our own masters once more, owners of our two Venetian weaving mills and a larger, more commercial, unit in Vicenza.

He wanted me to come and help him revive it, with the idea of inheriting the business in a few years' time when he finally retired to Sicily with his yacht and a companion yet to be discovered.

'Only if you want to, Nico,' he said with that wide-eyed gaze of innocence that won him so many conquests.

'I don't know anything about business.'

'Don't be ridiculous. You've more qualifications than I have.'

'They're not great qualifications.'

'Irrelevant. You know enough. You're presentable. You speak English, French, German . . .'

'My German's terrible.'

'It's better than mine. People like you. They see something in you. Something . . . genuine. Also' – he gestured with his right hand as if a decisive point was coming – 'you're an Uccello. Weaving's in your blood. And . . .' He grinned as if this clinched things. 'You can pillage our back catalogue and produce that book of designs. Three centuries of Uccello velvet . . .'

'A century and a half or so. Those earlier ones we inherited.'

'No one's interested in minor details like that. Three centuries of Uccello velvet . . .' He took my hand. 'Help me get going. Move back into the Colombina. Stay here for a little while and let's see how it goes.'

'Do I have a choice?' I asked and regretted it the moment I said the words. He looked so hurt.

'You've always had a choice. Haven't you? That's why I've spent most of the last twenty years wondering where the hell you were. You wanted something different. Now, just for a month or two, I need a favour in return. After that go and do what you want. Whatever it is you know I'll always support you. You're my flesh and blood. All I have. Well . . .' He frowned. 'Anything except parachuting into some stupid war. Where that insanity came from I've no idea.'

Of course he hadn't. And, of course, there was no way I could refuse. So we went through some of the practicalities and I agreed – my things would be shipped from London and I'd start work straight away with him, rebuilding the House of Uccello as an independent supplier of luxury fabrics around the world. When affairs were more settled we'd talk about what came next.

'Oh,' he said, as I was leaving. 'There's one small thing. A public event I was supposed to attend tomorrow. Can't do it now because of this stupid operation. No need to make a speech. They just need an Uccello there. We're paying for it after all.'

'What kind of event?'

He smiled, a fond memory returning.

'I don't think you've ever been there. The place where Nonno Paolo started us off near San Pietro. We sold it when you were little. The city never could work out what to do with it. Then some young people came to me with a few ideas. I put in a bit of money and now it's reopening. The Biennale are helping out. It's going to be one of these trendy new bars.' He hitched himself up in bed. 'You might get a surprise when you see it.'

'I bet . . .'

'There's a very forceful woman behind it—'

'The Giardino degli Angeli . . .'

'That's the spot. Don't look at me like that. She's not my type. Valentina Padoan. Left-wing firebrand. She threw a milkshake over your old friend Scamozzi the other day.'

'What?'

'Scamozzi. He's in the Senate now with all those other right-wing bastards we have to contend with. Don't you keep up with things? You're still Italian, you know.'

But I hadn't. I'd been drifting. Lost in work and the bustle of London. So Maurizio Scamozzi, the thug I once watched bullying a little Jewish kid and didn't do a thing to stop him, was now a politician of sorts.

'This country's changed, Nico,' my father said with a shake of his head. 'God knows how. I never saw it coming. Makes you think that evil old bastard Berlusconi wasn't so bad sometimes. The lovely Valentina threw a drink over your old school friend when he was giving some rabble-rousing speech about kicking out all the immigrants. I admire her sentiments if not her methods. Look . . . all you need to do is go along, be your usual calm, polite self. Talk to her. Cut a ribbon or something. Then you're done. The Giardino degli Uccello they're going to call it, not that it's ours, you understand, and I expect that's more to do with the birds than us. I gave them some money, a few other things too.

You'll enjoy it. She's quite a sweetie so long as you keep her away from the milkshakes.'

I couldn't take my eyes off San Michele, that shining white outline across the water.

'You really had me worried.'

'I said I'm sorry, didn't I? Don't go on about it. We've never been very good at communication. That's the trouble. Never mind . . .' He squeezed my hand again. 'We'll work on it. We'll make things right.'

I spent the rest of the day drifting around the city in a daze. Dad was right about one thing. Venice had changed. It wasn't just the size of the crowds milling aimlessly around San Marco and the Rialto. The neighbourhood shops I knew so well – bakers, butchers, greengrocers – had mostly gone. In their place was all manner of small establishments – mask shops, jewellers, scores of places selling trinkets and cheap glass that were surely never made in Murano. There seemed to be a cafe every few steps along the principal streets that led to and from the Rialto. Our new housekeeper, a charming and very loud Filipino woman called Madge, complained that it was simple enough to buy an Aperol spritz or the mask of a Plague Doctor a minute from our door. But if you wanted toilet cleaner or a fresh chicken for the pot you had to walk ages.

Then there was the atmosphere. Something about it that reminded me of the tensions I'd noticed lately in England. Gone was the sleepy, idle Venice of old. There were soldiers with weapons and armoured vehicles guarding the bridge as it led from terraferma into the busy hub of Piazzale Roma, something I'd never seen before. More armed men patrolled the ghetto, watching visitors as they arrived. A plaque now stood on the wall of Aldo Diamante's house, recording his role in defending the Jewish community and praising him for his courage and – in spite of what I'd read in Nonno Paolo's story – his faith as well. Across the way the old people's home still looked much as it did when Luca Alberti saw pensioners being dragged from there by Nazi troops.

When I went to the Jewish Museum I had to go through a security scanner as if I was checking in at the airport. Once inside I spent a quiet hour wandering the corridors and the synagogue hidden away in the tall tenement buildings of the campo. There was an advert for a tour of the ancient Jewish cemetery on the Lido later that day. I bought a ticket straight away, feeling Nonno Paolo's story coming to life again. I knew the time was coming when I could avoid facing it no more.

Time to spare. I walked to the vaporetto on the Murano side of the lagoon, past a couple of Africans hanging around street corners asking for change and an elderly woman dressed in ragged black robes, a veil over her bowed head, kneeling on the hard cobbles, begging the way you saw in drawings from centuries ago. Where she came from . . . I couldn't guess.

On the boat I read a newspaper someone had left. There was a story about a black kid, an immigrant, getting beaten up by his fellow school pupils on a bus in Treviso. It made our bullying of the Jewish boy, twenty years before, egged on by a boy who was now an Italian senator, seem petty if no less cruel.

Then we docked in the Lido and I took the long walk along the waterfront to the iron cemetery gates at San Nicolò. A young guide unlocked them and let us in. She was giving the tour in English, not that she spoke it so well. The place was extraordinary, vast and went back centuries, lichen-covered memorials written in Hebrew scattered everywhere beneath the shadow of sprawling trees.

Towards the end I asked the guide where were the graves of the victims of the Nazis? There were three names I was interested in. Mika and Vanni Artom. A woman from Castello called Isabella Finzi. She was a student, perhaps a little out of her depth, and perplexed that questions about the war weren't in her script. So she called someone, came back and said there were no graves from that time. Mussolini had stopped Jewish burials in the cemetery with the Racial Laws of 1938 and they'd never resumed.

'Where would they be buried then?' I wondered.

'I don't know, mister. That's a long time ago.'

'But it isn't.'

'It is,' she said, 'to me.'

I took the number one boat back, the slowest there was. Fifty minutes from the Lido to San Stae, my nearest stop. I wanted time to think. Back home I bought myself a pizza, ate it alone in our kitchen with a glass of wine, remembering the tranquil days in the Palazzo Colombina when there were three of us rattling around the big, old place, two happy bachelors and a young boy whose grandfather would read to him, history mostly, in my bedroom, the third floor on the right.

One storey below his mansard study.

That place of his looked no different. Not even a fresh lick of paint, although the housekeeper made sure everything was polished and free of dust. The key he gave me was at the bottom of the Grand Canal so I got a crowbar out of the toolbox in the shed and took it to the old wood instead.

Nothing had changed since the night I hurriedly pushed everything in there, the gilt box, the gun and six envelopes, one of them still unread, and threw the key into the canal. Watching the dust rise from the drawer as I opened it I felt as if I'd opened someone's grave. But whose?

The lid on the box was still stiff. The blood on the torn banner looked darker though I could touch it now. I was no longer scared.

The gun I left where it lay. It was just Nonno Paolo's final chapter I took with me down to the kitchen where, the rest of a bottle of Soave by my side, I placed the pages on the table and started on the final chapter of his secret life.

ORDINARY MONSTERS

Vanni Artom had heard distant gunfire and the cries of soldiers as they approached, but a single, louder shot was much nearer. After that came the stamping of boots through the building above him. German voices, men who sounded angry and aggressive. Drawers were noisily emptied, their contents thrown to the floor. The soldiers didn't stay long. There wasn't much to loot from Paolo Uccello's modest home judging by their gruff remarks. Given the chaos and slaughter on the streets they were probably called away for support.

All the while he'd sat there in the dark, silent, trying not to move, to give himself away. Was that cowardice? He wasn't sure. He had no weapon, no means even to climb the steep staircase to the trap door. The wound hurt and itched like hell. There seemed no point in asking himself the obvious question: if things were different and he was fit and armed, would he be like Mika and go straight for them, knowing this was suicide but hoping to kill a couple of Nazis along the way?

There was no food, no water, only the faint winter light from the tracery window after the torch failed. On what he believed to be the third day, when he was beginning to think he might starve to death with the stink of the lagoon in his nostrils, he heard the carpet above move away, the trap door creaking open. Vanni dragged his aching body to the foot of the steps, blinked against the searing light of a probing torch and wondered if he was about to die.

'Paolo?' a woman's voice asked.

No Germans. She seemed to be on her own.

'Paolo? Are you there?'

'I'm sorry. Paolo's dead, I think.'

She opened the heavy door all the way and let it slam on the kitchen tiles. Chiara Vecchi stared down at him in misery, tears starting to trickle down her cheeks.

'They said it was you. The Germans found your ID. They put it in the paper. They said the terrorists, you and your sister, were dead.'

'I wish I was. I wish it was Paolo here. Honestly . . .'

He was weeping too. There were no more words for either of them. She came down and helped him up the steps.

For days he lay in bed, sweating feverishly in a freezing room, watching the snow fall outside. Christmas came and went. Chiara moved into Paolo's old room on January the sixth, Epiphany, concerned about the state of him. A timid, nervy doctor arrived a few days later at her insistence. When he left she told him, Look after the leg or lose it. Then gave him new medication, not that he knew how she paid for it.

She started to call him Paolo and when he asked why she said, Because that's who you are now. Everyone assumed the solitary final member of the Uccello family had either fled when the Crucchi came or been murdered by his partisan guests. The doctor apart, no one knew he was living in the Giardino degli Angeli. She told anyone who inquired that she'd been given the job of looking after the place in the event anything happened to the family. The story went unquestioned. No one cared much about a failed weaving firm on the edge of San Pietro. Nor were they in much of a mood to ask hard questions in Venice that difficult winter.

One day, feeding him warm white polenta with a few onions and dried mushrooms in it, she said, 'If they ever find you here you'll tell them that evil terrorist Vanni Artom made you take him and his wicked sister in. You ran and hid. Then you came back. Maybe they'll believe you. If they come . . .'

She sounded doubtful about that last and he wondered why.

'They're losing the war,' she said with a shrug. 'They're beginning to know it too. The man they sent to replace the German your sister shot . . . he's useless. The Crucchi spend their time drunk mostly or with their whores. Those bastards in the Black Brigades are still rounding up what Jews they can find. Shooting partisans. Even they're starting to wonder what happens after. When others are doing the shooting.' She put down the bowl and lifted the sheets to look at his leg. 'I think you'll be fine.'

'The doctor—'

'He won't be back. He's run off south with all the money people like me have given him. He's not the only one.'

'Why are you doing this? Not that I'm ungrateful but—'

She looked astonished by the question.

'Who else is there to look after you, Paolo? I promised your father.'

'My name's not—'

'I know your name and so do you.'

Spring arrived and with it warmth and sun. By then he was walking round the place with barely a limp. During the day Chiara would vanish into the city, cleaning for people, looking after the elderly in her old parish, coming back with what food she could find and scraps of gossip.

He spent the time reading every book in the place. When he was finished with those she fetched him more from somewhere. Poetry books. American and British crime stories. History too. Lots of history.

Then one June afternoon she returned beaming and placed a bottle of Prosecco on the table along with some bread and prosciutto.

'What's happened?' he asked.

'They chased the Germans out of Rome.' She popped the cork, poured two glasses and made some panini. 'The Crucchi are on the run, Paolo. Not long now.'

They toasted the future. He felt happier than he had in months. Better in himself too. The guilt, the memory of that last bleak day by the campanile, remained but framed into perspective by Chiara's sacrifice and the risks she'd taken saving him. He'd always be haunted by the events of that bleak winter, but their bitterness was tempered by the decency of a stranger, unasked for, perhaps even undeserved.

'Now,' she said when they'd finished the bottle. 'You need to go back to earning a living.'

He laughed.

'I was a student. Of poetry and literature. I've never earned a living. I'm not sure I ever can.'

She wagged a finger at him.

'You're the offspring of the finest weavers to use a Jacquard loom here in ages. I've seen you work. You've promise. I'll teach you the finer points. As your father taught me.'

He pushed the bottle across the table and wished there was another one. A case. An endless flow of booze to take away the memories.

'I can't pretend like this. Not forever.'

'Soon it won't be pretending, Paolo.'

'Not my name,' he whispered.

She seized his arms.

'The war's not over. If they hear Vanni Artom's alive they'll come hunting. And they'll find you. Me too.'

'But it will be . . .'

'We think about that when the time comes. Right now I need you on that loom. I've got work for us. A rich lady in Dorsoduro in need of curtains. I can't do this on my own.'

'I'll do my best, Chiara,' he said and the following day he was there, seated at the middle Jacquard, just the two of them now in front of the bullet holes in the conservatory glass which she'd covered with black tape.

Later that month, as the weather turned warmer, he saw a tiny shape flit across the garden and heard a snatch of birdsong.

Si-dah-si-dah-si-dah-sichi-si-piu.

Soon it echoed his rapid movements on the loom.

Liberation didn't come quickly. On April the twenty-ninth the following year, 1945, soldiers from Britain and her colonies finally rolled over the bridge from terraferma and rounded up the surrendering Germans. Four days after most of the country had found itself free of Nazi rule.

It was the first time she allowed him out into the street. San Pietro was deserted. They had to walk to the foot of via Garibaldi to find the crowds, waving at their liberators, ripping flowers out of the public gardens to throw at them.

Chiara seemed to know everybody. She introduced him to all the curious as Paolo Uccello, gave him a hug and declared she'd managed to hide him from the Crucchi ever since that grim day sixteen months before when the Nazis murdered the priest Garzone, the grocer Gallo and all those other innocents. No one seemed surprised. No one questioned her story. Paolo was a stranger to them all in any case. Besides, the city was in turmoil, different parties fighting for control. They had bigger things on their mind.

News was slow to arrive and often doubted. It was only when people saw the photographs that they truly believed Mussolini and his mistress had died the day before Venice was liberated, shot and hanged from girders in the Piazzale Loreto, Milan, three fellow

Fascists alongside them. Locals had gathered to spit and piss on their corpses and cut at them with kitchen knives. Then came the best news: Hitler had killed himself in his bunker in Berlin. They heard the announcement on the old radio while they were at the looms, busy on a fresh commission, expensive soprarizzo for an aristocratic family on the Lido.

Chiara stopped work immediately. She had a bottle of good Franciacorta stolen when a friend of hers had helped himself to the goods in the Gioconda as the Germans fled.

They drank it outside in the garden, listening to the goldcrests and the cheers from distant houses. Chiara said the birds were singing more loudly and he believed her too, ridiculous as that seemed.

'You should marry again,' he said and realized immediately that was the drink.

'Me?' She waved her glass at him, amused. 'No. I'm done with men. You're the one who needs to find yourself a smart, young wife. Then, with your charm and good business sense, you can bring in the sales.'

'Jews being good at commerce,' he said, and there was the wine again.

She stared at him and for once there was no warmth in her eyes.

'Why do you say such things? You're Paolo Uccello. A Venetian. A good young fellow who's come through hard times. Call yourself another name and you invite attention. There are partisans fighting among themselves out there. The relatives of some of those who were shot in San Pietro are no fans of a brother and sister called Vanni and Mika Artom. They think their kin never deserved to die for what others did. Put the past behind you, Paolo. Go out there, find us more work. I'll train us new weavers. There's our future. Bright and clear. Unless you have a better idea?'

The commissions came sporadically at first, but turned into a steady stream when he started to go out into the city and show their wares. The Veneto wealthy were willing to spend their money now the Germans had gone. All the same he couldn't forget Mika. So, in a sleight of hand he suspected Chiara knew about all along, he engineered a sales trip to Milan.

On the free Sunday he took the train to Turin and looked around his old neighbourhood, banging on the doors of families the Artoms used to know.

When the seventh visit produced the same, a set of strangers shaking their heads, he made contact with the local rabbi who'd returned from exile in Spain. Quite why he didn't know – perhaps it was concern about Chiara's reaction – but he posed as a friend of a Jewish family who'd vanished in the war. His own he knew were all dead. Someone in their circle must have survived, surely. That miserable afternoon in the home of the apologetic rabbi told him otherwise. It was as if the realization that the war was lost made the murderers of the Nazis and the Black Brigades more bloodthirsty than ever. Even the wife and daughters of the traitor Salvatore Bruno were taken after Mika killed him. They were raped, robbed and shot screaming in the hills.

When he returned he brought back a folder full of orders and some wine and local biscotti for Chiara, who was now back in her own apartment near San Francesco della Vigna. She went through his job book, gasping at the numbers, saying they'd need to recruit and train yet more weavers and work shifts to meet demand.

Then, ever observant, she asked him what else he'd found on his travels.

'Only that the Artom family are dead, every last one of them,' he said with a heavy heart.

Chiara kissed him once on the cheek, the quick peck of a loving aunt, comforting a hurt child.

'I'm sorry to hear that, Paolo. You must mourn them, naturally. But it's the living we must think of first. They have much to do.'

Three years later a young woman accountant called Maria Ricci was summoned from Rome by the company's bank and asked to put the fast-growing company straight with its books which were, she said on her first day, more chaotic than any she'd ever seen. Her candour and strong will reminded him of his sister. When he began to show her round the city and take her to the beaches of the Lido, she stirred in him an interest outside accounting procedures, velvet, looms and commerce. The past, the experiments, the doubts, were forgotten in the whirlwind of a sudden and quite unexpected romance. He proposed at the foot of the Eiffel Tower feeling a little foolish and one year later they were married in the splendour of the Frari, Maria's parents looking on proudly, and always sympathetic to the loss of his own in the war.

Being wed suited him. It was the emotional anchor he needed, one that confirmed his identity. How could he now tell anyone he was a fugitive Jewish partisan from Turin? Who would believe him? Even his accent had adapted to the rougher tones of the lagoon. Nor did people wish to revive memories of the past. Maria's father was a Roman banker who never once spoke about what he did under Mussolini. Still, he had access to sources of finance that the fast-growing weaving company could never have found on its own, and endless contacts throughout Europe.

Five years later the House of Uccello was established internationally, with agents in New York, London and Tokyo, their luxury fabrics travelling a world fast putting to one side the calamity of war, thinking only of the bright and peaceful future that lay ahead. The company had long outgrown the Giardino degli Angeli which was sold to the city for a pittance since no one else wanted it. A growing army of weavers, women mainly, trained by Chiara personally, assembled in new workshops in Santa Croce and Giudecca. Buoyed by rising profits and with a little help from Maria's father the couple bought the freehold for a rundown and historically unimportant palazzo called the Colombina on the Grand Canal between the Scalzi and the Rialto bridges.

A decade after the war came to a close, Venice was celebrating liberation with a holiday. Parties in the street. Wreaths for the fallen. A plaque had been unveiled to the victims of the Nazis on the campanile in San Pietro, not that he'd been able to go there to witness the ceremony. The memories remained too sharp, too painful.

Instead that morning Maria had told him the news they'd been praying for. She was pregnant. Paolo Uccello kissed her over the breakfast table in the room by the canal which, after their own quarters, was the first they'd renovated.

One hour later the post arrived and with it a letter from a man with a task he'd placed at the back of his mind. The private detective in Milan hired years before with a single mission.

He read it, kissed Maria again then apologized. There was a sudden sales trip he needed to make. To Lausanne, by car he thought, since he might check out a few places for family holidays by the lake along the way.

The puzzled look in her eyes left him guilty. He'd never lied to her before and never would again if he could help it. But she demurred, naturally.

The wartime gun he'd bought from a shady dealer in Mestre was still in the locked bottom drawer of the desk in the private study he'd created for himself upstairs in the mansard.

Just after four the following morning he got his car out of the garage the Fascists had built at Piazzale Roma and set off north.

Over the years he'd made discreet inquiries about events that winter, asking round, hunting for information. One important source turned out to be a retired cardiologist from Giovanni e Paolo, a secret friend to both Aldo Diamante and the priest Garzone. He'd provided plenty of insight into the pair, including details of Diamante's determined state of mind and the conversations they'd had towards the end.

Finding Luca Alberti was a much more desperate effort to quell his conscience that he'd undertaken before Maria came along, when the memory of his sister and the sacrifice of the real Paolo Uccello continued to itch like open wounds.

There'd been recriminations aplenty after Venice fell to the liberating Allies. No one could stop them. The Germans had been taken as prisoners of war, some to face trials, others to be shipped home to freedom. For the Venetians who'd collaborated there was no such escape. The leaders of the local Fascist government had been rounded up for brief show trials, some executed in the public square in Mestre. Their names and their infamy were recorded in the newly liberated newspapers. Alberti's wasn't there and when he set a local investigator on the case the word came back: the man who'd killed his sister and his friend fled the city days before it fell, where no one knew.

Ten hours after leaving Venice in his speedy Lancia Appia convertible, he drove down from the snow-covered heights of the Alps into Montreux. The lake ran out in front shining in the afternoon sun like an inland sea, steamers criss-crossing the water. The address he had was the Auberge Raveyres, Caux. It turned out to be a modest two-storey, wooden hotel high up in the hills, a short way along from the mountain train that climbed through the peaks soaring above the town.

There was a 'closed' sign by the car park. When he drove in a woman in a pink, nylon housecoat came out immediately and began to speak French he couldn't understand.

'I'm sorry,' he said, taking out his small case. 'I'm from Italy.'

'*Allora*,' she said. 'In that case I'll get my husband.'

She looked about thirty-five, rural, red-cheeked, handsome and happy. As she wandered back to the house calling, 'Ettore, Ettore,' a young girl of four or so ran out laughing and threw her tiny arms around the woman's knees.

Ettore Romano.

That was the name the detective had come up with.

He'd only seen him the day Mika died, and then briefly. A face in the crowd. Not someone he could easily recognize nearly twelve years on, or so he expected. But when the man came out, washing his hands as if he'd been busy in the kitchen, a sturdy, fit-looking fellow, middle-aged but with the gait and confidence of a cop, he knew.

'Can I help you, sir?' he asked, looking puzzled.

'I came from Venice. We need to talk.'

There was a long moment and he thought to himself, perhaps he should have done what Mika would in the circumstances. Just killed the bastard, there and then, no matter that his wife and kid were around.

'Laura.' The man who was Luca Alberti called out to his wife and said it would be a good idea if she took herself and Sophie, their daughter, into Montreux to pick up some supplies. The hotel would be opening for summer soon. There were some things he'd ordered. He'd sensed something. It was obvious.

She looked puzzled but she soon left with the kid, driving an old Citroen van that had seen better days.

'Nice machine,' Alberti said, nodding at the Lancia. He'd noticed him thinking about their own decrepit vehicle. 'Whatever business you're in, friend, you're doing better than me.'

'My name's Giovanni Artom. Twelve years ago you shot my sister in the back. You probably thought you'd killed me too.'

Alberti blinked, nodded, looked around, grimaced.

'Ah. I wondered how long it would be before someone came.' He gestured at the hotel. 'Come inside. I'll make some coffee. Or a drink. You want a drink? Not wine. The Swiss wine's shit. Nothing like as good as back home. The brandy though . . .'

The old Citroen was gone, rattling down the rough dirt road.

There was no one around. He opened the case and took out the gun.

'I didn't come here for a drink.'

'Well,' the man said, turning his back on him, walking nonchalantly for the door. 'All the more for me.'

The kitchen was huge, with commercial cookers and a gigantic fridge. Everything looked as if it hadn't been used in ages.

'We close for the winter. There's no point in opening except Easter to the end of October. It's a living. Just.'

He took a bottle of white wine out of the fridge, got two glasses and gestured at the work table next to the sink.

'You ran straight here from Venice? After the Germans lost?'

Alberti shook his head.

'You really want to know?'

'That's why I asked.'

He took a gulp of wine and thought about his answer.

'I wasn't going to wait. The writing was on the wall. The place was crawling with partisans. Crawling with people who said they were partisans too, not that they ever did a thing. A few of them would string you up from a tree if someone said they saw you lighting a Nazi's smoke.'

'You did a lot more than that.'

'True.' He looked at the gun. 'If you shoot me, a favour, please. My wife and kid will be back in an hour or so. Don't let them find me here. There's plenty of places in the hills.'

Paolo shrugged and poured himself a glass anyway. The man across the table raised his in a silent toast, then narrowed his eyes and looked him up and down.

'I was pretty sure it wasn't you. When they came into that place and started shooting. Didn't make sense at all. No partisan was going to walk round with an incriminating ID in his pocket. That wound on his leg seemed too fresh. Also . . .' He squinted as if trying to remember. 'I dealt with a few suicides back when I was in the police. I never saw anyone shoot themselves straight in the face like that. Just isn't done. I'd seen the kid. I knew what he looked like. He wanted to make damned sure we couldn't identify him. Did a pretty good job too. His face was a real mess. Still . . . if Oberg had still been alive I doubt you'd have got away with it. He was one smart guy. Anyway, they left it to me.

When they turned suspicious I took in that woman who worked for him.'

'Chiara? Chiara Vecchi?'

'She said the Uccello kid had been taken hostage by those two wicked partisans from Turin. Maybe they'd killed him, dumped him in the lagoon. Maybe he'd got away. I didn't believe a word but I wasn't going to push it. We had corpses everywhere. Who needed one more? So I closed the case. I told the Crucchi the kid was either dead or missing and he was nothing special anyway, not someone to worry about.'

Paolo stayed silent, toying with the gun.

'You never knew she risked her neck saying that?' Alberti asked. 'Oh well. People don't like talking about things sometimes. Plenty of reasons.'

Still he kept on and on, as if this was a conversation he'd been holding in for years, waiting for the right person to come along and tell. The good deeds, naturally. About how he'd tried to warn off Aldo Diamante. The priest Garzone too. How neither of them took much notice. Any more than Mika that night he spotted her in the Gioconda and told her it was all a trap.

'Thing is, Giovanni—'

'Paolo. They call me Paolo Uccello now.'

Alberti smiled and said, 'So I'm not the only imposter round here. What I was going to say is . . . war's like this road you find yourself trapped on and you can't get off. You maybe get one choice at the beginning but by the time you realize it was on offer it's gone. It makes us monsters. Some of us were monsters to begin with. Some of us just ordinary. So we're ordinary monsters and maybe that's worse. I don't know. I went to work for the Crucchi because there didn't seem anything else to do. I thought from time to time I could save a few people. Trouble is no one sees it that way, not when the chance is coming from a man like me. Diamante was never going to change who he was. He wasn't going to bend. He was too proud. He hated us so much. Same with that priest in a way.' He took another sip and stared across the table. 'Same with your sister. Can't help anyone if they won't help themselves. So in the end you look after number one. I'm not saying I was a hero, even a little one.'

'Good.'

'I killed people when I had to. When it was that or get killed. No excuse. Just how it was. I'm not asking for forgiveness.'

'I wasn't offering it.'

The gun. He hadn't used one since that last time in the mountains with Mika. Alberti was looking at it, wondering.

'I've got something to show you,' he said getting up and dragging his chair along the floor.

'Keep your hands where I can see them.'

He laughed at that.

'Don't worry. The only weapon here's the one you've got. I've seen enough of those damned things for one lifetime. Don't want to see any more.'

He put the chair against a set of tables by the gas hobs, then clambered up on it. There was a small cupboard at the very top over lines and lines of cooking pans. He opened it, took out a gilt cardboard box and blew off the dust as he came down again.

'Here,' he said, placing it on the table. 'I kept it as a reminder of those days. Something I could look at when no one else is around. A way of keeping the bad things alive in my head because if you let them go you do no one any justice. Not Diamante. Not Garzone. Not your sister.' He hesitated. 'Go on. Take a look.'

There was silver lettering on the lid: *Uccello, Fine Weavers. Venice.* A couple of moths flew out as he opened the thing.

'Been a while,' Alberti said. 'Now I've got a daughter around. I don't want her coming in and seeing me staring drunk and weeping at that.'

Inside, wrapped in tissue paper, was a piece of fabric. Soprarizzo velvet from a Jacquard loom in the Giardino degli Angeli, the rampant lion of Venice repeated. One of the three he'd worked on under the tutelage of Chiara in the quiet days before the world fell.

The background was barely recognizable, the shiny silk soiled with something dark and dense. Dried blood, so much of it the stain reached through the tissue to the lid.

'After they shot those people in San Pietro . . . after I killed your sister . . . they called me back to San Marco. She'd found that evil bastard Salvatore Bruno and his little rat, Vitale. The woman got off lightly. A few bullets. Quick, I guess. Bruno . . .' He closed his eyes. 'I've seen a lot of things but nothing like that. Your sister carved him apart like he was a piece of meat. Couldn't really call it stabbed. More like butchery. Then she stuffed this thing in his mouth. He'd had it made, special, for the night before. Gave some matching ones to the Germans as if it made them equal or something. That they'd look at a piece of velvet and think, OK, he can live. Him and his Jew family. They're different. Fat chance.'

Paolo Uccello ran his fingers across the stiff, stained fabric.

'Why did you keep it?'

He looked around the kitchen.

'To remind me there's nothing here I deserve.' His voice had fallen a tone. 'Not a wife who loves me and my little girl. Why else?'

'You haven't shown her? Told her who you really are?'

'Would you?' He rapped his finger on the table. 'I did the only thing I thought I could do at the time—'

'You shot my sister in the back. I saw you—'

'She'd killed a German officer in front of them all,' Alberti cried. 'She was waving that gun round like she'd do it again. She—'

'Mika was brave.'

'She was dead already.' Then, more quietly, 'I did the kindest thing I could think of. I put her down. Do you know what would have happened if they'd got her back to Ca' Loretti alive? Do you have any idea? I do. I saw it. I wouldn't wish that on anyone. You wouldn't have thanked me for that.'

'And she'd have given you away.'

'Maybe,' he said with a shrug. 'Believe it or not I really didn't care. I didn't care about anything back then, any more than she did. I saw the look in her eyes when she went for Oberg. She knew what she was doing. She knew the cost and she wanted it. She *craved* being some kind of martyr. I just saved her the agony of getting crucified along the way.'

He nodded at the gun, then reached for the glass again and took a long swig.

'If you're going to do it, do it now. Before my wife and kid get back. There's a tarpaulin in the garage. You wouldn't want blood on the seats of your nice new car.'

'Will you tell her?' he asked. 'One day?' He put the lion banner back in its box. 'Will you show her this?'

'No.'

'What about your girl?'

'Sophie? Nah. She's four. Bright little thing. So long as the

Russians and the Americans get along she's going to grow up in a world where ordinary people don't kill each other just because some big guy told them to.' He thought of another drink, then pushed the bottle away. 'Maybe when she has a kid though. Or that kid has a kid. They should know. Do you think we stopped it? Really? Do you think we can just shake it off and put it down to experience? Tell ourselves that's what old people, primitive people do? We're better now? We're smarter?'

Straight away Paolo said he hoped so.

'Maybe you're right,' Alberti muttered.

'My wife's pregnant,' Paolo added and didn't know why. 'She told me just before I left.'

The man across the table smiled and Paolo had to stop himself thinking, I could like him.

'That's good. Children make men of us if we let them. Took me two goes to learn that but I'm stupid. By the looks of you, you're not.'

There was a long silence between them, then Alberti nodded at the gun and said, 'The longer you wait the harder it gets. I speak from experience.'

He couldn't stop thinking of Maria, back on her own in Venice. How he'd left her the day after she told him she was pregnant, driven all this way on a lie, intent on killing a man out of anger and vengeance, nothing more. He knew Mika. He understood they'd said farewell to one another that dreadful morning. If it wasn't Alberti it would have been another, and perhaps in circumstances yet more cruel.

'I can't shoot you,' he said, pushing the gun to one side.

Too late, Paolo saw the trick. An old cop's one maybe. Or a collaborator's. There was still that part of him inside.

Before he could do a thing Alberti snatched the gun, held it like a familiar thing, pointed the barrel in his face, arm straight, face cold and hard.

'The longer you wait the harder it gets,' Paolo said. 'Doesn't it?'

'You come here . . .' Alberti snapped. 'My home. I spend all these years working to put that shit behind me. You march in. Expecting what?'

'I don't know,' he said. And that was true.

'Your sister would have shot me without a second thought. Shot my wife and kid too.'

'I don't know about that last part.'

'You didn't see what she did to that bastard Bruno. He was a mess of meat.'

'I can't forget . . .'

'None of us can.' Alberti was waving the gun around as if he didn't know what to do. 'Think about your wife. Your kid. The world they got coming to them.'

'I'm trying . . .'

The man across the table shook his head. His eyes were glassy now.

'Try harder,' Alberti said. 'People now . . . they're already rewriting everything. Sanitising it. Saying, look the British won. The Americans won. We all lost. We always do. That's what war means. There are never any winners. Here . . .' He tossed the gun across the table. 'Shoot me if you like. If you think it'll make anything better.'

Paolo picked up the pistol and dropped it back in his bag.

Alberti wiped his eyes with his arm and nodded.

'That's a relief. We've got bookings next week. Need to clean this place up first. What are you going to do?'

There was only one thing when he thought about it.

'Leave you here. With your memories.'

'They're our memories, Giovanni . . . Paolo . . . whatever I'm supposed to call you. They belong to both of us.'

He got a pair of scissors from the table drawer, cut Salvatore Bruno's bloody banner in half, put one section back in the gilt box and shoved the other to one side on the table.

'Take this with you.'

'I don't need it.'

'You know what keeps me awake at night?'

'Lots, I imagine.'

'Not what you think. What keeps me up is this big conundrum. Here we are, we lived through it, and more than anything we'd like to bury all that horror, all that blood. Pretend it never really happened. But my little girl here . . .' He tapped the table as if that made her real. 'One day, if this all comes back, she's going to need to remember. And all they're going to tell her about are the heroes. People like you.' Alberti jabbed a finger hard in his chest. 'It's me they need to remember too. *Me.* How do you square that one, Mister Bright Guy? How do you fix that?'

'I'm no hero,' he murmured. 'I never was.'

'Doesn't matter. They'll make you one. It's all turning into a story now. A fairy tale. Good and bad. Black and white. Nothing in between. Except it's the in between that matters.'

Paolo Uccello flipped the case shut, got to his feet and took out his car keys. Alberti went and stood in front of the door.

'There's no way I'm going to let you drive through the mountains at this time of night. Even in your fancy car. Too dangerous. I'll make up a room. Laura will be home soon. She cooks this Swiss thing. Macaroni and potatoes and cheese and apples. You won't get that back home.'

'You want me to eat with you?'

Alberti opened his arms.

'The fighting's over in case you hadn't noticed. But if you like it's not unknown for guests to dine on their own.'

There was a sound outside. Tyres on gravel.

'Please. We'll talk about Switzerland. And Venice. Never the war, not with them around. No one's going to say a word about that in here. Maybe it's best they never do. I don't know.'

He hesitated which was as good as a yes.

'Oh. And if you could remember to call me "Ettore" that would be much appreciated too. OK . . . Paolo?'

The next morning, as the sun was rising over the great lake below, he set off for home. The three of them stood in the drive of their little hotel and waved goodbye, Ettore Romano, his wife, still bemused by the quiet meal they'd shared the night before, his charming little daughter. There was a gift, a piece of cheese from the mountains, in the boot alongside the gilt cardboard box which, later on, he hid behind something he bought at a souvenir shop near the border.

Ten hours later he parked in his private space in Piazzale Roma, bought an expensive bouquet of roses from the florist's in the campo and a box of chocolates from the fancy shop around the corner.

'Did you sell much?' Maria asked as he took her in his arms on the steps of the palazzo.

'Not a thing.'

She tapped his hand lightly.

'A wasted trip! You don't make many of those.'

'It wasn't wasted. Not really.'

'Then what?'

He'd left the present outside as a surprise. She clapped her hands in delight and laughed when she saw it.

A wooden cot, old-fashioned, very Swiss, with rockers, hearts and carved flowers on the side.

The child to come was all that mattered. The life before them. And one more obligation he'd been thinking about all the long drive home.

'I've been thinking of names,' he said.

'I thought we agreed we'd wait a while.'

'I know. But I couldn't stop myself. If it's a boy . . . Giovanni. A girl . . . Micaela.'

She leaned on the outside wall. He knew that look. It was the same one she gave him when she first got sight of his ham-fisted attempt at bookkeeping. Puzzlement and curiosity.

'What happened in Switzerland?'

'I drove too far. Too fast. It was the car. Sorry.'

Maria placed her hands on the wooden cot.

'I could like Giovanni. If it's a girl we think again. Since we're talking presents . . . what do you want on Saturday?'

'Saturday?'

'It's your birthday! You're the only man I've ever known who can forget the day he was born.'

He wanted to say it. To tell her. It wasn't his birthday at all but that of a dead man, a friend, a brief lover who sacrificed himself so that he could live. But Alberti was right. His generation wanted to blank out the harsh memories of the war and replace them with the Technicolor fantasies that were filling the cinemas. Then, at the same time, plead with the next generation to remember the horrors somehow. To conjure them out of next to nothing.

Maria came close, smiled, kissed his cheek.

'Such a strange husband I have at times. So what do you want? For this birthday you always forget?'

He didn't know where it came from. Perhaps the memories of being a student in Padua, struggling to write before he possessed any story to tell.

A typewriter, he said. An Olivetti portable, the Lettera 22.

The kind of thing his father would have worked on if he'd lived.

That would do.

* * *

It was almost one in the morning by the time I finished the final piece of the jigsaw Nonno Paolo had left for me. At seven I got up, went for breakfast in some kind of hipster cafe that had taken the premises of our old, beloved butcher, came home and read it again.

Late that afternoon I walked to Piazzale Roma and took the 5.2 boat to San Pietro, walked through narrow streets I barely knew except from a story first told to me a long time ago by a man I loved. The basilica was as I recalled, as it was to Filippo Garzone too: vast, grey, not pretty at all. Any more than the white campanile that sat, leaning a little, in the dry summer grass in front.

There was a memorial at the foot marking the events of December the fifth, 1943, not new but shiny. Someone kept polishing it. Alongside a brief description of the massacre were the names of thirteen 'martyrs'. The ten condemned along with Mika Artom, listed as a 'brave partisan', and two locals killed in the ensuing fracas. Next to that was a second, smaller bronze tablet dedicated to Father Filippo Garzone, naming him 'righteous among nations'. This, it said, was an honour given by the ghetto of Venice to a gentile who risked his life to save Jews from the Nazis and the Black Brigades.

I stood in front of that curious white tower for a long while, waiting for their ghosts. But somehow they weren't there, not in the way they used to be. Not shadows taunting me for my timidity, my fear, my inability to understand Nonno Paolo's story and what it truly meant. Twenty years, perhaps a quarter of my life, had passed between him secretly handing on that tale of his and the day I finally found the courage to stand again on the spot his sister died as he watched, crippled, helpless, from the bridge across the canal towards the Arsenale.

It was a new bridge now, fresh wood, smart grey railings, as yet untainted by the harsh salt air. On the other side the walls of the Giardino degli Angeli gleamed a rich ochre in the late afternoon sun. The ledge which Mika had used to escape the place had fallen away and was far too sheer to cross in safety. On the side was a red and white sign for the Biennale: *Il Giardino degli Uccello*. People were milling over the smaller bridge that led through into the side of Paolo Uccello's old home.

I fell in with the crowd.

* * *

A young woman was waiting at the door bearing a card with my name. She had very short hair and a serious, sunburnt face. There was a tattoo of the winged lion of Venice on her left arm and the scarlet design of a raised revolutionary fist on her right. With her ragged jeans, torn at the knee, and a white T-shirt bearing a loud anti-capitalist slogan she looked every inch the student revolutionary.

Valentina Padoan, it turned out, was a professor of twentieth-century Italian history at Ca' Foscari and a published author.

'I regret to say I'm a capitalist by birth,' I said, looking at the message on her shirt as I introduced myself. 'Please don't throw a milkshake at me.'

'I only throw them at Fascists. It's an English thing. Milkshakes. My boyfriend came from London. Well the last one. Blame him.'

'If I get the chance.'

'You won't. He's gone. Besides . . .' A smile did come then, quick, mischievous and very captivating. I could see how she could worm money out of Dad. 'If you lot weren't capitalists we wouldn't have been able to sting you for all this, would we?'

She waved her arm at the garden behind. It was nothing like the grim collection of spare trees and grass and wreckage I imagined. There were ornate flower beds, tall rose bushes, patches of exotic lilies. Next to a newly paved winding path that led to the conservatory stood a classical stone fountain where nymphs danced over grinning dolphins and water bubbled out of a vase held by a naked Venus. Rising above the gleaming glass of our former weaving workshop was what looked like a new terracotta-tiled roof for the house. Beyond was the ruined octagonal sentry tower, its reflection rippling in the grey-blue of the summer lagoon. The horizon was marked by the low, shrubby outline of the little island of Certosa where a vaporetto was docking – something new, that had never happened in my day I felt sure.

The broken statues, the heads and shoulders and wings of the lost angels, were still there, scattered across the lawn. Signs by them said that, as part of the Biennale, they'd been decorated by children from local schools, each putting their names to the rainbow garlands and ribbons and crowns that adorned their brows and fractured limbs. Beneath the fruit trees tables and chairs were set, most of them occupied by people lounging in summer clothes, sipping drinks and chattering away.

I turned back to the gate and tried to imagine what it was like that distant winter day when a man called Luca Alberti, half-traitor, half something else, came here with a group of German soldiers after he'd shot Mika Artom. How they'd approached the glass conservatory only to see the man behind it shoot himself in the face, then miss altogether the fact that the partisan they really sought was locked away in the cellar.

Past and present seemed to sit together side by side now, in my mind at least. Those ghosts weren't buried. They were a part of us all, shades locked to our footsteps, companions on the same journey.

She took my arm and showed me round. We walked through the conservatory where three looms – Jacquard they had to be – had been installed at the front as showpieces. A woman in a long, historical dress sat at the nearest fiddling with silk thread. Examples of classic Uccello velvet adorned the walls, framed like paintings. Next to them were photographs of Venice. It took a moment for me to recognize them. They were mine, shot that summer of 1999 with the camera outfit Dad had bought me. He must have found the negatives and produced new prints for the exhibition.

'These were a gift from your father. The machines that made you rich. Your father gave us lots of nice pictures too. We're very grateful.'

I smiled at the weaver and, with a nod of permission, ran my finger along the old wood, the soft silk, and asked where on earth they'd found them.

'Didn't he tell you? They came from here originally. They were the ones they used during the war.'

'I've been abroad,' was all I could find to say.

The house was now a modern, trendy cafe. On the left side, where the real Paolo Uccello's grandparents once slept, was a counter with a kitchen and storeroom behind. To the right ran a line of tables where a couple of young people tapped away at laptops beneath yet more of my photographs. Along the outer wall a panoramic glass window offered a view back to the basilica and campanile of San Pietro across the canal. It was all as pretty as a tourist postcard.

'And this,' she said, leading me to the steps, 'is what we're most proud of. We built it pretty much from scratch.'

I hesitated as we stopped at the top of a set of steep new stairs. The cellar.

'Come on,' she said and almost dragged me down.

It was now a basement floor for the cafe, with double doors that opened out to the platform over the lagoon where people could sit and enjoy the view. The breeze outside was welcome. I felt light-headed and she must have noticed.

'Are you alright, Signor Uccello?'

'My name is Nico. Please call me that.'

'Are you alright, Nico? You look like you might faint. Or throw up. Neither of which would be terribly convenient right now. We have work to do.'

No, I said. I wasn't going to throw up. But I did want a drink. A Negroni. A good one.

'Good ones are all I make,' Valentina Padoan told me. We went upstairs and she raced behind the bar to grab some glasses. 'After that,' she ordered while juggling the bottles, 'I speak. You smile and cut the ribbon. Then . . .' That smile again. 'We can talk some more.'

'*Si, signora*,' I replied with a salute.

There was a small crowd outside. The mayor, or so they said later, and a few local politicians, though no one from the party of Maurizio Scamozzi. With any luck he was still smarting from the unexpected violence of a milkshake.

I should have known there was more to it than I was told. Valentina gave a brisk speech thanking the Uccello family for bringing their old home back to life for the benefit of the city. Then the Biennale for its help in providing artworks for the garden. Finally, the schools who'd decorated the statuary, which brought a round of giggles and applause from a group of kids in the audience.

When everyone thought she was finished she said, 'And now . . . a surprise.'

On the far wall was a scarlet curtain decorated with the lion emblem of Venice, a product of our looms I didn't doubt, held in place with a gleaming satin ribbon.

'Nico.' One of her helpers handed me a pair of scissors. 'Please.'

I'd no idea what was going on but Valentina Padoan was not a woman to be denied. When I snipped the ribbon the curtain fell to the floor to reveal a bright new bronze plaque attached to the wall. I read it and once again felt giddy.

> Here, one cold winter's day in 1943, a partisan called Giovanni Artom fell, a martyr to the Fascists like his better-known sister Micaela. Patriots of a free Italy, dedicated to justice and liberty. We will remember them always.

'War is full of stories,' Valentina said to the audience in the confident tones of a born academic. 'Some known. Some unknown. Giovanni Artom was one of the latter. He was not a Venetian but came from Turin. He died here and was forgotten over the years. It's our belief we must keep alive the memories of all the fallen. Even those who, for whatever reason, have fallen through the cracks.'

For a moment the audience seemed to listen as Valentina set forth her explanation of how she and her students had discovered there'd been another victim that bloody December Sunday in 1943. A man whose sacrifice had never been acknowledged. Perhaps because there'd been so much death that day. And he was a stranger, not a Venetian.

They didn't listen long. This audience wasn't here for distant history. They wanted free drinks, some selfies, the opportunity to see a small part of the city that was usually kept from view.

I watched her start to lose their attention, and the way she realized this was happening, how much it hurt. And I found myself thinking of the world I grew up in, an easy, lazy one, where no one talked much of war and poverty. All those years we took for granted.

'Please,' Valentina begged them. 'A moment's silence for Giovanni Artom and all those who died so that we might live in freedom.'

At least they gave her that. Even the birds and the boats on the lagoon seemed to acknowledge it, though doubtless that was my imagination. Then, on cue, it was back to normal and everyone was talking, wandering round the garden, looking at the statues and the children's decorations, my photographs from twenty years before, queueing for more free drinks.

By then I was remembering Maurizio Scamozzi, a school bully I'd fallen in with for a little while out of nothing but laziness and fear. A man of some power now in this strange, new world that had succeeded those idle years of old.

I thought of soldiers at Piazzale Roma bearing weapons as they stood by their armoured cars. Of men with rifles in the ghetto, beggars ignored in the street and a teenager getting beaten up on a school bus in Treviso for no reason except the colour of his skin.

The spell was broken by something familiar, eternal, real and haunting.

Si-dah-si-dah-si-dah-sichi-si-piu.

A goldcrest flitted across the garden, always busy, always alive.

'I'm sorry, Nico,' Valentina said, her eyes welling with tears. 'People don't really listen sometimes. They're too . . . busy.'

I was astonished by my own blindness. At how long it took for the scales to fall from my eyes.

I thought Grandfather meant this story for me.

'Let me get you a drink,' she whispered.

Of course he didn't. He placed his memories in my hands for safekeeping. The voice of an old and long-dead Venetian doctor was in my head then, saying something to a turncoat policeman in a chilly alley in San Marco. Though perhaps the words were Nonno Paolo's all along.

It wasn't enough to remember the fallen. You had to remember how and why they fell.

This story – *his* story – wasn't for me.

It was for now.

For today.

For you.

'I've a tale to tell as well,' I said, glancing at the plaque on the wall and the name there: Giovanni Artom. 'A big one. I'm going to need your help.'

'Of course,' said Valentina Padoan.

And here, at last, it is.

AUTHOR'S NOTE

This is a work of fiction though it takes some inspiration from events that followed the German occupation of Venice in September 1943. Up to that point the city's Jews had been persecuted by the Italian Fascist authorities but few had been interned. From the moment the Nazis took total control, however, the oppression became all too real. Professor Giuseppe Jona, the president of the Jewish community, committed suicide on September 17th after refusing to hand over to the Germans a list of members of the city's qehillà. In November Mussolini declared all Jews foreigners of a hostile nationality, ordered the confiscation of their estates, and marked them down for arrest. For the sake of a fictional narrative I have changed the real-life timeline of events and invented much. While Aldo Diamante owes something to the courageous Jona, all characters in this story are inventions.

During the German occupation some 230 Venetian Jews were deported to German concentration camps. Only eight of them returned alive. According to Susan Zuccotti (*The Italians and the Holocaust, Persecution, Rescue, Survival*) wartime Italy's relatively small Jewish population lost 6,800 of its 38,400 members to Nazi and Black Brigade murderers after the persecutions.

Some 200,000 Italians are estimated to have taken part in the resistance efforts against the Nazi and Italian Fascist regimes. Around 70,000, both civilians and partisans of all backgrounds, are thought to have been killed. L'Istituto Veneziano per La Storia della Resistenza (iveser.it) has recorded many stories of partisan activity in their research archives on Giudecca.

The weaving of fine velvet is a long tradition in Venice. There is still one manufacturer using the technique of ancient Jacquard looms – Tessitura Luigi Bevilacqua (www.luigi-bevilacqua.com) based in a palace on the Grand Canal in Santa Croce. I'm grateful to the company for showing me round its fascinating weaving room there, though I should say the real process is far more complex and time-consuming than it appears within these pages.

David Hewson
Kent and Venice
December 2018 to April 2020